Other Works by David A. Wells

The Sovereign of the Seven Isles
- THINBLADE
- SOVEREIGN STONE
- MINDBENDER
- BLOOD OF THE EARTH
- CURSED BONES
- LINKERSHIM
- REISHI ADEPT

The Dragonfall Trilogy
- THE DRAGON'S EGG

The Dragon's Codex

Dragonfall: Book Two

by

David A. Wells

THE DRAGON'S CODEX

Copyright © 2016 by David A. Wells

Edited by Carol L. Wells

This is a work of fiction. Characters, events and organizations in this novel are creations of the author's imagination.

www.DragonfallTrilogy.com

The Dragon's Codex

Chapter 1

Ellie and Olivia were sneaking into the house well after their father's newly imposed curfew, taking their favored route through the shuttered back wall of the kitchen root cellar. Suddenly Ellie froze, straining to hear, her eyes going to her sister almost automatically. Each motioned to the other for silence.

Olivia carefully lowered the heavy hinged board and latched it, casting the room into an even deeper darkness. Ellie eased forward, finding the staircase and slowly ascending to the top, stopping in a crouch about a foot away from the kitchen door.

"I know it's short notice, Gwen, and I'm sorry," their father said. "Cascade Manor is a day on horseback. I'll spend a day there and be back in three."

Olivia moved silently up the stairs, stopping behind Ellie. She took a quick breath at the sound of her father's voice.

"Is this about that?" Gwen asked.

A moment of silence passed.

"Yes," Dom said.

"It's too dangerous. You should send someone else."

"Who?" Dom asked. "I've been through a lot with this guy. I owe him a thousand different ways. I have to go myself."

"At least wait until morning," Gwen said, her voice softening.

"I can't. The sooner I get there, the sooner I can determine if there's a threat."

"Dominic Flynn, don't treat me like I'm stupid. You know damn well there's a threat. He wouldn't be back after all these years if there wasn't."

"All right, fair enough," Dom said. "I just didn't want you to worry."

"Too late."

More silence. Ellie and Olivia could just make out each other's eyes in the dark as they shared a look.

"Who's going with you?" Gwen asked.

"Just Ty. Kat is already there with Belle and Adam."

"You got Belle mixed up in this? What the hell were you thinking?"

"Gwen," he said, a hard edge in his voice. "This is deadly serious business. I needed people I trust."

"That's not very reassuring."

"No, I don't suppose it is," he said, quietly, "but it wasn't meant to be. I know better than anyone what's at stake here. I need you to be prepared for what might be coming."

"Dear God," Gwen said, her voice little more than a whisper.

"Just be ready to go if you have to," Dom said. "Have the girls ready too."

"They're sleeping," Gwen said. "Should I wake them? Do we have to leave now?"

Ellie and Olivia tensed.

"No, no," Dom said. "Let them sleep. Just be ready."

Ty Winter strode into the kitchen—the rhythmic click of his boots on the tile distinctive enough to identify him.

"Ma'am," Ty said. "I have two of my best men at your disposal, day and night."

"Thank you, Ty."

"Our horses are ready, Dom."

"All right. I'll be out in a few minutes."

"At least let me make you a sandwich for the road," Gwen said.

"Deal," Dom said. "I have to grab a few things."

The waiting was interminable. They could just barely hear their mother preparing a lunch for their father.

Ellie had wondered about her father's recent behavior. He was a man who relished routine, yet lately, his travels and meetings and the hours he kept were anything but. Ellie had, of course, talked to Olivia about it and they had agreed to keep an ear open.

Footsteps announced their father's return.

"I made one for Ty, too," Gwen said.

"Of course you did," Dom said with a chuckle.

Silence.

"Three days and it'll be over," he said.

"Or not."

"Or not," he agreed with a hint of resignation in his voice.

"I'll walk you out."

"I was hoping you would."

Footsteps faded down the hall, then the door opened and closed.

"What the hell is going on?" Ellie and Olivia asked at the same time in harsh whispers.

"Cascade Manor won't be in production until next spring," Ellie said. "Why would he go there?"

"And who is this mysterious person they keep talking about?" Olivia asked.

"And why is Belle in the loop and we're not?"

"I know, it's so unfair."

"Want to follow him?" Ellie asked.

"We should follow him," Olivia said, almost before Ellie had completed her sentence.

They crept back down the stairs and climbed outside, staying behind a few conveniently located bushes as they quietly closed the shutter behind them. They could hear hoofbeats fading into the moonlit night.

They headed for the stables, both moving through the night with practiced ease. They arrived to find two stablehands just closing the door after having prepared horses for Dom and Ty. They waited until they were out of sight.

"What about your sword?" Olivia asked, once they were safely inside the stable.

"It's with my travel gear," Ellie said with a shrug. "I only need it on the road anyway."

They lit a lamp and set to work saddling up and loading their gear. Within a few minutes they were leading their horses out of the barn and into the night.

"We should leave a note for Mom," Ellie said.

"You're right, if we just go missing there's no telling what she'll do."

"I'll go," Ellie said.

"No, I'll do it. I'm sneakier." Olivia flashed her sister a smile as she handed over the reins and vanished into the night.

Ellie tied the horses to a tree and slipped into the brush, going still, watching and listening to the night. She knew her sister well enough to know that she would try to sneak up on her. It was a game their father had encouraged them to play since they were children.

She heard a twig break and smiled to herself as she focused her attention on the direction of the noise. Olivia was almost invisible in the dark, moving slowly, keeping to the shadows.

"Nice try," Ellie whispered, stepping out into the open, looking straight at her sister.

"Damn," Olivia whispered under her breath, abandoning her attempt at stealth.

"What did you tell Mom?"

"I said we went into town for a couple of days to go shopping."

"Think she'll buy it?"

"Probably not, but I couldn't come up with anything better."

Ellie nodded before mounting her horse and patting him on the side of the neck. He was small, but sturdy and strong, surefooted and smart. They set out slowly, not willing to risk injuring one of their animals in the dark.

As dawn broke, they picked up the trail of their father and Ty.

"How far ahead of us do you think they are?" Olivia asked.

"Hard to say. We probably pushed a bit faster through the night so they might be close."

By midmorning the road meandered over a rise. They approached cautiously, leaving their horses below as they crept up to a large tree at the crest.

They scanned the landscape, searching for travelers. A glint of light atop another rise about a mile away caught Ellie's eye.

"Crap," she said, pulling Olivia behind the tree.

"Do you think he made us?"

"Probably. It's Ty, and he was looking right at us with his binoculars. The real question is, did he recognize us?"

"Yeah," Olivia said, peeking out from around the tree with one eye. "Doesn't look like they're coming back this way."

Both breathed a sigh of relief.

"So what do you think?"

"We can't keep following them," Ellie said. "You know they'll ambush us or double back."

Olivia nodded, frowning deeply.

"We can't just give up," she said. "If we do, we'll always be on the outside wondering what is going on."

Ellie smiled. "So let's go the other way. We know where he's going. The mountain trail is shorter and we won't have to worry about them getting the drop on us."

"I like it," Olivia said. "If we're quick, we might even get there before they do."

They returned to their horses and backtracked to the trail that led up into the forested hillside toward a far more rugged and treacherous road that switched back and forth up to the ridge and then down again into the next valley. While their horses were well suited to the journey, they still proceeded with caution. The trail was uneven and rocky, even washed out in a few places, but passable.

Ellie found herself smiling at the beauty of the forest, the cool breeze and the blue sky. A detached sense of serenity distracted her as they rounded a bend and her horse reared in sync with Olivia's.

Ellie pulled on the reins and leaned into her horse, trying to regain control, not yet even aware of the reason for the sudden skittishness. As the animal's front hooves returned to the ground, she saw the man on the bridge.

And then both of the horses calmed, as if someone had thrown a switch.

Ellie scanned the area, alarm blaring in the back of her mind. Her sword came free almost instinctively.

The man was deathly pale with shock-white hair. His black spiked armor was burned along one side, several spikes on the shoulders having melted to dull points. His face was scarred with a horrible burn, disfiguring one side. Despite his apparently recent injuries, he faced them with confidence and no hint of pain.

On his right was a creature that stood three feet tall and looked almost human, but not quite. On his left was a mountain lion, the source of their horses' dismay.

Thoughts swirled through Ellie's mind. The horses should still be frantic, given the presence of a cougar, but they weren't. It was almost as if they'd been given a sedative.

Ellie and Olivia shared a glance.

"Ah, there you are," the man said. "I've been expecting you."

"Who are you?" Ellie asked.

"What do you want?" asked Olivia.

"My name is of little importance and I doubt you could pronounce it correctly anyway. I believe I am referred to as the Warlock by those I have come into contact with in this world. That title will suffice. As for what I want … I would like you to deliver a message for me."

Ellie scanned the area again, confusion driving her fear.

"What message?" Olivia asked.

"Tell Benjamin Boyce that I require the egg and his blood. If he gives me what I want, I will leave him alone. If he refuses, I will rain down hell upon everyone he holds dear."

Ellie and Olivia shared another look.

"We don't know anyone by that name," Ellie said.

"Not yet," the Warlock said, "but you will."

"How do you know?" Ellie asked.

"I heard a whisper in the dark."

Ellie felt a chill. She began to question the wisdom of following her father. But, looking at the Warlock, the seriousness of the situation began to sink in.

"And if we don't?" Olivia asked.

"Well then, young Benjamin will have no opportunity to preserve his family. I will come and take what I want, and those who try to stop me will die screaming. Your choice."

He walked into the forest, his unusual retinue following without a sound.

"Oh, I almost forgot," he said, turning back. "An hour or so up the trail is a bandit party camped in the forest. Wouldn't want you to be waylaid before you can deliver my message."

Without another word he set out along the stream bank and vanished into the trees.

"What the hell?" Ellie said.

Olivia just shook her head slowly, her big blue eyes wide with fear.

"Maybe we should turn back," she said.

"I don't think we can," Ellie said. "Not and live with ourselves anyway."

"What do you mean?"

"That guy was all magic," she said. "He knew we would be here, so it's a good bet that he knows we're going to meet this Benjamin person sometime soon. If we don't warn him, then he won't have a chance to save his family."

"Some salvation," Olivia said. "The Warlock said he wants this guy's blood—"

"And the egg!" both of them said at the same time, their faces going pale in unison as the magnitude of the situation penetrated into their consciousness.

"Oh God," Olivia whispered.

"No wonder Dad's so freaked out. His past is coming back to haunt him."

"If the egg is back in play, the dragon will be coming for it with everything he's got." Olivia took a quick breath. "Do you think Benjamin is the Wizard?"

Ellie nodded slowly. "Probably. We have to hurry."

"Yeah, but let's not forget about those bandits."

"No," Ellie said, spurring her horse forward, thoughts spinning in her head and her heart pounding in her chest.

For most of her life, she had dreamed of fighting the dragons like her father had. His stories seemed so romantic and heroic. She had longed for such experiences throughout her adolescence. Now, on the cusp of twenty, and having just encountered a being that she knew instinctively was well beyond her, she wasn't entirely certain she really wanted to go to war after all.

But then, she doubted that her father had wanted to go to war either … yet he had. He'd fought and he'd experienced unspeakable loss as a result. Deep down, she knew that she wouldn't exist if her father hadn't suffered so, but it still pained her that she had three brothers she would never know.

They pushed hard for half an hour, riding as quickly as the terrain would permit until they reached the top of a ridge. Ellie reined her horse in and dismounted, tying the animal to a tree near a patch of grass. She walked out onto a rock outcropping that jutted over a steep descent to the heavily forested valley below.

The sun and the breeze felt good, but this time she dismissed those simple pleasures in favor of concentration. Closing her eyes, she cocked her head and listened. She could hear the gentle breeze through the trees, the horses enjoying the green shoots beneath their feet, the sound of her own heartbeat … then a voice in the distance. She focused on it, waiting. Another voice filtered through. She had a direction.

"I don't see any smoke," Olivia said.

"Me neither, but I can hear them off that way."

"You think they've got an ambush set?"

"No," Ellie said, shaking her head, peering into the forest below. "This trail isn't used often enough. If I had to guess, I'd say they're hiding, which means someone is looking for them."

"Great, so they're probably paranoid and cautious."

"Yeah, let's try to see them first."

They mounted up and slowly proceeded down the switchback trail, taking care to be quiet. As they descended into the valley, the trees rose up around them, throwing shade across the path and lending a chill to the air. Half a mile later, the trail turned back the other direction. Ellie stopped and listened … voices, several of them wafting through the trees. Perhaps they weren't as cautious as she first thought.

"Sounds like they're having a party," Olivia whispered.

"Yeah, and it's not even noon yet. Problem is, it sounds like they're camped where the trail crosses the creek."

"If they don't have horses, we might be able to run through and be gone before they can react," Olivia said.

"Unless one of them has a gun."

"So, sneaky then?"

"Yeah," Ellie said with a grin. "Sneaky is better than fast."

"What do you have in mind?"

Ellie handed her sister the reins to her horse and dismounted. "When the shouting starts, ride hard. Meet me on the trail on the other side of the creek."

"What are you going to do?" Olivia asked, a tremor of worry in her voice.

"Distract them," she said, heading down the slope on foot.

"Be careful," Olivia whispered.

Ellie flashed her a smile. The terrain was steep and difficult, but within a few minutes she'd reached the stream several hundred yards down from the bandits. She cleared a spot and built a fire ring, then quickly gathered a bundle of kindling and a few larger pieces of wood. After building a teepee with the larger branches, she filled its interior with smaller twigs, then drizzled lamp oil over everything.

With a few strikes of her flint, the fire caught, rising quickly to engulf the entire stack of wood, flames dancing four feet into the air. Ellie hurried across the creek and up the far bank. Before she was even out of sight of the fire, shouts reached her from the camp. They'd seen the smoke. She picked up her pace.

It wasn't long before she reached the trail leading up out of the valley toward the far ridge. She hid in a cluster of trees. The sound of men traipsing through the brush reached her from below.

A shout of warning rose up from the camp. Ellie could just make out the sound of horses. A minute later, Olivia came around the corner, riding as quickly as the terrain would permit. Ellie stepped out from her hiding place.

"They have a couple of horses," Olivia said. "And one of them has a crossbow, but he's not a very good shot."

"Thank God," Ellie said, swinging up into her saddle.

They rode hard, shouts behind them fading into the distance. At the top of the ridge, they stopped and listened for sounds of pursuit but heard nothing.

"Do you think they'll follow?" Ellie asked.

"Hard to say," Olivia said. "From the looks of their camp there were at least six men, but only two horses so they can't mount much of a pursuit."

"Still, let's get to the road as quickly as possible."

By midday, the trail meandered out of the forest and met an old road. The black pavement was cracked and deteriorating, grass and moss growing through a spider web of fissures over the entire surface. An ancient truck, rusted, weathered and slowly disintegrating, had been rolled off the road into the ditch.

Cars and trucks from before Dragonfall had mostly been scavenged for metal. Old derelict vehicles like this one were not as common as they once were, but they weren't exactly rare either.

Ellie handed her sister the reins and dismounted, taking a moment to search the vehicle for anything of value. It had been pretty well stripped of everything that didn't require tools to remove. She smiled in triumph when she came up with a small bottle from under the seat. It was almost half full of whiskey.

"You aren't actually going to drink that, are you?" Olivia asked, crinkling her nose.

"No, but I might use it to light someone on fire," Ellie said, climbing into her saddle.

Olivia laughed under her breath. "Another few hours, you think?"

"Provided we don't run into any more obstacles."

"What are we going to tell Dad when we get there?"

"The truth," Ellie said with a shrug, "especially if this Benjamin person is there. Even if he's not, I think our encounter with the Warlock is way too important to keep from him."

Olivia nodded. "That guy gave me the creeps."

"Yeah, who wanders around with a dwarf and a cougar for pets?"

"And what melted half his face?"

"I really don't want to think about that," Ellie said.

Olivia looked at her sister, her eyes wide. "You think it was the wyrm."

Ellie nodded solemnly. They rode in silence for a few minutes.

Then Olivia said, "Dad's going to be pissed that we followed him."

"I'm a lot more worried about Mom."

Olivia winced.

Chapter 2

"Where is everyone?" Frank asked.

Annabelle had led them into a paddock bordered on two sides with old wooden fences made of quarter-round timber. The barn served as the third side of the paddock with the wall of the house completing the rectangle.

Emotion threatened to bubble up from Ben's frothy subconscious into his deliberately calm mind. He shoved it away again. Annabelle had helped them, she had saved them and brought them to this place of refuge, yet he didn't feel safe. He felt like an animal on the run, desperate for a place to go to ground, if only for long enough to catch his breath, to grieve his grandfather's death and figure out what to do next.

"The few hands working here are living in a ranch house on the other side of the property," Annabelle said. "We're all alone here."

"This must have been a really nice house at one time," Zack said, picking at a spot on the wall where the yellowing stucco was crumbling.

"And it will be again," Adam said. "This vineyard has some of the finest grapes I've ever seen. Most of the vines are older than I am."

Annabelle smiled at her husband's enthusiasm.

"Let's get our horses unsaddled and brushed out," she said as she dismounted. "Then I'll show you to your rooms and get some food going."

"Don't have to tell me twice," Hound said, sliding to the ground and following her into the empty barn.

"There hasn't been a horse in here for ages," Homer said in Ben's mind.

"It does seem a bit musty," Ben said, while he unbuckled his saddle. "But, all things considered, I'm glad they brought us here instead of into town where we might be spotted."

Homer curled up in the corner, laying his chin on the floor while he watched Ben work. It wasn't long before the horses were brushed and turned out into the paddock.

Annabelle led the group into the manor house. Zack was right—at one time the place had been a house fit for royalty. Today, it was in disrepair and in need of a thorough cleaning, but that didn't diminish the high arched ceilings painted with idyllic landscapes or the crystal chandeliers dulled by dust or the rich dark wood of the walls.

"So, you mentioned putting this property into production," Frank said.

"Yeah, my father acquired it last year, but we've been so busy with our other properties that we haven't had the time or manpower to get this place up and running. We will though. I expect it to be one of our prized vineyards within a few years."

"Other properties?" Frank asked.

"My father owns several pieces of land and a number of buildings in town," Annabelle said with a hint of pride. "He's a widely respected businessman in this territory, and he's been pretty successful. I don't remember a project he's invested in that returned a loss."

"Impressive," Frank said. "I've always dreamt of owning a business one day. Maybe your father could give me some advice."

Annabelle and Adam laughed out loud as one. "I doubt you could avoid hearing my father's advice if you tried," Annabelle said. "I've certainly never been able to."

"Is he here?" Ben asked.

"Not yet," she said, leading them into a large sitting room and throwing open the curtains to let in some light. The room was empty, save for a large table and a matching set of wooden chairs. "I expect him to arrive by dark." With the early afternoon light streaming into the room, the thick layer of dust was even more pronounced. She wrinkled her nose.

"Someone want to help me with dinner while the rest of you clean the table off?" she asked, running her finger through the dust and holding it up to show them the dirt.

"I'll help you cook," Imogen said, her voice somewhat subdued.

Ben grimaced inwardly. Imogen was hurting, even more so than he was, and there was precious little he could do to alleviate her suffering—or his own for that matter. The feeling of helplessness was beginning to become far too familiar.

"Belle," Ben said, before she could leave the room.

She turned.

"Thank you. We wouldn't have made it out of Rogue City without you."

She smiled, nodding as she turned away and vanished into the manor with Imogen. Ben set his pack against one wall, unbuckled his belt and sat down, cross-legged, closing his eyes and focusing his mind on the image of his lucky coin. It was the most reliable way he knew to stave off the yawning pit of grief welling up inside, threatening to consume him every time he let his mind wander close to it.

He had feared this moment—the moment when he stopped moving and was alone with his thoughts and feelings. He knew he had to grieve, but he also knew that not enough had been settled yet. He didn't know the intentions of the Dragon Slayer.

Annabelle was kind and she'd saved them, but that didn't mean anything. Until Ben had a safe place where he could emotionally fall apart for a while, he didn't dare open that door.

"Your brother is looking at the egg again," Homer said.

"I wouldn't expect anything else from him at this point," Ben said without opening his eyes. "Keep an eye on him."

"Always," Homer said.

"So what are we going to do now?" Zack asked.

"Now, you're going to help me clean this place up," Hound said. "After that, we're going to have a hot meal … I hope."

Ben turned his focus inward, blotting out everything save the safe, familiar image of his coin. Some time later, how long he didn't know, Homer nudged him with his nose.

"I smell food."

When Ben came back to his outward awareness, the scent of stew set his stomach rumbling. He opened his eyes and tried to remember the last time he'd eaten a hot meal ... at a table.

Not long after, Annabelle and Imogen pushed a cart into the room carrying a big pot of steaming hot beef stew and a basket full of fresh biscuits. After a hasty setting of the table, conversation ground to a halt while they ate.

When he started to feel full, for the first time in weeks, Ben sat back and sighed.

"You want some more?" he asked Homer, looking down at his pristine bowl.

"Of course. What kind of question is that?"

Ben smiled to himself as he ladled stew into his dog's bowl and set it on the floor next to his chair. He ignored the look of disapproval Frank gave him.

"That was the best meal I've had in a long time," he said. "Thank you again, Belle."

Hound muttered something that sounded like praise around a mouthful of food. Once everyone had eaten their fill, Belle and Adam cleared away the dishes and left them alone with Kat.

Ben looked at her and said, "Tell me about the Dragon Slayer."

She started to say something, but then closed her mouth as if she thought better of it.

"I guess the first thing you should know is that he hates to be called that," she said. "He goes by the name Dominic Flynn, but he prefers to be called Dom. He's fiercely loyal to those he cares about, but he also won't hesitate to tell you what he really thinks, especially if he's in a bad mood—which is what you should expect. Your presence puts his family at risk and that always makes him a bit testy."

"Will he help us get my baby back?" Imogen asked, her voice very small.

Kat took a deep breath and let it out slowly. "I don't know. As long as I've known him, he's made it a practice to avoid contact with all things dragon."

Imogen looked down at the table. Ben could almost feel the angst radiating from her. She'd lost nearly everything. He knew how overwhelming his own grief was, swirling deep within, threatening to surge forth and consume him. He couldn't even imagine having to contend with the loss of a child as well. The feeling of helplessness welled up again. He shoved it aside, deliberately repudiating the paralysis that inevitably followed the belief that he had no power to make things right. He slipped his hand into his shoulder bag and laid it on the egg, noting the slight warmth of its smooth scales.

He wasn't helpless—like it or not, he was the Wizard now. He would have laughed out loud at the absurdity of it, had the situation not been so serious. The weight of it pressed down on him. His hand rested on a power like no other, a power that gave him abilities that he had yet to discover, abilities that his grandfather had used to help defeat three dragons. With that thought, his greatest fear revealed itself to him.

What if he failed?

Whether they knew it or not, humanity's future rested squarely on his shoulders, and deep down he didn't believe for a second that he was adequate to such a monumental task. How could he be? How could anyone be?

And yet, his grandfather had been. His grandfather had risen to the challenge, and he had succeeded more wildly than seemed possible, even in hindsight. And he had paid for that success with horrific suffering and pain. And even with all of the hardship that he had endured, all of the loss that he had suffered, his grandfather had never revealed a shred of regret for his part in the war against the wyrm.

Ben was committed to his course, there was no question there. He just wished that he could see something other than a very bad death at the end of the road that he'd chosen. He kept those thoughts to himself. If he was to make an attempt against the dragon, he would need all the help he could get.

A pang of guilt assailed him at the thought of leading his friends into a lost cause.

"Stop that," Homer said.

Ben nodded, half to himself. Objectively, he knew that anything was possible. He might even find a way to defeat the dragon—and if he was to have any chance at all, he had to preserve at least a small spark of hope within himself. If he let that light go out, he truly was lost.

He looked around the table, assessing the state of mind of his friends and family. Imogen was lost in her despair and worry—he could understand that well enough. John was by her side, quietly supporting her without question or complaint. He smiled inwardly at the Highwayman. Though he'd never spoken of it, he clearly loved Imogen—his actions revealing that truth more plainly than any words could.

Hound didn't seem to be too worried about their situation, perhaps because he knew there would be more violence in their future and he was looking forward to it, or perhaps because his temperament was simply immune to worry. Either way, Ben was glad to have him. Whatever else he was, Hound was both loyal and a good man in a fight. Qualities that would no doubt prove invaluable in the coming days and weeks.

Zack was entirely out of his depth. Ben felt sorry for him. He'd bumbled into this situation when he should have just gone home, and now it was probably too late for him to salvage his old life. One more victim.

That left Frank, his brother, the one person he wished he could trust with anything and yet couldn't trust at all. Frank would eventually make a move to get the egg, of that Ben was certain. How and when were the only questions.

Annabelle and Adam returned with a tray filled with cups and a steaming hot kettle of tea. He thanked them with a smile. The tea was warm and soothing, a brief respite from his inner turmoil.

"We should talk about what we're going to do next," Frank said, dispelling the moment of peace that Ben was savoring.

"That's a conversation that should probably wait until my father arrives," Annabelle said.

"She's right," Ben said.

"Is she?" Frank asked. "It doesn't sound like he's going to help us any more than he already has. Don't get me wrong, I'm grateful for all your family has done, but without his help, I don't know how we can possibly hope to kill the dragon."

"The wyrm has my baby," Imogen said.

Frank held up his hands, palms out. "I know, and I'm not saying we abandon him, I'm saying we go get him without confronting the dragon."

Ben clenched his jaw, but remained silent. Imogen's baby was important, he was family and he was helpless. Ben wanted to help him, even if only to help Imogen, but when he stepped back from his feelings and looked at the situation with cold eyes, he knew that his real duty was much, much bigger. The egg gave him a better chance against the dragon than any other person alive.

If he didn't rise to the challenge, then no one would. Humanity would be forever enslaved.

No pressure, he thought.

"And then what?" Hound asked.

"We run," Frank said with a flippant shrug. "We get as far away from the wyrm as we can and we live our lives."

"Do you really think the dragon is going to give up on the egg?" Hound asked.

"What can he do if he can't find it?"

"How sure are you that we can hide it?" Hound asked. "I don't know a damn thing about magic. What if we think it's well hidden but the dragon comes anyway?"

"So we put it back where it was," Frank said. "The dragon didn't find it for all those years where the old man kept it hidden."

Ben schooled his emotions, finally chuckling softly to himself.

"And after I put it back where our grandfather had hidden it, would you like me to draw you a map?" Ben asked.

Frank glared at him. "You're insane if you think I'm going to follow you into a dragon's lair. Leading us to our collective suicide won't do anyone any good."

"Who says I'm asking you to follow me?"

Ben and Frank glared at each other until Frank finally smiled to diffuse the tension.

"You're my brother, where else would I go?"

Ben knew with perfect certainty that the only way Frank would leave now was with the egg.

"Maybe we should ditch him," Homer said.

"The thought crossed my mind," Ben said.

"Look, I'm just trying to be realistic," Frank said, his voice dripping with reasonableness. "We all know that we don't stand a chance against a dragon, egg or not. The truth is, you don't even know how to use it, and it's not going to do us any good to waltz in there and get ourselves killed."

"I'm not going to knock on the wyrm's front door," Ben said.

"All right, so what is your plan then?" Frank asked.

"I'm not sure yet," Ben said, with a shrug. "I don't have enough information."

Imogen tensed almost imperceptibly.

"My father might have some insights," Annabelle said.

"I'm hoping he does," Ben said. "The truth is, I'm out of my depth and I need all the help I can get."

"If you feel that way, maybe you should let us help you carry your burden," Frank said.

Ben snorted. "Never give up, do you?"

"That's not what I meant, but it's obviously weighing on you. That egg is really more of a curse. As long as you have it, the wyrm will hunt you."

"And I suppose you'd be happy to take that risk."

"I'd be happy to share it," Frank said. "You don't have to do this alone."

"Do what alone?" a voice from the hall asked.

"NACC technology detected," the augment said, flashing a diagram of a wristband in Ben's mind.

All eyes turned to the two men standing at the threshold, scrutinizing them. The augment highlighted the tech weapon worn around the wrist of the older man.

"Where's Robert?" the man asked, a hard edge in his voice.

Kat stood with a deferential nod. "The Wizard was killed," she said without emotion.

Alarm ghosted across both men's faces.

"Robert's dead?" the older man asked, a tremor in his voice.

"I'm sorry, Daddy," Annabelle said, going to her father and hugging him.

He closed his eyes for a moment before he took a quick breath and composed himself.

"Where's the egg?" he demanded, stepping past his daughter.

Ben stood, facing him as he drew the egg from his shoulder bag and held it out.

Some small portion of the tension etched into Dom's face eased.

"And exactly who the hell are you?" he demanded.

"My name is Benjamin Boyce. My grandfather was the Wizard, though I didn't know that until very recently."

"*Our* grandfather. My name is Franklin Boyce, at your service," Frank said.

Dom scarcely noticed him, his eyes still locked on the egg. After a moment of tense silence, he seemed to come to a decision, nodding to himself before scanning the rest of the faces around the table.

"Imogen? Is that you?"

She nodded, forcing a half smile.

"You were just a kid the last time I saw you," Dom said. "I'm sorry about your father."

"Me too," she said.

He strode to the empty chair at one end of the table and sat down. The man who had arrived with him leaned up against the wall just beside the entrance.

Dom folded his hands on the table and said to no one in particular, "Tell me everything that's happened."

What followed was a somewhat sanitized version of the past few weeks. Ben was careful to leave out any mention of the augment. Frank still didn't know about it, and Ben didn't want him to. He couldn't really put his finger on why, except that he just didn't trust his brother.

Dom quizzed them on various points, focusing on their contact with the Warlock and then even more intently on their experiences with the dragon. Once they had finished their story, he sat back and shook his head.

"Chen, too," he muttered. "I'm the only one left." He sighed sadly as he eased himself away from the table. "Annabelle will see to your quarters. We'll talk more over dinner."

"Wait, that's it?" Frank asked.

"For now," Dom said. "You just told me that two of my oldest friends are dead. I think I'd like to be alone."

He left without another word.

Chapter 3

Annabelle showed them to their rooms, still musty, but dry enough. Ben was just happy to have some solitude. He closed the door and gently pushed the bolt into place before laying out his bedroll on the matressless bed frame. The room was small. A single window looked out over the vines covering the north slope of the hill. Satisfied with his accommodations, he lay down and closed his eyes.

As much as he was trying to avoid thoughts of his grandfather, he found himself thinking about him ... thinking about his lessons, his wisdom, and his steady unconditional love. All his life, Ben had taken Cyril for granted. He'd just always been there—and now he wasn't. It felt like a vital part of the world had been taken from him.

Unbidden, the augment replayed the moment in the bunker when Cyril had first revealed his past. Ben could see and hear his grandfather in his mind's eye. For a moment, he simply enjoyed the perfect memory, taking solace in the realness of it, but it didn't take long for the horrible reality of Cyril's passing to overwhelm his reverie with grief.

"Stop," he said in his mind. The images of his grandfather vanished as if turned off by a switch. Ben rolled onto his side and wept. Homer jumped onto the bed and curled up with his back to Ben's.

He wasn't sure how long he cried, but eventually the sadness and loss began to subside. It was cathartic to weep, to release the pent-up emotion he'd been struggling to keep at bay. When his tears ran out, he slipped into a fitful sleep, waking somewhat confused.

"Someone's at the door," Homer said.

Ben sat up, rubbing his face.

Another knock.

"Yes?"

"Dinner will be ready in half an hour," Annabelle said.

Ben stood, filling his lungs with air in an attempt to clear the cobwebs from his mind. He opened the door, still a bit unsteady and not fully awake.

"Thanks," he said.

"You all right?" she asked. "It looks like you've been crying."

He nodded sadly.

She put a hand on his upper arm, offering him a sympathetic smile. "If you want to talk about it, I'm a pretty good listener."

"Thank you, but there's really nothing to say. He was always there for me—and now he's gone. I didn't know that anything could hurt like this."

"I can only imagine," she said.

He nodded again.

"There's a washroom down the hall with some hot water if you want to clean up before dinner."

"Thanks," he said, closing the door as she moved down the hall.

He opened the window and took several deep breaths of cool air to clear his head and wake him up before going to wash his face.

All of Ben's friends and family were already at the table when he arrived. One glance at Imogen told him that she had spent her afternoon crying as well. He put a hand on her shoulder in passing on the way to his chair. She forced a wan smile.

Dom arrived a few moments later, taking his seat at the head of the table. He surveyed the faces before him, but held his tongue, though it was clear that he had much to say. Annabelle and Adam arrived a minute later pushing carts full of hot food. At the smell of roasted venison with gravy and potatoes, Ben lost interest in his questions and even forgot his grief for a moment.

The meal was enjoyed quietly, all of them eating their fill. Only after the table had been cleared and wine had been poured did Dom raise his glass.

"To the Wizard and the Monk, champions of humanity. May they find peace."

Ben swallowed the lump in his throat and schooled his emotions, distancing himself from the raw pain still gnawing at his insides.

"Thank you for saving our lives, for taking us into your home, and for this meal," Ben said.

Dom nodded, pausing for a moment before speaking. "You're welcome and you're not. You bring danger to my doorstep. Your presence here puts my family in jeopardy. Yet, I can't in good conscience turn you away. Your grandfather was my friend. We rarely saw eye to eye, but there is no one that I would rather go into battle with. He saved my life countless times. We spilled blood into the same dirt. I sent help because he asked me to, and I will continue to help you out of respect for him, but I will decide what assistance to offer and I will expect you to live by my rules as long as you remain in my care."

Ben nodded. Frank took a breath to say something but Dom continued, cutting him off before he could speak.

"You may stay here for as long as your presence remains a secret. You will stay in the house or the courtyard. Do not leave. Do not allow anyone to see you. Do not go into town. When you're ready, I will arrange for discreet transport to your destination of choice, within reason. After that, you will never speak of me again and you will never return to my home.

"I will not challenge the dragon. My days of such recklessness are well past. I have paid a terrible price for my part in the war and I will not risk my family again."

"I thought you were going to help us," Frank said.

"I have helped you," Dom replied, a hard edge to his voice, his eyes holding Frank until he looked away.

"Thank you," Ben said. "My grandfather told me of your loss." He paused, looking down at the table and shaking his head. "I can only imagine, and still you choose to help us. I will be forever grateful for what you've done. And still, I need your help."

Dom's expression hardened but Ben met his glare without flinching or apology. "I understand that you won't face the dragon with me, but your counsel and guidance might prove invaluable."

Dom snorted, the severity of his expression softening. "You want my advice? All right. Destroy that damned egg and get as far away from the wyrm as you can."

"Finally, some common sense," Frank said.

"What about my baby?" Imogen said.

Dom closed his eyes, nodding sadly. He took a deep breath and sighed helplessly.

"I know you don't want to hear this, but your child might be beyond your reach. Trying to rescue him will probably lead to your death and deliver the egg and humanity's doom to the wyrm.

"Having lost three children myself, please know how horrible I feel telling you this. But, if there's one thing that war has taught me, it's that denying truth because it's too painful to face is a certain path to ruin."

Imogen shook her head, tears streaming down her face as she stared at Dom in horror and disbelief.

"Wise advice is typically unheeded," John said. "In fact, I'm sure some wise fool told you to flee the dragons rather than fight them, and we're all better off for your foolishness."

Dom couldn't help but smile. "You're right. Truth is, I don't expect you to take my advice, but these things need to be said."

"Can we back up for a minute?" Ben asked. "You said I should destroy the egg. My grandfather told me he didn't know how."

"He knew exactly how," Dom said. "He just didn't want to."

"Why would he lie to me?" Ben asked, a bit defensively.

"If you asked him, I'm sure he'd say that he didn't," Dom said. "He was always good at picking just the right words. The truth is we did try to destroy the egg, and we failed. But then, we never tried the one way that would work—hatch it and kill the whelp before it takes its first breath."

"Don't we need the egg to get Imogen's baby back?" Zack asked, his face flushing slightly as all eyes turned toward him.

"Pretty sure we do," Hound said.

Ben looked pointedly at Dom and said, "I appreciate your advice. And I will destroy the egg, but only after we've rescued Imogen's baby and killed the wyrm."

"I figured as much," Dom said.

"Someone's here," Homer said. "Out in the hall."

Ben surged to his feet, knocking over his chair, drawing his sword, point down, with his left hand and his pistol with his right.

"We're not alone," he said.

Hound was on his feet a moment later, followed by Kat and Dom.

As Dom stood, three darts an inch long and a quarter-inch wide lifted off his wristband and began orbiting over his head, gaining speed quickly until they were just a blur.

A diagram of the wristband and darts, along with a list of specifications, appeared in Ben's mind, followed by the words "Access Denied" in bold red letters. With a thought, he dismissed the informative image.

"Reveal yourself!" Dom said.

"It's just us, Daddy," Olivia said, stepping into view with Ellie right behind her.

"Goddamn it! What the hell do you think you're doing? I could have killed you!"

The darts slowed and reattached themselves to his wristband, seemingly unbidden.

"We're just playing sneaky," Olivia said.

"That excuse might have worked a few years ago, but not anymore. You're both grown women."

"So why don't you treat us like adults then?" Ellie asked, stepping into the room and facing her father. "You've kept us in the dark like children."

"I've kept you out of harm's way," Dom said. "And this is not the time to indulge your defiant streak, young lady." He stopped and shook his head. "Was that you following us?"

"Yeah, right up until Ty made us ... then we took the mountain trail."

"What?! You know there are bandits up there. I thought I taught you better."

"You taught us well enough to get past a bunch of half-drunk bandits," Ellie said.

Dom started to say something, but stopped and turned away from his daughters, taking a moment to rein in his anger. He turned back around slowly, staring each of his two wayward children down in turn.

"You will go to the working house on the other side of the property and stay there for the night. Then, tomorrow at first light, you will go back home." His tone was measured, even reasonable, but there was an undercurrent that made Ben a bit nervous and he wasn't even the focus of Dom's wrath.

"No," Ellie said.

Dom clenched his jaw as he stared at his daughter.

"Kat, shoot them both, tie them up in the back of a wagon and take them home."

Kat looked at Dom questioningly. "You sure?"

Both Ellie and Olivia looked a bit shocked at the command.

"Yes," Dom said, turning to Kat so she could see just how serious he really was.

She shrugged and started to draw her dart pistol.

"Wait," Ellie said. "Which one of you is Benjamin Boyce?"

Dom's eyes snapped back to Ellie, his raised hand staying Kat.

"Where did you hear that name?" he demanded.

"On the way here," Ellie said. "We were confronted by someone."

"Or something," Olivia added.

"A man was waiting for us on the trail," Ellie said. "He told us to deliver a message to Benjamin Boyce."

Ben felt ice flow through his veins. He swallowed his fear and stepped up beside Dom. "I'm Benjamin Boyce. What was the message?"

"Surrender the egg and your blood or he will rain hell down upon everyone you love," Ellie said.

"What did this man look like?" Ben asked, knowing the answer.

"Albino-white skin, pale blue eyes, shock-white hair, black spiked armor—and he had a cougar and a strange little man that didn't look quite human with him."

"Also, it looked like half his face had been melted off," Olivia added.

"The Warlock," Ben said, shaking his head. "I was hoping he was dead." He went back to his chair and sat down heavily. "Dom, I'd really like to hear everything they can tell me about this guy."

Dom harrumphed, shaking his head. He glowered at his daughters and said, "The two of you, sit down and start talking."

They obeyed, talking a few minutes to detail everything they could remember about their encounter.

"I got the feeling that he could have killed us both if he'd wanted to," Ellie said, wrapping up her report. Olivia nodded in agreement.

"You're both lucky to be alive," Frank said. "We've had a few run-ins with him and I can tell you from personal experience that he's dangerous."

"Yeah, we gathered that," Ellie said.

Ben almost smiled. He decided that he liked her. She was pretty, though not as beautiful as Olivia. While they both carried themselves with confidence, he got the impression that Olivia's self-assurance was born of an ability to charm and seduce. Ellie, on the other hand, carried herself like she could hold her own in a fight. And she wasn't afraid to speak her mind. All good things.

"It looks like you have more enemies than just the dragon," Dom said. "Is there anyone else hunting you that I should know about?"

"Just the demon Magoth, who's in possession of a Dragon Guard named Dominus Nash," Ben said with a helpless shrug.

"Yeah, that was part of your story that I wanted to clarify," Dom said. "Robert would have never summoned a demon. He always steadfastly refused to use bargaining magic."

Ben frowned for a moment before nodding. "I've always known my grandfather as Cyril Smith. The fact that that wasn't his real name is going to take some getting used to." He paused, then said, "As for the demon, my grandfather said that it was the only way to get Imogen's baby back. And it killed him."

The table fell silent until the tension became uncomfortable.

"Would someone please tell us what's going on?" Ellie asked.

Dom glared at his two daughters, stood up and left the room without a word.

Annabelle shook her head at her sisters. "You think he's mad? Just imagine what you're in for when Mom finds out what you've been up to."

They both cringed.

"We just wanted to be included," Olivia said.

"Well, I guess you got your wish," Annabelle said. "You might think otherwise after you hear the whole story."

"So tell us," Ellie said.

Annabelle looked to Ben.

"Thank you for warning me about the Warlock," he said, "but your father's right. You don't want any part of this."

He got up and headed for the door.

"Wait," Ellie said, coming to her feet quickly. "Where did you get that sword?"

It was only then that Ben noticed the blade buckled to her waist—an exact duplicate of the sword his grandfather had given him.

"I suspect it came from the same place yours did," he said, leaving the room before she could ask any more questions.

"I think she likes you," Homer said.

"How do you know?"

"You'd be surprised what an adequate sense of smell can do for you."

Ben snorted under his breath, shaking his head. "If you say so."

He returned to his room and locked the door before lying down to think about his options. He had hoped that the Dragon Slayer would help—even lead them against the dragon. With that hope dashed, he would have to decide his own course, a daunting prospect considering what he faced. Worse, he didn't have nearly as much time as he'd hoped given the appearance of the Warlock.

When he considered facing the dragon, he couldn't imagine a good outcome, at least not with his current resources and capabilities. He needed more power. That led him to magic and tech—both of which he had, and both of which were less than they could be.

He wanted to talk with Dom about magic. It was possible that the Dragon Slayer could offer some insight that could lead him to greater mastery of his fledgling manifestation abilities. He also wanted to talk with him about the augment in the hopes that he might know of an NACC facility that was still functional. He wasn't sure what new capabilities the augment might provide once it was satisfied with the truth of the world, but he was certain that anything would help. And, if he found a few tech weapons in the bargain, that would go a long way toward evening the field.

He lay there thinking for several hours. Part of him knew he should try to get some sleep, but he just couldn't seem to turn his mind off. There were so many unanswered questions and so much uncertainty. He kept circling back to worries that he had already thoroughly explored, only to work through them again and arrive at the exact same conclusions.

Homer lifted his head, his ears perking up as he sniffed the air. "Dom is coming—very quietly."

Ben went still, stopping his breathing so he could focus on listening.

"I don't hear anything."

There was a gentle tapping on the door.

"How about now?"

Ben gave Homer a sidelong look as he rolled to his feet and drew his sword before going to the door.

"Yes?" he asked in a loud whisper.

"We need to talk, alone."

Ben considered the request for a moment and then sheathed his sword and strapped on his belt, throwing the bag with the egg over his shoulder before quietly sliding the bolt and easing the door open.

Dom motioned for silence. Ben nodded and followed. Dom led him into the main house and then outside to an outbuilding adjacent to the manor on the opposite side from the stables and paddock. He unlocked the door and entered, motioning for Ben to follow. He frowned when Homer slipped in as well.

Ben started to speak, but Dom silenced him with a gesture in the growing light of the lamp he'd just lit. Ben looked around and saw pallets of supplies lining the space—bags of cement and plaster, stacks of lumber, buckets of nails, and an assortment of tools.

Dom eased a pallet jack under a skid and pulled it out into the center of the room, letting it down slowly. It had been resting on a trapdoor, which Dom unlocked and opened, revealing a steep wooden staircase.

Ben waited until Dom had reached the level below and held the lamp up before he followed. Homer descended right behind him, but far less gracefully.

"You know I don't like heights."

"Is the dog really necessary?" Dom asked.

"What kind of a question is that?" Homer protested.

Ben ignored him, answering Dom instead.

"Yes, he is."

Dom shook his head, climbing back up the stairs to close the trapdoor before leading Ben down a narrow tunnel to another door. He unlocked its three locks and led them inside, closing and securing the door behind them. The room was a workshop of sorts with several large tables, racks of tools hanging on the walls and a variety of other equipment that Ben didn't recognize.

Dom took a minute to build a fire in the wood stove, gesturing to one of two chairs. Ben sat down, wondering at the purpose of the place. Dom found a bottle and two glasses, pouring each half full before sitting down himself. He took a deep breath and let it out slowly as if marshaling his thoughts.

"We have a lot to talk about, not the least of which are my daughters," Dom said. "I've tried to teach them to be independent, to think for themselves and to make their own choices. Looks like that's coming back to haunt me.

"The truth is, they're young and filled with idealism. All three of them want to go to war with the wyrm, if only because they think it's the right thing to do. Annabelle is beginning to show some sense, I suspect mostly due to her husband and the prospect of having a family of her own. But the other two are just as delusional as most young people. They think fighting the dragon would be romantic and glorious. If I read you right, you've discovered that it's anything but."

Ben nodded, taking a sip of the brandy that Dom had offered.

"The odds are pretty good that you're going to get everyone near you killed," Dom continued. "And the thing that terrifies me the most is the idea that one or both of my younger daughters might choose to help you. I think we can safely say that they aren't going to listen to me, so I'm asking you to refuse them if they offer. Turn them away. Send them home. Make them hate you if necessary. Just please, don't lead my daughters to their doom."

Ben blinked a few times as he absorbed Dom's plea. He hadn't even considered that Ellie and Olivia would join him—and the idea of asking them to help would never have crossed his mind. Looking into Dom's eyes, he could see genuine fear.

"The last thing I want to do is cause you or your family any harm," Ben said.

"I know, and I don't question your intent, but good intentions don't matter for shit when you're looking a dragon in the eye. He's going to eat you if you're dumb enough to give him the chance. Worse, he'll kill my daughters if they're standing next to you."

Ben shrugged helplessly.

"Give me your word that you won't involve my daughters."

"I promise that I won't involve your daughters."

Dom nodded with a mixture of satisfaction and skepticism.

"Well, I guess that's all I can ask for. Now, let's talk about your plan of attack. You do have a plan, right?"

"I'm not sure I'd call it a plan at this point. I know that I'm not ready to face the dragon … so I need to get ready. I'm hoping you can help me with that."

Dom snorted, shaking his head. "You'll never be ready to face the wyrm. The best you can hope for is to get lucky."

"That's not very encouraging."

"It wasn't meant to be."

Ben fell silent, staring at the flickering fire through the vent on the front of the stove.

"My grandfather told me about a book called the Dragon's Codex."

Dom half-smiled. "I guess that's as good a starting point as any. At least you're thinking strategically. Shame it won't do you much good."

"Why?"

"The Codex is in the deepest levels of Shasta Base, and that place is stalker central. And that's provided that the dragon didn't find it—though I doubt he did."

"So it's still there, then?"

"Maybe, but getting to it will be a bigger challenge than fighting the dragon. It's locked in a vault that was spelled by Sephiroth to ensure that magic couldn't open it. I can give you my entry code but the vault also has a set of biometric scanners that requires two of us."

"Us who?"

"The original four. Since I'm the only one left, I doubt that door will ever open again."

Ben felt like he'd been kicked in the gut. Since his grandfather had died, he'd been holding out hope that the Codex would provide him with the guidance he needed to wield magic as a weapon. He didn't realize just how much he'd been counting on that until now.

"There has to be a way."

"And maybe there is, but I don't know it. Even if you could get through the door, getting to it is probably impossible. The entire base was burned out. Most of the top levels collapsed into a maze of unstable rubble, and then the wyrm sent in his minions. And not just stalkers. He summoned some things that make the horrors you've witnessed look positively tame."

"I can't fight the dragon without magic. If I can't get the Codex, then where can I go for the answers I need? Can you teach me?"

Dom laughed humorlessly, shaking his head. "I was the least magically inclined of the bunch. If I had to guess, I'd bet that you already know more about magic than I do. Whether you realize it or not, your grandfather spent years teaching you the things he thought you needed to know, even if he didn't tell you what he was up to. Typical Robert."

"He taught me Tai Chi and meditation, but I don't know how that's supposed to help me beyond simple manifestation."

"So you have used magic then?"

Ben nodded, fishing his lucky coin out of his pocket. "He gave this to me when I was twelve and taught me to visualize it in my meditations. Since we retrieved the egg, I've been finding coins exactly like this one."

Dom chuckled. "It's funny, we were always in need of money to keep fighting. I guess it doesn't surprise me that he'd make that the one thing you won't have a problem with."

"But how do I fight a dragon with gold?"

"Every war in the history of the world has been fought with gold. You'd be surprised what you can get people to do for you if you can afford to pay them."

"I'm not going to win this fight by hiring mercenaries. I need something more direct."

"Don't underestimate the power of people working for you," Dom said. "Half of war is intel, and people have always been the best source of intel there is. You can get a lot with surveillance—capabilities, positions, armaments. What you can't get by watching and listening is intent and strategy, or better yet, an inside man. That comes from people in just the right place who can be had for the right price.

"Consider the dragons' initial attack. They didn't use magic to attack, they used it as currency to buy the people they needed—with devastating effect.

"More to the point, manifestation is a skill—one that you've developed to at least some degree if you're able to attract gold coins to you. My advice, focus on honing that skill until you can bring about events on the fly as circumstances dictate.

"That was your grandfather's forte. I can't tell you how many times he created little changes that made all the difference. The trick is being able to do so quickly and reliably. Also, having the imagination to think of just the right tweak to reality that will lead to the outcome you desire is vitally important."

Ben frowned. "I saw him do that a few times, but it always seemed so mundane."

"Perhaps, but I bet if you look back, you'll realize that without his intervention you would have had a much harder time of it."

"I guess you're right, but … well, it just seems like magic ought to be able to call lightning or brimstone or something down on the wyrm and his minions."

Dom laughed, taking a moment to sip at his brandy.

"Ah to be young again," he said, chuckling to himself. "I used to think exactly the same thing. Robert and I argued about it often in the early years, but over time I came to see the wisdom of his approach. We had a few operatives with dragon artifacts who tried to attack the dragon directly with magic." He shook his head and fell silent.

"What happened?"

"They died. If you hear anything that I tell you, hear this: You will never be able to match the dragon with magic … not ever."

It was Ben's turn to fall silent. He felt what little hope he had drain away. For a moment he even considered giving up, going into hiding and just trying to live his life. But then he thought of Imogen and her baby. He remembered that his grandfather had prepared him for this. He forced himself to face the fact, as preposterous as it was, that he was humanity's best hope.

He tried to ignore the gibbering insanity that accompanied such monumental responsibility and returned to the problem at hand.

"So what can magic do for me?"

"It can do a lot," Dom said. "The gold you're manifesting is no small thing. Don't be afraid to use it. It won't run out so long as you keep focusing on it. Aside from that, you should start using your magic in conjunction with your sword."

"How?" Ben asked, a spark of excitement igniting within him.

"Robert didn't choose Tai Chi by accident," Dom said. "He learned it from Chen, who often said that Tai Chi is meditation in motion. I know from experience that magic can make you far more effective in battle. When you become one with your blade, when you lose yourself in the flow of the fight, the magic will make your sword sharper, your movements effortless, your attacks hard and true, time itself will seem to slow for you. Perhaps more than any other thing, magic will make you lucky. When you're in that flow, that state of grace, events will fall your way with uncanny frequency."

"How do I learn that?"

"The same way you learn anything else—practice."

"I'm not sure I have time."

"You already have the skills you need—the ability to manifest and training with your sword. All you have to do is put them together. The courtyard makes for a good practice area."

Ben nodded, considering his advice and beginning to make plans for testing this new perspective on his training.

"I'll certainly give it a try, but I'm not sure it will be enough."

"I'm certain that it won't," Dom said. "I'll say it again: The dragon will kill you if you go up against him."

Ben felt a squirming sensation in his belly that morphed into anger.

"What choice do I have? The wyrm abducted Imogen's baby. He killed my grandfather. He drove us from our home. His tyranny is spreading like a plague. It won't be long before he's knocking at your door. What will you do? Run? Hide?

"Someone has to stand up to him or he'll take this whole world for himself, and everybody, everywhere will suffer for it. I thought you of all people would understand that."

Dom took his anger without offense, smiling sadly and nodding to himself.

"You're right. About all of it. Many years ago, I made much the same argument. But that was before…" He stopped, his eyes going distant, a haunted look ghosting across his face.

"You're young and filled with delusions about the very nature of the world. And maybe the world is a better place for youthful exuberance and the seemingly infinite ability of young people to exempt themselves from even the most obvious consequences of foolish choices. Maybe you will prevail. I hope you do, but I doubt you will.

"As for me and mine, when the dragon comes calling, we won't be here to answer the door. I'll take my family and we'll run or hide. I've learned my lesson all too well."

In spite of the frustration that Ben felt, he couldn't help but sympathize with Dom's position. And, truth be told, he had no right to ask any more of the man. He'd already fought his war, and done more to free humanity from the tyranny of the wyrm than any other person still living. He was an old soldier back from the war, and he deserved to live the remainder of his life in peace.

"Don't you think I want to be safe and happy?" Ben said. "That I'd rather just live my life? Trouble is, I can't bring myself to do it, not with what I know. I have to try. I have to do everything I can for Imogen's baby, for everyone, or I just won't be able to live with myself."

"I can understand that," Dom said. "More about Imogen's baby than the rest of it anyway."

"What do you mean?"

"Look around. Who else is fighting this fight for the sake of humankind?"

Ben looked at him blankly.

"No one," Dom said deliberately. "No one else is risking their life for you, aside from your friends and my family at any rate. Those people out there," he gestured toward the wall, "they're just trying to get by. None of them are planning to storm the dragon's lair on your behalf. If they can't be bothered to stand up for their own liberty and the future of their children, then why should you?"

Ben looked into the fire for a moment before he withdrew the egg and held it up in the flickering light.

"Because my grandfather gave me this, because he died for all those people out there, because I can't let his death be in vain. It has to matter, it has to lead to a better world."

Dom shook his head, sighing heavily. "More delusions. In many ways, I knew your grandfather better than you did. Trust me when I tell you that he wasn't thinking of all those people out there when he decided to take up the moniker of the Wizard again—he was thinking about his grandson, period.

"As for challenging the dragon to avenge your grandfather, he'd slap you upside the head if he heard you say that. As far as I can tell, the only legitimate motivation you have in this whole thing is saving your own blood. That, I understand. The rest of it, the fate of the world and all that nonsense, that's too big a burden for any man to carry. Trust me, if you try to pick up the weight of the world, it'll crush you."

"Even if my only objective is to save my nephew," Ben said, "I still need to face the dragon. For that, I need all the power I can get."

"Yes and no," Dom said. "Your objective should be to rescue the baby without confronting the dragon. With a little bit of creativity and a lot of luck, that may actually be possible. As for power, you have money. Find an inside man."

Ben considered his suggestion. It was certainly a more workable plan than charging into the dragon's lair and confronting him with a sword that couldn't even penetrate his scales.

"They call you the Dragon Slayer," he said, gauging Dom's reaction to the title. The man frowned, clenching his jaw. "My grandfather said you didn't like to be called that."

"No, I don't."

"But you did kill a dragon."

"Yes, but it was pure dumb luck. By all rights, I should have died that day."

"But you didn't," Ben said, drawing his sword and resting the point on the ground in front of his chair. "Your daughter has a sword exactly like this one."

Dom nodded, one side of his mouth turning up mirthlessly. "You want to know about the Dragon's Fang."

"This is a good blade," Ben said, "but we both know it's useless against the dragon."

"Mostly ... you might be able to poke the wyrm's eye out with it, right before he eats you."

"But the Dragon's Fang can penetrate his scales."

"Yes, it can ... and no, you can't have it."

When Ben didn't respond, Dom continued.

"We had those swords made to exacting specifications. The length, weight, and balance are precisely the same as the Fang. The pommel even screws off to accept a staff so you can turn it into a spear." He smiled at Ben's look of surprise. "The thinking was that we should all have experience wielding the one weapon that we knew could kill a dragon. That way, if I fell, someone else could pick up my sword and make good use of it. Little did we know that the dragon would defeat us by breaking our spirit rather than our bodies.

"Much like your grandfather did with the egg, I've put the Fang well out of reach. As you might imagine, it's one of the items that the wyrm is very interested in acquiring. And, while it doesn't represent nearly the danger that the egg does, it would still be very bad if it fell into his possession."

"What if it's the one thing that could make the difference?"

"*What if* is for children," Dom said, with a derisive snort. "If you try to face the dragon with a sword, any sword, you're going to wind up little more than a spot of indigestion."

Ben took a breath to speak, but Dom continued.

"That sword would give you a false sense of confidence. It would lead you to believe the delusion that you can kill the wyrm, and you can't. If you try, you will die. I don't know how to say it any more clearly."

"You've made your point, and I reject it," Ben said. "You killed a dragon with that sword. If you can do it, then it can be done. If it can be done, then I can do it."

Dom chuckled to himself. "I see some of your grandfather in you ... not the wise parts, mind you, but the self-assurance. Robert always believed that anything was possible with sufficient motivation, preparation, and will. And maybe it is, but I'm still not giving you my sword."

"Fair enough," Ben said. "I didn't really expect you to, and I'm not sure I was even asking you for it. I guess I just need to know that the wyrm can be killed."

"Oh, he can die, all right. Killing him is something else entirely."

Ben sipped his brandy while he considered his next question.

"Is there another way into Shasta Base besides the main entrance?"

Dom laughed, shaking his head. "Just when I think I've gotten through to you—"

Ben held his hands up and shrugged. "I need all the information I can get, even if I don't use it."

"I guess that's fair," Dom said. "The answer is yes. One of the things that made Shasta so useful was the tunnel system it connects to. Most people aren't even aware of the hundreds of underground bases with tunnels connecting them into a network that stretches across the entire continent.

"The old government built the first generation of this network, most if it in what was the western United States. When the nation-states bankrupted the world with the magic of electronic currencies, some of these bases were used to shelter the wealthy elite from the wrath of everyone else. Over time, they either came out or died in hiding and the bases went dark for decades. Once the corporations managed to consolidate power, they revived the underground network and began to expand it, for all the good it did them.

"Most of the corporate resistance to the dragons arose from the resources and personnel they had hidden away beyond the reach of the neural-pulse bombs. For a while, they put up a fight, but ultimately the dragons defeated them in exactly the same way that they murdered nine billion people in an afternoon ... they bribed bureaucrats to turn on their own."

"I still find that hard to comprehend," Ben said.

"That's probably because you've never had to deal with very many bureaucrats," Dom said. "Anyway, the short version of my very long answer is, there are several tunnels leading to the lower levels of Shasta Base. Trouble is, they haven't been maintained for decades ... oh, and the dragon knows all about them. They're full of things that go bump in the night. You'd probably have better luck getting to the Codex if you knocked on the front door and fought your way through a few dozen levels of stalkers."

"I was really hoping this conversation would be more encouraging," Ben said.

Dom laughed out loud, draining his brandy and pouring another glass, topping Ben's off as well.

"I'm trying to encourage you to survive."

"And I appreciate that," Ben said, scratching his eyebrow as he considered another line of questions.

Chapter 4

He decided that now was as good a time as any to tell the Dragon Slayer about the augment.

"The Warlock, the one your daughters met, he was summoned with my blood. I almost bled out as a result." He stopped talking, his eyes losing focus as the memory of the coldness seeping into his bones came over him. He shivered involuntarily, taking a quick breath to bring himself back to the present moment, savoring the warmth of the stove on his face and the brandy in his belly.

"My grandfather saved me with a serum he found in one of the NACC bunkers."

"Holy shit!" Dom said, looking at him in shock. "He actually made you drink that?"

Ben shrugged. "I was dying. He used the egg to take as much of my injury onto himself as he could—so much that he almost died too. But it wasn't enough. I'd lost so much blood that my heart was failing.

"At any rate, the serum healed me … and more. It built a computer in my head. It's been useful, to a point, but it doesn't recognize me as an NACC agent, so it won't give me access to all of its capabilities until it can link with a corporate computer."

"Huh," Dom said, eyeing Ben as if he were a curiosity. "I always wondered what that stuff would do. I mean, I read some of the information that came with it, but it all sounded so farfetched."

"More than dragons?"

"I guess that's a fair point. Still, I wasn't about to be a human guinea pig. None of us were. The other items we recovered from that lab were far more useful—your grandfather's drone and my dart band, for example." He held up his left hand so Ben could see the wristband with darts affixed to it.

"Yeah, my augment pointed that out to me the moment you entered the room."

"Interesting. What else does it do for you?"

"It heals me when necessary, and it provides me with information. It's like having a whole library in my head. It also allowed me to see through my grandfather's drone. And it records everything I see and hear, so I can play it back in my mind whenever I want to."

Dom whistled. "Impressive."

"I think it will allow me to use NACC tech if I can link with a computer."

"Ah, so you want to know where to find a functioning corporate bunker."

Ben nodded. "My grandfather said that I should rely on tech more than magic. This is the best tech I've got," he said, tapping the side of his head.

"I can't argue with that," Dom said. "Truth is, tech won't do much against the wyrm either, but most of his minions aren't so well protected, and you're going to have to get through a bunch of them to get to the child. Also, that computer in your head can probably open the vault in Shasta." He scratched his stubble, frowning deeply. "Off the top of my head, I don't know of any facility that's still intact, but I do know a few people who might. Let me look into that."

"Please be discreet," Ben said, pausing for a moment, pursing his lips as he debated with himself how much to tell Dom about Frank. "My brother is unaware of the augment, and I'd prefer that it stayed that way."

"You don't trust him?"

"No," Ben said, shaking his head sadly. "In fact, I believe that he's the reason our grandfather didn't tell us about his past. Frank can always be counted on to do what he thinks is best for him. He also can't stand the idea that I might have anything that he can't take from me."

"I've known a few people like that over the years," Dom said. "They tend to gravitate toward positions of power. The Dragon Guard is full of them."

"Yeah, I thought he was one of a kind until I met Nash," Ben said.

"So I bet he's happy as a clam that Robert left you the egg," Dom said with a wry smile.

"Yeah, he's already tried to talk me out of it a few times. If our history is any indication, he'll try to steal it next."

Dom sighed.

"That explains a few things," he finally said. "I wondered why Robert didn't tell you more. As if you didn't have enough to worry about."

"Yeah," Ben said again.

"Well, I may actually be able to help you on that count," Dom said. "Wait here."

He left the room and returned a minute later with a bag of plaster over his shoulder, flopping it down on one of the worktables.

"We had a few acquaintances who thought they would be able to better serve their own interests if they were in possession of the egg. Rather than fight them, your grandfather made a duplicate egg and let them steal it." He chuckled. "Robert was a wily one. We had a good laugh imagining them trying to work magic with a lump of plaster."

Ben smiled. "You want to make a decoy."

"Yep. Come on, give me a hand."

"All right," Ben said, a little unsure but willing to learn.

Dom mixed a bucket of plaster and poured a small wooden box half full of the white paste. Then he pointed to a tub of bearing grease on a nearby shelf. "Smear that all over the egg," he said.

Ben did as instructed, deciding to hold his questions until after they were finished, on the theory that most of them would be answered by the process. He wasn't disappointed.

"Good, now press the egg down into the plaster, right in the middle of the box."

Once in place, Dom laid a few strips of paper on the plaster all around the egg and poured more plaster over the top of it.

"There, this stuff sets pretty fast," he said. "We should have just enough time for another glass of brandy."

After a few moments of silence, Ben said, "Thank you."

"You're welcome," Dom said, raising his glass. "I know I haven't told you what you wanted to hear, but sometimes that's exactly what you need to hear."

"We haven't really talked about the Warlock," Ben said. "If he found your daughters, then he can find me."

"Yeah, I'm sure he already knows where you are," Dom said.

"How so?"

"Your blood," Dom said, looking over at Ben with deadly seriousness. "If he was brought here with a circle consecrated by your blood, then he will always be able to find you. You and he are bound by magic."

Ben felt a chill wash over him in spite of the pleasant warmth emanating from the stove.

"I didn't know that," Ben said, the implications ratcheting his fear higher still. "How do I break that bond?"

"Kill him or send him back where he came from," Dom said with a helpless shrug. "Both of which are probably beyond you."

"No wonder my grandfather was so concerned about him."

"You could always give him what he wants," Dom said.

"What do you mean? He wants my blood."

"Probably not all of it. If your blood brought him here, then he needs your blood to get home. A small jar would be enough—provided that's what he wants if for, anyway."

"I'm not sure he wants to go home," Ben said. "I got the impression that he wants this world for himself."

"Even better," Dom said. "Give him the egg and let him go at it with the dragon. Maybe they'll kill each other."

"He tried that already. He called the dragon out and stood his ground. After the battle, the guy or thing or whatever was riding the dragon had the Warlock's staff. We hoped he was dead."

"Describe the staff."

"It looked old, and it had a dragon's claw affixed to one end," Ben said.

Dom nodded to himself. "That was his source, or at least one of them. He'll be weaker now. Probably why he wants the egg so badly. Without a more substantial dragon artifact, he doesn't stand a chance against the wyrm, or Noisome Ick for that matter."

"Who?"

"The dragon's high priest."

"That's his name? Noisome Ick?"

Dom chuckled, nodding with mirth. "Not the name his mother gave him, mind you. That's the name the dragon gave him. He's the only person permitted to have an audience with the wyrm. As I understand it, everybody else that goes into his lair doesn't come back out."

"Why would the dragon name him that?"

"Contempt. The dragon hates us. We're beneath him. He refers to Noisome Ick as his slave. Everybody else, he calls food."

"He wasn't human," Ben said. "He had wings and claws and a dragon-like snout."

"The rest of the priests are fed a concoction containing ground-up dragon scales, but Ick, he's been drinking dragon blood, straight up. It's changed him into something else, rewritten his genetic code.

"He's dangerous, and completely loyal to the wyrm," Dom said. "Rumor has it that he was once the Chief Healthcare Officer for the NACC—one of the original sellouts."

"How is that possible? Dragonfall was seventy-five years ago."

"Dragon magic can prolong life," Dom said with a shrug, "if you're willing to pay the price. All Ick had to do was give up humanity."

"I still can't bring myself to understand how anybody could do that."

"If I read things right, I suspect that he's a lot like your brother—maybe a bit more of a big-picture kind of guy, but the same where it counts."

Ben felt a chill race through him again. He knew that Frank couldn't be trusted, but he wasn't ready to accept that his own brother might turn his back on humanity itself for personal gain. He dismissed the thought, if only to banish the nagging worry that accompanied it.

"I'm afraid that the Warlock will attack us here, and soon," he said.

"I'm expecting it," Dom said.

"Aren't you concerned?"

"Concerned? Sure. But that's not going to change anything. Besides, you said he had a hard time defending against tech. If he comes from a version of Earth that was conquered by the dragons millennia ago, that makes perfect sense. More importantly, it makes him vulnerable in ways that he isn't even aware of."

"Your dart band?"

"For starters," Dom said with a knowing smile. "It's not the only trick I've got up my sleeve. You know, I wasn't kidding when I suggested giving him what he wants."

"What good would it do to trade one tyrant for another?"

"The warlock is human," Dom said. "If he kills the dragon, he'll reign for no more than a hundred years and then he'll die of old age. You might just save humanity from thousands of years of oppression. Also, without the egg, you're just another snack as far as the wyrm is concerned. But with the egg, you're enemy number one."

"What about Imogen's baby?"

Dom winced. "Yeah, there is that."

"Maybe Rufus, John, and I should go after the Warlock tomorrow," Ben said.

"No, you shouldn't," Dom said. "First, you're not leaving the house until you're ready to leave for good. Second, why kill him when you can use him?"

"What do you mean?"

"He's a powerful piece on the board and he's a natural enemy of the dragon," Dom said, as if he were talking to a child. "Why sacrifice him for nothing?"

"You say that like I have some control over him."

"Control is a strong word," Dom said. "But you do have influence because you have two things that he wants. Hell, you might even be able to make an alliance with him."

"You said yourself, he's like Frank. If I can't trust my own brother, how on earth can I trust the Warlock?"

"Oh, you can't, but that doesn't mean you can't make use of him," Dom said. "People like that, those without conscience, are predictable. Like you said, they'll always do what's in their perceived best interest, regardless of the consequences to others. That predictability makes them vulnerable, provided you have the imagination to exploit it.

"For example, I doubt very seriously that the Warlock will attack us here in person. He'll send a proxy to do his dirty work. His fight with the dragon and Ick left him weakened and vulnerable. And he knows that his defenses won't hold up to tech weapons. He won't risk himself unless he thinks he has the upper hand."

Ben shook his head. "I'd feel a lot better if he was dead."

"You're at war now, so I suggest you get used to it because this won't be the last time you feel that way. Learn to see your enemies as sources of power to be used against other enemies. Play one against the other."

"That all seems so ... dishonest."

Dom laughed out loud, taking a few moments to indulge his mirth, shaking his head and wiping a tear from his eye.

"Ah, if only your grandfather could see you now," he said, stifling another round of laughter. "He'd be torn between pride at your decency and dismay at your naiveté.

"Listen to what I'm about to say to you and make it a part of your being," Dom said, all hint of humor gone from his visage. "Deception is the beating heart of war. If you refuse to use it as a weapon, you will lose."

Ben opened his mouth and then closed it again, frowning deeply as he deflated slightly.

Dom leaned in. "More wars have been won with a well-placed lie than with any weapon ever invented. Hell, most wars are started with a well-placed lie."

"The dragons didn't use lies to kill us, they used our own weapons."

"Wrong! They used lies. Do you really think the bureaucrats in the NACC thought the dragons were plotting to have the other conglomerates attack them right back? Isn't it far more likely that the pawns in each corporate government thought they were going to wipe out the rest of the world while their corporation remained intact? Believe me, self-preservation is right at the top of the list of bureaucratic skills. None of them would have gone along with the dragons if they'd known their lives would be forfeit in the bargain."

Ben couldn't argue with his reasoning, but he hated the notion just the same.

"I know, you wanted war to be glory and honor—it's not. Never has been. Never will be. That's just a line of bullshit that leaders use to encourage young, idealistic dupes to spill their blood in the dirt. And for what? To grow the wealth and power of old and cynical assholes. Just one more lie."

Ben felt like he'd been kicked in the gut. Worse, he couldn't find a valid argument to refute anything that Dom had said, even though he desperately wanted to.

Dom patted him on the shoulder.

"Maybe that's enough hard truth for one day," he said. "The mold should be set by now anyway."

He got up and went to the box and carefully pulled the boards away until he had a cube of plaster. He selected a putty knife from the rack of tools on the wall and pried the mold apart where he'd laid the paper, then gently tapped the egg out and handed it back to Ben.

"Yeah, this will do nicely," he said, inspecting the mold before smearing a layer of grease over the inside. After rummaging around for a minute in a tool box, he returned with a hand drill and bored a hole in the side of the mold.

"Mix up some more of that plaster, and make it wet," he said. "It has to be thin enough to flow through this hole."

Ben did as instructed while Dom fit the two halves back together, ensuring that they lined up with one another perfectly before binding them with tape.

"Good," he said, giving the plaster a stir. "Here, hold this." He handed Ben a funnel and motioned to the hole in the side of the mold. It took several minutes to fill the egg-shaped cavity, shaking the mold and tapping it occasionally to ensure that there were no air bubbles. Satisfied with their work, Dom motioned to the chairs and they sat back down.

"Do you remember what my daughters said when we caught them listening in on us?"

Ben thought about it for half a second and the scene played back in his mind, courtesy of the augment.

"You mean the part about playing *sneaky*?"

"Exactly," Dom said. "It's a game I taught them when they were young. The premise is, you try to learn things that others want to keep hidden without them knowing about it. All three of my daughters are good girls, but all of them can lie to your face without any kind of tell. They're light on their feet, know how to hide in the shadows and move in the dark. I taught them these things because I want them to have the best chance of survival possible, no matter what comes their way.

"I could have focused on a hundred other things. They all know how to fight to one degree or another, but I never pushed them to learn those skills because fighting is a good way to get yourself killed. It's far better to defeat your enemy without a fight, and sneaky does that better than anything else.

"A thief in the night can accomplish far more than a warrior in the light. Embrace deceit and you might just get through this alive."

"You should listen to him," Homer said.

"You too?" Ben said.

"He's right," Homer said. "You can't beat the dragon in a fair fight."

"Much of the advice he's given you has been proven on the battlefield," the augment said. "Historical records suggest—"

"Enough," Ben said in his mind, cutting off the augment, as he reconsidered Dom's suggestions. When he started with the idea of confronting the dragon directly, the concept of winning without a fight started to sound more appealing. Then he considered his own skill set and deflated a bit.

"I'm not a very good liar," he said.

"I never imagined that you were," Dom said. "More often than not, deception in war doesn't involve a face-to-face lie—and if and when it does, have your brother do it for you. Sounds like he's a natural."

"I hadn't thought of that."

"Start thinking about your friends as weapons too," Dom said. "I know, I know, that's cold and calculating and unfeeling … and absolutely necessary. You can't afford to give up any of the precious few advantages you might have because it makes you feel bad to make use of them. Trust me, you'll feel far worse when the dragon eats you.

"Like it or not, you're the Wizard. And a wizard has to think strategically. He must be keenly aware of his strengths and weaknesses. He makes use of deception, trickery, manipulation, and misdirection at every turn.

"Believe it or not, your grandfather was the sneakiest, most underhanded and duplicitous person I ever knew. And, he was also one of the most honorable men that I ever called a friend. Those characteristics aren't mutually exclusive. He was honest to a fault with the people he loved, but the enemy never knew if he was coming or going."

"I wish I'd had the opportunity to see that side of him," Ben said.

"No, you don't," Dom said. "Knowing Robert, I'm quite sure that you saw the best he had to offer. Remember him as the kindly grandfather he was. That's what he would've wanted."

Ben swallowed the lump in his throat, searching his mind for something, anything, other than his grandfather to ask about.

"Maybe I should give the Warlock the decoy egg," he finally managed.

"Are you kidding? He'd see right through that," Dom said, shaking his head. "You really are a bad liar."

"I know … I hate lying to people almost as much as I hate being lied to. It always bothered me when Frank would deceive people. I learned to see through his outright lies early on, but then he started to get creative with his dishonesty, twisting words and using partial truths to mislead. I never wanted to be like that."

"Good, don't become that, just learn to do it when you have to," Dom said. "I suggest you look back over your brother's lies and think about the more effective deceptions that he managed to pull off. Find commonalities in the methods and techniques he used. Lying is a skill like anything else. Bad liars have tells, they twitch, look up and to the left, they fidget and blush. All of which stems from the self-consciousness a good person naturally feels when they deliberately deceive.

"Good liars are so sincere, you'd give them your coat in a rainstorm. Some, like your brother, don't have much of a conscience to get hung up on. The rest of us have to practice. Fortunately, there are a few basic principles. First, learn your tells. No one is going to believe you if you can't look them in the eye when you say something. Choose your lies carefully and use them rarely and for strategic purposes. The most devastating liars are people who are widely believed to be honest to a fault. You can't build that kind of reputation by lying about little things all the time.

"The most powerful lies always contain elements of the truth. Not only does it make it easier to tell sincerely, but parts of your deception are easy to verify and that lends credibility to the rest of your story.

"Above all, know what your intended target wants, and I mean truly, genuinely desires. People will believe a lie far more readily if they want it to be true. Figure that out and you have your in. The flip side of that is, know what you want and be wary of people who offer it at too low a price. Make no mistake, the dragon is a deceiver. He'll try and play you every way he can."

"That's a lot to think about, but I'm not sure how to make use of it," Ben said.

"You've already started," Dom said, pointing over his shoulder with his thumb. "The decoy egg is a deception. It's the prop for a lie. Now, you have to decide how you're going to use it."

Ben started to reply.

"Stop," Dom said, raising his hand. "I don't want to know. A secret isn't a secret if other people know about it. Even those you trust the most can betray you, so don't share important information with anybody unless they absolutely need that information."

"Imogen wouldn't—"

"Really?" Dom asked, cutting him off again. "What would she do to save her baby? She has powerful motivation, maybe the most powerful there is. You don't know what she might do if the wyrm forces her hand. We've already talked about your brother. The Highwayman is so obviously in love with Imogen that the only person who doesn't see it is her. Hound looks like a good man in a fight, and he seems loyal, but a man can always be broken. It might take a lot, but once he breaks, he'll give up everything he knows. And your buddy Zack, he'll fold faster than a pair of twos at the first hint of trouble. That leaves you with your dog, and the only reason he's not a risk is because he doesn't know anything."

"Hey!" Homer said, grumbling under his breath.

"Easy," Ben said silently.

"Hell, that computer in your head might even betray you," Dom said. "The point is, don't trust anyone with anything unless you absolutely have to."

"That sounds pretty lonely," Ben said.

"Like it or not, that egg makes you the Wizard and that makes you a general officer, a commander. There are few jobs in life more lonely than that."

Ben snorted, shaking his head. "That just sounds absurd. I'm not even twenty. And I'm certainly not in command of anything."

"Oh, but you are," Dom said. "You command the most powerful dragon artifact in the entire world. You might as well have an arsenal of neural-pulse bombs at your disposal. You also have a handful of people who are willing to follow you—and more will come. Once it gets out that the Wizard is walking the world again, people will beg you to lead them. Be wary of that as well. The wyrm will send infiltrators."

"I never wanted any of this," Ben muttered.

"If you did, you wouldn't be worthy of it," Dom said. "And, whether you want it or not, you've got it. Which brings me back to the Warlock. Maybe you make a bargain with him. Offer to give him the egg in exchange for Imogen's baby. Let him do the heavy lifting for you."

Ben thought about it for a moment. Simple and practical … and yet his conscience rebelled at the thought of empowering the Warlock, even if it meant that he could live a safe and comfortable life.

When he looked up Dom was watching him with a knowing smile.

"You know I can't do that. What's more you know why I can't do that."

"I do," Dom said. "I just wanted to make sure you know what you're fighting for. Ultimately, this isn't about Imogen's baby or the death of your grandfather. It's about obeying the dictates of your conscience. If that's truly what's driving you, then so be it. It's going to get you killed, but you'll die honorably. For some, that's a far better fate than living dishonorably."

"You just don't let up, do you?"

"Nope," Dom said. "The path you're walking leads to heartache and loss. You might just get lucky and save the world, but it'll cost you in ways you can't even imagine. In the end, you'll ask yourself if it was worth it."

"There were five dragons when you started, now there's only one. Don't you think what you did was worth it?"

Dom fell silent for a moment.

"I'm sure that there are countless people in the world whose lives are immeasurably better for what we did, but none of them are my sons."

He got up and went to the mold.

"It should be set by now," he said, carefully unwrapping it and prying the two halves apart. He tapped the plaster egg out and examined it carefully, taking a piece of sandpaper to the rough edge along the seam as well as to the plaster left by the fill hole.

"Well, it won't fool anyone experienced with magic," Dom said, "but your brother might buy it, especially if he has to work for it."

"Yeah, I'm not sure what to do about him," Ben said. "Sometimes I think I'd be better off if he just went his own way."

"Maybe," Dom said, "but I doubt he's going anywhere until he has what he wants. Better to keep him close. He might be useful."

"That'd be a first," Homer said.

Ben gave his dog a sidelong glance.

"You've given me a lot to think about."

"We'll talk more," Dom said, closing the draft ports on the stove. "It's late, you'd better get some sleep."

He led the way back into the storeroom, locking the doors as he went, taking a moment to conceal the trapdoor again with the pallet of building materials.

"Can you show me the courtyard on the way back to my room?" Ben asked.

"Sure," Dom said quietly, leading him along a different path through the house. The manor was built around the central courtyard with doors to the house on each wall and a gated tunnel through the ground floor leading out into the vineyard. The grass was lush and green and a bit unkempt. A seven-foot-tall, three-tiered fountain stood as the centerpiece with successively smaller bowls set one above the other around a single support pillar. The periphery of the courtyard was planted with rose bushes, all thorns and no flowers this time of year.

"Your room is right through there," Dom said, pointing to one of the doors. "Goodnight, Ben."

"Goodnight. I think I'm going to take a moment to get some air."

"I thought you might," Dom said over his shoulder.

Ben went to the fountain and sat down. He waited for several minutes, listening intently.

"Are we alone?"

"I don't hear anyone … or smell them," Homer said.

"Good," Ben said, taking the dragon's egg out of his shoulder bag and putting it into the top bowl of the fountain. A bit of water spilled over into the second bowl and then in turn into the base.

He sat back down and waited, searching the night for a thousand imagined threats, but all was quiet. He put the decoy egg into his bag and quietly returned to his room. He locked the door and lay down on the hard bed. In spite of all the worries plaguing his mind, he was asleep within minutes.

Chapter 5

He woke early with the first light of day streaming through his window. A flutter of fear brought him to his feet a moment later. The worry that hiding the egg in the fountain had left it exposed seized his imagination. He dressed quickly, stopping by the washroom briefly before heading straight to the courtyard.

It was a crisp morning with a clear sky. The grass was wet with morning dew and all was quiet. As much as he wanted to check on the egg, he didn't dare climb up on the fountain and peer into the top bowl for fear of revealing its hiding place. Instead, he sat on the edge of the fountain and closed his eyes.

After a few moments of deep breathing, his emotions began to settle and his mind cleared. He smiled to himself when he realized that he could feel its presence. He'd never given it much thought before. Since they'd retrieved it from his grandfather's bunker, the egg had always been nearby. Now, having spent a night away from it, he could sense the difference. It was subtle, almost imperceptible, but it was there for those with the will and the knowledge to see.

And that made it a threat.

If he could sense it, then so could others. He sighed. It was never easy. Fortunately, the person he was hiding the egg from at the moment was Frank.

He went to his pile of gear and drew his sword. It took a few minutes to begin to feel the flow of the egg's magic while he practiced his sword form. At first he found his mind split between doing the exercise and feeling for the egg's influence. It was only when he lost himself in the familiar sequence of movements that he suddenly realized he could feel the magic moving with him, almost like a partner in a dance.

It all hinged on the most difficult part of learning his forms—losing his sense of self, forgetting that he was a person doing an exercise and becoming the flow of movements that comprised the form.

Words sprung unbidden into his mind from a lesson learned long ago. "Only once you lose your mind can you tap into its true power." Ben never really understood what his grandfather meant with those words, until now. But understanding and implementing were two different things. He had often strived to reach that coveted state of mind where doer becomes one with the thing being done and all sense of self vanishes, but he learned early on that it's elusive. The harder he tried to reach it, the farther away it got.

It took him a long time to realize that that state of mind can't be the goal. Whenever he set out to reach it, he always failed. It was only when he focused on the task at hand to the exclusion of all else that he found himself in that place of pure doing, realizing only after the fact that he'd succeeded.

He returned to the beginning of the form and gave himself permission to let go of all of his other concerns, for the moment anyway. He told himself that they would all be there, waiting for him, once he finished his practice. He began again, this time with his eyes closed.

He forgot about the egg and the dragon and the loss of his grandfather as he brought his whole mind to bear on executing the next movement. He had memorized the form years ago. He knew it without having to think. Soon he was flowing through each step and into the next—and then he was each movement, he was one with his sword, lost in the moment. He completed the form and came to rest, taking a slow breath to bring himself back before opening his eyes.

Ellie was standing next to Homer watching him with an expression of bemusement at his surprise.

"Good morning," he managed after a moment of self-consciousness. "I didn't know you were there," he added with a reproving look at Homer.

"What? She wasn't hurting anything," Homer said.

"It is, isn't it?" she said. "You're pretty good. Looks like you've had a lot of practice."

He shrugged. "I guess I have, more than most anyway."

"We should spar," she said.

Ben hesitated for a moment. He liked the idea. She was pretty and forthright and confident and he liked her.

And he'd given Dom his word that he would keep his distance. Thoughts of Britney came to him.

"Maybe some other time," he said, apologetically.

"Great, I'll see if I can find a couple of practice swords," she said, completely brushing off his brush-off. "How about this evening?"

"I was planning on working through my forms again later," he said.

"Perfect, after dinner then," she said.

Before he could reply, Frank and Olivia came out of the house together, laughing about something. Frank was at his most charming. The moment he saw Ben with Ellie, his target changed. It was so obvious to Ben. He wondered if anyone else could see it.

"Here it comes," Homer said.

Olivia was wearing a powder-blue dress with delicate white lace. She looked stunningly beautiful, almost too beautiful—and more than a little out of place.

Ellie, by contrast was wearing her riding clothes and had a well-crafted knife on her belt. She smirked at her sister.

"Good morning, princess," she said, with a mockingly deferential tone.

"Oh, stop," Olivia said, "you know Daddy won't yell at me when I dress like this."

Ellie laughed gently, tugging at one of the lace frills on her sister's dress as if it were hanging on a mannequin.

"Always playing sneaky," she said. "So how do you get into something like this anyway? Don't you have to tie it on?"

Olivia smirked back.

"Besides, I think our father is done yelling at us, for this transgression anyway," Ellie said.

"Right up until he tells us to go home and we refuse again."

"There is that," Ellie said.

"I for one thinks she looks beautiful," Frank said, inserting himself into the conversation. "I bet the two of you would make a stunning pair in evening gowns."

Ellie cocked her head, a flicker of annoyance dancing across her face.

"Be nice," Olivia said before Ellie could respond.

"Actually, I was just watching Ben practice his sword forms," she said. "Are you as good as he is? You should come spar with us tonight."

"This ought to be good," Homer said, sitting up attentively.

"Oh, no, sparring isn't for me," Frank said. "I find a rifle to be a far better weapon."

"Really? How about after you run out of bullets?" Ellie asked.

Annabelle stuck her head out of a door. "Breakfast in ten," she said, stopping short before closing the door when she saw how Olivia was dressed. "Really, Liv?"

Ellie laughed out loud.

"It's the only dress I had," Olivia said a bit defensively.

"I should get washed up," Ben said, gathering his gear and heading for the house.

"Be careful with him," Frank said to Ellie, just loud enough for Ben to hear. "He's a killer."

Ben schooled his emotions, refusing to give Frank the satisfaction of letting him see his anger.

When he arrived at the breakfast table a few minutes later, both Ellie and Olivia were looking at him differently. They were guarded and almost hostile. Ben had to wonder what else Frank had said to them. But then he realized that whatever it was, it was probably for the best. Even if he hadn't promised Dom that he would stay away from them, he didn't want to get them involved any more than they already were.

He decided to ignore them, mentally preparing himself for the conversation to come as he ate his eggs and sausage. Once the table was cleared and hot coffee was poured, Dom cleared his throat pointedly, looking at his two younger daughters.

"Time for both of you to go home," he said. "I want you on the road within the hour."

Ellie looked him right in the eye and said, "No."

He clenched his jaw.

"We want to be a part of this," Olivia said. "Stop excluding us."

He looked down at the table and shook his head, visibly calming himself. "You're not a part of this and you're not going to be a part of this. As soon as transportation is arranged, you're leaving and you're not coming back."

Ellie glanced at Ben with a flicker of growing anger.

"Maybe you don't know—"

Frank cut her off. "They warned us about the Warlock. Maybe they're already a part of this."

"He's right," Olivia said.

Now both Dom and Ellie were glaring at Frank.

"I just think we'll come up with a better plan with more smart people thinking about it," he said. "After all, my nephew's life hangs in the balance. I think we can all agree that he deserves the best chance that we can give him."

"He's just a baby," Olivia said. "Let us help."

Dom offered a withering glare in response. Both young women began to fidget and then looked down.

"If I hadn't already sent Kat to tell your mother where you ran off to, I'd have her knock you both out and cart you home in a wagon."

They looked at each other, both flushing a bit.

"Oh, yeah. You think I'm pissed off about all this, just wait. She didn't even want *me* to come here."

The table fell silent.

"Can you get us to Denver?" Imogen asked very quietly, filling the silence with her pain.

Dom glanced at Ben before answering. "I can get you close if that's where you want to go. Regardless of your destination, it's going to take a day or two to make the necessary arrangements."

"Maybe we should just buy some horses from you and be on our way," Frank said. "Ben has plenty of money."

"You're being hunted," Dom said. "If I let you ride off out in the open, I'd be killing you all, not to mention alerting the wyrm's minions to my involvement. No, we wait until I can smuggle you out in a regularly scheduled supply caravan."

"How close to Denver can you get us?" Imogen asked.

Ben looked down, letting out a deep breath. "We're not going to Denver," he said.

"What? Why not? You said you'd help me."

Ben could hear a tremor of panic in her voice. "And I will," he said, "but I'm not ready yet. I need the Codex. I need to know how to use magic better."

"Really, Ben?" Frank asked. "You're going to abandon your own family? And what is this Codex you're talking about anyway? Just one more thing you're keeping from us?"

"Not from 'us.' From you," Ben said.

Frank looked at him with an expression of surprise and sadness. "I've been nothing but supportive, and this is what I get from my own brother."

Hound snorted mockingly, but otherwise remained silent.

"My baby is all alone," Imogen said. "I can't stand to think about what they're doing to him. Please, Ben, you promised."

"I know, but I'm not ready," he said.

"Well, then maybe you shouldn't be the one carrying the egg," Frank said. "If you're not willing to do what needs to be done, then give it to Imogen so she can."

"Not going to happen," Hound said, giving Frank a hard look.

"Who says it's your decision, Rufus?" Frank asked.

"Bertha," Hound replied.

"I don't know why you're all of a sudden siding with him over me," Frank said. "We've been friends for years. Maybe Ben knows how to use magic better than he's letting on. Maybe he's got you under his spell, 'cuz you're not acting like the man I know."

"Enough!" Imogen said. "None of this matters."

"Hey, Sis, we'll get him back," Frank said. "I promise."

"How?" she asked weakly.

"First, we need to get to Denver," Frank said.

"And do what, exactly?" Ben asked. "Are you going to knock on the dragon's door and ask him nicely? We don't stand a chance against the wyrm right now, but we might with the right preparation."

"At least I'm willing to try," Frank said, turning to Dom. "What do you think we should do?"

Dom regarded him coolly. "Mourn your losses, destroy the egg, and get as far away from the wyrm as you can."

"You can't really mean that," Ellie said.

"Your daughter's right," Frank said. "You of all people—"

"Stop talking," Dom said, cutting Frank short before turning to Imogen. "I'm sorry. I know how painful this is, but your chances of success against the dragon are virtually nonexistent. Worse, you're going to hand him humanity's doom if you try. As for you," he said, turning to Frank, "Don't ever try to play my daughters against me again. You're a guest in my home, I suggest you act like it."

"I ... I meant no offense," Frank said.

"I won't abandon my son," Imogen said, pushing away from the table. "Even if I have to do this alone, I'll find a way."

"You're not alone," John said, moving to follow her.

Ben stopped him with a gesture. "Let me talk to her," he said, following her out of the room.

He caught up with her in the paddock between the house and the barn.

"Hey, wait up."

"Leave me alone, Ben."

"No, we need to talk," he said, following her into the barn and stopping her with a gentle hand on the shoulder. "You know that we both want the same things, but I can't walk the egg into the dragon's lair without knowing how to use it."

She nodded, struggling to keep from crying again. He pulled her to his shoulder and gave her a hug, letting her cry until she had collected herself.

"So what's your plan?" she asked, wiping her face clean of tears.

"I need to find an NACC computer to fully activate my augment," he said. "Dom is going to look into it for me. After that, we need the Codex."

"That seems like an awful lot standing between me and my son."

"I know, but I don't know what else to do," Ben said, helplessly. "This is all so beyond me, but because I have this damned egg, everybody thinks I can do the impossible. And maybe I can, but I sure as hell don't know how."

She blinked a few times, seeming to recognize the fear in his eyes before nodding.

"I know I said that I would do this alone, but I think we both know how that would end," she said. "I need you, Ben. My son needs you. And I trust my father's judgment. He wouldn't have left you the egg if you weren't worthy of it. But ... every time I think about my son, I lose my mind. I can't stand it."

"I know," Ben said. "And I wish there was more I could do, but I don't have the strength to face the wyrm ... not yet, anyway."

"You think the Codex will teach you what you need to know?"

"I hope so," Ben said. "It's the only book of magic that I know of."

"My father said it's in Mount Shasta and that place is crawling with evil."

"That's why I need to upgrade my augment first, and hopefully find a few weapons in the process."

She nodded reluctantly. "I don't like it, but I'm with you. I'm not sure I have any other choice."

It wasn't what he was hoping for, but it was enough.

"Thank you," he whispered. "I can't do this alone either."

"What are you going to do about Frank?"

He shrugged helplessly. "I don't know. Maybe I can give him some money to go away."

"That's wishful thinking and you know it," she said. "I'm afraid he'll do something stupid and get us all killed."

"I smell the youngest sister," Homer said. "She's right outside."

"Sneaky," he said to Homer.

Homer headed over to the inside of the barn wall, barking and growling. "She's leaving," he said, wagging his tail. "I scared her off."

"What got him riled up?" Imogen asked.

"I think someone was listening to us."

"Frank?"

"I doubt it, he's not that quiet," Ben said. "We'll be on the road soon. Take this time to get rested up and ready. There's no telling when we'll have a chance to stop again."

"What are you going to do?"

"Work on magic," he said, patting the shoulder bag containing the fake egg.

"Maybe I'll do the same," she said, leaving him alone with Homer in the barn.

Chapter 6

Olivia slipped back into the house through a service door. Frank was waiting for her.

"Any luck?" he asked.

"I'm not sure," she said. "He convinced her to go after the Codex ... he also mentioned something he called an augment."

Frank frowned sadly. "More secrets. It's always secrets and lies with him. I wish ... I just wish I could trust my own brother the way you trust your sisters."

"It sounds like he genuinely wants to help Imogen get her baby back," Olivia said.

"God, I hope so," Frank said. "But I'm terrified he's going to vanish in the night with the only hope we have of rescuing little Robert."

"I don't—"

"You don't know him like I do," Frank said, cutting her off. "He says that he doesn't know how to use magic. What he didn't tell you is that he's been using it all along ... to make money."

She looked at him blankly.

"I know, it's crazy. Our family is in crisis and all he can think about is putting gold in his pocket."

"Why would he do that?"

"I'm afraid he's planning to abandon us," Frank said, shaking his head. "I just wish I knew what to do."

"We could go to my father," Olivia said.

"And say what? We don't have any proof. Besides, I get the impression that he wants us gone anyway."

"He's afraid of the wyrm," Olivia said. "For what it's worth, he has good reason."

"Oh, I don't doubt him in the least. He took us in when we needed help, but I don't think there's anything he can do to make Ben see reason. Going after the Codex is crazy. For all we know, it's not even there anymore, but all Ben sees is the power it will give him."

"I didn't get that from him," Olivia said. "It seems like he wants to help but he's in over his head."

"There's no doubt about that second part," Frank said. "He's always getting himself into trouble. I usually have to step in and clean up after him. But this mess ... I don't know if anyone can clean it up, especially if he loses the egg to the dragon."

"Maybe if you talked to Imogen."

"Maybe, but I'm afraid that his command of magic is far greater than he's let on," Frank said. "You saw how Rufus sided with him at breakfast. Rufus and I have been best friends for years. Now, all of a sudden, he's become Ben's lapdog.

He never even liked Ben before. The only way that makes any sense is if he's under a spell. And if he is, I'm certain that Imogen is too."

"If that's true, then he probably shouldn't even have the egg."

"That's what I've been saying all along. I've tried to convince him to do the right thing, to give it to Imogen. After all, it's her baby, she should have the power, not him."

"Maybe we could steal it," Olivia said.

"But then what?" Frank asked, shaking his head. "Ben's good with a sword and he'll stop at nothing to keep his power. I don't want to have to shoot my own brother."

"What if he doesn't know it's gone?" Olivia said with mischief in her eye.

"How would we do that?"

"We switch it with a duplicate … a fake."

"But where would we get a fake dragon egg?"

"Leave that to me," Olivia said. "My father has an exact copy of the real egg in a glass case in his den at home. He said that the Wizard made it to fool a would-be thief. I've spent hours staring at that egg. I know it intimately. I can see it when I close my eyes. And, I'm a pretty good artist."

"What are you going to make it out of?"

"This house is scheduled to be renovated. There's a whole shipment of building supplies in the shop, including several dozen bags of plaster."

"Do you really think you can pull it off?"

"I know I can, but we'll need a plan," Olivia said. "Your brother carries that bag with him everywhere and I doubt we can sneak up on him at night with his dog sleeping next to him."

"No, you're right about that," Frank said. "I'll think of something. You have no idea how much this means to me."

"You can thank me later," she said, laying a hand on his arm. "Figure out how to make the switch. I'll get to work on the egg."

Imogen returned to the house and went to her room. John was leaning up against the wall next to her door.

"How're you holding up?"

"I'm all right, I guess," she said.

"You need anything?"

"No, but thank you," she said. "I think I want to be alone for a while."

He nodded, making no move to leave.

She went into her room and closed the door, waiting for several moments until John's footsteps receded into silence.

She sat down cross-legged on her bed and took the amulet from around her neck. It was such a simple thing, just a piece of bone. She laid it into her right palm and wrapped the thong around her hand before closing her eyes and settling in to meditate.

"Please, Dragon, don't hurt my baby," she whispered, taking a deep breath.

"Please, Dragon, don't hurt my baby," she whispered again, inhaling fully and repeating the phrase.

Ben sat down on a bale of hay. It felt good to be alone for a moment. He thought about his conversation with Dom the night before. They'd discussed a lot. The part about trust and lies stood out. Ben wanted to trust Imogen, but she would always put her baby first, and perhaps rightly so. As he considered his friends in his mind, a feeling of loneliness and isolation seeped into him. Ultimately, he was alone in this.

He was his own master.

He couldn't count an anyone else to set his course anymore. He had willingly followed his grandfather; he would have followed him anywhere. Even though the man had kept so much from him, Ben realized that his grandfather was the one person in the world that he'd ever really trusted completely.

And he was gone.

The loss tore at his soul, left him with an emptiness that was nearly unbearable.

Homer laid his chin on Ben's knee, looking up at him with his big brown eyes. "I miss him too," he said.

"I know," Ben said, scratching his dog's ear. "I think he would want me to grow up and start making my own decisions instead of looking to others to do it for me."

"Pretty sure," Homer said. "So what are you thinking?"

"I need to do something about my brother."

"Like what?"

"Well, I think I'll let him steal the egg," Ben said. "Maybe he'll run off with the fake."

"That's risky," Homer said. "He'll probably get caught and spill everything to the wyrm."

Ben winced. "Hadn't thought of that. And now it's probably too late to convince him that we're going somewhere other than Shasta."

"Probably ... still, he's never been willing to let you have anything that he couldn't take from you. That's why he hates *me* so much."

"That and the pile of shit you left in his shoe that one time."

"He had it coming," Homer said.

"I can't argue with that. I guess, for now, I'll wait and see what he does."

He took a deep breath and closed his eyes, centering himself and releasing all tension from his body. After a few minutes of breathing and clearing his mind, he reached out for the feeling of magic. He wanted to know the range of the egg's influence.

Being this distant from the source of magic that he'd been traveling with for the past several weeks gave him a new perspective on how it made him feel. As his awareness searched out the magic of the egg, he felt another source of power nearby.

It was lesser in strength, static rather than vibrant, but it was active, radiating magic and will into the world. The feeling was so subtle that he wouldn't have noticed it had he not been searching for it. Imogen said she was going to work on developing her command of the amulet. He hoped that that was the source he was sensing.

Extending his mind farther, if only in his own imagination, he began to feel the raw power of the egg, dormant but alive with potential. He made a point of remembering that feeling, taking note of the difference in the world when he was in the presence of magic. Then he turned his mind to the familiar image of his lucky coin and lost himself in meditation.

The barn door creaked and his eyes came open. Annabelle stuck her head inside and smiled.

"Found you," she said. "My father has some information for you."

He stood and stretched.

"Imogen seemed pretty upset at breakfast," she said.

"Yeah, I can't say I blame her. I wish there was more I could do."

"All we can do is all we can do," she said. "I'm sure she knows you're doing the best you can under the circumstances."

"Thank you for that, but I can't shake the feeling that my best isn't going to be good enough."

"You've set some pretty lofty goals for yourself," she said. "It's only natural to have doubts, and fears in this case. Come on, my father's waiting."

He followed her out of the barn and into the house, checking the position of the sun and frowning to himself.

"What time is it?"

"Almost lunchtime," Annabelle said.

"Wow, I must have really lost track of time."

As they walked across the paddock, a glint caught his eye. He bent down and picked up another coin, mentally saying "thank you" as he slipped it into his pocket.

She led him to what used to be a library. Shelves lined the walls but the only tomes in the room were piled up on one end of the central table. Dom was leaning over a large map.

"Come take a look," he said, motioning for Annabelle to close the door.

"We're here," he said, pointing to the eastern slope of the Cascade Mountain Range. "I sent Ty into town to talk to an old-timer about NACC bunkers. The best lead is here." He pointed to the opposite side of the map. "It's rumored to be a door in the side of the mountain, and it's well defended by automated tech. Every now and then some enterprising scavengers will make a run at it. The ones that return tell stories that sound like gravity and laser weapons. If the defenses are still active, then there's bound to be a computer inside."

"How close can you get me?"

"I have a supply caravan leaving for Burnt day after tomorrow," he said. "That's the best I can do without drawing undue attention."

"Attention?"

"Ty also tells me that there are Dragon Guard poking around town."

"They're here? Already?"

"He said they were led by a blond woman—looks like an Amazon. His words."

"That's Magoth," Ben whispered, a thrill of fear racing up his spine.

"Figured as much," Dom said.

"I watched her become what she is now," Annabelle said. "She's dangerous. Liv and Ellie should go home."

"Why don't you tell them that," Dom said with a snort. "No, I think we're past that. I'm pretty sure your mother will be arriving this afternoon. We'll stay here until we see them off and then we'll head north."

"We're going to abandon the business?"

"We'll sell our properties in the Deschutes Territory and set up shop in the gorge on the north slope of Mount Hood. We have a few hundred acres of apples up there. Maybe we'll switch to cider."

"But … we've worked so hard here," Annabelle said. "We can't just leave our lives behind."

"We're not," Dom said, laying a hand on his daughter's shoulder. "Our lives are why we're leaving. This isn't about Ben and his friends either. It's been in the works for some time now, ever since the wyrm took over Rogue City and started making noises about moving north."

"There must be something we can do," Annabelle said.

"There is. We leave. I already have buyers lined up for most of the properties. Recent developments just sped up the timetable a bit."

"This is home," she said.

"Wrong. This is just a place. Home is where the people you love are."

"Do Ellie and Olivia know?"

"No, just your mother and a few of my operatives."

"What if I don't want to leave?"

"Don't you start, too," Dom said, pulling her into a hug. "If we stay, we risk everything. The dragon still has people working for him that will recognize me on sight. Truth is, I've put this off longer than I should have."

"This is all so wrong," she said, stepping back from her father and looking up into his eyes. "We should help them kill the wyrm so nobody ever has to run from him again."

"No! Don't even start thinking along those lines. You have a husband now, and hopefully you'll have a child soon. Think about that. Focus on keeping the people you care about safe. The rest of the world isn't yours to save."

"He's right, Belle," Ben said. "You've already helped me more than you know. Protect your family."

"This sucks," she said.

"Can't argue with that," Dom said. "Belle, why don't you go check on lunch?"

She left with a frown.

"So how are you going to smuggle us out?" Ben asked.

"Pretty much the same way we got you out of Rogue City. This time should be easier since we don't have any Dragon Guard checkpoints to worry about. Once you arrive in Burnt, you'll be unloaded in our warehouse. I'll have horses and supplies waiting for you there. After that, you're on your own."

Ben nodded, looking more closely at the map. "This looks like pretty rough terrain."

"It is," Dom said. "The Steens Mountain area is mostly high desert, a lot of sage and rock. Not much forage up there so you'll need to go in well provisioned. Take old highway 78 from Burnt and head south until the road turns left just past the lake. You'll have to go cross country from there. I'll get you a map, but I can't give you more than a general area and a few landmarks to look for."

"I'm hoping that'll do," Ben said, tapping the side of his head. "I'm pretty sure I'll have some help finding what I'm looking for once I get close."

Dom sighed. "You could always come north with us."

"You are persistent."

Dom shrugged. "Robert would want you to live."

"I know," Ben said, certainty settling in on his mind. "But he's not here anymore. I have to make my own decisions now, decisions that I can live with—even if they kill me."

"Well, if nothing else, you can stubborn the wyrm to death."

"Does that work?"

"You might be surprised," Dom said. "Let's go get some lunch."

They made their way to the dining room, trailing Homer behind them, and found everyone else already there. Ben took his seat, glancing at his family and friends. Imogen seemed resigned to the situation. John sat beside her, silent as ever. Hound was eager for a hot meal and Zack looked like he was trying to avoid being noticed. Frank stopped telling his story to Ellie and Olivia just long enough to nod to Ben.

He sighed inwardly. He'd lived with Frank his whole life. While most others would be taken in by his machinations, Ben knew his tells. He was up to something. So be it, Ben thought.

Aside from a furtively hostile look or two, Ellie and Olivia ignored him. Part of him hated the idea that they were judging him based on Frank's word, even though he knew that his feelings stemmed from nothing more than ego. Still, it stung.

He thanked Adam for the bowl of stew and ate quietly. When the dishes were cleared, he thanked Dom and pushed away from the table.

"What, you're not even going to talk to us?" Frank said.

Ben stopped and shrugged. "What do you want to talk about, Frank?"

"I'd just like to know the plan," he said. "After all, I'm a part of this too."

"Honestly, Frank, you really don't have to be," Ben said. "You've made it pretty clear from the beginning that you don't want anything to do with the dragon. I think your exact words were 'That's crazy' when I said I wanted to kill the wyrm. And you're probably right. Thing is, I don't feel like you're completely on board with what I have in mind. And that's a problem."

"Whoa, what are you talking about?" Frank said, holding up his hands in protest. "The dragon has Imogen's baby. He's family and he needs us. I know I've said some things over the past few weeks. You've said some things too, and you broke my nose, but we're brothers. If we can't count on each other, then who can we count on? We're in this together, no matter what."

"Fair enough," Ben said. "Day after tomorrow we'll travel to Burnt in a caravan. From there, we'll head south to Steens Mountain to look for an NACC bunker that's rumored to be intact. I'm hoping to find some tech weapons there. Then we head for Shasta to recover the Codex."

"Okay," Frank said. "Was that so hard? I just wanted to know the plan."

"He's up to something," Homer said.

Ben was thinking the same thing.

"What I'm planning is dangerous, maybe even fatal. Rufus, John, Zack, you have no obligation to do this. All three of you have given up your homes already. I can't ask any more of you. If you choose to go your own way, I'll understand."

"I owe Cyril," Hound said. "I wouldn't feel right if I didn't see this through."

"I don't have anywhere else to go," Zack said.

"I'm in," John said.

"Thank you, all of you," Ben said, walking away from the table. Out of the corner of his eye he caught Ellie glance at him with a look of uncertainty, as if she wanted to be angry but wasn't quite sure it was justified. Olivia, on the other hand, had lost all hint of her earlier hostility and was almost overtly flirting with him. He tried to ignore them both and left in a hurry.

He returned to his room and lay down, his mind turning back to his grief. Rather than indulge the sadness, he got back up and went to the courtyard, dropping his belt and the shoulder bag containing the fake egg.

"Keep an eye on these for me," he said to Homer, drawing his blade and beginning his sword form. The movements came more easily this time. They had been a part of his muscle memory for years, but always before he'd needed to focus to fully immerse himself in the form.

This time, he simply let go—stopped thinking and let the sword move as if it were guiding his body. The first time through he worked at about half speed, gliding through the motions, one to the next with a feeling of effortless flow. When he finished, he felt buoyant and light, filled with a sense of power and calm.

He started again, this time allowing himself to perform every strike, every block and every transition with all of his physical and mental strength. He could feel the magic working within him, guiding his hand, driving his blows with precision and power like he'd never felt before. His blade whipped through the air, flashing in the sunlight.

It felt good. Effortless. Yet, he knew that there was power behind his blade like nothing he'd ever felt before. He had no opponent save the air, but he knew that his sword was sharper, almost as sharp as his mind in this newfound state of being.

He sensed Ellie, Olivia, and Frank more than saw them. All three came into the courtyard. They entered talking, but soon fell silent. He ignored them in favor of the simple joy of losing himself to the moment.

And then the form was over and he came to rest.

Olivia clapped, giggling girlishly. Ellie looked at her like she was trying to figure out who had replaced her sister.

"That was amazing," Olivia said. "I had no idea you were so graceful."

Ben tried to conceal his annoyance that his practice had been interrupted.

"I have to say, that was impressive," Frank said. "I've seen you do that form before but never with such … energy."

"Yeah, it's one thing to fight the air, another to face an opponent," Ellie said, tossing a wooden practice sword at him. He caught it easily in his off hand, testing its weight almost reflexively.

"I'm not sure this is a good idea," Ben said.

"What? Afraid of a woman who can defend herself?" Ellie said. "Put your blade down and we'll see if you're as good as you think you are."

He paused for a moment, sizing her up. She had fire. Her ice-blue eyes flashed with passion … and anger. Ben considered walking away, but he didn't want to. Partly because he wanted to prove himself to her, but also because he wanted to face an opponent in the presence of the egg and see if the power at his disposal would serve him.

He shrugged almost imperceptibly, a gesture that only served to irritate Ellie even more, before going to his things and returning his sword to its sheath.

"You sure about this?" Homer asked. "She's pretty hostile right now."

"I know," Ben said. "But it might be instructive."

He stepped out onto the grass and bowed his head to her respectfully. She lunged, quick and hard. He parried her strike easily, circling toward her off hand. She adjusted and attacked again but her poor position forced her to rush her strike. He slipped out of the way, whipping his blade around and checking the swing just short of her neck.

He still felt the lightness, but there was more of an edge to his mind, a sharpness that he knew was deadly, even with a wooden sword. He reminded himself that this was just practice—had to remind himself in the face of something new. A feeling of visceral, almost animalistic aggression flowed into him, filling him with a kind of bloodlust that he'd never experienced before.

She advanced again, driving at him with a flurry of attacks. She was good, skilled and driven, but he was better. Each attack was thwarted by his blade, moving almost of its own volition, each thrust parried, each strike stymied. He didn't bother to counterattack. He didn't dare.

As he defeated her every advance, her anger seemed to recede. Bit by bit, determination and single-minded focus replaced it until she was fighting with a kind of reckless abandon that would have been impressive if it didn't leave her exposed to his as-yet-unoffered counterattack.

He brought his will to bear on the aggression flowing through him, reining it in, gaining control of it, mastering the power behind it so that he could put it to use as he chose rather than letting it drive his actions. It was a battle within a battle, the bloodlust of the dragon's egg driving him to strike, his will restraining his hand and guiding his actions according to his conscience and reason.

The aggression offered him power. Unbridled and wild, overwhelming and potent, yet without any purpose save the spilling of blood. He knew that he would be deadly beyond measure if he succumbed to its influence. He also knew that he would strike out at anyone and everyone around him if he allowed the fury to gain control.

Another flurry of attacks drove him back until he ran out of space. He countered, slapping her blade aside just enough to circle, bringing the flat of his blade around and slapping her on the back of the leg. She yelped, turning on him, more anger than focus now.

He felt strangely detached. Memories of lessons from long ago surfaced, words and lectures that only partially made sense at the time sprang into his mind full of new meaning. His grandfather had always come back to control. Ben thought that he was talking about physical control, moving the blade precisely, performing each technique correctly.

His lectures on emotional control and mental discipline always seemed so out of place. Sure, Ben understood that a contest of violence contained within it the possibility for a terribly final outcome, but he always felt that his grandfather had spent far too much time and energy on the mental aspect of the fight. After all, a fight was a physical thing, movement and metal.

Now he understood.

He wasn't being trained to fight with a sword, he was being trained to fight with magic. More importantly, he was being trained to retain command of his faculties in the face of the unborn dragon's lust for blood.

Ellie's attacks came swift and sure. His defenses held. He checked another blow that would have left her sprawled unconscious on the ground. She got through, her blade landing hard across his ribs. He felt them crack, his chest constricting, a stab of pain radiating through his chest.

A flash of rage washed through him, driving him to attack. Almost unbidden, he savagely brought his blade up into hers, opening her guard as he thrust, open palmed, into her solar plexus with his free hand, knocking her back and stunning her momentarily. He brought his blade down, a kill strike on the side of her neck.

In the last possible moment, he caught himself, stopping the strike and staggering back, terrified by what he'd almost done. Even a wooden blade propelled by such rage and magic would have killed her.

He shook his head, bringing himself back from the bloodlust that had almost consumed him. She was still living in the moment of the fight and she was coming for him. He reined in his feelings and focused his mind, giving over to the flow with only one mandate—defend.

She lunged, driving hard at his heart. He slapped the blade aside and grabbed her by the wrist, pulling her forward and off balance, sweeping her feet as she passed and sending her face first into the ground.

"What the hell are you two doing?!" Dom shouted, racing into the courtyard.

She came up, fury and focus, but Dom caught her practice sword by the blade and yanked it out of her hand, tossing it aimlessly across the courtyard. She stopped, facing her father, the anger and energy dissipating slowly.

"I taught you better than that," he barked at her. "Use your anger, don't let it use you, remember? And you," he said, rounding on Ben, "I told you to practice your sword skills but not on my daughter."

"He likes to hurt women," Ellie spat out, anger still gripping her. "Isn't that right, Ben? Tell them what you did to Britney. I bet she couldn't fight back."

Ben froze as if he'd been slapped in the face. Ellie stopped short when she saw the look on his face. It looked like she was trying to hold on to her anger but couldn't.

It was only then that Ben realized that they had a much larger audience—everyone in the house stood silently watching them. Frank looked worried. Ben turned back to Ellie and flipped the practice sword into the ground.

"I wondered what he'd said to you. Good match." He gathered his things and walked away without another word.

"Holy shit, Ben," Zack said following behind him. "I didn't know you were that good. I mean, I always knew you were good, but that was amazing."

"Thanks, Zack," he said, tenderly probing his ribs. "She got me pretty good. I think I need to lie down."

"Hey," Zack said, as he reached his door. "Do you think you could teach me? Your grandfather never would, and now … well, I think I might need to learn how to handle myself."

Ben nodded with a pained smile. "I'd like that, but later," he said, stepping into his room and closing the door gently, taking a moment to lock it before easing himself into bed.

"Augment."

"You have sustained a minor fracture of the eighth rib on the left side. I'm beginning repairs now. Remain immobile for the next two hours to maximize recovery time."

"Right," Ben said, closing his eyes and trying not to breathe.

"I really want to be there when Ellie learns the truth about Britney," Homer said. "She might just solve our Frank problem for us."

Ben started to laugh and then winced. "Poetic justice is a beautiful thing," he said. "Now let me rest."

Homer curled up on the floor next to his bed.

Chapter 7

Ben woke some time later. The light of day was fading, flooding the room with shadow. There was a timid knock at the door.

"It's Ellie," Homer said.

Ben rolled to a sitting position, only remembering after the fact that his ribs were cracked. When they didn't protest, he looked at his side, probing gently for pain. A bit of prodding produced a dull ache.

"Your fracture is nearly healed," the augment said.

"Nicely done," he said, going to the door and opening it.

Ellie stood in the hallway, looking a bit sheepish.

"I wanted to apologize," she said. "Belle told me what really happened with Britney. I feel like such an idiot."

"It's not your fault," Ben said.

"But it is. I let myself get lied to and played for a fool. My father taught me better than that. Worse, I let myself lose control in a fight. You had me half a dozen times, mostly because I was letting my anger get the best of me. And I hit you. I'm sorry."

"My brother is … well, let's just say he's a damn good liar. Honestly, I'm surprised he used Britney to play you against me. He's usually more careful."

"He made us both promise to keep it secret," she said, shaking her head. "And I would have, if I hadn't been so angry. I still don't know what came over me."

"I do," Ben said. "Magic. We were both fighting under the influence of the egg."

She frowned up at him, her brow furrowing deeply. "But how? I don't know how to use magic."

"I'm not sure it's a matter of knowing how to use the magic as much as it is knowing how to prevent the magic from using you."

"Oh God, that's terrifying."

He nodded somberly. "A lot of my grandfather's warnings are beginning to make sense now. The truth is, I think you helped me more than you know. Having an opponent seemed to ignite a bloodlust within me like nothing I've ever felt before. If I'd felt that for the first time in a real fight, I'm not sure how I would have handled it. Now I know what to expect."

"How did you control it?" she asked, her eyes going distant. "My father was right, I let the anger use me, and I know better than that."

"I'm not really sure," he said with a shrug. "Probably a combination of things. I was practicing with the intent of using the magic to fight, so I was aware of its influence when we started. Also, my grandfather drilled me on control a thousand times. Today, I finally figured out why."

"There you are," Dom said from down the hall. "Dinner in ten."

Ellie nodded to him. "We'll be there."

"See that you are," he said, an undercurrent of anger still lingering in his voice.

"He had a few things to say after he broke us up," Ellie said.

"I'll bet," Ben said, looking down at the floor for a moment, collecting his thoughts. "I think I might owe you an apology, too. I knew you were angry before we started but I agreed to spar with you anyway because I wanted to see how the magic would work. If I'd known—"

"Stop," she said, both hands raised and open. "You pulled your punches, I didn't. Speaking of which, how are you ribs?"

"Tender."

"I got you pretty good," she said. "A real blade would have gutted you."

"I'll be all right," he said, patting his side gently and offering a slightly exaggerated wince.

"Maybe we could practice again tomorrow," she said. "I promise I'll go easier."

Ben hesitated.

"I understand if you don't want to."

"It's not that, I just don't want to upset your father."

"Yeah, he's been grumpier than usual lately."

"He's afraid," Ben said. "We brought danger into your home."

"I cornered Belle after she told me what really happened with Britney and made her tell me everything else she knew. It doesn't sound like you had much choice about anything."

"No, I guess not, but that doesn't change the fact that my presence here puts your family in danger. That's enough to make any man unhappy."

She harrumphed. "Just wait until you meet my mother. She got here about an hour ago."

"So dinner should be interesting, then."

"More like tense," Ellie said. "Mom didn't even want my dad coming here, never mind me and Liv."

"Well, in that case, I probably ought to get washed up. I wouldn't want to be late."

"I'll see you there," she said, smiling over her shoulder as she left him.

He gathered his things and made his way to the dining hall with a brief stop at the washroom on the way.

"Now I see where your daughters get their extraordinary beauty," Frank said to Dom's wife, just as Ben entered the room.

She was pretty, at least twenty years younger than Dom, with long blond hair and blue eyes like her daughters.

She turned those eyes on Frank and stopped him cold. "Save your bullshit. Belle told me all about you."

He smiled his most charming smile and tried to brush off her glare.

"This is going to be fun," Homer said.

Dom's wife turned to Ben.

"Think so, do ya?" Ben said to his dog.

"So you're the one," she said, looking Ben up and down like she was sizing up a piece of meat.

"Yes, ma'am, I guess I am," he said, making his best effort to look her in the eye, but without any hint of challenge.

She looked away, glancing over at her husband before looking back at Ben.

"You're just a kid," she said, turning back to Dom, a look of helplessness ghosting across her face.

Dom put his arm around her. "This is my wife, Gwen," he said. "This is Benjamin Boyce."

"Pleased to meet you, ma'am," Ben said.

"Under other circumstances, I might agree," she said. "Now, if you want to win me over, stop calling me *ma'am*. My name is Gwen."

Ben nodded mutely, glancing almost involuntarily at Ellie. She offered the hint of a smile in return.

"Sit down, dinner's ready," Gwen said.

Stew again, but seasoned far better than lunch. Ben was more hungry than he should have been.

"Healing your rib fracture depleted a number of nutrients within your system," the augment said.

Ben pondered the implications while he spooned another mouthful.

"Why were you able to heal a broken bone so easily, when it took much longer to heal my stab wound?"

"Lost blood must be replenished," the augment said. "Doing so required more resources and hence more time. Healing a fracture requires comparatively little in the way of raw materials."

Ben sopped up the remaining gravy with a piece of bread and Gwen took his bowl, ladling another helping without asking. He smiled his thanks. By the time he finished his second helping, his belly was slightly past full. He sat back and stifled a belch.

"Thank you," he said, "that was delicious."

"I'm glad you liked it," Gwen said. "So, do you want to tell me about the blond woman with scary eyes that I met on the way here?"

"You ran into Nash? Where?" Ben asked, leaning forward.

"Just outside of town," Gwen said. "She had a squad of Dragon Guard and the mangiest dog I've ever seen."

Ben glanced at Hound.

"Told you she'd be back," he said with a humorless grin.

"You think this is funny?" Gwen snapped.

"No, ma'am," Hound said. "Far from it. I am looking forward to putting her in the dirt, though. Nice of her to save me the trip."

"She'll be here soon," John said. "We should probably get ready."

Dom sighed.

"She didn't follow us," Gwen said. "I doubt she knows you're here."

"She doesn't have to," Ben said, pushing away from the table. "Her stalker will find us for her. That, and she's not entirely human."

"What do you mean by that?" Gwen said.

Hound was up and following Ben. Neither bothered to answer.

Both went to their rooms and collected their weapons. Kat came trotting up the hall from the opposite direction, arriving at the entrance to the dining room with them.

"Cleve spotted … something … watching the house," she said, the uncharacteristic uncertainty in her voice distinctly unsettling.

"Something?" Frank said. "What do you mean by that?" He was on his feet, looking around a bit wildly.

"He said it stood like a man but then ran like a dog when it saw him," Kat said.

Dom's face went pale, sending a thrill of fear through Ben. He closed his eyes as if his greatest fear had just become real.

"Bring everybody inside," Dom said to Kat. "Get your weapons," he said to everyone else.

"Dom, you're scaring me," Gwen said, after everyone but Ben, Zack, and Hound left to arm up.

"That was Mandrake," Dom said, "Hoondragon's tracker."

Her face went white.

"What's a Hoondragon?" Zack asked.

"I told you to get your weapons," Dom replied, visibly annoyed.

"I … I don't have any," Zack said.

Dom looked at him, mouth agape.

Ben unbuckled his grandfather's sword and handed it to Zack along with his shotgun and what shells he had.

"Don't lose these," he said. "Hound will show you how to shoot. If we get into a fight, keep your sword between you and whatever's trying to kill you."

Zack nodded, fear mixed with wonder shining in his eyes.

Just then John, Imogen, and Frank returned, followed a few moments later by Dom's daughters and Adam.

Ben looked at Dom and said, "Tell us about Mandrake and Hoondragon."

"Mandrake is a made creature—part man, part dragon, part wolf. He serves as Hoondragon's tracker and scout. He can run for days without stopping, he fights with claws and teeth, and his skin is tougher than most armor. I've shot him before, more than once. He just took it and ran away like it was nothing."

"Wait, are you saying this thing is out there?" Frank said.

"What's the matter—scared?" Ellie said.

Gwen silenced her with a look.

"You should be, too," Dom said. "Mandrake is deadly on his own, but he's nothing compared with Hoondragon."

"I thought we were worried about Nash," Frank said.

"We are," Ben said. "This Mandrake was just spotted as well."

"As I was saying," Dom continued, "Hoondragon is the real threat. The name means 'dragon hunter.' The wyrm created Hoondragon to kill Sephiroth. It didn't work out that way in the end, but apparently, that was the plan."

"Another made creature?" Ben asked.

"Technically, Hoondragon is a sword," Dom said. "Your grandfather believed that the dragon summoned a named demon and bound it into a blade. The sword remembers all of the fights that it's ever been in and confers all of that experience onto its current wielder.

"The wyrm keeps an arena where he makes men fight to the death. His champion wields Hoondragon and takes the name for himself as well. That blade has been spilling blood for years. Whoever wields it is the most deadly swordsman you will ever meet."

"Good thing I'm just gonna shoot him in the face with Bertha," Hound said.

"He also wears a suit of black dragon-scale plate armor," Dom said. "Bullets are useless."

Hound frowned. "He didn't mean it, Bertha," he muttered to his shotgun.

"We should run," Gwen said.

"No, it's too late for that," Dom said. "We don't stand a chance in the dark. Besides, we probably have time before Hoondragon arrives. Mandrake is much faster than his master's horse, which is a stalker, by the way, so he usually ranges out ahead by a day or so when he's on the hunt."

"How can we be sure that Mandrake knows we're here?" Imogen asked.

"He knows," Dom said. "He can sense the egg. It's a shame Robert didn't have time to teach you how to cloak it."

"What do you mean?"

"Your grandfather could make the egg's magic less detectable to those with the inclination for magic. Left unshielded, that thing is like a beacon to anyone nearby that has much experience with magic."

Ben tensed slightly, reminding himself to relax.

"Fortunately, it just gives away its general area, but that's enough."

Kat, Ty, and two other men entered the room.

"This is Cleve," Dom said, gesturing to the smaller of the two men. He was wiry with intelligent eyes. "And this is Baxter," he continued. The second man was almost as big as Hound. He was armed with a broadsword and a rifle. "How're we looking?" Dom asked.

"All quiet," Ty said.

"A bit too quiet," Cleve added.

"Hopefully, it'll stay that way," Dom said. "We'll double up tonight, two to a room. I'll post a watch. We'll reassess tomorrow. For now, stay in the dining hall until you're ready to sleep. I don't want anybody wandering around except my people."

Ben sat down at the table, scanning all of the faces in the room, all here, in harm's way, for him. He didn't feel guilt for their predicament so much as a deep sense of responsibility. Enemies circled in the night and he was their quarry. Everyone else was just in their way.

He thought about the egg, wondering if he should retrieve it from its hiding place, but decided against it. He could feel its presence … that was enough. He started wondering if his grandfather had taught him how to cloak the egg without telling him the real purpose of the lesson, but found nothing promising when he searched his memory.

The evening passed slowly, tension palpable in the air. There was little conversation since most were listening for some sign of an attack. After an hour of worrying, Ben closed his eyes and tried to meditate but he found his mind too distracted to focus so he turned to thoughts of his fight with Ellie. As he tried to recall the experience, his augment came to life, replaying the scene with perfect detail.

Blow-by-blow he relived the fight, but with the benefit of hindsight and detachment. His form was good. He had fought well, though there were a few points where he found opportunities to learn from his mistakes.

Once the augment finished, it began to analyze his fighting style, offering suggestions in the form of alternate techniques that he might have employed— each playing out as a simulation in his mind. At first he was annoyed, but as he watched each engagement play out in a variety of different ways, he came to see the incredible value of such an exercise.

"My analysis is troubling," the augment said. "At several points during your battle you moved with unnatural speed and force. An evaluation of your physiology suggests that you are not capable of such action, yet the record is clear. Again, I fear that my programming is flawed or damaged."

"I doubt it," Ben said. "You're just too stubborn to accept the truth."

"You refer to your belief in magic."

"Yep."

"Such beliefs have existed for the whole of human history, yet there has never been conclusive scientific evidence to support them."

"Is it so hard to believe that there are forces at work in the universe beyond what is scientifically provable? Isn't that what science is? The pursuit of unknown knowledge?"

"Yes, but I am not programmed to accept such theories as fact unless sufficient evidence exists to support them."

"You saw the dragon," Ben said. "You saw the summoning of Magoth. You saw the Warlock. And you just said that I shouldn't be able to move as fast as I did. What more evidence do you need?"

"Confirmation from an NACC uplink."

"Yeah, I'm working on that," Ben said. "In the meantime, can you provide the same tactical suggestions in real time that you offered during the review of my match with Ellie?"

"Yes, but those capabilities are currently restricted."

Ben took a deep breath and sighed, shaking his head.

"What good will it do you if I get killed?"

"None, but that concept is meaningless to me. I am not programmed to act in my own interests, but instead in the interests of my host and the NACC."

"Never mind," Ben said. "Show me the match with Ellie again."

The scene replayed in his mind, vivid as a picture. He found that he could control the flow of the replay with a thought, slowing or even completely stopping a moment at will—even viewing the scene from different angles based on the augment's extrapolation of the participants' positions and motion.

"How are you so calm?" Ellie asked, pulling a chair up next to him.

He opened his eyes, the images in his mind vanishing. He shrugged. "I was thinking about our match."

She winced. "How are your ribs?"

"They're fine. You really don't need to worry about that."

She glanced over at Frank, a spark of anger igniting in her eyes. "I'm more worried about getting played."

"I wouldn't worry about that either," he said. "Now you know."

Dom and Gwen exchanged a worried look.

"I think it's time for bed," Gwen said, coming to her feet. "Ellie, Olivia, I want the two of you to share a room."

Ellie offered Ben a quick smile before obeying her mother.

"I'm not tired yet," Olivia said.

"Too bad," Gwen said.

Olivia didn't argue.

Ben stood as well, stifling a yawn. He was tired from lack of sleep the previous night.

"I'll bunk with you tonight," Hound said.

Ben nodded, heading for the hallway. Hound retrieved his bedroll from his room and laid it out on Ben's floor, lying down without a word.

"The girl likes you," he said after a few moments.

"I don't know about that," Ben said. "Besides, her father made it pretty clear where he stands on that subject."

"Fathers always do," Hound said with a chuckle.

"You'd know more about that than I would."

"Ain't that the truth," Hound said. "Night."

"Good night," Ben said.

It didn't take long before he was drifting in that place between waking and sleep, floating in that detached, gauzy world—warm and safe. But then everything changed. Coldness flooded into him and he couldn't breathe. Still not quite awake, he felt panic rise in his belly as he struggled against some unseen force.

He heard Homer bark, but it seemed far away.

He struggled with his fear as much as he struggled to breathe, failing on both counts. The darkness was complete, blackness like nothing he'd experienced since his otherworldly confrontation with the stalker.

Homer barked again. "Something has you," he said.

Ben registered his dog's warning, coming completely awake in a blind panic. He fought against something over his face, cold and insubstantial, yet all too real. Somewhere in the background he heard Hound curse, scrambling to take action against the threat.

All at once, the cold darkness lifted away from him. Lamplight flooded his eyes. For an instant he thought he saw a shadowy figure, dark as soot yet not quite solid, float away as if fleeing from the light—dark red eyes glared at him out of the shadow, communicating hate and malice more completely than words ever could.

It hit the window and passed through, leaving only a splotch of frost on the pane.

"What the hell was that?" Hound asked, holding the lamp high.

"Ben? Are you all right?" Imogen asked through the door.

Hound threw the bolt and tossed the door open.

"Something attacked him in the dark," he said.

Ben was still a bit disoriented, chills racing over his skin.

"Are you hurt?" she asked, kneeling next to his bed.

He tried to speak but only managed a croak, shaking his head to answer her question while working up some saliva in his mouth to salve his throat.

"I couldn't breathe," he finally managed. "And it was so cold."

"Did you see what it was?" she asked.

"Some kind of shadow," he said with a shudder. "It had eyes."

"How did you drive it off?"

"It didn't like the light," Hound said, going to the window and touching the frost, leaving a fingerprint where his body heat melted the cold away. He held the lamp to one side and cupped a hand against his face, peering through the window into the night. "I think it's gone."

"For now," Ben said.

Dom and Kat appeared in the hall.

"Do we have a problem?" Dom asked.

"Pretty sure," Ben said, taking a moment to recount his experience.

"Sounds like someone or something summoned it to kill you," Dom said. "Question is—who?"

"Probably the Warlock," Ben said. "Nash would have sent men or a stalker, and Hoondragon would have come himself."

"I suppose that's fair," Dom said.

Cleve came trotting up. "Something's got the horses spooked."

"A big cat would rile them up," Hound said.

Ben reached for his belt, strapping on his weapons and pulling on his boots.

"What are you going to do?" Imogen asked.

"I'm thinking about calling the Warlock out," he said.

"And then what?" Dom asked.

"I thought maybe I'd shoot him until he's dead," Ben said, checking the cylinder of his revolver and flipping it closed before returning it to his holster.

Dom chuckled, nodding and then shaking his head. "I understand how you feel, but we don't know if he's the one ghosting us and we don't want to draw any more attention than we have to. Your demon-possessed Dominus is still out there, never mind Hoondragon."

"What do you suggest?" Ben asked.

"Let's move everybody into the dining hall and keep some lamps burning until dawn. If we're going to face off against a demon-summoning Warlock, I'd rather do it in the light of day."

"Fair enough, but he's not going away," Ben said. "Odds are, he'll make another attempt on us tonight."

"All the more reason to be together in a secure place," Dom said.

Ben nodded his assent, though he didn't really agree.

The commotion of bringing everyone into the dining hall did little to clear the fog of recent waking from his mind. Despite the fear that had gripped him, or perhaps because of it, he was tired enough to sleep standing up.

And then a thought occurred to him.

"Augment, can you check to see if I've been poisoned?"

"Beginning diagnostic."

He laid out his bedroll where Gwen told him to, on the other side of the room from her daughters, and sat down to remove his boots.

"No anomalous substances detected."

"Good, run periodic checks through the night," Ben said, easing himself onto his bedroll. "Also, replay the visual record of the encounter with the shadow."

"Understood."

The scene came to life in his mind. He only had a few seconds of disoriented imagery available, but that was enough to send chills through his entire body. As it fled the light, its eyes radiated such penetrating malice. And then it flew through a window with no trace of its passage save the spot of frost.

"How do I kill something that isn't even there?" he thought.

"Unknown," the augment said. If Ben didn't know better he would have thought the augment sounded worried.

Zack and Frank came into the room, shepherded by Kat, both still bleary-eyed from recently waking. Zack dropped his crumpled blankets next to Ben and sat down heavily.

"What's going on?" he asked.

"I'm not really sure," Ben said, opening his eyes but not bothering to sit up. "Something attacked me in the night."

"What do you mean, 'Something'?" Frank asked.

"Whatever it was, it didn't like the light," Hound said. "Get some rest. We'll probably be on the move tomorrow."

"I thought—" Frank said.

"Doesn't matter," Hound said. "Things just changed."

Frank hesitated, but obeyed after a moment of Hound's unflinching gaze, tossing his bedroll out and lying down with his rifle next to him.

Ben drifted off in spite of the light cast by several lamps hanging from the walls. He slept fitfully, dreams of the shadow invading his slumber.

He woke suddenly, a scream of pure terror flooding the room. Imogen sat bolt upright, trembling and sweating, trying to catch her breath. Hound was on his feet along with John and Kat within the second, all three with weapons at the ready, even though they had no target for their wrath.

Ben scrambled to Imogen.

"What is it?" he asked, holding her by the shoulders, forcing her to look him in the eye.

She shuddered, trying to shake off a chill, every hair standing on end. "The wyrm," she managed, before she started sobbing.

Ben pulled her to him and held her until she stopped crying.

"Tell me what happened," he said gently.

Everyone else was awake, some standing around her, others checking the hall and windows.

"The dragon came to me in my dream," she said. "He was horrible—so evil that I could feel it. He said he'd trade my baby for the egg."

"It was just a dream," Frank said.

She shook her head. "It was more than that, I know it was." She stopped, clenching her eyes shut and shaking her head. "Oh God, what have I done?"

She broke down again. Ben waited, motioning for Frank to be quiet until she was ready to talk.

"Tell me," Ben whispered.

She sniffed back her tears. "Chen told me to meditate on getting my baby back—so I did, only it was more like I was praying to the dragon to keep him safe. I think he heard me."

"Shit!" Dom said under his breath.

"Is that even possible?" Frank asked incredulously.

"Oh, yeah," Dom said. "It wouldn't be the first time the wyrm has tried to get into a person's head through their dreams."

"What do I do?" Imogen asked, tears in her eyes.

"Stop praying to the wyrm, for starters," Dom said. "After that, learn how to draw a magic circle and start sleeping inside one every night."

"Is there a way to keep him out of her dreams?" Ben asked. "Other than a circle?"

"I don't know," Dom said. "She invited him in. He might be hard to banish."

"Oh God," Imogen whispered.

"What the hell is that?!" Kat snapped, pointing toward the shadows in the hall outside the dining hall. All eyes followed her finger.

From the darkness, a pair of eyes watched them, red with hate.

Ben came to his feet and strode toward the shadow, taking care to remain within the light.

"Tell your master that I have a bargain for him, but him alone," he said. "Tell him to come at first light, in person."

The eyes narrowed and then fled into the darkness.

"What are you talking about?" Frank asked. "What bargain?"

"I'm going to offer the egg for Imogen's baby," Ben said.

"But ... the dragon can't be trusted," Frank said.

"No, but that shadow doesn't work for the dragon, it serves the Warlock," Ben said.

"How do you know?"

"Because the dragon would be here if he knew where we were."

"The Warlock can't be trusted either," Frank said.

"Probably not," Ben said, returning to Imogen. "Do you remember anything else about your dream?"

"Nothing except the feeling of pure hatred and contempt he has for all of us," she said. "To him, we're less than insects."

A big cat screamed in the distance and the room fell silent.

"Well, I guess we have a date," Ben said.

"Not exactly a friendly answer," Hound said.

"No, but I'm pretty sure it is an answer."

"And just what exactly do you plan on telling the Warlock if he does show up tomorrow?" Hound asked.

"Just what I said."

"Think he'll go for it?"

Ben shrugged.

"We should ambush him," Frank said. "There are more than enough of us to take him."

"Probably, but he's dangerous enough that he might get a few of us, too," Ben said. "I'd rather see if we can turn him into a problem for the dragon."

"The enemy of my enemy," Hound said.

"We can hope," Ben said. "Dom, do you have some charcoal or chalk, anything I can draw on the floor with?"

"Yeah, in the map room."

"I'll get it," Kat said.

"What if he doesn't agree?" Frank asked. "Shouldn't we have a plan?"

"I got a plan right here," Hound said, patting Bertha.

"Seriously," Frank said. "He's dangerous."

Ben sighed and stepped close enough for Frank to hear him whisper. "He'll wait until morning to see if my offer is worthwhile. He'll pretend to agree, then he'll circle around and try to steal the egg." Frank started to interrupt but Ben stopped him. "The important part is that he'll wait until morning."

"So you're just buying time?"

"Yes, now don't speak of it again. He might be listening."

Frank looked around quickly just as Kat returned.

"What good will that do?" Frank asked.

Ben pulled him closer. "He has a stalker cat. If he sends it to spook the horses, they'll tear themselves apart trying to get out of the barn."

Frank frowned, taking a breath to say something else but Dom spoke first.

"Like it or not, Frank, your brother is the Wizard now. You'd do well to back his play."

Frank glanced around the room and went silent.

"Here you go," Kat said, handing Ben a big piece of chalk.

"Thank you," he said, handing the chalk to Imogen. "It's important that you follow my instructions exactly."

She nodded.

"Start here…"

Five minutes later she'd drawn a magic circle on the floor around her bedroll. He checked with his augment's memory files to ensure that she'd duplicated the circle just as Cyril had taught him.

"Tomorrow, I'll help you create a meditation to get your son back that doesn't involve the wyrm."

She nodded sheepishly.

Chapter 8

Ben lay down and tried to sleep, but his mind was too active, so he started replaying the fight with Ellie again. After the first time through, the augment interrupted.

"I believe it wouldn't violate my programming to offer you combat simulation training."

"What's that?"

"Virtual reality training."

"I still don't know what that is."

Quite suddenly, Ben found himself standing in an open field of hard-packed dirt. The landscape was barren and flat, stretching in every direction to the horizon. The sky was a steel grey and the air was calm. He held his sword.

"What the hell?" he said, looking around a bit wildly.

"Don't be alarmed," the augment said. "This is a simulation that I have created within your mind. In reality, you are still resting safely."

The initial fear faded quickly, replaced with curiosity and then a sense of wonder.

"So, what now?"

Two men appeared twenty feet away, both dressed in Dragon Guard armor and both armed with swords.

"I can offer a wide variety of simulated combat environments and opponents. While you will feel pain, you are in no danger of actual injury."

The two men began to advance, the first coming straight at him while the second began to circle. Ben brought his blade up instinctively, moving at an angle away from the circling man, his mind slipping almost involuntarily into a state of effortless flow, thought giving way to instinct honed by training, his blade becoming an extension of his will.

The first man charged. Ben reversed course, slipping inside his thrust and lunging at the second man, catching him off guard and stabbing him through the wrist. The man shrieked in pain, crimson dripping into the dirt next to his sword as it clattered to the ground, his left hand holding his right wrist tightly to staunch the bleeding.

Ben raced past him, the sound of a sword slicing through the air behind him. He spun, putting the injured man between himself and the other attacker. The first man angled to get around the second, who was bending down to retrieve his blade with his off hand. Ben kicked him in the back, sending him sprawling into the first man's path. As the first attacker tripped over his companion, Ben thrust, catching him under the chin and driving his blade through his throat and spine.

He pulled his bloody blade free, whipping it around and placing the point against the downed man's neck just under his helm as he stepped into the middle of his back and drove the blade through his spine as well.

The two men vanished, along with the blood coating Ben's blade. He looked at it in wonder.

"This feels so real."

"While useful for training your mind, this environment does little to train your body. Tactics, technique, and a limited version of experience can be honed within this construct, but muscle memory, strength, and endurance cannot."

"Can you make my opponents better?"

"If by better you mean more skilled, then yes."

"Good ... do it."

Two men appeared...

Ben sat up gasping. The pain faded almost instantly but the memory of it lingered.

"Holy shit," he said in his mind. "You said it would hurt, but not that much."

The second fight had been more difficult, though he was still victorious. The third fight ended when one of his opponents stabbed him through the belly.

"Pain is a useful teaching tool."

"You all right?" Homer asked.

"Yeah, the augment has a training simulator," Ben said, waving off Kat's concern when she looked at him questioningly. He eased himself back onto his bedroll. "It feels real."

"What's that do for you?" Homer asked.

"Let's me train without actually training."

"So why did you sit up like you were in pain?"

"Because I got stabbed and it hurt like hell."

Homer grumbled audibly, rolling onto his side. "That's just stupid. You should get some sleep instead of pretending to get stabbed."

Ben closed his eyes and cleared his mind. He woke with the growing light of day. Most everyone else was still asleep. He gathered his weapons and the egg and headed for the door.

Ty intercepted him. "Where are you going?" he whispered.

"Just out to the courtyard," Ben said, not giving him time to object.

A gesture sent Baxter following after Ben. The man-at-arms didn't try to stop him, instead taking up a post beside the door while Ben piled up his gear next to Homer and began his sword form.

Now that he knew how to achieve the state of effortless flow, it came far more easily. He moved through the form with grace and even joy, a feeling of calm centeredness permeating his consciousness. When he finished, he noticed Ellie sitting on the steps watching him, two practice swords beside her.

"I promise I'll go easier," she said, standing and offering one of the wooden blades.

"I'm not sure your father will care one way or another," Ben said.

"Good thing it's not up to him."

"Why do I feel like I'm going to regret this?"

"Probably 'cuz I'm gonna to kick your ass," she said with a challenging smile.

"Huh," he laughed. "Think so, do ya?" He returned his blade to its scabbard and took the practice sword, facing off with Ellie and bowing respectfully before stepping into his favored guard.

"Mind the egg," he said.

She nodded, moving at an angle toward his off hand and attacking. He blocked fluidly, testing his feelings and the magic that permeated the area. It felt different—less hostile.

They met in a flurry of thrust and parry, each striving to best the other. Without the anger that Ellie had brought to the previous fight, the quality of the magic was entirely different, fostering more of a cooperative energy instead of the wrathful aggression he'd felt the first time he'd sparred with her.

It felt good, more like an elaborate dance than a contest of violence. Each managed to get through the other's guard, but all blows were checked and then acknowledged. After a while he found himself completely lost in the exercise, his mind, body, and sword becoming one.

And then he started to feel her will and mind as well. He could sense what she was going to do next, feel her intention. The dance became more dynamic, more nuanced, and far more energetic, both of them moving with blinding speed, surrendering to a kind of trust that could only be possible between two people sharing the same mind.

As one they both stopped, staring at each other in wonder and bewilderment.

"That was incredible," she said.

"I've never felt anything like it, either."

"It was like I was inside your head," she said. "I mean, I couldn't read your mind or anything, but I just knew where you were going next."

They only noticed Dom when he started clapping slowly from the porch. He sighed, shaking his head sadly.

"You've both just experienced something that few others ever will. It was Chen who first figured it out. He called it *overlapping flow*—leave it to Chen to come up with a boring name for something so powerful. It's a kind of melding of the minds. After the four of us practiced and mastered the technique, we were far more effective in battle, each of us coordinating our efforts almost subconsciously.

"Not everyone can do it, only those with a natural aptitude for dragon magic. Something both of you clearly have in abundance."

"Indeed," the Warlock said, through a tear in the fabric of space not thirty feet away. Ben whirled on him, raising his wooden blade reflexively, scanning the area for any other hint of danger.

The Warlock smiled. Ben could see forest behind him through the rift. He had to check his sanity. Things like this weren't supposed to be possible, and yet…

"You have a great deal of raw talent—wild and uncontrolled, mind you, but powerful. If you had been born on my world, the dragons would have taken you as an acolyte … or eaten you as a child."

The darts on Dom's wristband floated into a fast orbit overhead as Ty came out of the house, rifle at the ready.

"There's no need for any of that," the Warlock said. "You requested an audience. Here I am."

"So you are," Ben said. "I wasn't really expecting this."

"Word to the wise, never play into an enemy's expectation unless you can use it against them."

"Fair enough," Ben said, glancing at Dom to see if he would let things play out, turning back to the Warlock when Dom nodded.

"Looks like the dragon did a number on your face," Ben said. "I was hoping you'd kill each other."

The Warlock smiled humorlessly. "A young dragon would normally have posed little problem. The priest on his back was … unexpected. Where I come from a dragon would never let a human ride him. But then, where I come from there are thousands of dragons. I suppose one must find allies where one can. You mentioned a bargain."

"The dragon has my Aunt Imogen's baby. Bring me the child, healthy and alive, and I'll give you the egg."

The Warlock smiled again, cocking his head to one side.

"A single child for the greatest treasure your entire world has to offer," he said, laughing to himself. "Unlikely."

"That's the deal. All we want is the baby and to be left alone after that."

"No treasure, no keep, no army, no land, no magic … just a baby." He tipped his head back and laughed, a singularly mirthless sound.

"When I learned how to part the veil, I looked into many worlds before settling on this one to take for my own. A few didn't even have dragons, but those had so many people. I settled on this one because it appeared to be a jewel just waiting to be plucked, not too many people and but a single dragon. I had no idea how right I was. Here you stand, the only person who passes for a champion in this entire world and you would sell it all for the price of a single child.

"Bargain struck. But know this, you have enemies pursuing you. If they catch you, then our deal is off. Also, if you betray me, I will teach you the fate of your beloved Britney."

Ben's expression of horror and surprise betrayed him.

"Ah, yes indeed, how could I possibly know about her? More importantly, what else might I know?"

The rift closed, leaving no trace of its existence.

"Well, I'm glad to see you're making friends," Dom said, darts returning to his wristband.

"That was the guy we saw on our way here," Ellie said.

"Yeah, he might be a problem," Ben said.

"He's probably a far more manageable problem than the wyrm," Dom said. "Come on, breakfast should be just about ready."

"He seems less and less manageable every time I run into him," Ben said.

"If you'd gotten that close to the wyrm, he'd have made a snack out of you," Dom said. "And who knows, you might have just turned an enemy into an ally, for now anyway."

"One can hope," Ben said.

Gwen and Annabelle wheeled a cart full of food into the dining hall—eggs, sausage, and biscuits. Ben shared a smile with Ellie when her mother directed them to opposite ends of the table.

After the meal was finished and coffee poured, Dom cleared his throat, drawing everyone's attention.

"It seems pretty clear that we can't stay here another night. Cleve and Baxter will go with the family back to the homestead. Ty, Kat, and I will escort our guests to the warehouse east of the cinder cone. The convoy should be arriving today so you'll stay there for the night and leave at first light."

"Come home with us, Dom," Gwen said. "Ty and Kat can take them to the warehouse."

"No, I have to see this through," Dom said. "But you knew that."

She closed her eyes, nodding as she sighed. "You come home to me, Dominic Flynn," she said.

"I always do," he said, taking her hand.

"I want to help them," Ellie said.

Dom and Gwen both turned dour as they looked at their daughter.

"Absolutely not!" Gwen said.

"She's right," Dom said, somewhat softer. "This isn't our fight."

"Of course it is," Ellie said. "This is humanity's fight."

Dom laughed bitterly, shaking his head. "Then where are they? Where are the hosts of humanity? Where is the army of freedom-loving people ready to risk their lives against this tyranny?" She tried to interrupt him but he cut her off with a look. "I'll tell you—they're huddled in their homes waiting for someone else to save them. They're cowering in fear, unwilling to risk themselves, hoping that someone else will die for them. And I'm here to tell you, that someone is not going to be you."

"But what if she's right?" Olivia asked.

"Don't you start, too," Dom said. "And don't either of you think to disobey me in this. I've told young Ben here what he should do—destroy the egg, let the dragon reign until he grows old and dies. That is humanity's best hope. He's chosen a different course. I disagree with him, but I understand his choice—hell, I even respect it, but I won't see one more drop of my family's blood spilled to buy salvation for people who won't lift a finger to save themselves."

"Not another word from either of you," Gwen said. "Go pack your things. We're going home."

Both stormed out of the room.

Dom chuckled under his breath after they'd gone. "I wonder where they get their tempers from?" he said, giving his wife's hand a squeeze.

The anger in her eyes softened as she looked at her husband. "Do you think they'll listen?"

"They'd better," Dom said.

"I'm sorry that I've brought strife into your home," Ben said. "You've already done more for me than I can ever repay."

"You've got it backwards, kid," Dom said. "I'm the one who's repaying a debt, and I'll consider it paid in full once I see you off."

"Thank you," Ben said, pushing away from the table. "I should gather my things."

"All of you should," Dom said. "My people will prepare the horses."

Ben stepped out of the house, pulling the hood of his cloak up to ward against the penetrating drizzle.

"Looks like we're going to get soaked," Zack said, standing just inside the doorway, peering up at the heavy grey sky.

Frank was just inside the barn talking with Olivia while she saddled her horse. Kat, Ty, and Annabelle were busy deeper inside the barn preparing horses for everyone else. Ben looked around for Ellie but didn't see her. Frank and Olivia went silent when he approached.

"How's your hand?" Ben asked, motioning to the burn on his palm from attempting to use a Dragon Guard's rifle.

"It still hurts, but it's healing," Frank said, shaking his head. "I never would have fired that rifle if I knew it would burn me."

"Will you be able to ride?"

"Yeah, I'll be fine," Frank said. "You really think that Warlock will help us?"

"No, but he might see my offer as the best way to help himself."

"I worry what he might do with the egg," Frank said.

Homer shook the rain off his coat, spraying everyone nearby.

"Homer," Ben said out loud.

"What? You know I don't like the rain," he said, trotting over to a dry corner and curling up.

Frank wiped the water from his face and glared at Homer. "Damn dog," he muttered.

"No, he's cute … all scruffy looking," Olivia said.

"Right up until he pees in your shoes," Frank said.

"It was one time," Homer said.

Ben stifled a chuckle.

"Anyone seen Adam?" Annabelle asked from across the barn.

Zack hesitated, his eyes flickering to Olivia before he answered. "I thought I saw him heading toward the kitchen."

"Oh, okay, he's probably packing lunch," Annabelle said, going back to her work.

Suddenly Olivia's horse became skittish. "Whoa, easy girl, what's wrong?" she asked in soothing tones, but her horse became even more agitated.

The horses not in their stalls broke free and raced as one into the paddock, prancing and protesting some unseen threat.

"Smell anything?" Ben asked Homer.

"Something dead is coming," he said.

"Stalker," Ben said aloud, drawing his pistol.

Hound came out of the house, racking a round into Bertha when he saw Ben with his gun drawn.

Ty and Kat came out of the barn, weapons at the ready. Ben trotted over to the front fence of the paddock and scanned the vineyard blanketing the rolling hillside to the front of the manor. He didn't see anything except for row after row of grapes, all good cover for an approaching enemy.

"Anything?" he asked.

Hound turned away from the back fence and shook his head.

"Guys," Zack said, pointing into the barn. All eyes turned to look.

Adam stood behind Annabelle, holding a knife against her side.

"What are you doing, baby?" Annabelle asked, a trace of panic in her voice, and a look of disbelief on her face.

Dom came out of the house at just that moment, taking in the scene with a glance, his darts spinning up off his wristband into orbit over his head.

"What the hell are you doing, Adam?" he said, striding toward them both, ignoring the spooked horses that were dancing back and forth across the paddock.

"He doesn't smell right," Homer said.

Ben brought his pistol up. "It's not Adam," he said, taking careful aim.

It looked like Adam but Ben could sense that it wasn't. It was subtle—so subtle that he probably wouldn't have noticed if Homer hadn't warned him.

"Quite perceptive ... for a dead man," Adam said, then turned to Dom. "I will happily release your daughter unharmed and leave you in peace."

"If?" Dom said.

He smiled and gestured toward Ben and Frank. "If you kill both of them and give me the egg."

"I'll give you the egg," Ben said, lifting his bag off his shoulder with his free hand and holding it out. "Just don't hurt her."

"What are you doing?" Frank whispered harshly.

"Not good enough," Adam snapped, morphing into Nash with a less-than-human snarl. "You were there when your grandfather called me forth. You heard what he said to me, how he insulted me. Such insolence cannot go unavenged. I won't permit it. His bloodline must die."

"I'm the one you want," Ben said, stepping forward. "Take me and the egg. Let her go."

"You think me a fool? Stop! One more step and she bleeds," Nash said.

Ben stopped midstride.

"You're surrounded," Dom said, motioning to Hound who had circled the barn, entered through a door on the far end and was pointing Bertha at Nash from her left flank.

Nash whistled, not too loudly, but with piercing shrillness. A stalker howled in response, sending the horses into a panic. Those still in stalls struggled to break free, one leaping over the railing and landing in the middle of the barn. Another broke the door open, coming free and heading for the paddock along with the first, obstructing Ben's view of Nash and Annabelle.

The horses in the paddock crashed into the gate, breaking it open and dashing out into the vineyard, running wildly in all directions. Ben dove out of the way of those barreling down on him, landing hard, and dropping both the bag and his pistol.

He looked over at Nash. She smiled at him as she stabbed Annabelle in the side and shoved her face first onto the hay-strewn floor. Olivia screamed, fear and horror quickly transforming into rage. Hound shot Nash square in the chest, knocking her back half a dozen feet, her armor holding easily. Darkness swirled around her, wisps of unnatural blackness forming out of nothingness.

Ben got to his hands and knees as a dozen streamers of darkness leapt forward, hitting Hound in the chest and shoving him violently out the door into the rain and out of Ben's line of sight.

Dom regained his footing after narrowly avoiding the horses just as several more broke free, coming out of their stalls and bolting for the paddock. Ben heard the ring of steel as he gained his feet. Dragon Guard were coming from both sides. Ty, Kat, and Ellie were fighting to keep them from reaching Dom, who was focused on Annabelle, his eyes never leaving her bleeding body.

Ben drew his sword, lunging toward Nash, blocking her from the bag with the fake egg in it. She extended her hand before he could reach her—a plane of translucent darkness, just barely visible stopped him cold, holding him frozen in front of her.

"You are an insect challenging a god," she said, her voice dripping with disdain.

Homer bit her ankle, snarling and shaking his head. She shrieked in pain, turning her attention to the dog as he raced out the door.

Her spell broke, freeing Ben. He swept into her, bringing his blade down with all the rage-fueled force he could muster.

She raised her left arm to defend against the blow, trusting her bracer to withstand his blade, but it didn't. Ben's sword cut halfway through the dragon metal, half severing her arm in the process. She cried out in pain and surprise as he kicked her in the chest to free his sword from bone and steel.

A moment later three darts flew past Ben like bullets. The first hit her breastplate so hard that it knocked her back a few feet, though without penetrating. The second hit her upper arm, driving clean through and then through the back wall of the barn. The third grazed her head, taking a chunk out of her ear. She barked a word and the area around her exploded in a sooty cloud of blackness.

"Look out!" Zack shouted.

Frank tried to take out a Dragon Guard with the butt of his rifle, but missed his jaw and caught him on the shoulder. The Dragon Guard stabbed with his sword, narrowly missing as Frank brought his rifle back in a wild bid to block the strike. His flailing attempt to defend cost him his balance, sending him falling backward against the wall of the barn.

Another Dragon Guard fixed his eyes on the bag with the egg. Zack saw his objective and raced for the bag, snatching it up and racing to the back of the barn and out the door opposite where Hound had entered.

The Dragon Guard that had just bested Frank turned on Olivia. She dodged a downward blow, rolling out into the paddock away from him, then scrambled under the fence as another enemy tried to hack at her.

Ben let go of everything else save his rage and hurled himself into the two men, swatting the first man's sword aside with ease, using the momentum created by hitting his blade to turn the butt of his sword toward him before lunging forward, striking him in the throat with his sword's pommel. Ben shoved him aside, obstructing an attack by the Dragon Guard who had chosen to face him over finishing Frank.

Ben caught a downward blow with his sword whipping it around to open the man's guard while circling to cover Dom's mad dash to his daughter. Ben's sword ended the circular parry high, well over the Dragon Guard's ability to block, and then came down on the side of the man's neck, his blade sticking in bone. Panic and pain mingled with disbelief in the dying man's eyes.

Ben kicked him, but the blade held fast, pulling Ben forward and off balance while he struggled to free it. A whoosh, followed by a wave of orange washed over the side of the barn, igniting it all at once. Ben freed his sword and surveyed the battle.

Frank had just managed to regain his feet.

"Cover Dom," Ben barked to his brother, seeing that Dom was oblivious to the rest of the scene unfolding around them, his entire focus on Annabelle.

Ty was down and bleeding from the belly, three Dragon Guard dead at his feet. Kat was down with Baxter standing over her and fighting another Dragon Guard to a standstill, his big broadsword slashing back and forth, the Dragon Guard's armor thwarting his blows. Ellie faced two men, one trying to circle her.

Two more came through the open paddock gate. Ben hurled himself into the fray, racing to Ellie's side to stand with her, attacking the circling man with a flurry of blows that set him on his heels. Ben kicked him in the chest, sending him falling backward into the door to the house. He turned his attention to the remaining Dragon Guard.

Side by side, he and Ellie faced three men in a shoulder-to-shoulder battle line. He could feel her mind and her tightly controlled rage. They moved in unison, playing off each other's strengths, fighting with an almost instinctual knowing of the other's thoughts. Ben parried a well-placed swing by the man on the right side of the enemy's line, stepping past him into the center man, kicking him in the knee, causing him to lurch forward.

Ellie stabbed him in the face through his helm's visor, twisting and turning her blade to drop the corpse at the feet of the man on the left end of the line. Ben slipped through the opening, flipping his sword point down and stabbing into the back of the right Dragon Guard's knee in passing. The man shrieked in pain, falling forward, pitching onto his hands and knees.

Ben spun around on the flank of the last man standing, swinging his blade in a wide arc, not to land a blow but to draw him into reacting, and react he did. Flailing to block Ben's blade, he left himself open to Ellie's thrust. Her sword plunged into the side of his chest through the weak spot where breastplate met backplate. He fell, blood sputtering from his mouth.

Ben scanned the battlefield in a glance. Dom was carrying Annabelle toward the house with Frank in tow. John rolled the man that Ben had kicked into the doorway out onto the paddock lawn, dead from an arrow thrust into his eye socket. He followed him out, arrow nocked and a sheepish look on his face seeing that the battle was all but over. Dom carried Annabelle into the house, leaving Frank behind.

Flame licked up the side of the barn. Zack and Olivia were nowhere to be seen. Nash was gone. Ty and Kat were down, with Ty looking like he'd gotten the worst of it as he held his guts inside his belly.

Baxter was busy ministering to Ty. Kat rolled onto her back and groaned, holding her head. Cleve came racing up from behind the house. One Dragon Guard remained, on hands and knees. Ben kicked him over onto his back and stepped on his sword arm.

"Get his helmet," he said to Ellie. She drove her sword into the ground scant inches from his head and wrenched the helm off, tossing it aside.

"Where's Nash? What did she do with Adam?" Ben barked, placing the point of his blade on the man's throat.

"You're just going to kill me anyway," the man said, his voice trembling with fear.

"I have a trail," Cleve said.

"I can help track them," Homer said, running up next to Ben.

"What the hell happened?" Hound said, leaning against the paddock railing, still a bit unsteady. "One minute everything goes black, the next your dog is licking my face."

Ben looked down at the Dragon Guard. "I guess you were right," he said, pushing the point of his blade into the man's throat, looking him in the eye as his life faded.

"Rufus, can you move?"

A wail came from the house, Gwen's voice trailing off in despair.

"Oh God," Ellie said, darting inside.

"I'm good," Hound said, eyeing the scorched barn, the fire burning into smoke under the steady drizzle.

"Me too," John said.

Ellie came out of the house, fear and anger etched into her face.

"She's alive, but she's hurt, bad. We need to find Adam."

"Cleve, lead the way," Ben said, trotting into the barn to retrieve his pistol, glancing at the still-smoldering roof as he backed out of the unstable building. He ran to catch up with the hastily formed hunting party.

"What about me?" Frank said.

"You and Imogen help with the wounded," Ben shouted over his shoulder.

Chapter 9

Olivia scrambled to her feet, glancing back to see if the Dragon Guard was following her over the paddock fence. Ben swept into him, giving her a moment to gather her wits. She got to her feet and saw Zack running away from the barn into the vineyard—he had the egg.

A Dragon Guard was between them, raising his rifle, taking aim at Zack. She raced toward him yelling "Hey!" a moment before crashing into him. He turned, trying to bring his dragon-fire rifle to bear on her before she reached him.

She hit him broadside, knocking him off balance and causing his rifle to fire, a wave of orange flame hitting the barn and igniting it with a whoosh. She stabbed at him but her knife was turned aside by his armor. He tried to hit her in the face with the butt of his rifle, but she ducked under his stroke and stabbed him in the hip, just under the lower edge of his breastplate, her thin blade penetrating deeply. He yelped, flinching backward, slipping on the rain-soaked sod and falling on his back.

Olivia scanned the rows of vines and found Zack, heading down the hill, away from the house. She started after him, leaving the injured Dragon Guard to bleed. Another source of motion caught her eye—it looked like a dog on the hunt. It was tracking Zack by sound, looking for a break in the vines that would allow access to the row he was running down. She picked up her pace, racing almost recklessly down the rain-slick grass.

She picked the row Zack had taken and followed, his head just visible over the shallow slope of the hill. He stopped suddenly, falling out of sight a moment later. She poured all of her energy into speed, hurtling down the hill. Zack had fallen when he tried to stop too abruptly, his feet slipping out from underneath him. He sat in the middle of the row pointing his sword at a coyote that looked like it should be dead.

Olivia had heard about the stalkers, but the stories didn't do the creature justice. Its lifeless eyes never left Zack as it moved toward him, crouching low, ready to spring.

"Get away from me!" he shouted.

It kept coming, and then, seeing Olivia approaching, it lunged into a charge. Zack kept the tip of his blade pointed at the stalker even as it leapt onto him. He hit it square in the chest, his blade penetrating to the breastbone and turning it aside as he scrambled to his feet, slipping but quickly regaining his footing.

The stalker fell to the ground, black blood splattering the grass before it surged to its feet, turning its side to Olivia as it faced Zack. She hurled her knife, the blade flipping end over end until it buried to the hilt in the stalker's haunch. It turned, snarling at her with such ferocity that she struggled to stop, losing her footing and falling hard.

Zack stabbed it again in the side of the neck, a blow that should have killed it. Instead, the unnatural creature skittered backward, snapping at him and then snarling at Olivia. A shrill whistle wafted in over the gentle sound of the rain. The stalker barked once and turned away, limping off with the knife still stuck in its haunch.

Orange bloomed behind her. She ducked instinctively as droplets of fire splattered the vines on either side of her, a few landing randomly across her cloak.

"Look out!" Zack shouted, pointing at the injured Dragon Guard behind her. She glanced back, only then realizing that her cloak was on fire. She stripped it off, dropping it to the ground as she ran toward Zack.

"Come on!" she shouted, snatching up the bag with the egg and taking his hand, leading him farther down into the vineyard until they reached a break in the rows, both of them stopping to look back at the slowly pursuing Dragon Guard stymied by a fire of his own making.

"This way," Olivia said, ducking low and racing across the rows along a service road that ran perpendicular to the vines.

"I hate those things," Zack said, when she slowed to glance behind them. The Dragon Guard hadn't yet reached the service road. She turned back toward the house.

"Hush, we don't want him following us," she whispered harshly.

Zack nodded, trailing behind her.

She led him to the house, and then along the outside wall until she reached a window.

"Here," she said, searching the vineyard for any sign of their pursuer. "Boost me up."

He laced his fingers together and offered her his hands. She stepped up and opened the window, crawling into her bedroom.

"What about me?" Zack whispered.

"Let me get something to help you climb up."

Leaving Zack to wait, she quickly opened her footlocker and pulled out the wool blanket on top, throwing it onto her bed. She smiled at the two fake dragon eggs that she'd made the day before, taking the egg out of Ben's bag and comparing it with her duplicates, nodding in approval. She took one of her fakes and slipped it into the bag, carefully placing the egg from Ben's bag into the trunk and closing the lid.

She dropped the bag onto her bed and grabbed the blanket, unfolding it and tossing one end out the window. Zack frowned at it for a moment but took hold and looked up at her. She nodded, holding on to the blanket and placing one foot against the windowsill. Zack climbed inside the room and stumbled into her, nearly knocking her to the floor, then stepped back once he'd caught his balance.

"Sorry. Are you all right?" he asked, blushing.

She giggled, patting him on the arm in passing, taking a quick look out the window before closing it.

"I'm fine. Are you okay? Did that thing hurt you?"

"No … I think you saved my life."

She smiled, deepening the red on his cheeks.

"I'm glad I was there," she said. "Let's go see what's happened. Don't forget the egg." She pointed to the bag on her bed.

"Oh, yeah, Ben would kill me if I lost that."

When they headed out into the hallway, they could hear urgent voices coming from the dining room.

"Quickly, hand me the cayenne," Gwen snapped. A scream followed. Olivia and Zack shared a look, both running toward the voices.

"Oh, no," Olivia said when she saw her sister lying on a table, bleeding from a wound in her side. Gwen was holding the wound closed with a compress of dried cayenne pepper pressed against it to staunch the bleeding.

"What can I do?" Olivia asked.

Dom noticed the two of them and took his daughter into his arms.

"She's hurt, but she'll make it if we can get her to the doc in town," he said. "Go find a horse and hitch it to a wagon." She nodded, turning toward the door and then stepping aside as Baxter and Frank carried Ty into the room. They laid him out on the floor. Kat followed behind them, pulling out a chair and sitting down heavily.

"Oh, Ty," Dom said, kneeling next to his friend, looking back up at Olivia. "Go!"

She nodded, motioning for Zack to follow. They emerged into the empty paddock.

"Shit," she muttered, scanning the vineyard in the front of the house for any sign of a horse, putting two fingers into her mouth and whistling shrilly. She stepped up onto the railing to see farther.

"There she is," she said, pointing at the horse trotting toward the house.

"What about the Dragon Guard?" Zack asked.

"I don't see him," Olivia said, waiting impatiently for her horse to arrive. The mare was still a bit spooked but calmed down readily enough after a few soothing words. Olivia led her through the paddock and behind the barn, going to work hitching her to the wagon parked there.

"Hey, there's another horse," Zack said.

"See if you can get him to come to you," Olivia said.

Zack headed off, returning with a horse in tow a few minutes later. Olivia took the reins and led the animal into the charred but still-standing barn.

"Help me saddle him," she said. "My father will want someone to ride escort."

"I wonder where Ben went?" Zack mused while they worked.

"That's a good question," Olivia said. "I haven't seen Ellie either."

They finished and headed into the house, back to the dining room and the wounded.

"Wagon's ready and Zack rounded up another horse," Olivia said.

"Good. Baxter, I want you to ride with them," Dom said.

"How is she?" Olivia asked.

"The bleeding's stopped, but she's lost a lot of blood," Gwen said tightly. "Ty is in worse shape."

Both were lying on the table, both were bandaged around the belly, and both were deathly white. Olivia gave her sister's hand a squeeze, looking over at her father.

"Ellie? Ben? We haven't seen them."

"They went after Adam," Dom said. "Bring the wagon around so we can get them loaded."

"I'll help," Frank said, stopping Zack with a hand on his shoulder. Zack looked a bit dejected but didn't argue.

Once outside, Frank stopped Olivia, stepping close so he could speak quietly.

"Did you make the switch?"

"Yeah, but my sister's lying on a table bleeding right now, so let's get her taken care of first, all right?"

Frank blinked a few times, nodding agreement and offering a smile that she ignored.

"Get the horse in the barn and follow me around to the courtyard," she said over her shoulder.

Ben crouched low, scanning the woods, seeing nothing but dripping greenery.

"Smell anything?" he asked Homer.

"Nothing but rain."

"Looks like they went this way," Cleve said.

They set out again, slower and more deliberately this time. The trail had been easy to follow through the wet and muddy grass between the rows of grapevines, but once they'd reached the woods, tracking became more difficult.

The ubiquitous drip, drip, drip, obscured what noise they made moving through the trees, but it also made picking out the enemy by sound nearly impossible. Several hundred feet inside the forest, Cleve stopped, pointing to the tracks he'd been following. John knelt down next to him, nodding at the small blood droplets on the leaves of a shrub.

They moved more carefully for another fifty feet, cresting a gentle hill with Cleve in the lead. He crouched quickly, motioning for silence. Ben crept up next to him, lying down in the damp moss and peering through the ferns.

Adam was sitting against a tree, his arms tied to it behind his back, his head lolling forward. Nash stood over him, looking angry, holding the wound on her arm. A Dragon Guard stood watch facing toward them, but judging from his lack of reaction, he hadn't noticed them. A second Dragon Guard sat against another tree, holding his hip, blood seeping through his fingers.

"Can't you use him to heal us?" the bleeding Dragon Guard asked.

She looked at him, her face a mask of annoyance. "Quiet, I'm thinking."

Drip, drip, drip.

"I'm bleeding here," he said.

She glared at him until he looked away nervously.

"No, I can still use him," Nash said. "You, on the other hand…" She faced him, raising her arms in spite of the through-and-through wound she'd suffered.

"What … what are you doing?" the Dragon Guard asked, his eyes going wide.

Blackness began to form around her, wisps of cold darkness.

"Don't," he said, struggling to regain his feet.

The darkness began to flow into him, holding him fast, his eyes wide with fear and pain as the black magic flowed from her arm to the Dragon Guard and back again. He screamed. The other Dragon Guard looked back and then quickly looked away, his face going slightly pale.

The injured man struggled in vain as Nash's wounds were transferred to him, fresh blood oozing from his upper arm. The magic ran its course and Nash smiled down at the man for a moment without any hint of sympathy before inspecting her arm and her ear.

"Much better," she said.

The stalker came limping into the clearing, a knife still buried to the hilt in its haunch.

"Ah, there you are," Nash said, kneeling next to her stalker and inspecting the knife.

"That's Olivia's," Ellie whispered.

The stalker turned, looking straight at them. Then it barked, snarling as it advanced.

She winced, apologizing with a glance at Ben.

He drew his pistol and looked back at Hound, motioning for him to flank. The stalker leapt into a run, the blade in its haunch slowing it down, but not enough.

John came up on one knee, drawing an arrow and loosing it, hitting the possessed animal in the shoulder just below the neck, penetrating deeply, but only slowing it marginally.

Nash snatched up a dragon-fire rifle and turned it on Adam. At the same time the other Dragon Guard took aim at them.

Cleve fired his pistol at the stalker, hitting it just below John's arrow. His bullet tore the coyote's left front leg completely off, toppling the creature into the mossy forest floor, but it didn't stay down for long.

Ben took careful aim at Nash, remaining prone to steady his hand, and fired, missing completely. Hound fired from the flank, hitting the Dragon Guard across the arm and hand, causing him to drop his weapon with a grunt. Ben quickly fired again. This time his round hit Nash in the forearm, forcing her aim wide and causing her to unleash fire across a patch of ferns.

Ellie was up with her sword drawn when the stalker reached them. It lunged at her but she caught it in the mouth with the point of her blade, driving straight through and out the back of its head. It landed on her, knocking her flat on her back. She slid down the hill still holding on to the hilt of her sword while the stalker frantically tried to bite her despite the steel in its mouth, its eyes beginning to lose intensity. When they finally came to a stop, she rolled the beast off her and wrenched her blade through the side of its head.

Hound fired again, this time aiming low at the Dragon Guard's relatively unprotected crotch, eliciting a scream of abject torment from the man as he collapsed to the ground, followed by the mewling denial of his grievous injury.

Ben was up, taking another shot at Nash, hitting her in the breastplate, knocking her off balance. Hound turned Bertha on her, firing again, blowing her off her feet. She hit the ground and then rebounded through some force of magic that brought her to her feet a moment later.

She locked eyes with Ben and shouted a word, thrusting her hand at the ground. A wave of translucent shadow radiated away from her in all directions, holding Ben and his friends fast while she bolted into the forest, injured and alone. The spell only lasted for a few seconds, but it was long enough for her to get away.

Ellie came over the ridge, sword in one hand and Olivia's dagger in the other, black blood staining her riding leathers. She raced to Adam, gently lifting his chin and looking into his slack face, opening one eye to see if he was still alive.

"He's breathing, but he won't wake up," she said. "What did she do to him?"

"Black magic," Ben said, cutting Adam's hands free. "Let's get him back to the house."

"What about them?" Cleve asked, motioning toward the two Dragon Guard, both bleeding to death in the rain.

"Kill them if you want … leave them to die slowly … I don't really care," Ben said.

"Nash might be able to use them to heal herself," John said.

"Good point," Ben said, holstering his pistol and drawing his sword.

They carried Adam, dripping wet and unconscious, into the house and laid him on the table still stained with Annabelle's blood.

"Where's Belle?" Ellie asked.

"Your mother took her into town," Dom said, leaning over Adam and checking his eyes. "What happened? And what's that all over you?"

"We tracked Nash and found her with Adam and a couple of her men," Ellie said. "This … is stalker blood."

"Did it draw blood? Even a scratch?" Dom asked, suddenly very concerned.

"No, I don't think so."

"You should burn those clothes," Ben said. "Stalker blood is dangerous."

"He speaks from experience," Hound said.

"Go get cleaned up," Dom said.

Ellie nodded, heading for the door.

"This reminds me of John in the bunker," Imogen said, leaning over Adam.

"She was definitely using black magic," Ben said. "Maybe we can help him with a little magic of our own."

"You're going to need this, then," Zack said, holding out Ben's bag.

"Thank you," Ben said, taking the bag and slinging it over his head and shoulder just as Olivia and Frank entered together. Ben could tell in a glance that something had happened between them. Where before, they were very friendly, now there was coldness coming from Olivia and Frank seemed overly satisfied, though he was trying to hide it. Ben knew his brother well enough to know that victory was never enough for Frank—he had to make sure you knew that he'd beaten you, even at the expense of his own machinations.

Ben filed his suspicions away and looked around the room, his eyes landing on the piece of chalk that Imogen had used to draw her circle the night before. He began drawing his own without a word.

"What do you have in mind?" Dom asked, watching him work.

"I'm going to try to break the spell he's under," Ben said, looking over at Adam.

"How're you going to do that?" Frank asked.

"Magic," Ben said with a shrug.

Frank twitched involuntarily.

"Help me put him in the circle," Ben said, after inspecting his work. Hound and John carefully lifted Adam from the table.

"Don't step on the lines."

They both nodded, laying him on the floor within the confines of the magically protective diagram.

Ben sat down inside the circle, crossing his legs and closing his eyes. He cleared his mind as if beginning meditation, but instead of focusing on his coin, he reached out for the feeling of magic that he'd come to know from the egg's presence. It came to him easily. After a moment, he directed his focus to Adam, probing with his mind, or maybe just his imagination, trying to determine what was wrong.

At first he felt like he was floundering. He couldn't tell if he was doing anything at all or if he was just pretending that he knew what he was doing. Frustration welled up in his belly, disturbing his calm and forcing him to begin anew. He mastered the emotion quickly, calming his mind once again, but this time he simply listened, probing the stillness for some insight, opening himself up to a flash of inspiration that he hoped would lead to a solution.

When it came, it came quickly—and it wasn't at all what he expected.

A dark and cold consciousness invaded his mind, pushing its way into his psyche and supplanting his will in an instant. He slumped forward, unable to command his body, completely helpless as some dark and hateful being invaded his mind and usurped control.

He was fully aware. He could feel and hear everything. He just couldn't move or speak. He was cut off from himself—a prisoner in his own body.

"What's happening?" Ellie asked.

Adam sat up with a gasp as he came back to himself.

"Stop!" Dom said. Adam froze, Ben's forehead resting on his lap. "Stay inside the circle."

"Are you still in there?" Homer asked, uncharacteristic worry in his voice.

"I'm here," Ben said, panic scratching at the periphery of his mind. "Don't let anyone break the circle."

He heard Homer bark.

The presence within him began to assail him with emotion, dark and despairing, sapping his will and railing against his life and his very existence. At first, the onslaught of hopelessness was nearly overwhelming, but he caught his mental balance quickly, having experienced such unwelcome feelings before.

He thought of his grandfather, and the unconditional love that he'd always given Ben. The thing within him shrieked in the face of it, fury and fear. Ben held up his love for his grandfather and then reached out to the magic of the egg, binding both feelings together into a ward against the invading spirit.

It railed against him, pushing harder and more furiously, trying to infect Ben's mind with despair, but Ben had been here before, he'd fought this kind of enemy and he'd won. He knew the secret was control over his emotions. Love was the one thing that the darkness hated and feared. It was the one thing that had the power to undo it.

Ben turned it into a weapon, transformed it into a talisman and held it up in the face of the invader. He let it pour all of its hate and rage into him and accepted it, staring down those empty emotions with the unshakable confidence of a man who knew what it was to love and to be loved.

The assault against his mind and soul grew more ferocious, driven by the desperation of the disembodied demon. As the beast's fury grew, Ben's calm centered clarity rose to match and surpass it until, with a final howl, its claim over him broke.

He sat up, his eyes snapping open. Adam sat next to him, both of them inside the circle. The room was silent, all eyes on Ben.

Dom chuckled gently, drawing everyone's attention. "Looks like Robert chose well," he said. "That was impressive."

"What just happened? And what was that shadow that came out of him?" Frank said, his voice unsteady.

"I'm pretty sure that shadow was what had me," Adam said. "I could hear and see and feel, but I couldn't do anything. And … whatever that thing was, it seemed to feed on my fear."

Ben nodded, slowly getting to his feet. "When I opened my mind to it, it took me instead."

"How did you get rid of it?" Ellie asked, stepping past everyone else.

"Love," he said with a shrug. "The darkness hates that more than anything else. I always wondered why my grandfather put so much emphasis on learning emotional control. Once again, it seems that he taught me more than I thought he did."

"Robert always was the master of sneaky," Dom said.

Adam looked around the room.

"Where's Belle?"

Dom sighed, pulling him aside.

"So Nash is still out there," Frank said.

"Yep," Hound said. "She has a few more holes in her, but she's out there."

"Fortunately, she doesn't have anyone left to help her," Ben said.

"But she has magic," Frank said. "And she knows how to use it one hell of a lot better than you do."

"I can't argue with that," Ben said.

"So what are we going to do?" Frank asked.

"The plan hasn't changed."

"Maybe it should."

Ben clenched his jaw, regarding his brother for a long moment before nodding slowly. "What do you have in mind?"

"I don't know. It just feels like you're making decisions for all of us."

"That's because I am," Ben said. "But you don't have to be a part of this if you don't want to be. I'll give you some gold. You can go where you want and make a life for yourself."

Frank hesitated. "No, I can't abandon you."

"He wasn't so quick to reject the idea of leaving this time," Homer said.

"Yeah, I noticed that too," Ben said.

Kat came striding into the room. "I've rounded up four more horses."

"Good," Dom said. "Adam, Ellie, and Olivia will be taking three of them into town. We'll take the last one for a pack horse on our walk to the warehouse."

Adam hurried out of the room heading toward the stables, a look of fear etched into his face.

"You girls better hurry," Dom said. "I don't think he's going to wait long."

"Daddy, I need a minute to talk to you, alone," Olivia said.

"Oh, we're going to have a talk, all right," Dom said. "Both of you can count on that, but now's not the time. Get your things. I want the two of you on the road with Adam inside of ten minutes."

Olivia's eyes darted to Ben and then to Frank. Ben thought he caught a hint of guilt in her expression. She seemed to struggle with something before obeying her father.

"The rest of you should gather your things as well," Dom said. "We'll be leaving as soon as possible."

Ellie came up to Ben, sadness in her eyes. "I wish we had more time," she said.

"Me too."

She stood on her toes and kissed him on the cheek, turning away and leaving the room quickly.

He pulled Zack aside as everyone else filed out of the room.

"Did you have the egg in your possession the whole time?"

"Yeah ... I mean, well, no. Olivia had it for a minute."

Ben nodded to himself.

"Is it all right?" Zack asked.

"Yeah, everything's fine. You go on ahead. I'll be out in a minute."

Once everyone else had left the room, he grabbed his pack and headed for the courtyard. While revealing his hiding place no longer mattered, he was careful to keep it a secret just the same, if only to avoid revealing his ruse. He didn't want the others to begin thinking of him as duplicitous lest they become overly suspicious—especially Frank.

He looked around the courtyard, scrutinizing each window.

"Are we alone?" he asked Homer.

"I think so."

Ben stepped up onto the fountain and scooped the dragon's egg out of the top bowl. He stuffed it into his pack, pulling clothes over the top of it, then hurried to catch up with the others.

The drizzle had let up, but the sky was still grey and heavy. Ben stepped out into the paddock, feeling a twinge of loss that Ellie was already gone. Dom had the last remaining horse saddled and loaded with supplies. It was only a day-and-a-half walk to the warehouse, but given recent events, it seemed prudent to be prepared.

Ben checked his revolver, removing the spent casings and reloading the empty chambers before following Dom out the gate into the vineyard. He did a mental inventory of his weapons and ammunition, the augment assisting with a list in his mind's eye: a tech revolver with twenty-seven rounds and five seeker rounds; a shotgun with ten shot shells and four slugs; a sword and a knife; two grenades and an ex-plus charge; thirteen bullets that didn't fit anyone's weapon.

Hound still had a grenade round for Bertha along with a number of shot shells, and John's quiver was full of arrows. Imogen and Zack had swords. Not bad, he thought, even though he felt like no amount of weaponry would ever be enough given the array of enemies they faced.

Even with all of his tech weapons, Ben believed that his sword was his best weapon, or at least the one that he was most adept with. He decided that he needed to practice with his pistol, even if that practice took place in the virtual reality created by the augment.

He winced when he recalled missing Nash with his first shot. If she hadn't hesitated, Adam would have been burned to death—not a pleasant thought.

"Stop fretting over things that didn't happen," Homer said. "There's plenty to worry about that's real—like the probability of rain."

Not ten steps later, Ben felt a raindrop on his face.

"You had to say it," he said to Homer.

"You can't blame me for the rain."

They reached the edge of the vineyard and moved into the forest. The air was heavy with moisture and the dripping from the trees might as well have been rain. Ben pulled his hood up and cinched his cloak. After a few hours of walking along a muddy and rocky trail, they came to a road—broken pavement pocked with potholes and sections that had been entirely eroded away. Dom turned onto it.

"Shouldn't we stay out of sight?" Frank asked.

"Yeah, but this is the way we have to go to get where we're going," Dom said. "Besides, this road is so bad that traders almost never use it."

Ben's mind turned to the egg and his brother. As he worked out what had likely happened, he frowned to himself, stopping to tie his boot.

"I'll catch up," Ben said, kneeling at the side of the road. Once everyone had passed, he quickly took the fake egg out of the bag and inspected it. It was close to the fake that he'd made, but not exactly the same. He smiled wryly to himself as the certainty hit him—Olivia had switched it for another fake.

His mind began to race as he trotted to catch up with the others. Did she keep the other fake or give it to Frank? If he'd made a play for the egg, that changed things. Ben knew that he could never really trust his brother, but this was a betrayal that put everything in jeopardy.

He knew better than to try and confront him. Anything short of knocking him on his butt and rifling through his pack would fail—Frank could talk his way out of almost anything else.

The kernel of an idea began to form. Ben smiled to himself, testing the weight of the pouch of coins that he'd accumulated since the egg had come into his life.

When they stopped for lunch, he stepped into the forest to relieve himself and took a couple of gold coins out of his pouch, slipping them into his left pocket, opposite where he kept his lucky coin. He always kept that one separate for sentimental reasons.

"We're making good time, considering the weather," Dom said. "Should be there by evening tomorrow."

"Do you think we're being followed?" Imogen asked.

"Hard to say," Dom said. "I haven't seen or heard anything, but that doesn't mean much."

"No sign," John said.

"Nash is out there somewhere," Ben said. "I can't imagine that she'd stop hunting us now."

"Way to lighten the mood," Homer said.

Ben gave him a look.

The drizzle picked up and the conversation died. Ben worked his idea over in his mind while he trudged through the rain, trying to tease out all of the ways that it could go wrong, finally deciding that it was worth the risk. The longer they marched, the more convinced Ben became that it was dangerous to allow Frank to remain part of the group. If he was willing to steal the egg, he was willing to do anything.

He slowly repositioned himself second in the march order right ahead of Frank. After a few minutes of walking, he dropped a coin—and Frank walked right past it.

"Would you pick that up for me, please?" he asked Homer.

It took six tries and over half an hour, with a grumbling Homer playing surreptitious fetch with overlooked gold coins, before Frank finally found one of them. He stopped cold, staring at the ground, a wide smile on his face, before leaning down slowly and picking it up.

"I just found a gold coin," he said, drawing everyone's attention.

Ben nodded with a smile. "I told you, all it takes is proximity and a little practice," he said, patting the egg and watching his brother's reaction, while schooling his own.

He saw a flicker—just a hint of doubt, or suspicion, or something in Frank's eyes.

"I think you just managed to lie to your brother by telling him the truth," Homer said. "You're better at this than you thought."

"Thanks."

The hook was set.

They walked on, the drizzle dampening any talk. As dusk approached, Ben came up alongside Dom.

"Do you have a campsite in mind?"

"I do," Dom said. "Half mile ahead with pretty good tree cover. There's a little bridge over a creek."

"Sounds good," he said, stopping to tie his boots and slipping Homer a gold coin.

"Take this ahead to the camp and leave it for Frank to find. Somewhere near the fire ring should do. He's been complaining about the cold all afternoon."

Ben watched while they approached, smiling to himself as Frank hurried ahead, arriving in camp well before the rest of them. When Ben arrived, Frank locked eyes with him for just an instant, but there was a finality to the look that made Ben question his ploy.

Whatever else, Frank now believed something different than he did before about the egg, and about Ben.

"Did he find it?" Ben asked Homer, knowing the answer.

"Yep. Pocketed it in a blink."

"No fire," Dom said when Frank started to assemble a pile of kindling.

"What do you mean, no fire? Why not?"

Ben checked with Hound about his watch before lying down for the night. He wondered what his brother would do … and felt a faint stab of guilt for deceiving him.

Chapter 10

Ellie tied her horse to the railing, the tension building in her mind, tightness in her chest. She hurried into the doctor's office. The waiting room was empty—even the woman that greeted patients was absent. Two doors led to exam rooms. She chose the one with more light emanating from under the door, striding to it without hesitation, tossing the door open and then stopping cold at the threshold, Adam and Olivia gently crowding in behind her before they too fully stopped, peering over her shoulders.

The doctor and his two assistants were working furiously to put Ty Winter's innards back inside his belly. The receptionist was holding an array of lamps and mirrors steady while watching with detached fascination.

Ty's dead-still face was as white at the few parts of the doctor's smock that weren't stained with blood.

The doctor looked up at Ellie and stopped what he was doing. "Get out!"

He held his glare on her like a morally righteous challenge until she backed out, closing the door and turning away aimlessly, her hand going to her forehead.

"Holy shit!" Olivia said.

"That's bad," Adam said.

Annabelle.

Gwen hurried out of the second exam room.

"Oh, thank God!" she said, rushing to take both of her daughters into a hug. "I love you both so much I could just about kill you. I don't know what the hell you were thinking." She never let go while she scolded them.

"What about Belle?" the sisters asked at once.

"She'll mend," Gwen said, stepping away from her daughters reluctantly. "She's in here."

They filed into the exam room and surrounded Annabelle's bed. She was bandaged and sedated but breathing strongly.

"Doc says she'll heal," Gwen said, looking at Annabelle with glassy eyes. "He gave her something to make her sleep through the night."

Adam grabbed a chair in passing, dragging it like an afterthought before plopping it in place next to his wife's bed. He sat down, took her hand, put his forehead on the edge of the bed and started crying.

Gwen herded Ellie and Olivia out with her arms stretched wide. Ellie sat down in the waiting room and leaned her head back against the wall. A flood of tension washed away with a single deep breath.

Annabelle was going to be all right.

Olivia sat down next to her and lay her head on Ellie's shoulder. Gwen pulled a chair up in front of them both.

"How's Ty?" Ellie asked.

"Bad," Gwen said, looking down sadly. "Doc says he's not sure he'll make it."

"Damn it," Ellie said.

"Shit," Olivia said.

"Language, both of you," Gwen said.

"Really, Mom?" Ellie said in a weary tone. "After all we've been through?"

Gwen stopped short with an annoyed frown, paused for a long moment, then regarded her daughters sternly before chuckling. "You're my babies," she said. "You always will be. Even when you're old. As for Ty ... do you really think, for one second, that an ornery old cuss like him is going to lay down for a belly wound?" She forced a smile, quickly wiping away a tear.

Ellie pulled her into a hug, all three of them crying on each other's shoulders.

Ellie was fighting the dragon. With Ben.

They were in a dark cavern with many enormous chambers. The wyrm blew fire in the distance, a flash of orange stinging her eyes.

She followed Ben, a hand on his shoulder, he followed the wall. Another flash, closer this time. She thought she saw light—an indistinct dull reddish-orange smudge in the distance. Ben led on. She followed, puzzled as to why. There was a dragon where he was going. Death awaited—yet, she wanted to follow him.

All in a rush, they arrived in a chamber filled to dazzling with light from a thousand fires—candles, lamps, braziers, and fire pits lining dozens of shelves cut into the rock walls of the giant cave. The glare was overwhelming. Ellie clenched her eyes shut, opening them again in the hope of seeing her adversary.

She didn't know where he was—only that he was real, and that he was hunting her.

A shadow appeared in the blurry light before her, black as death, powerful—a universal symbol of predatory prowess cast as a silhouette against overwhelmingly bright light ... and then the light was all around her ... and then she was on fire.

She sat up, gasping and thrashing.

"It's me," Olivia said. "It's just me."

Ellie calmed as she came fully awake, taking a few deep breaths and flopping back down onto her bed.

"What the hell are you doing?" she finally asked with almost no energy, rolling over and burying her face in her pillow.

"I need to talk to you."

"Now?"

"I couldn't sleep," Olivia said.

"I was sleeping just fine."

Olivia went silent for almost a minute, sitting on the edge of Ellie's bed.

"You wouldn't be if you knew what I know," she finally said in a very small voice.

Ellie took a deep breath, willed her mind to become alert and sat up, rubbing her eyes and facing her sister.

"Tell me."

Olivia winced.

Ellie cocked her head, looking at her expectantly. "What did you do?"

"Promise you won't get mad," Olivia said.

"Yeah, 'cuz that always works. Tell me."

"I thought it was what Daddy wanted," Olivia said.

"Tell me."

Olivia looked down, her hands clenched tightly together.

Ellie waited for half a minute before putting her hand on her sister's white knuckles. She waited for a dozen seconds more until Olivia looked up and met her eyes.

"Tell me," she whispered.

"I stole the egg," Olivia blurted out in a rush, standing up and walking away in a circle, stopping to face Ellie from a few feet away.

Ellie closed her eyes and shook her head just slightly, willing the last vestiges of sleep from her mind.

"Say that again."

"I stole the egg—from Ben. It was Frank's idea but I decided that I don't like him either so I gave him a fake, too."

Ellie rolled into a seated position on the side of the bed, put her hands on her knees and willed her temper into check.

"You're telling me that you have the dragon's egg … here … right now."

Olivia nodded.

"And Ben has a fake but thinks that he still has the real one."

She nodded again.

Ellie leaned her eyes on the heels of her hands and took a deep breath, and then another. A wave of anger at Olivia welled up in her, but she dismissed it with uncharacteristic ease, setting it aside for later.

Right now, she faced a combination of danger and responsibility. The simple presence of the egg might bring those seeking it right to her sister's hospital bed. Also, Ben was walking into danger without his most important weapon, and he didn't know it.

She stood up quickly, facing Olivia and locking eyes with her.

"Show me," she said.

Olivia nodded sheepishly, going to her saddle bags and removing a leather shoulder bag. She handed it to Ellie as if giving it to her were an act of absolution.

Ellie opened it and rolled the egg out onto the bed, staring at it in disbelief.

"What the hell were you thinking?"

"At first we hated him," Olivia said, talking quickly. "And I'd already set the plan in motion. Then we found out that he's not so bad after all. But then the perfect opportunity fell into my lap—you should've seen it, like God touched me on the head—I couldn't resist. It was just too easy. But, by then, I didn't like Frank either, so I kept it and gave him a fake too."

"Olivia, you're my sister, and I love you, but one of these days, I'm going to bust you right in the mouth," Ellie said, her eyes never leaving the egg.

"I know you're mad, and I'm sorry," Olivia said. "Once it was done, I didn't know what to do."

"I do," Ellie said, snatching her bag off the floor.

"What are you doing?"

"If I hurry, I can catch Ben at the warehouse," Ellie said, packing her travel gear.

Olivia sighed. "I was afraid you'd say that. Let me get my things."

"No, it's just a quick ride across town. I need you to handle Mom."

"I don't like you going alone."

"And what if Ben takes offense at you stealing his greatest family heirloom? Let me take care of this. I'll be back by dark." She sat down on the bed to pull on her boots.

"I feel like shit," Olivia muttered, leaning dejectedly against the doorjamb and looking at the floor.

"Good," Ellie said, not bothering to look up from tying her laces.

Chapter 11

Frank struggled against waking. "Just one more minute," he tried to mumble but nothing came out.

A sharp stinging sensation across his left cheek jarred him awake. His face hurt. Hound was leaning over him holding up a candle lamp with only one window partially open.

"Damn, did you have to slap me?" Frank said, rubbing his face.

"Shook you three times and you didn't wake," Hound said.

"Still ... it hurts."

"It'll pass," Hound said. "Your watch."

"Yeah ... great," Frank said, sitting up and reaching for his boots. "Who do I wake?"

"Ben, but give him at least an hour."

"Got it," Frank said, gathering his cloak around himself and settling in for his watch. The night was cold and still, the air crisp and clear in spite of the cloud cover blotting out all light from above.

"Never doubted it," Hound said, climbing into his bedroll.

Silence settled onto the camp.

At first, Frank took it as a curiosity, listening for sounds from the denizens of the night. After a while, the penetrating stillness began to become unsettling. After a while longer, he broke a twig just to make sure that noise could still be made. His nerves began to tense. His fear started to build.

He eased open the window on the candle lantern, casting a dim, flickering glow across the campground, panning the dim ray of light across the shadows, peering intently into the impenetrable night.

"Why stay?" a voice in the dark whispered from somewhere behind him.

Frank spun to his feet, turning and looking for a threat, or at least an explanation for the voice. Everyone was asleep, breathing rhythmically. There was no one behind him, no matter how hard he looked. He stood, stock-still, watching the shadows, looking for any hint of movement, listening for any noise.

Silence.

After a while, he sat back down, wondering about the whispering voice.

"It wasn't in my head," he said, barely audibly. He started to wonder less about who had spoken and more about their message.

Why stay? He thought about it. He had the egg. And he certainly didn't need all the hassle of the Dragon Guard chasing him.

He mulled the question, finding no satisfactory answer no matter how he looked at it. Ben didn't trust him anymore and everyone else was wrapped around his finger.

He had the egg.

The most powerful object in the world.

If Ben or the others discovered that he'd stolen it, they'd take it back ... at best. No ... there was nothing left here. Taking the egg would be his last con at home.

No one trusted him anymore.

Really, every moment he stayed was just added risk ... a chance to get caught.

It was so quiet.

Frank agonized over the decisions before him, watching his breath in the light of the candle lamp.

"Take the horse," the voice whispered from behind him.

Frank froze, every hair on his body standing on end. Chill after chill raced up his spine. He schooled his breathing and reached out with his hearing while slowly turning and scanning the shadows behind him for movement.

Stillness settled onto the campground again. The loudest noise he could hear was his own pounding heart. He sat back down.

Why stay?

Take the horse.

Fear drove him back to "Who?" Someone was out there, yet the night was still and silent as a tomb. Frank knew without any doubt that he would have heard someone get close enough to whisper to him like that.

He stared at the thin light of the lamp and tried to make sense of the whispers in the dark.

The forest was still and black.

That left only one explanation.

Magic.

He had acquired the egg just before they left the vineyard. Since then, he'd found two gold coins. Ben always said that proximity and will would produce results, that Frank could use magic if he focused on it while he was around the egg, but that was all just a load of bullshit that Ben put out to throw everyone off the track.

Frank never found a coin until he had the egg.

He'd never heard a voice in the night either.

Why stay? Ben was going to get everyone killed. He snorted derisively to himself when he thought about Ben's plan to pick a fight with a dragon, but only after they returned to a base filled with stalkers to find a book buried in a mountain of rubble.

Sounded like a long hard road to a certain death. And for what? A kid that no one but Imogen had ever even met.

I have the egg, he thought.

What else is there for me here?

Nothing worth the risk of getting caught with the egg.

Take the horse.

If he was going to make a break, he'd need a clean getaway and a good head start. Leaving on his watch with their only horse would give him both of those things. He nodded to himself, quickly formulating a plan to get out of the camp without being detected.

After collecting his gear, he scanned the sleeping figures sprawled out across the campground, listening carefully for any sign that someone was awake. After nearly a minute of eerie silence, he made for the horse, all the while watching the night like it was coming for him.

Slowly, deliberately placing each step by the light of the narrowest crack of the lantern, he made his way to the tree and the horse tied to it. She protested at being disturbed, but settled quickly enough, obeying the hand directing her with a firm touch.

When Ben's dog lifted his head, Frank thought for sure that he would bark, but instead he just watched Frank lead the horse out of the camp and into the tall grass running along the side of the road. The first time the mare stopped to munch on the long green shoots, he tugged her into following him. The second time, he stopped and waited, listening to the night.

Silence—save for the sounds of his horse grinding grass. But normal silence, a breeze through the trees, the crack of a twig, an occasional animal noise.

He was a good half mile away from camp ... and nobody had even woken up. A clean getaway. He smiled to himself.

They would figure it out. Ben would doubt. He would question. Sooner or later, he would examine the egg—very carefully.

Then he'd know.

Frank looked up at the inky black sky.

When the sun rose, questions would be asked.

They'd be on to him within an hour after first light. His horse tugged him forward, reaching for more fresh green grass.

Where to go? He was already east of camp. He didn't want to double back. And the road went east.

And Ben was going east.

He tugged the horse away from the tall grass and onto the eroded and uneven surface of old Highway 20, his eyes well adjusted to the frail beam of light that he allowed to escape from the candle lantern. The horse followed amiably, settling into an even clip-clop.

He really didn't have a choice, he thought, fretting about the consequences of his decision to steal the egg and abandon his family. It was just going to get everyone killed anyway. And besides, Ben was planning on hand delivering it to the one creature that really shouldn't have it.

The more he thought about it, the more he realized that what he was doing was necessary, heroic even. After all, he'd sacrificed his relationship with his own family to ensure that the dragon would never have an heir. In the grand scheme of things, that was a pretty important accomplishment.

The darkness pressed in around him, the sound of each step feeling like an intrusion in the night. The cold demanded that he continue moving. His fingers and his nose stung. His breath formed sharply defined clouds in the lantern light.

Now that he had the egg, he could take it somewhere that nobody would find it and keep it safe. He would use it carefully, learn its secrets, and guard it jealously. He needed somewhere free of the dragon's influence.

He would head north.

Except, the night was dark … and the road went east. He stayed on the road.

Another complication occurred to him. Ben might come after him. In fact, when he realized that Frank had the real egg, he would almost certainly come after him. As much as Frank hated it, he had to admit that Ben was more than his match … in a fair fight, anyway. Plus, Rufus had made his thoughts on the matter pretty clear, and Frank had no doubts about how that fight would end.

Traveling along the same road as Ben was a bit nerve-wracking but he thought it through and realized that he had no better choice at the moment. He wasn't going to go back. Leaving the road in the dark was stupid. Also, the road diminished evidence of his passage, especially when he stuck to chunks of pavement. All the better. He didn't need John tracking him.

He'd made his choice.

Now he just needed to figure out how to win his fortune. He adjusted the weight of his pack, noting the added heft from the dragon's egg and smiling to himself.

Luck is just preparation meeting opportunity, he thought, smiling at what he'd just pulled off.

He'd made his own luck—and now he owned the single most powerful item in the entire world. The possibilities that lay in his future seemed nearly limitless. He began to consider his many options as the coming dawn smudged the horizon ahead with purple and black.

This road had to cross highway 97. When it did, he'd go north, maybe up into Columbia or even Alaska. It would be years before the wyrm expanded that far. By then, Frank would find a way to Europe or maybe even Australia. The farther from the dragon, the better.

He didn't need much, just a comfortable place to live and plenty of spending money. Even without the egg, he knew that he could do well for himself. With it, he could be a king—even though he'd have to settle for becoming a shopkeeper, or some other such innocuous profession. He had to protect the egg and that meant keeping it a secret—from everyone, forever. That meant not drawing attention. He could do that.

He'd always known that he could make it on his own. He'd imagined it a thousand times. He knew exactly what to do—steal enough for a stake and find a game, and then win … even if it meant cheating. After he had some coin, he'd find a crew looking for a good man and earn a reputation.

So much for that, he thought, picking up his pace as the building dawn defined the road more clearly. The energy of a new day filled him with promise and possibility. He was free to succeed on his own. No one to hold him back—no one to interfere with his plans.

Predawn diminished the impenetrable black of the night, replacing it with shadows in the trees, but still not providing enough light to risk riding. There were too many holes and gaps in the pavement and one wrong step could break the horse's leg.

"Hello."

Frank nearly jumped out of his skin, searching wildly for the source of the voice, this one entirely different from the earlier voice. After a moment of rapidly diminishing panic, his eyes fell on the Warlock, sitting on a log along the side of the road.

"I apologize if I startled you," he said amiably, not bothering to get up.

Frank backed away, his horse skittish from the sudden excitement. He took a few moments to soothe the animal before facing the Warlock again.

"What do you want?"

The Warlock regarded Frank calmly, his albino skin standing out in stark contrast to the shadowy forest behind him.

"There's no need for alarm," he said, so calmly and assuredly that Frank relaxed a bit. "I thought we could help each other."

Frank stared at him, unsure of what to do, looking all around in an apparent fit of panic, before taking a few more steps back.

"What do you want?"

"Little bit of light," the Warlock said, finding a pine twig on the ground with a dozen end branches and blowing gently into it. He took a breath and spoke a series of strange words, blowing on the twig again. Embers formed, growing quickly but not igniting the twig … instead dozens of them floated up six or eight feet into the air, glowing with soft orange light, casting a warm, golden glow over the immediate area.

Frank watched, looking up, mouth agape, his eyes dropping back to the Warlock after the last of the embers had taken up station floating overhead.

"I won't hurt you," the Warlock said, with the utmost sincerity.

"Why should I believe you?"

"Your suspicion is fair," he said. "Allow me to prove my sincerity. Ask me anything you'd like. I will answer honestly."

"You tied me up, gagged me and blindfolded me. Why should I trust you to answer a question honestly?"

"All good points," the Warlock said. "And you're wise to be wary. Perhaps you should try me. After all, what do you have to lose by asking me a question?"

Frank frowned, looking around again before focusing on the Warlock.

"How does magic work?" Frank asked, grimacing a moment after he asked the question. "I mean, how do you use it?"

"Well, that's quite a complicated question," the Warlock said. "Perhaps we should talk while we walk."

"What do you mean?"

"Well, I'm headed east and it appears that you're headed east as well. I suggest we walk together while I tell you about magic."

"Why should I trust you? You could be leading me into a trap."

"Oh, no. Had I set a trap for you, it would have already sprung."

"I guess that makes sense," Frank said, reluctantly. "What do you want with me, anyway?"

"To make friends."

Frank blinked, shaking his head.

"You've got to be kidding."

"Not at all," the Warlock said. "Your world was not entirely what I was expecting. The truth is, I need a guide, someone who knows the customs and expectations of people here, maybe something about the various factions, or the dragon or any others of note."

"You can get basic stuff like that from anyone. Why me?"

The Warlock smiled, nodding in admission of his deliberate omission. "Your brother, of course."

Frank nodded for a moment and then shook his head in disgust. "It's always about him," Frank said. "What do you want with him?"

"Your brother is necessary for me to accomplish two of my most important objectives."

"What objectives?"

"There will be plenty of time to talk about all of that later. For now, I'd like for us to be friends ... allies even," the Warlock said. "I can offer a great deal."

Frank frowned deeply, looking about furtively but finding only forest in the fading night.

"Like what?"

"Wealth and power, what else?" the Warlock said, still sitting calmly on the log running along the side of the road. "More than you've ever even imagined."

"I don't know about that," Frank said. "I can imagine a lot."

"I have no doubt, and all of your wishes and dreams can be fulfilled..."

"If?" Frank asked, after the Warlock didn't continue.

"Well now, that depends on you," he said. "You have a number of qualities that I look for in a man. To begin with, I can employ you as my personal guide. Your duties would be to take me where I want to go and to help me navigate your customs and communities so as to minimize attention. I would pay you quite well, or..."

Frank cocked his head. "How well? And, or what?"

"Let's just say that coin wouldn't be a problem. As for the *or*, I'm not entirely certain that you are ... adequate."

Frank bristled, stopping to face the Warlock.

"What the hell do you mean by that?"

"Ah, my apologies, I meant no offense. This is the type of thing I could use help with. When I say I don't know if you are adequate, I mean, I don't know if your blood is descended from the wyrm, and if so to what degree."

"What?"

"Some of the dragon's vital essence must have intermingled with one of your ancestors in order for you to be able to use magic."

Frank frowned, his expression turning to one of curiosity and even wonder. "How do I find out if I have the blood?"

"I can test you easily," the Warlock said. "I just need a place to sit down. My camp is not far."

"So, if I pass your blood test, will you teach me magic?"

The Warlock motioned toward his little camp a hundred feet off the road, under a small grove of trees. Frank was all the way inside the grove before he noticed the horse tied to a nearby tree.

"Nice spot," he said. "Secluded."

"I thought so as well. Please tie your horse next to mine and come sit," the Warlock said, motioning to a log on one side of a stone fire pit. By the time Frank returned and sat down, a small fire was burning brightly, and a kettle was warming next to it.

"Give me a few minutes to prepare this," the Warlock said, opening a large bag filled with small pouches and vials, selecting several and setting them out, then choosing a few more, searching for a moment before selecting the last ingredient.

Then he went to work, placing a pan by the fire, but not too close. He poured just a few spoonfuls of water into the pan and started measuring ingredients and adding them according to some recipe that baffled Frank almost as much as it fascinated him.

Once all of the ingredients were in, the Warlock stirred them into a slurry, letting them come to a bubble before adding more water, stirring thoroughly, and setting it back on the fire.

"Once it comes to a boil again, I'll need you to cut yourself and drip blood into the pan," the Warlock said.

"What?"

"I require your willingness in order to test your blood. What did you think was going to happen? Magic always has a cost."

"And the price of knowing if I can use magic is a few drops of my blood," Frank said.

"Precisely. It's important that you make the cut yourself and that you direct the blood into the vessel. Do you have a suitable knife?"

Frank drew his belt knife and frowned at the neglected and dull blade. He had his sword … he could press his finger onto that.

"Allow me," the Warlock said, offering him a thin-bladed dagger.

Frank took it suspiciously, drawing the seven-inch long, half-inch wide, double-edged, charcoal-grey blade from its sheath and admiring its balance. The hilt was easy to hold and the cross guard weighed just enough to center the balance perfectly. The point was needle sharp and the edges would slice hair.

"Nice knife," Frank said. "How do I know it won't do something to me?"

"You don't. But then, the potion won't work without blood, and it's coming to a boil now, so make your choice."

Frank started forward, stopped, hesitating for a moment, before holding his finger over the pot and stabbing it with the knife, blood dribbling out as soon as he pulled the blade free. The Warlock immediately offered to take the knife in exchange for a bandage. Frank took the bandage, holding it on his finger while the Warlock put the dagger into a case in his bag of ingredients and closed it up tight, immediately returning to the bubbling potion and stirring carefully.

"It's just about ready," he said, removing a piece of folded cheesecloth from a pouch in his bag. "Do you have a cup?"

"I have to drink that?"

The Warlock sighed, fixing him with a cold, uncompromising stare.

"All right, I want to know," Frank said after a few seconds, digging his cup out of his pack.

"Good, hold it here," he said, directing Frank to a flat rock away from the fire, "and hold very still."

He wrapped the cloth over one edge of the pot and carefully poured the liquid through it into Frank's cup, discarding the spent ingredients along with the piece of cloth and setting the pot aside before kneeling in front of him and producing a dragon-bone amulet, holding it up for him to admire.

It was an inch long and a quarter-inch square with delicate runes etched into all four sides. A hole was drilled through one end, a piece of heavy woven silver wire running through it and forming a loop on the end for a leather thong.

"Is that dragon bone?"

"Yes, it's my initiate talisman," the Warlock said. "On my world, when initiates complete their training in the arts of mind and war, they are given a series of tests, some of them quite dangerous. Those who survive are granted a talisman—their first dragon bone, and the only one that will ever be given to them.

"But with that talisman comes training in the magical arts … an expansion of consciousness … access to new worlds … power."

He placed the bone in his left palm and wrapped the thong around his hand until it ran out of leather, holding out his hand, palm up, dragon-bone talisman in the center.

"Lay your hand on the talisman and take a drink of the potion. Do not remove your hand from mine, no matter what happens."

Frank nodded, placing his hand into the Warlock's and raising the cup, sniffing thoroughly before taking a drink, swallowing and waiting. The Warlock took the cup and set it aside quickly, taking a firm grip of Frank's hand.

Frank's face contorted in a silent scream of agony and he crumpled to his knees, the Warlock guiding him to the ground gently, laying him over. Frank curled into a ball and began whimpering.

The Warlock released his hand and stepped back, watching Frank for a moment before sitting down by the fire. Frank spent several minutes mewling, curled into a ball, before he gradually uncurled and took a seat by the fire, breathing heavily with the effort, his face glistening with sweat.

"What the hell did you do to me?"

"I tested you … and you passed, with high marks in fact."

"Wait … you mean I can learn to use magic?"

"You have the aptitude. Learning the craft is another matter."

"After what you just did to me, if I can learn it, then I want to."

"Understandable, but perhaps you should begin as my guide. While we travel together, I will learn more about you and then I will know."

Dawn broke and light filled the forest. The Warlock handed Frank a purse half full of silver and gold drakes.

"An advance," he said. "Now tell me, where is your brother going?"

Frank glared at him, hefting the purse, staring at the Warlock and weighing his options. He couldn't go home. He could go it alone. Or, he could follow the Warlock—a practiced wizard from a world dominated by magic.

"I'm going to expect a lot more than this to betray Ben."

"As I said, simply an advance. Now, we have the matter of direction of travel. You were headed east. Shall we continue in that direction? I have paid you to be my guide, so guide me to my desired destination—along your brother's intended path."

Frank tried to hold his own against the dead, cold stare that the Warlock fixed on him, but failed quickly.

"He's going to a warehouse east of town to be loaded into a smuggler's caravan bound for Burnt."

"There, don't you feel better now?" the Warlock said. "Mount up."

"Why is my brother so important?" Frank asked, untying his horse.

"The egg and his blood," the Warlock said. "The dragon's egg is the most powerful artifact that exists in this world. And your brother's blood opened the portal to my world. I'll need his blood to do it again. Not a lot, if he's willing."

"Ben will never cooperate with you," Frank said. "Whatever you want from him, you'd better make a list, because he'll fight with everything he's got to stop you."

"Will he talk to you?"

Frank thought for a moment, nodding. "Probably."

"So that's one play," he said, watching Frank intently.

"What? You thought I was going to flinch?" Frank asked.

"I wondered," the Warlock said. "But then, you have no concept of what I have to offer you."

"What's that supposed to mean?"

"It means, I can give you more than any other person that you've ever met," he said, his ice-blue eyes steady and unwavering. "But … you have to want it."

"I do."

"Good, we'll start small. While we travel, I'll give you a few magical experiences, nothing serious, just a few simple things to get you used to the feel of magic."

"When do we start?"

"We can begin during our journey."

Frank mounted his horse.

After riding for half an hour, the Warlock pulled up alongside Frank, matching his horse's speed.

"Feel the horse," the Warlock said, his voice carrying over the tumult of the two horses trotting, side by side. "Allow the animal to become an extension of your will."

Frank felt the horse between his legs, but he had no feeling for the beast's will. He tried to relax. That seemed to be at the heart of most of the nonsense that Cyril had tried to teach him. As he relaxed, he slid sideways, slipped off the horse and fell, tumbling into a mud puddle with a splash, scrambling to get up quickly and falling for the effort.

The Warlock stopped and turned to watch him regain his feet. It wasn't a quick process. His first attempt was thwarted by slick mud, his feet slipping out from underneath him, flipping him onto his back into the puddle.

He rolled onto his belly and crawled out of the water and onto the pavement before standing, water draining from his clothes and into his boots.

"You should get your horse," the Warlock said, gesturing to the animal grazing three hundred feet away.

Frank stared at him in disbelief, finally nodding and stomping off. Half an hour later, he returned with the animal in tow.

The Warlock sat next to a small fire contained entirely within a six-inch-diameter ventilated metal cylinder that stood nine inches tall. A pan rested over the flame and the Warlock was drinking tea from a metal cup.

"Good, tie her to that bush and come have some breakfast."

Frank felt better about the situation as his belly filled. The Warlock fed him sausage patties, bread-like pancakes, and eggs. They ate like they didn't have a care in the world, savoring every bite and washing it all down with tea sweetened with honey. The chill finally faded in spite of the fact that his clothes were soaking wet.

"What would you do to get what you want?" the Warlock asked, easing back and waiting with rapt attention.

Frank looked at him for several seconds.

"Oh, you actually want an answer," he said, thinking for a few more moments. "I guess I'd have to think about what I really want. Then, I'd have to decide what it was worth."

"Sounds pretty straightforward," the Warlock said. "So what do you want?"

Frank stopped cold for a full second, then smiled with every bit of charm he could muster.

"Now, that's quite a list," he said. "Wealth and power, like you said, but also, women and security … and magic."

"Well thought out. And ambitious," the Warlock said, pausing to hold Frank's eyes for several uncomfortable seconds. "If you'll kill a man for me, I'll make you wealthy and powerful," he said.

Frank hesitated, his eyes scanning the forest. He swallowed the piece of sausage he was chewing. "Who?" he asked.

"This man here," the Warlock said, raising his hand as if in introduction. A man with hollow eyes stepped out of the forest and stopped stone-still two dozen feet from them.

"What's wrong with him?" Frank asked, cocking his head as he regarded the man, wondering idly where he'd come from.

"He's dying," the Warlock said. "He's been possessed by a being that your mythology would call a demon—this demon is one of my servants. People can only survive for so long when possessed by such a creature. It's time for my pet to find another host."

"Wait … you don't mean me, do you?"

The Warlock turned, smiling at Frank as if he were a rat in a trap, chuckling without humor, before slowly shaking his head.

"That is not my intention, though I suppose it's always a possibility," he said. "But it doesn't have to be that way. If you help me, I'll help you. I'm a powerful friend."

"What did this man do?" Frank asked.

"Nothing," the Warlock said with a shrug. "He was a target of opportunity—wrong place at the wrong time, for him anyway. He won't last much longer. I have a spell that can heal your injuries. But this spell requires you to take a person's life in order to liberate the life energy necessary to heal you."

"You can do that?" Frank asked. "Wait, why would you help me?"

"Because you have knowledge and information that would be very helpful to me."

"But, first you want me to kill this guy," Frank said.

"Yes."

"And then what?"

"Then we'll talk."

"And if I don't take your deal, then you'll have your familiar possess me?" Frank said.

"No, of course not," the Warlock said. "The information in your mind is far too valuable to risk with such harsh treatment. No, I would use a potion to magically enslave you. It's far less invasive—you retain everything and there are no side effects, save a wicked headache. Compliance is nearly certain, provided that the subject understands the commands given."

"So, I do what you say or you'll give me a potion that will make me do what you say anyway," Frank said. "Some choice."

"I would much prefer that you help me of your own free will and in the pursuit of your own reasonable self-interest," the Warlock said. "A willing ally is a powerful asset, especially in so unfamiliar a place as this one is to me. My gratitude will be both genuine and bountiful."

Frank looked at the shell of a man ambling toward them, a faint whiff of rot emanating from the near-corpse. He took a deep breath, grimacing at the smell of death but enduring it nonetheless. He let it out slowly and then nodded, at first to himself as he stared at the dirt at his feet, and then to the Warlock.

"If I kill him, you'll heal all my injuries and I'll get power," Frank said.

"Yes, for a time, though the healing will remain."

"God, he looks dead already."

"He is, more or less."

"I'll do it."

"Excellent," the Warlock said, all business. He held up the hilt of his perfectly balanced knife. "Please, use this blade. Stab him through the heart."

Frank grasped the hilt and drew the knife slowly, noting a smudge of his own blood on the tip. Then he looked at the empty man, wondering if he could see and hear what was happening to him.

Frank had made his decision—he would have magic. He placed the point of the blade against the man's chest, directly over his heart and put his other hand on the man's right shoulder before looking to the Warlock for a command.

"Excellent ... now hold," the Warlock said, conjuring a magic circle made of soot around Frank, the man, and himself with a few arcane words. It fell into place all at once, as if all the soot in the entire circle had been dropped from a height of half an inch in the same moment.

Next he withdrew a thong from around his neck and lifted it over his head, dangling a black nine-inch tooth suggestively and muttering a chant over and over again.

When he stopped his rhythmic chant, he stood up straight and looked directly at Frank, placing one hand on his shoulder and the other on the doomed man's shoulder.

"Kill him!" he said intensely, his grip on them both freakishly strong.

Frank looked at the man, walking dead really.

"Kill him!" the Warlock said, watching Frank intently.

Frank thrust the blade into the hollow man's chest, slicing his heart in half, pulling the blade out and leaving a gaping wound. The man's dead eyes widened momentarily and he slumped to his knees before falling sideways, his blood pouring onto the ground. Frank stepped back, watching him die.

The Warlock began chanting another set of phrases over and over, all the while holding his enchanted tooth right above the body. Frank thought he saw a shimmer, almost like a mirage, flow from the corpse into the tooth.

Then the Warlock held the tooth against Frank's chest.

"You have to accept what I give you," he said.

Frank held his breath and nodded tightly.

"Good," the Warlock said, beginning to chant again.

After several moments had passed, Frank thought that nothing would happen, but then energy began to flow from the tooth into his body. The Warlock chanted in the background. Frank felt all of his injuries heal, as health and energy and lightness flowed into him. After the spell had run its course, the Warlock withdrew the tooth.

"I feel better than ever," Frank said. "What did you do to me?"

"I took the life energy remaining within him and I gave it to you."

"I feel so good," Frank said. "Like I can do anything. How did you do that?"

The Warlock held up the tooth again. "On my world, dragons create creatures to serve them. One such creature was hideously deformed, but magically gifted. When it killed people, it harvested their vital life energy, energy that it could use to heal, cure disease, or even reverse the aging process. This is one of its teeth."

Frank looked at it with intense curiosity.

"This tooth was enchanted by one of my long-dead forefathers. He killed the beast that was unleashed on his homeland by the wyrm and fashioned an amulet from its right canine. The story is that he thought on the tooth for a year until it told him what it was to become. After much preparation, he bathed the tooth in water infused with ground dragon scales, then bathed it in dragon blood, then washed it in pure water and applied one drop of dragon's tears. Then he summoned the tortured spirit of the beast that had been made by the dragons and unmade by my ancestor. He bargained with the demon for the entire night. At dawn, they struck an agreement. The demon spirit would be released from its tortured form and inhabit the tooth. In exchange, the owner of the tooth would be able to transfer life energy from one living being to another—the process is slow and a bit tedious, but quite effective."

"That was amazing!" Frank said. "I've never felt so healthy, so clear-headed ... and light." He bounced into the air.

"And your concerns for this man?" the Warlock asked.

Frank shrugged as he regarded the corpse lying before him. "You said yourself that he was going to die, and you were just going to give me some magical potion to make me do it anyway. This way is better."

The Warlock smiled, nodding appreciatively. "Indeed," he said. "And that was just a trifling taste of the power that I can offer you. Power beyond wealth or position—the power to change the very fundamentals of reality."

"Well, I just killed a man because you asked me to," Frank said. "And I have to say, it was a hell of a rush."

"Excellent. Please, sit," the Warlock said. "Let's have a look at your weapons. Tell me everything you know about how your firearms work."

At one point during Frank's mostly rambling explanation, the Warlock stopped him.

"You're telling me that this weapon can only work by expending one of these," he said, holding up a bullet.

"Well, yeah..."

"How many do you have?"

"Fifteen, I think," Frank said.

"Show me."

Frank found the box of bullets for his brush gun and dumped it out onto a dew rag. Next he emptied the magazine. Thirteen rounds total.

The Warlock folded up the rag and put it in his pocket.

"Hey, I need those," Frank said.

"I'll give you a bullet when you need one," the Warlock said. "Now the pistol."

Frank handed it to him. "I don't have any rounds for it at all."

"Shame," he said, handing it back. "Don't lose it. We may be able to procure more bullets."

Frank slipped it back into its holster, handing over his sword when prompted with a gesture.

"Very nice," the Warlock said, looking closely at the edge. "This is unlike any metal I have ever seen. Light and sharp. Are you any good with it?"

"Well ... I've been trained."

"Yes, but are you any good? Compared to say ... your brother."

Frank glared at him.

"Fair enough," the Warlock said. "If you follow my instructions and practice when opportunity presents itself, I can train you in the basic use of this weapon."

"I'd like to get better with it."

"Then it's settled. You'll gain the added benefit of experiencing my instructional methods. That will help you decide if you really want me to teach you about magic. For now, we mount up and ride east."

Chapter 12

By dark, Frank was saddle-weary and tired. The Warlock had spelled the horses, allowing them seemingly endless endurance. They had ridden past the warehouse and many miles down the highway that Ben would be traveling the following morning.

As a consequence of the spell placed on the horses, they both lay down at sunset and slept until dawn. Camp was dim and quiet. The Warlock cooked sausage links over his stove, stabbing one when it was done and juicy—he handed the fork impaling the sausage to Frank and took the other link for himself.

He looked at it closely, examining the skin for a moment before smelling one end intently. "I recognize many of these spices," he said, taking a deliberate bite and chewing slowly before swallowing and testing his palate. "Wonderful. So many seasonings in one simple dish. Spices must be abundant here. I look forward to a wide and thorough sampling." He took another bite and became lost in the process of experiencing and savoring it.

Frank ate quietly. It was good sausage, but it was sausage.

After dinner the dwarf abruptly appeared out of the darkness, startling Frank terribly, which amused the dwarf to no end. He leaned in and whispered something to the Warlock.

"Excellent," he said. Then he looked at Frank and said, "We're quite alone. I would recommend you sleep. We'll be riding at dawn. There's no need to worry, we have guardians watching over us."

"I don't doubt it," Frank muttered, rolling out his bedding and climbing inside. Morning came quickly. He woke to a dim sky and the sounds of the Warlock stirring. He slowly got to his feet and gathered his things.

One shitty situation to the next, he thought, shivering in the early morning cold. As much as he wanted magic, he hated sleeping on the ground, and he hated being cold even more.

They saddled up as soon as it was light enough to ride. An hour past dawn, they reached the head of Dry River, a canyon two and a half miles long with steep walls and a rocky riverbed. Bluffs lined both sides of the valley.

The terrain had transformed over the course of the morning. They were no longer surrounded by mountain pine and cedar. Shortly after they'd left town, high desert had engulfed them. Sage and wide-open emptiness greeted them, marred by an occasional geological blemish in the otherwise pristinely flat and empty expanse.

"This looks promising," the Warlock said, urging his horse on. A mile up the road he found his spot, stopping his horse and surveying the landscape. The road ran along the south bluff of the canyon.

"Yes, this will work nicely," he said. "The embankment overlooking the south side of the road … The section of road that's eroded into the canyon slope

… Once they're over the edge, they won't stop till they hit river rock … that's my window of opportunity. We'll watch from that bluff over there." He pointed across the canyon. "We'll have to backtrack, but we have time."

Frank hurried to catch up as the Warlock spurred his horse back the way they'd come. It took a couple of hours to reach the north bluff, secure the horses out of sight of the road, and move down the edge of the bluff onto a rocky outcropping studded with hardy evergreen bushes that offered much-needed cover. They both got down on the ground and crept up to the edge.

"The wagons should come off the road just over there," the Warlock said, pointing across the ravine. "This location is perfect. Keep watch and tell me if you see anything."

"All right," Frank said, trying to decide if he wanted to be a wizard badly enough to put up with being ordered around all the time. After all, he could probably figure it out on his own.

He glanced back. The Warlock was kneeling before a foot-wide magic circle embroidered into a crimson square of silk with gold thread. A single bullet stood in the center of the circle and the Warlock was focusing his will on it very intently.

Frank watched a desolate road, across a desolate ravine. He wasn't even really sure how the plan was supposed to work, or what he was supposed to do … besides watch the road.

The Warlock crawled out on his belly next to Frank. "Quiet?"

Frank nodded, pausing for a moment before rolling onto his side to face the Warlock. "What happened with the dragon?" Frank asked, hesitating for a moment before continuing. "And your face?"

"Both fair questions. I called out the dragon never expecting a rider, and a mule at that. I was outmatched and his fire got through, scorching me in passing. I was able to flee the battle after that, through I did lose my staff … and a grievous loss that was."

"You called the rider a 'mule.' What's that?" Frank asked.

"It's either a made creature from birth or it's a creature that has consumed so much dragon blood, tears, meat, or even ground-up bone, teeth or scales that they've transformed permanently. They can gain a number of interesting abilities, but one thing they always lose is the ability to reproduce, hence we call them mules."

"So who's the rider? And how dangerous is he?"

"I don't know, but if he's riding the wyrm, then he was probably made with blood or tears—and that makes him potentially very powerful. With my staff, he's a force to be reckoned with, especially on the back of a dragon."

"I'll bet," Frank said. "I truly hope I never see what you just described. Let's avoid them."

"For now, that's the plan," the Warlock said.

"Well, tell me when it isn't the plan so I can go the other way. I want no part of that dragon—except the magic part."

"Oh, you'll know without question when I begin to prepare to challenge the wyrm again. I've taken his measure, and alerted him to my presence. Now, I will wield patience."

Frank's brow furrowed for a moment.

"Tell me about your world," he said, after the silence had become intolerable.

"The dragons came to my world thousands of years ago. They conquered everything, building idyllic sanctuaries for themselves and their slaves, causing them to flourish with their magic, burning everything else. Those of us who chose free will fled underground. Dozens of civilizations grew in the deep dark. I am the master of one of the greatest of these."

"There," Frank said, pointing toward the road. The first wagon of the caravan had just rolled into view.

"Excellent," the Warlock said, closing his eyes intently for several moments.

Frank watched a seemingly endless stream of tumbleweeds come off the southern embankment, piling up on the road just across from the spot of erosion that flowed into the canyon.

A glint of bright orange, then another as two bottles of flaming oil shattered into the fifteen-foot-tall pile of tumbleweeds.

Moments after the flame began to rise, the driver of the first wagon called for a halt to the rest of the caravan still a few hundred feet behind him.

A cougar trailing the wagons screamed a moment later, and the horses panicked, bolting forward in a jumble, a twelve-foot embankment rising to their right, and an increasingly brilliant conflagration directly in front of them.

The cat screamed again.

The horses' panic was complete. They turned left, into the section of road eroded away and flowing into the canyon. A couple of drivers jumped clear at the top, but the rest were thrown, tumbling and broken, into the rocky riverbed at the bottom, followed quickly by the rolling cluster of mangled horses and shattered freight wagons.

The entire tortured mass slid off the edge of what used to be a riverbank, dropping ten feet into the forty-foot-wide riverbed, crashing with such tumult that Frank was certain people in the town miles away would hear it.

Once the dust had settled, one horse squealed in pain and fear, struggling to get free from the wagon pinning her down. The flaming tumbleweeds had burned out quickly, leaving only a column of fading smoke in the sky to mark the location of the ambush.

"What if you killed him?" Frank asked.

"Then he was unworthy," the Warlock said. "A goodly sample of his blood, even shortly after death, is all that I require."

A box broke open and Hound emerged, shouting a challenge to the world in general, looking around wildly before seeming to gather his bearings.

"Watch for your brother," the Warlock said.

"Naturally."

Not long after, another box broke open and Homer came tumbling out, limping away from the mess. Ben crawled out next, rolling onto his back as soon as he was free.

"Perfect," the Warlock said, closing his eyes intently again.

Chapter 13

Ben stared up at the uniformly grey sky, half expecting it to start raining. He was beat up and still a bit rattled from the crash. He heard a thud and lifted his head just in time to see the Warlock's dwarf race up, thin-bladed knife in hand, and stab him right in the thigh, withdrawing the blade quickly and dancing backward.

He sat up screaming, his hands going reflexively to the wound.

Then the dwarf darted in and cut the strap on his shoulder bag, pulling it free and racing away with the fake egg.

Homer tried to bite the nasty little creature but missed, his snarling bark transforming into a yelp as he tested his leg. The dwarf was already gone up the riverbed.

John scrambled out from a pile of crates and wagon parts, sliding down to the ground.

"Help!" Imogen cried out.

He sat up, listening.

"Hey! Can anybody hear me?" Zack yelled.

Hound and John began looking for the two of them, working feverishly to find them. They found Zack first, freeing him relatively quickly.

They could hear Imogen calling to them from underneath a mound of shattered freight. After some frantic digging, John reached down and pulled her out, unharmed.

Soon they were all sitting in a tight group next to the remains of a wagon that partially blocked their view of the north bluff.

"Horses and drivers are all dead," Hound said, peeking out from behind the rubble to scan the ridge to the north.

"Seems like a pretty well-executed ambush," Ben said as Imogen put the finishing touches on the bandage around his leg.

"Yeah, I'll give him points for style," Hound said, "but I'm still gonna shoot him in the face."

"How's your leg?" Zack asked.

"It hurts," Ben said. "I probably won't be on my feet for a while."

"Augment," he said in his mind. "Report."

"Your wound isn't life-threatening but it is deep. Assuming optimum rest and currently available materials, heal time will be approximately twelve hours."

"Available materials?"

"Yes, the raw materials required to repair your tissue. You are currently deficient."

"You mean I haven't eaten in a while?"

"Yes, ingesting the proper nutrients will speed the tissue-repair process."

"Good to know," Ben said. He pointed at his backpack and said, "Could you grab that for me, Zack?"

He smiled his thanks as he fished out a bag of dried fruit.

"Food with higher protein content would be better."

"Thanks," Ben said in his mind, putting the fruit away and finding a bag of jerky instead. Hearing no internal protest, he ate the entire bag while his friends fretted about their situation.

He began to worry that his ruse might be discovered. With the fake egg gone, someone might ask questions.

"Yeah, never mind about your leg," Homer said, laying his chin on Ben's good leg.

"It'll heal," Ben said to Homer. "I'm more worried about what happens when the Warlock realizes that he stole a fake."

Just then Zack pointed up the road. "Who's that?" he asked.

John had his monocular out in a blink. "Looks like Ellie," he said. "She's alone."

"Shit," Ben whispered. "This complicates things."

Ellie made her way down the slope, leading her horse, taking her time and picking her way until she reached the ten-foot drop at the edge of the dry riverbank.

"Are you all right?" she yelled.

"Mostly, but we're pretty sure that the enemy is still out there," Ben said.

Ellie looked around the canyon, scanning the ridgelines.

"I'll find a way down," she said, moving along the edge of the bank, walking her horse carefully.

"Just like a woman," Hound said. "Make decisions for you without so much as a by-your-leave."

"What are you talking about?" Ben said.

"She's here, isn't she? I'm pretty sure she's not supposed to be, but there she is."

"I'm sure she has her reasons," Ben said, his eyes watching her pick her way along the rugged slope.

"Oh, me too," Hound said, chuckling.

Ben leaned his head back and closed his eyes. He didn't have twelve hours—especially not with the Warlock examining the egg, probably at this very moment. He needed to move. And there was only one horse.

But he'd made a promise. Ellie shouldn't even be here.

Rather than race headlong into the rabbit hole of wondering about the reasons for her presence, he focused on the pain in his leg, an easy enough subject to put his mind to. At first, it was terrible and intense, but after a while of focusing on it, Ben found that he was able to manipulate it to some degree, diminishing the intensity, changing the quality or even detaching from it altogether.

"Hey," Ellie said.

He opened his eyes and she was there, kneeling beside him, smiling sympathetically.

"You all right?"

"Mostly," he said. "But I'm not really in fighting shape at the moment. What brings you around?"

She smiled, stifling a laugh. "Olivia and her damn sneaky." She stopped, trying to form a word before shaking her head angrily. "Oh, hell, she stole your egg."

Ben schooled his expression and took a deep breath, carefully working through his opportunities and risks, given this recent turn of events.

"What do you mean? The Warlock just stole it a few minutes ago." He felt a pang of guilt at misleading her.

Ellie shook her head. "No, he stole a fake. Olivia switched it." She dug a leather shoulder bag out of her backpack and handed it to Ben.

He took it with a frown, shaking his head while his friends all looked on, before gently dumping the egg out onto his backpack.

"I don't know what to say. Your sister betrayed me and saved me at the same time. Except now I suspect that the Warlock might make another attempt, as soon as he realizes that he stole a fake."

"Let him come," Hound said. "Bertha's lonely."

"She's going to figure you out," Homer said.

"Not if I send her home," Ben said.

"Good luck with that."

"Where's Frank?" Ellie asked, looking at the faces surrounding her.

"Gone," Ben said. "He stole your father's horse and ran off in the night."

"Shit, that's probably because Olivia gave him a fake egg, too," Ellie said, wincing. "Don't hate her. She's not bad—she just likes to see what she can get away with."

"Well now, I'll bet her ears are burning," Hound said, pointing up to the road.

"What the hell?" Ellie said.

Olivia and Baxter dismounted and walked their horses down the treacherous slope, reaching the edge of the riverbank before stopping.

"Mom sent us," Olivia shouted.

Before anyone could respond, a sharp crack shattered the calm afternoon air, echoing down the ravine. Baxter's head exploded. He fell backward and then slid toward the edge of the riverbank, landing with a thud. The horses were spooked by the shot, both bolting, Olivia's knocking her off balance as it broke free of her control. She fell on her butt and slid off the edge of the riverbank, yelping in fear as she slipped over and crashed to the rocky bed below. She hit and rolled onto her side, crying out in pain.

"What the hell was that?" Zack said, his eyes never leaving the gruesome form of Baxter's mostly headless corpse lying not twenty feet away.

"Sounded an awful lot like Frank's gun," Hound said, leaning into the mass of wagons and freight, peeking carefully at the ridge looming over them.

Ellie scrambled across the riverbed toward her sister.

"Rufus!" Ben snapped.

"Yeah," he said, racing after Ellie.

"Liv ... Liv! Are you all right?" Ellie asked, kneeling next to her sister.

"I think so. Baxter?"

"Dead."

"Just the way you're going to be if you stay out here in the open," Hound said, taking Olivia by the wrist and tossing her over his shoulder. He carried her to the cover of the wagons and laid her down next to Ben.

"How bad is it?" Ellie asked.

"Just a sprain," Olivia said. "Why kill Baxter? And who?"

"Regardless, they've got us pinned down," Ben said. "If we're going to get out of here, we'll have to get to the north bank without getting shot. It should give us enough cover to get out of this canyon."

"You're in no shape to run, either of you," Ellie said.

"No, we'll need help," Ben said. "Once we're under the cover of the bank, Olivia and I will ride the horse while you guide her. We'll make best speed down the river until we can find a way back up to the road."

Chapter 14

"So, what now?" Frank asked.

"We wait."

"For what?"

"For him," the Warlock said, pointing to the dwarf as he came running up with the bag. He lay down next to the Warlock, placing the bag on the ground in front of them both.

"Huh," the Warlock said, frowning. "Something's not right." He backed up a few feet behind a screen of bushes and dumped the egg out. Frank looked back just as he slammed it into the ground. It broke into chunks and left a stain of white plaster.

"What the hell?" Frank said.

The Warlock lay down next to Frank again.

"Looks like he was carrying a decoy. At least he's making an effort to be interesting."

Frank was silent, his eyes fixed on the scene below, while his mind was fixed on the egg in his backpack. He really didn't want the Warlock to discover it.

"I know he has it down there somewhere, though. I can feel it," the Warlock said.

"What do you mean?" Frank asked.

"One trained in dragon magic can detect the general presence of dragon artifacts. Those of greater skill and experience can discern the power and quality of such a detected artifact. There is a powerful dragon-magic presence coming from that mess of cargo."

Frank held very still, his mind racing. When he looked over at the Warlock, he was looking back with his implacable eyes and Frank knew that he knew.

He smiled thinly. "It makes perfect sense that you'd be involved in a theft of the egg—maybe even a caper where it gets replaced to throw people off track. The trouble is, you've stolen a fake egg, too."

"What?" Frank said, a little too loudly. He tore his pack open, digging the egg out and examining it closely.

"Oh, those bastards," he said, quieter this time, heeding the Warlock's gesture for greater silence. "They tricked me." He tapped the egg against stone, rolling it over and examining the broken point of impact—plaster. He hit it harder and it broke in half. He set it aside in disgust.

"Son of a bitch!" he whispered harshly. "One of those sneaky, underhanded schemers tricked me." He rolled over onto his back and fell silent.

Finally he said, "Someone I trusted tricked me."

"Who did you trust?" the Warlock asked.

"Nobody. Well, I mean Olivia made the switch … and Zack had it for a couple of minutes. Otherwise, it was all Ben all the time."

"Which of those three is most likely playing you for a fool?" the Warlock asked.

Frank scowled at him.

The Warlock chuckled under his breath past a thin smile. "Facing a mistake, and all of the glorious agony that accompanies failure, is the only sure way to learn from it." He chuckled again. "Your ego is bruised by the suggestion that you are a fool. As well it should be. Not because I suggest it, but because it is so. You were tricked. The question remains: By whom?"

Frank considered the question, rubbing his chin. "Probably Olivia," he said, after some thought.

"Why?"

"She had the best opportunity and it wouldn't occur to Zack."

"What of your brother?"

"Why would he switch it? No, he'd never let it out of his sight. I know I wouldn't."

"A fair point," the Warlock said. "Tell me about Olivia."

"She comes from a rich family. They make wine, and I mean a lot of wine. Lots of properties and lots of money. She's pretty, like conquest pretty, and still young enough to be almost ignorant of the true power of her beauty.

"She's a willing thief—likes stealing for the sake of it, I think. She was only too happy to go along with my plan to take the egg from Ben—now I'm starting to see why. She gave us both fake eggs."

"And yet the real one is still down there."

"What?" Frank said. "What do you mean?"

"I just told you that I can feel its presence—even at this distance."

"How can it be down there if Olivia gave us both fakes?" Frank asked.

"Perhaps your brother has played you both?"

Frank grimaced in rejection of the idea, shaking his head. "No, Ben is way too honest to pull something like that off. It had to be Olivia."

"All of that privilege must change the way a person thinks," the Warlock said.

"Yeah, she certainly had it better than I did."

"But more than that," the Warlock said. "Olivia didn't earn any of her own wealth. She was simply given everything she wanted when she wanted it. Perhaps it's only natural for her to believe that she can take from others so casually."

"Yeah. You know, she always did come off as 'better than,' like she knew something that the people around her didn't. Maybe we should pay her a visit. She's probably still in town."

"Perhaps, but only after we've completed our business with your brother. Tell me, what do you think he'll do in this situation?"

"Probably bandage his leg, make a crutch and head east along the riverbed."

"Is that one of the Flynn girls?" the Warlock asked, suddenly.

"Yeah," Frank said. "That's Ellie, Olivia's sister."

"Ah, another player."

They watched her pick her way down the slope and then vanish behind the mound of freight and wagons. Frank started to get bored, wondering what he was going to do, now that his greatest treasure had been stolen right out from under his nose.

That's when he saw Olivia.

"There she is," he said, pointing and then scrambling to get his rifle. "I need a bullet."

"No."

"What do you mean no? She tricked me. She has it coming."

"Perhaps, but she won't die today."

"Why not?"

"She's far too valuable a piece to remove from the board so early in the game," the Warlock said, his eyes never leaving the figures of Olivia and Baxter making their way down the slope.

"What are you talking about?"

"She has powerful relationships with powerful people," the Warlock said. "She can be leveraged. She lives. Her man though, is perfect. His death will send a clear message that we are unhappy at being deceived by a fake egg."

"You want me to kill Baxter? What did he do?"

"Nothing," the Warlock said, handing Frank a bullet. "He doesn't die today for what he did, but for what your brother did. Sometimes the best way to punish an enemy like your brother is to kill others of no import whatsoever. He'll carry the guilt of it by his own accord."

"You're right about that," Frank said, taking the bullet. "I'm not sure my rifle will shoot this far."

"I am," the Warlock said, laying a hand on Frank's back. "Just breathe easily and fire when you have the shot."

Chapter 15

Every step the horse took was painful, each step swinging the intensity and quality of his pain from dull ache to sharp, stabbing agony and back to ache again. Ben focused on breathing, trying to keep the rhythmically stabbing torment somewhere, anywhere, other than at the center of his focus.

Olivia rode behind him, her ankle too sprained for her to keep up on foot. They had been moving along the north bank of the riverbed for nearly an hour. Ben had really been worried that someone would get shot racing away from the cargo mound, but they had all managed to reach the cover of the north bank without incident.

"Water," Ben heard John whisper. His mind returned to the present at the promise of it.

"You awake?" Olivia asked.

Only then did Ben realize that her hands were holding him across the chest, keeping him from falling.

He'd been half asleep

"Yeah," he mumbled.

"You sure?"

"Yeah," he said, regaining control of his balance and his mental faculties with a quick breath.

The canyon was deep and rugged. In some places the walls sloped steeply from the tops of the surrounding ridges only to abruptly transform into rocky cliffs falling hundreds of feet into giant scree piles built up over time. In others, the loose, rocky ground sloped precipitously all the way into the ravine. Still others offered a gradual descent that looked like a perilous climb out, especially with a wounded leg.

John stopped at the edge of a spring, ice-cold water bubbling freely out of the rocks of the riverbed. Ellie helped Olivia down and then both of them helped Ben down. He landed, favoring his wounded leg, the jolt sending a shock of pain through him.

"Continued travel will delay healing time," the augment said.

"Yeah, I figured."

Ben sat on his pack next to the little pool of crystal-clear water. Under other circumstances it would have been almost idyllic. A small grove of scrub pine clinging to the sloping south bluff provided shade and some cover.

"You think they're tracking us?" Zack asked.

"I doubt it," Ben said. "The Warlock will probably ride ahead and set another ambush."

"He seems to be cautious that way," Hound said.

"Do you think it was Frank that shot Baxter?" Zack asked. Ellie and Olivia both looked down.

"Yep," Hound said.

"Probably," Ben said, "but we don't know the whole story." Another pang of guilt assailed him. He'd sent Frank away only to have him fall into the lap of the Warlock. And the result was Baxter's death.

"I will say this," Hound said, stripping off his armor and tossing it onto the rocks, "you look for the good in others—even when it's not there." He knelt down and dunked his head in the spring, whipping it back out of the water and spraying everyone. "Holy shit, that's cold!"

Ben wiped the water from his face as Ellie sat down next to him.

"How's your leg?" she asked.

"Hurts," he said, "but it'll heal." He looked at her until she looked back. "How are you feeling?" he asked.

"You mean Baxter? It doesn't seem real, until I try to imagine telling my parents. It gets pretty real then."

"I'll bet."

"He was a good guy. Always had my family's back … always. And it was so senseless. I still don't understand why he died."

"Me neither," Ben said, though he had his suspicions.

Imogen brought him a bowl of water and a cloth. He washed his face and then changed his bandage, inspecting the wound in the process and nodding approvingly at the progress of the tissue repair, though there was still a ways to go. No sooner had he finished dressing his wound than Olivia sat down in front of him.

"Are we going to talk about this?" she asked.

He sighed, motioning for her to speak.

"I thought you were bad," she started. "And my father thinks the egg should be destroyed. And your brother," she scowled, "your brother tricked me into stealing from you."

Ben sat looking at her without emotion.

She winced. "I'm sorry! I shouldn't have done it and I'm sorry," she said.

"Did you give my brother a fake?"

"Yes," she said, in a very small voice.

He nodded, appraising her until she began to fidget.

"This is going to be hard to hear," Ben said. "Frank left us the night after you gave him the fake egg. We're pretty sure he killed Baxter, sounded like his rifle anyway."

Her eyes opened wide, she shook her head, a tear spilling down her cheek as one hand went to her mouth, the other to her stomach.

"No," she mumbled past her hand, staggering to her feet. She sobbed, limping away.

"That was pretty harsh," Ellie said. "She didn't mean any harm."

"I never imagined that she did," Ben said. "But that doesn't change reality."

"You sound like my father," she said.

"He probably got it from my grandfather," Ben said. "He was death on facing reality, no matter how much you didn't want to."

"I can see why they were such good friends," she said.

"Bird," John said, putting his monocular on a circling raptor high overhead. "Falcon."

Ben and Hound shared a look.

"You don't think it's one of those, do you?" Imogen asked.

"I hope not, but if it is, it's probably Hoondragon," Ben said.

"We should get moving," Hound said.

Back to the rhythmic pain of riding over uneven ground, but this time with the added tension of a fairly distraught Olivia periodically crying behind him. Ben endured, though he knew that each step away from the advancing enemy was one moment more it would take him to heal. They found a way out of the canyon, a switchback path leading up to the road.

It was a harrowing ride, Ellie carefully leading the horse until they reached the top of the ravine and the road stretching out straight and level for as far as the eye could see into the high desert to the east.

The falcon circled overhead.

"Nowhere to hide," John said.

"We keep going," Ben said. He looked at Ellie and Olivia. "But you two should go back home. Your parents will be worried."

"No!" both said at once.

"I owe you," Olivia said. "And I can't let Baxter die for nothing."

"You're on my horse," Ellie said.

Ben smiled at her, nodding defeat. "I guess I can't argue with that. You two can turn around as soon as we find another horse."

"We'll talk about that then," she said, leading the animal onto the road. "Nearest stop is Oasis." She checked the position of the sun in the sky. "It'll be well after dark before we get there, though."

Chapter 16

Frank looked up as he mounted his horse.

"Look!" he said, pointing.

"I see a bird," said the Warlock.

"I think it's a stalker tracking Ben," Frank said. "The Dragon Guard did this to us before."

"Ah … interesting," the Warlock said, taking a moment to mutter a few arcane words under his breath. A few moments passed. "Seems that you're right. That bird is indeed a stalker … but whose?"

"Whoever it is, they've got my brother's position," Frank said.

The Warlock pursed his lips, rubbing his chin for a moment before dismounting.

"Come along," he said to Frank, heading back to the rock perch on the bluff overlooking the wreckage of the caravan.

Frank hurried to catch up.

"What are we doing? We could catch up with Ben by dark if we hurry."

"And then what? Your brother is a skilled swordsman accompanied by at least two well-armed fighters—one of whom carries a firearm. No, he's wounded and his party has only one horse. We have more than enough time to catch up with them. I'm more concerned with the others who are pursuing the egg at the moment."

They reached the rock formation and the Warlock ducked, motioning for silence. Both of them crawled on their bellies out to the edge of the cliff and peered down at the riverbed below.

"That's Nash," Frank whispered, tensely. "She's been chasing us since the beginning."

She was alone, kneeling on the rock riverbed, a circle of blood splashed on the smooth stones around her in almost haphazard form. Her eyes were closed and she was swaying back and forth, chanting words that sounded like guttural barking.

Frank frowned when he saw the black cat wander out from the wreckage and flop over on its side nearby.

"What's she doing?"

"She appears to be casting a divination spell," the Warlock said. "I suspect she's found traces of your brother's blood and she's using it to predict where he will be in the future."

"Can she do that?"

Before the Warlock could answer, Nash abruptly stopped chanting and stood, barking a single word. The black housecat meowed and then began to transform. It grew larger, but not uniformly. Instead, one body part at a time grew—first its right front leg got bigger, growing to a size larger than the rest of the cat. Then its body started to grow, the cat wailing in agony as it morphed into something else entirely.

After a minute of tortured transformation, the cat was no longer furry and cuddly. It was six feet tall at the shoulder and fifteen feet long nose to tail—probably fifteen hundred pounds. Its skin was black and leathery, stretched thin over sinewy muscle. Its fangs had grown long, protruding from its deformed mouth.

Once her pet had fully transformed, Nash swung up onto its back and barked a command. The cat leapt ten feet up and twenty feet away, landing easily on the riverbank and bounding up the slope. Within moments the cat and Nash were gone.

"What the hell was that?" Frank asked.

"Your friend Nash is possessed by Magoth, the demon prince of transformation. It would seem that she has turned a stray house pet into a fearsome servant."

"Do you think the bird is hers?"

"No," the Warlock said. "She was casting a spell to determine Benjamin's future whereabouts, and it looks like she got an answer. Let's hope we catch up with your brother before she does."

"So who does the bird belong to?"

"That's what we're here to find out," the Warlock said, pulling his bag open and searching for a moment before withdrawing a small wooden box. He took a moment to break the seal and unwind the wire binding it shut, then carefully opened it to reveal a perfect glass sphere two inches in diameter. Within the sphere was an inky cloud roiling around with an occasional flash that looked like lightning.

He handed the orb to the dwarf.

"Hide this near the spot where you spilled Benjamin's blood."

The dwarf nodded and raced off, returning a few minutes later.

"Now what?" Frank asked.

"We wait."

"You do a lot of that," he said.

"Indeed. Patience is a powerful skill. It's amazing what you can accomplish if you wait for just the right moment to act."

"If you say so," Frank muttered.

Sunshine passed into a break in the clouds at the horizon, casting golden light over the canyon. A man on a black horse came into view on the road across the ravine. He wore armor so dark that it seemed to absorb the sunlight. Spikes jutted from his shoulders and elbows. His helm was horned and covered his face with the mask of a skull. His horse was equally armored.

"Ah, here we are," the Warlock said. "The dragon's hunter."

Hoondragon gestured and three creatures bounded down the slope to the riverbed. They looked like giant squirrels, maybe a hundred pounds each, but they had red eyes, fangs, and claws that left scars in the earth.

All three began sniffing around the wreckage. One began chittering, a loud and menacing sound.

"Pity," the Warlock said, placing a small glass bead on the ground and smashing it with a rock.

Stillness followed and then a sound reverberated out of the canyon, a sound like nothing Frank had ever heard before. It was loud and thrumming but also viscerally disturbing, as if human ears were not meant to hear such a thing.

Frank watched intently as a cloud of inky blackness interlaced with argent lightning dancing within it expanded to thirty feet across in a blink, completely engulfing the three giant rodents serving Hoondragon. A moment later, the lightning subsided and the blackness solidified into what looked like basalt.

"That was impressive," Frank whispered.

Cracks shot through the newly formed stone mound and then it abruptly shattered, turning to powder, leaving nothing but a black stain on the riverbed where the three rodents had been, taking a portion of the caravan wreckage along with it.

"Too bad you couldn't have gotten him with that," Frank said.

"True, but dragon-rodents are extremely dangerous," the Warlock said. "The dragons on my world create them to hunt us in our underground cities. They're fast and vicious, not the kind of opponent you want to face in tight quarters. And, they had your brother's scent. He probably wouldn't have survived the night."

Hoondragon watched his minions vanish into the Warlock's trap. He remained there for almost a minute before looking up to the falcon, still circling off in the distance. He spurred his horse into a gallop.

"Come, we must hurry," the Warlock said.

Chapter 17

The cloud cover that had been so ubiquitous for so many days broke in a strip along the western horizon, revealing the snow-capped mountains standing in a neat row describing the Cascade Range. The sun fell below the clouds, casting long shadows as it sank into night and dusk claimed the world.

The night was dark, cloudy and moonless. They traveled by the light of a torch that John had fashioned from scraps of wood he found along the road.

"Do you really think I got Baxter killed?" Olivia whispered from behind Ben, her voice still heavy with sadness.

"Yes and no," Ben said, after taking a moment to think about his response. "Your actions set in motion a chain of events that led to Baxter's death, but you didn't kill him. Someone else did that."

"I just keep thinking that things would have worked out differently if I'd made different choices."

Ben said nothing.

"I feel so guilty," she whispered.

"Good," Ben said gently. "That tells me two things. First, unlike my brother, you have a conscience, and that's no small thing. Second, you don't like what you're feeling, so you'll probably learn something from this, maybe something important."

They rode in silence for a while.

"You're not a very sympathetic person, you know that?" she said.

He chuckled mirthlessly. "No, I guess I'm not, at least not at the moment. But then, sympathy won't do any of us much good right now. You made a poor choice and there were consequences. You own that, like it or not. Now you have to decide if you'll face your guilt and endure it … or run from it … or lie to yourself about it."

"I thought I was doing the right thing, I really did," she said after a long silence.

"And now?"

She fell silent again.

"For what it's worth, I encouraged Frank to leave, so if you're to blame, then so am I."

"You don't seem that broken up about it," she said.

"I'm not. I didn't pull the trigger, and neither did you."

She fell silent and Ben's mind returned to the steadily diminishing pain in his leg. While it was taking much longer to heal than it would with rest, his wound was mending far more quickly than it would without the augment's repair capabilities.

"Do you hate me?" Olivia asked.

"No," Ben said. "Can't say I trust you much right now, but I don't feel any ill will toward you. After all, I brought this hardship into your home, and your family was gracious enough to take me in and help me when I needed it. It would be very easy for you to blame me for Baxter's death ... and Annabelle's wound for that matter. If I hadn't shown up on your doorstep, none of this would be happening."

"I guess there's plenty of guilt to go around," she said.

"No ... the guilt in this situation rests squarely on the wyrm and his minions," Ben said. "I will not accept guilt for protecting my family or for running for my life. You chose to steal from me because you believed your father to be a better guardian of the egg ... and he probably is. The truth is, I would've given it to him if he'd have asked me for it. But more importantly, I doubt he would have taken it even if I'd begged him to.

"He understands better than anyone the danger it represents, which is why he made me promise that I wouldn't involve his daughters. A promise that I've broken, though certainly not intentionally."

"He worries," Olivia said. "His mind goes to the worst possible outcome first."

Ben turned in the saddle so he could look Olivia in the eye. "That's because he's lived through the worst possible outcome and he doesn't want to do it again."

She frowned before answering. "It'll be different this time. Things will work out."

He snorted, shaking his head.

"You don't think so?" she asked.

"I don't know," he said. "A month ago, I would have thought the exact same thing ... it'll be okay, nothing bad is going to happen to me. Since then, I've been chased from my home, stabbed twice, I've watched my grandfather die, and I've killed people, starting with a woman that I wanted to love.

"Bad things do happen to good people," he said, almost to himself.

They rode in silence for a while, Ben's mind returning to the pain in his leg and the days ahead. His pursuers were close—far too close, and he was in no condition to fight, or to run for that matter. He needed to heal and that meant stopping to rest.

"Light up ahead," Hound said, shielding his eyes from the torch.

"Probably Oasis," Ellie said. "It's farther than it looks."

"Of course it is," Hound muttered.

"How long until we get there?" Ben asked.

"Another couple of hours," Ellie said.

"What do you know about this place?" Ben asked.

"Oasis?" she said. "It's a caravan way station owned and operated by an older couple named Harvey and Gladys Wright. They come across as sweet and friendly but they're tough as nails and shrewd dealmakers. My father has a pretty good relationship with them since his caravans pass through on a weekly basis."

"Can we get fresh horses there?"

"Sure," Ellie said. "They keep a pretty good stable. A few of the bigger caravan companies lease space with them to keep horses on hand as well—my father's included."

"What about security?"

"They have a garrison of guards and ten-foot walls around the whole compound, not to mention the caravan guards stopped for the night. All in all, it's not the kind of place you want to pick a fight."

"What are you thinking?" Hound asked.

"Whoever's holding the leash to that falcon will probably catch up with us at Oasis, especially if we stop for the night."

"Ben, we have to stop," Imogen said. "We're all exhausted and you need time to heal."

"I know," he said. "Doesn't change the fact that someone or something is right behind us. Also, what about the people who live there?"

"This conversation would be all well and good sitting around a coffee table with a bottle," Hound said, "but here in the real world we need a place to sleep and we also need the security of other people shooting at our enemies if they attack. We're stopping at Oasis."

They arrived several hours later, well into the night. Ben was struggling to stay awake, the pain in his leg offering unwanted assistance. Oasis was a small village off the side of the old highway. A makeshift wall surrounded nearly twenty buildings laid out in haphazard fashion within. Four manned towers stood above the walls, providing the guards with a clear view of all approaches.

The gate was closed but there were two men atop the wall watching over it.

"Hello," Ellie called out from a distance, drawing their attention.

Two lanterns opened wide, casting a dim glow on the area before the gate.

"What's your business here?" one of the men asked.

"We need shelter for the night and fresh horses in the morning," Ellie said. "My father has an account here—under the name of Flynn."

The man frowned, checking a book before looking back down at them.

"We were expecting one of your father's caravans but it never showed."

"We were ambushed," Ellie said. "The wagons and horses are all at the bottom of Dry River canyon. Drivers are all dead."

The two men looked at each other, and the one who hadn't spoken left in a hurry.

"Who attacked you?"

"Don't know," Ellie said. "We didn't stick around long enough to find out. We could really use some rest. Can you open the gate?"

"Not sure yet," the man said. "We're pretty careful about who we open up for after dark."

"What more do you need?" Ellie asked.

"My approval," another voice said, out of breath. A rotund man appeared, dressed in a robe, his round face ruddy from the exertion of climbing the stairs to the top of the wall. He peered down at them, holding his lantern high and squinting for a moment.

"Well, it's been over a year since you two young ladies stopped by," he said. "How's your father? As cantankerous as ever?"

"More so," Ellie said with a smile. "Hello, Harvey. How's business?"

"Open up," he said to his man. "Come on in and I'll tell you all about it," he said over his shoulder as he turned back to the stairs.

The gate creaked as it opened. Ellie led them inside and the gate closed behind them.

Harvey smiled at her and then looked at her friends, his smile fading quickly.

"You didn't tell me your friends were on the run," he said.

Ben felt a tingle of dread in the pit of his stomach.

"We just need some sleep and fresh horses," Ellie said. "We'll stay in my father's caravan barn and take our own horses in the morning."

"Now you know that's not the point," Harvey said. "You have some pretty dangerous-looking people after you. Three of those damned Dragon Guard came through just the other day handing out wanted posters on your friends here and at least one group of guests has been asking around about 'em—had the look of bounty hunters.

"You know I run a business here. I don't want trouble, certainly not with the wyrm."

"What are you saying, Harvey? Are you going to turn us out into the night?"

"Damn it, child," he said, running his hand across his bald head. "I certainly don't want to have that conversation with your father but you're bringing danger into my home."

Ellie looked down sadly and nodded. "I know. And I'm sorry, but we have nowhere else to go."

He glowered at her for a moment before sighing heavily.

"All right, let's get you to your barn, hopefully without anyone noticing you. You and your sister are welcome in the roadhouse, but your friends need to stay out of sight, and I want you gone at dawn—before would be better."

"Thank you, Harvey. You're a lifesaver."

"Oh, trust me, your father's going to pay through the nose for this one." He turned to his guards. "Don't open the gate for anyone without my permission. Also, neither of you saw anything."

"Yes, sir," both men said.

Harvey led them around the buildings, staying close to the wall to avoid the roadhouse and inn. At the back of the compound was a series of barns, each large enough to house a caravan's wagons, horses, and men. Several of them were occupied.

When they arrived at the Flynns' barn, a man sleeping in the hay woke with a start and came to his feet quickly, rubbing his eyes, trying with limited success to fully wake up.

"Where's the caravan?" he mumbled.

"Ambushed," Harvey said. "Go on back to your quarters. You're done for the night."

He nodded, still not fully awake, stumbling toward the door. He blinked a few times when he looked up at Ben, his brow furrowing deeply for a moment. He shook his head in passing and then vanished through the door.

Ben dismounted, taking a quick breath when his wounded leg hit the ground.

"Now remember," Harvey said, "stay out of sight. When you leave tomorrow, use the wagon gate in the back."

"Thank you," Ben said, holding out three gold coins.

"Not sure I've earned all that," Harvey said.

"Not yet," Ben said. "If anyone asks about us, tell them we bought some horses and left in the night."

"So you are expecting trouble to show up on my doorstep."

"I'm afraid so," Ben said.

"An honest fugitive. Not sure I've met one of those before," Harvey said, rubbing his hand over his bald head again and taking the coins. "I'll lie for you, but only because I don't want the people searching for you to stop here."

Harvey left, closing the barn door behind him.

Hound did a quick search, securing the doors and checking the exits. Ellie took a moment to inspect the six horses stabled in a series of stalls against one wall.

Ben sat down heavily, Homer curling up next to him. "How're you doing?" Ben asked.

"My feet hurt."

"I'll bet. Will you be able to keep up tomorrow?"

"Of course," Homer said. "I'm a dog."

Ben chuckled under his breath, gently stroking Homer's side.

"Let me take a look at your leg," Imogen said.

Ben nodded, sitting back as she went to work unwrapping his bandage.

"It's healing nicely," she said.

"How's that even possible?" Ellie asked, looking at his wound over Imogen's shoulder. "You were stabbed just a few hours ago."

"It's a long story," Ben said. "One I don't have the energy to get into right now."

"One of these days, you and I are going to have a long conversation," Ellie said.

"Yeah, but not today," he said, closing his eyes.

Imogen wrapped the wound with a clean bandage while Ellie watched, a look of confusion and curiosity etched into her face.

Once Imogen was finished, Ben tossed out his bedroll and lay down, exhaustion overcoming him quickly. Within minutes he was asleep. What felt like only minutes later, he woke with a start. Hound was kneeling over him, a finger over his lips. Ben nodded.

"What's going on?" he asked Homer.

"Some men are outside poking around the barn."

"How many?"

"I smell four."

Ben held up four fingers to Hound. He nodded, going to the main door, Bertha in hand, while Ben sat up and scanned the barn. John was awake, bow in hand. Everyone else was still sleeping. Ben remembered his injury only from the dull ache in his leg when he pulled on his boots.

"Your wound is eighty-six percent healed," the augment said. "Another two hours of sleep will complete the repair."

"Good to know," Ben said.

There was a loud knock on the door.

"We know you're in there," a voice said. "You're surrounded, so don't try anything stupid."

"Says who?" Hound said, racking a round into Bertha's chamber and then picking up the round he'd just ejected.

"That sounded like a shotgun," a muffled voice outside the barn said.

"If you try to fight, we're just going to barricade you in and light the barn on fire," the first voice said.

"You think Harvey is going to let you out of here alive after you set his business on fire?" Ellie shouted through the door.

Everyone else was awake and getting up.

"What time is it?" Ben asked the augment.

"An hour and a half before dawn."

Ben motioned for everyone to begin packing up and saddling the horses, while he went to the door and peered through a crack. He couldn't see anything except the inside of the compound wall thirty feet from the door.

"We'll give him a cut," the man said in response to Ellie. "I'm sure he'll understand."

"I doubt that very much," Harvey said from somewhere on the opposite side of the barn.

"Whoa … let's not get carried away here," the man said. "These people are wanted. We're just here to take them in."

"I've got five rifles that say otherwise," Harvey said. "Lay down arms and come out into the open."

"Doesn't have to go this way, old man," the leader of the bounty hunters said.

A shot rang out in the distance.

"Sounds like you've got your hands full," the bounty hunter said.

Several more shots, followed by a loud crash.

"What the hell was that?" Hound said.

"The gate," Ellie said.

All at once, gunfire erupted everywhere, a stray round shattering one of the barn's boards, spraying splinters in its wake.

"Imogen, Zack, and Olivia, get the horses ready to run," Ben said. "Everyone else, on me." He lifted the bar and tossed it aside, then eased the door open, looking down the wagon-worn dirt road running between the row of barns and the wall.

Most of the gunfire was coming from the far side of the barn, where the bounty hunters were fighting Harvey's men. A shotgun blast shattered the lock on the main door on that side. A second later it burst open and a man entered swinging his weapon around to take aim just as an arrow appeared in his chest, buried to the feathers. His eyes went wide with surprise as he looked down and fell over.

John nocked another.

"Come on," Ben said, throwing the door open and drawing his pistol before cautiously stepping outside.

One of the bounty hunters rolled out from the corner of the barn and leveled a crossbow at Ben. He spun backward inside the barn as the bolt zipped past, missing by inches.

"Shit, that was close," Hound said, rushing out past Ben to get a shot at the man. He caught him trying to cock his crossbow. Bertha barked. Ben didn't give the man a second thought as he turned in the other direction, heading toward the caravan gate in the back of the compound.

The gunfight between the bounty hunters and Harvey's guards seemed to have ended in favor of another fight taking place in the main courtyard. Alarm bells were ringing and lanterns were being lit, gradually driving away the darkness within the confines of the walls.

All of the caravaners were awake now and their guards were moving to assist against whatever had come through the gate. Ben raced up to the corner of the next barn, noting with satisfaction that the pain in his leg had become manageable. He peeked around the corner and every hair on his body stood on end.

From where he was he had a clear view of the main courtyard and part of the shattered front gate. Men lay broken and dying, cast to the ground in haphazard fashion. A single man fought in the center of the melee, surrounded by more than a dozen others trying to take him down.

He wore black armor, spiked and horned, and he wielded a broadsword, black as night and dripping with blood. He moved with deliberate assurance and deadly efficiency. He wasn't particularly fast, but he was unrelenting and powerful.

Ben watched a caravan guard unload both barrels of a shotgun into his back at a range of ten feet—a kill shot by any standard. The man in black lurched forward as if someone had gently pushed him. He spun, closing the distance quickly, cutting the shotgun man in half just above the waist with one stroke of his sword.

Ben felt a squirming, twisting sensation when he looked at that black blade. It whipped around, taking another man's head, then drove through the belly of another. Three men attacked him in unison with spears, all three hit hard against his breastplate. One shattered and the other two glanced away. He hacked all three of those men to pieces with an almost casual flourish.

Another man raced into view—he was big, almost as tall as the attacker—he wore a tech breastplate and wielded a two-handed sword. The man in black saluted him before they began circling each other.

The swordsman attacked, sweeping up and driving the man in black backward a step before bringing his blade down on his shoulder. The swordsman's blade fell hard between the shoulder spikes on his armor, but it didn't penetrate. Instead, the man in black turned quickly, twisting the blade free of his opponent's hands. It flipped away into the dirt. He rushed, thrusting hard, driving his sword through the tech armor and the man, lifting him off the ground with one hand so he could look him in the eyes as he died.

"We've got to go," Hound said, quietly.

"Yeah, but not yet," Ben said. "You're with me. Everyone else, get the caravan gate open and be ready to ride."

"Wait, what are you going to do?" Ellie asked.

"Just get to the gate," Ben said, heading toward the enemy, sticking to the shadows.

"You got a plan?" Hound asked from right behind him.

"Grenades."

"Right," Hound said, adjusting the round in Bertha's chamber.

Ben skirted a small building to remain hidden, rounding the corner carefully, imagining in his mind's eye a successful attack

Six more men charged the man in black. He met their attack with calm, cold and explosive violence, tearing them apart in a matter of seconds, carnage beginning to pile up around him.

Ben noticed the horse at the gate, eyes glowing red—and it noticed him, neighing loudly, drawing the enemy's attention.

"Hit the horse," Ben said to Hound, a grenade already in his hand.

"I am Hoondragon and I will have my prize!" the man shouted.

Hound fired his last grenade round at the stalker horse just as it broke into a gallop toward them. It hit the horse in the chest and blasted it backward, flipping it end over end through the air before it landed in a jumbled heap.

Hoondragon was distracted by the attack on his horse and looked away from Ben at just the right moment. The grenade landed close. He and Hound quickly withdrew behind the building a moment before another explosion tore through the early morning like a clap of thunder. They sprinted toward the back wall and the caravan gate, not bothering to look back, reaching the gate out of breath, the pain in Ben's leg now far more intense than it had been when he woke. He swung into his saddle, taking the reins from Ellie.

"Holy shit!" Zack said, pointing.

Hoondragon was staggering to his feet, little more than a few scorch marks on his armor.

"Ride!" Ben shouted, spurring his horse into a gallop, circling the compound toward the gate and then racing for the road.

They slowed once they were some distance from Oasis. A faint orange glow stained the sky behind them. Ben felt sick to his stomach. He'd brought war into the home of innocent people and then left them to burn. He considered going back, but the image of Hoondragon rising from the carnage after a close hit with a grenade was enough to persuade him otherwise.

So he rode, picking his path by the light of fading stars.

He'd hit Hoondragon with a grenade.

And Hoondragon had gotten back up.

Ben lamented the part he'd played in the lives lost at Oasis. Relived it, over and over. Finally, he resolved that he would bear the burden without dwelling on it. He was at war. It was time he started acting like it. And with that thought, the true enormity of war settled onto his psyche.

He had to make choices that would cost good people their lives. Maybe even people that he cared about.

Hoondragon would be coming. He would never stop.

The sky began to take on the colors of dawn, blood and fire staining the horizon. As the light rose, Ben reined in his horse atop a small rise, scanning the terrain. It was mostly flat for as far as the eye could see with only a few hills in the distance. Where the Deschutes area had been forested, this part of the world was the sole domain of sage and tumbleweed, jackrabbits and prairie dogs.

The road ran east to the horizon, a black ribbon of man-made stone, straight and pockmarked with disrepair, looking as if it stretched to the very edge of the world.

"Not much cover," Hound said.

"No," Ben said. "Hopefully, your grenade did more damage to his horse than mine did to him."

"Yeah, I have concerns about that myself," Hound said.

"Can we make it to Burnt by dark?" Ben asked, turning to Ellie.

"If we push it."

"All right, speed is our best defense then," Ben said. "Let's ride."

As the light came up, the wind did as well, a steady gale blowing from the south, dry and dusty despite the heavy, but patchy, black clouds. Sunlight stabbed down to the desert floor in a number of places, the light shifting as the clouds drifted across the sky.

Ben wrapped a rag over his head and face and rode hard, pushing his horse. The terrain got more mountainous, then became flat again, the road once again running straight to the horizon. All the while, the two abiding constants were the wind and the sage. Nothing else seemed to grow save for a few lonely, wind-stunted pine trees scattered here and there across the plain.

A splatter of rain whipped them, big, heavy drops that stung when they hit—but it passed quickly. They rode on, Ben beginning to feel growing pain in his leg again. He ignored it. Hoondragon was back there somewhere, though Ben was happy that he hadn't seen the bird overhead ... perhaps because of the wind, or maybe it was just obscured by the clouds.

The day dragged on, as interminable as the desert. Just at dusk, they crested a rise and saw the town of Burnt. The houses and buildings on the outskirts were all hollow burned-out shells, husks of former homes, destroyed and discarded.

The town itself was sparsely populated, a way station for travelers and a market for local ranchers. Few saw them ride into town and even fewer gave them a second look.

They reached the warehouse just after dark, exhausted and road-weary.

"Miss Flynn?" the man at the door said, a frown creasing his brow.

"Open up," Ellie commanded.

His demeanor changed with her tone.

"Right away, miss," he said, going to work with his companion to open the main gate, closing it behind them after all of the horses were inside.

Ben winced when he hit the ground. He expected it. He was tired, but he was more afraid of Hoondragon arriving in the night.

"How quickly can you have fresh horses ready?" he asked the warehouseman, who looked to Ellie.

"Are you sure?" she asked Ben. "Everybody's exhausted."

"I know. That's why we can't be here when Hoondragon arrives."

She blinked. "Do you really think?"

"I hit him as hard as I could and he got back up," Ben said. "Do you want to be here if he catches up with us?"

She nodded to the warehouseman. He went to work transferring their saddles and gear to fresh horses.

Olivia limped up.

"You're kind of a slave driver. I haven't ridden this hard ... well ever."

"I'm glad you brought that up," he said. "Your family has helped us more than I can ever thank you for, but we should part ways here."

"No!" both Ellie and Olivia said at once.

"Here we go," Hound muttered.

"Your father is going to come looking for you," Ben said. "You can go home now or when he catches up with us."

"Or neither," Ellie said. "I'm my own person and I believe that human freedom is worth fighting for. I'm in."

"Me too," Olivia said.

"No, you're not!" Ben said. "I promised your father that I wouldn't get you involved."

"It's not your choice," Ellie said.

"Or his," Olivia said.

Ben looked to Hound. He shrugged helplessly and shook his head. Imogen offered a sympathetic smile.

"You know what it feels like when we fight together," Ellie said, stepping just inside Ben's personal space, looking up at him. "Are you really going to give that up?"

"To preserve you and to keep my promise to your father? Yes," Ben said. "Please, go home."

"You are one of the most stubborn people I've ever met."

"I'm stubborn?" he said, shaking his head and turning away from her, taking a few tentative steps before turning back to face her. "Do whatever you want. That's what you're going to do anyway."

He walked away and checked his saddle and gear before leading his horse out of the stable and mounting up.

"You'll want to lock up and leave as soon as we're gone," he said to the warehousemen. "Dangerous people are following us. Don't be here when they arrive."

Both men nodded, their eyes going a bit wide.

Ben set out, traveling south along the road leading out of town toward Steens Mountain. He traveled as quickly as he could safely manage by lantern light. About two hours south of town, he found a half burned-out farmhouse not far off the road.

There was enough barn left to tie the horses out of view of the road, and enough house left to put a roof over their heads and give them three walls. Ben was asleep moments after he lay down.

Through a conspiracy of his companions, he was allowed to sleep through the night, his friends taking the additional guard duty on themselves. He woke feeling refreshed and hungry, but most importantly, his leg was healed and it felt strong.

After a quick breakfast, they saddled their horses.

"I had a dream last night," Imogen said, cinching her gear onto her saddle.

"A dragon dream?" Ben asked, stopping what he was doing to look at her.

She nodded. "I forgot to draw a circle. I was so tired. He asked me where we're going."

"What did you tell him?"

"I told him that we're coming to Denver to get my baby. He laughed and I woke up with images of fire in my mind."

"Are you all right?"

She nodded. "I hate him," she whispered. "I want to kill him so badly I can't stand it."

"I know, and we will, but we have to attack him on our terms or we're dead."

"I know," she whispered.

Chapter 18

They set out into another relentlessly windy day, the sky filled with an endless array of rapidly passing clouds dancing with rays of sunlight. After several miles due south, the road abruptly turned east, running at a steep angle down a cliff drawn across the landscape like a scar. At the bottom, the road turned due south again heading to the lake ten miles away.

With fresh horses and Ben feeling like himself again, the ride went quickly. They reached the edge of the lake by midmorning, stopping to assess the cluster of men camped out in the center of the nearly mile long bridge spanning the narrowest part of the lake—one of the few intact prewar edifices of its size that Ben had ever seen.

"What do you think?" Hound said, handing the monocular back to John.

"Not a good place for battle," Ben said.

"We could go around," Imogen said.

"They probably just want to get paid," Olivia said.

"Yeah … or maybe they're slavers looking for women," Hound said.

Ellie and Olivia shared a horrified look.

"Either way, we have to cross," Ben said, gently spurring his horse forward. "Be ready."

They approached at a walk, stopping within shotgun range. A jumble of old car frames and empty steel drums was built up across the road, forming a wall ten feet high with only one passage through.

Men stood atop the twisted steel battlements.

"Hello," Ben called out. "We wish to pass."

"Will you pay the price?"

Ben dismounted, handing his reins to Ellie before he approached the passage entrance, stopping well short. A few men bristled but none fired. After a tense minute, a man came out, stopping ten feet from Ben.

"How much?" Ben asked.

The man looked at Ben and his group, seeming to evaluate the worth of each person and animal. He nodded to himself and smiled, turning back to his companions with his hands held wide.

"I require one ounce of gold each for passage," he said loudly, walking full circle to face Ben again, his arms still held wide, his smile even wider. There was a smattering of laughter from his men.

"If I were to pay your price, what would I receive in return?" Ben asked, just as loudly. Silence fell on the bridge.

"Safe passage, of course," the man said.

"And you never saw us, no matter who asks."

The man's eyes narrowed as he regarded Ben. "You can pay this price?"

"Do we have a deal?"

"Yes," the man said, "If ... you can show me the gold."

Ben had already counted seven gold coins from the ten he had in his pocket. He stepped forward and gently placed the coins in the man's hand.

The brigand looked at the small fortune and then at Ben in wonder.

Ben looked back expectantly. There was a flicker of double-cross in the man's eyes, but he glanced at Hound and Durt and then back to Ben and smiled graciously, bowing out of the way.

"Let them through," he shouted. The men on the wall stood down, opening the way.

Ben nodded his thanks, mounted up and rode forward, looking straight ahead the whole way. Only once they had all reached the far end of the bridge, safe and traveling at good speed, did he feel like he could breathe again.

Money. He couldn't help but smile.

And then he saw the bird.

It was high, circling across a break in the clouds.

He pressed on. It was all he could do. Late in the afternoon they came to a vantage point looking out at Steens Mountain, as majestic and desolate a thing as Ben had ever seen.

"How do we know where we're going?" Hound asked.

Ben pulled out a map, folded to show just this part of the world. "It's supposed to be up there somewhere." He gestured to the mountain with the map.

"We might need more than that," John said.

"Yeah, I have an idea," Ben said. "Let's see if we can get to that hilltop by dark."

"That's farther than it looks," Ellie said.

"Probably," Ben said, urging his horse off the paved road and onto an old, nearly overgrown mountain trail.

It was rugged and unforgiving terrain which required a more deliberate pace. As darkness fell, it became clear that continued travel could easily be fatal, so they made a cold camp far short of Ben's goal, but still well off the main road.

The sky cleared, revealing a blanket of stars overhead. It was a bitterly cold night, but any fire would be seen for miles. Ben found himself waiting for dawn, shivering in his blankets.

"You awake?" Ellie whispered.

"Yeah," he said, adjusting his pack so he could lean against it. She crawled up and laid her head on his shoulder, snuggling in close to him and draping her blanket over both of them.

"For warmth," she said.

"If you say so."

"You still want us to go home," she said after a long pause.

"Yes."

"Are you mad at me?"

He thought about it for a minute before answering. "No, I'm afraid you'll get hurt and that's a lot worse."

She got closer. "Thank you ... and get over it. I chose this. Me. I can help you. So can Liv, if you'll let her."

"I don't doubt that."

"We've made our choice, both of us. Accept that and let us help you. We're going to do it anyway."

"Yeah," Ben mumbled, half asleep.

She smiled, adjusting the blanket to cover them better and closing her eyes.

When dawn woke them, Ben's arms were around her, and Hound was standing over them, smiling suggestively.

"Oh, piss off," Ellie mumbled, waving Hound away.

He chuckled, walking off. "I'm starting to like her," he said over his shoulder.

Ben got up after Ellie, both of them stretching the kinks out of their legs. The air was cold, each breath stinging Ben's nose. The terrain was just as desolate as anywhere else in this part of the world. He fixed his eyes on the hilltop he wanted to gain. It didn't look too far away, but he knew how little that meant.

The sky was clear. He did his best to ignore everything except his hilltop. It was indeed farther than it looked, but they reached it by noon, walking the horses for the last several hundred feet of elevation gain.

John pointed out the bird overhead and began scanning the horizon with his monocular.

"I need to know where the remote node is," Ben said to the augment.

"I must broadcast on several EM frequencies to answer your query."

"Use minimal time and power."

"Understood."

Ben waited. Several seconds passed.

"Location confirmed. Seven and a half kilometers at azimuth 104."

"So, that way then?" Ben asked, orienting himself to the augment's directions.

"Correct."

"So, about your plan," Hound said.

"Let's take a break for lunch," Ben said, looking up at the bird. "We still have a ways to go, but we're close."

"And we're still being pursued," John said, handing Ben the monocular and pointing toward the bridge. There was a streamer of black smoke rising from the center where the brigands had been camped. Ben handed the monocular back and got some food from his saddlebag.

They didn't rest long, taking only enough time to feed and water their horses and have a bite themselves before heading into the mountains. The terrain was so rugged that most of the time they had to lead their horses. All the while the bird circled.

Ben knew he was going the right way. He even knew how close he was to his goal, but it seemed very far away knowing what was behind him. The path wound through a field of rocks, some as large as a house, scattered down a shallow draw that ascended into the core of the mountain.

A howl rose up from a distance behind them, echoing through the rock field and setting the horses on edge.

"What the hell was that?" Zack asked.

"Whatever it was, I bet it bleeds," Hound said.

"Stay alert and keep moving," Ben said.

"Smells like Mandrake," Homer said.

"I thought we'd lost him."

"No ... and he's circling upwind of us."

Not long after, Ben rounded a giant boulder and saw the enemy. Mandrake was perched atop another rock of similar size a hundred feet away. Ben scanned the open space before him, and finding nothing, eased forward.

"Careful, Ben," Imogen said.

"Hound, keep an eye behind us," Ben called out without looking back.

"You got it."

Mandrake tipped his head back and howled, a deathly, keening sound that seemed to drain the warmth from Ben's body and the courage from his heart. His horse started to protest, bringing him back to the present moment and focusing his mind on the task at hand. He regained control of his mount and bolted forward, closing with Mandrake.

Mandrake looked at him curiously. Ben reined his horse in, stopping quickly, drawing his pistol and firing. He missed, but Mandrake fled deeper into the boulder field.

"We getting close?" Hound asked, bringing his horse up next to Ben's. "That bird and that dog are both making me nervous."

"I hear you," Ben said. "Should be up at the top of this draw."

"I sure hope you're right about this."

"Me too," Ben said, spurring his horse forward.

The boulder field narrowed until only one passage remained, a narrow winding path through the jumble of rocks. Ben hesitated at the entrance, but the augment told him that his goal lay on the other side.

Not fifty feet into the passage, Mandrake howled from behind them, barking and snarling in a blood-chilling display of ferocity—none of which was lost on the horses. They bolted, fleeing the predator behind them, as natural and primal as could be.

Ben held on for his life as his horse careened around a corner, bouncing off the wall before losing its balance and taking a bad step.

Ben heard the crack. It seemed to echo against the walls of stone. The horse squealed in agony as its front leg broke, sending the animal crashing to the ground face first, wailing in fear and pain. Ben pitched forward, narrowly missing a sharp stone outcropping as he was thrown. He tucked, rolling away from the panicked animal behind him.

A shout, and then another crash echoed past him. Ben rolled to his feet, hours spent tumbling in training saving him in one moment. He turned just in time to see Zack's horse manage to dodge the growing pile of fallen horses and head straight for him. He danced aside, throwing himself against the stone wall and making himself as flat as possible.

Zack raced by, followed by Imogen and Olivia. A moment later, Ellie's horse went by, without Ellie. Both Hound and John were struggling to get away from the pile of wounded horses, all flailing about in pain.

Ben's horse was beyond salvation. Her leg was horribly broken and she was bleeding profusely from a gash on her rump. The other two were equally bad off, Hound's with two broken legs and John's bleeding from the neck. All three animals formed an agonizing, shrieking mess of bloody horror.

Ben drew his sword, a sense of deep sadness filling the pit of his stomach as he advanced. Each kill was clean and efficient, though no less bloody for it. He felt sick as he retrieved his saddle bags and gear.

Ellie came trotting up.

"Oh, shit," she said. "Anyone hurt?"

"Just the horses," John said.

A snarl from above drew their attention. Mandrake backed out of view.

"Come on out!" Hound shouted.

"Where's Liv?" Ellie asked.

"She blew past us with Imogen and Zack," Hound said.

"Grab your gear," Ben said. "We have to go."

They set out on foot, keeping careful watch all around. Two hundred feet farther, they came to Olivia, Imogen, and Zack, all nursing minor injuries.

"Everyone all right?" Ellie asked.

"We jumped," Olivia said. "Horses kept going."

"Can everyone move?" Ben asked.

"Yeah … but my ankle hurts," Olivia said.

"Hound, can you help her?"

"Sure thing," he said.

The narrow passage in the boulder field opened to reveal a cliff face that bordered one side of the massive draw. A glacial stream ran from a field of blue ice along the cliff until the terrain forced it into the boulder field. The horses were grazing in the fields between the glacier and the boulders, easily a mile away.

Ben followed the cliff face, a growing feeling of failure welling up in his belly as he got closer to his destination.

A howl behind him added urgency to the tension in his gut.

He stopped at a break in the cliff. A four-foot-wide crack in the rock ran straight into the heart of the mountain, directly where Ben had to go.

"Here he comes," Hound said.

Ben turned to see Hoondragon coming for him. He rode a big horse, but not his horse, not his stalker. Mandrake ran next to him as they closed the distance.

Everyone braced for battle at the entrance to the chasm. The waiting was interminable. Ben found himself willing Hoondragon to ride faster, if only to dispel the tension.

A shot rang out, its echo eliminating any hope of locating the position of the shooter. Hoondragon's horse stumbled, then fell, tossing the dragon's hunter to the ground. Mandrake stopped, circling his master.

"Come on," Ben said, rushing headlong into the chasm. It ran straight for nearly a hundred feet before opening up to reveal a small grotto, water trickling down from one side, moss and ferns clinging to anything that resembled soil.

Mandrake came up behind them, staying just out of shotgun range. John loosed an arrow, grazing him and convincing him to stay back farther still.

Ben led them on.

"I really hope you know where you're going," Ellie said.

"Bit late to doubt me now," he said.

"Face me and die with honor!" a voice shouted from well behind them.

"Ya think?" she said.

If Ben hadn't been running for his life, he would have stopped to enjoy the extraordinary beauty of the confined space. Mosses and lichens of all varieties clung to the walls, covering the stone with a mosaic of wild variation in color and texture.

John's bow twanged. Ben looked back just in time to see Mandrake dodge the arrow. Hoondragon came into view behind him, striding toward them with relentless purpose.

"Shit," Hound said.

"Yeah," Ben said. "Try to slow him down with Bertha. I'll hit him with my last grenade, then we rush him."

"Right," Hound said, less enthusiastically than Ben would have liked.

"NACC technology detected," the augment said.

"Restricted area," a computer synthesized voice said. "You are required to evacuate the area immediately."

Ben saw three small cubes floating twenty feet overhead.

"Are you done running, little rabbit?" Hoondragon said, approaching on foot with Mandrake beside him. "If you hand me the egg and kneel, I will take your head cleanly."

He stopped twenty feet away, his black armor almost glistening in the shadowy light. Very little of the man was visible, each piece of armor crafted to fit him perfectly, covering nearly his entire body, leaving vulnerabilities only at the joints and the face.

"This is a restricted area," the three drones repeated in the same emotionless voice. "You are trespassing. Leave the area now."

Hoondragon drew his sword.

Hound fired, hitting him squarely in the chest, knocking him back several feet, but doing no real damage. Ben quickly pulled the grenade out of his pocket, but Mandrake leapt at him, covering the distance in one bound and landing on him, forcing him to drop the grenade before he could pull the pin.

Ben landed hard on his back. When Mandrake reared back to strike, Ellie stabbed the creature in the shoulder, penetrating his armor-like hide deeply, spraying blood across the lichen, adding to the kaleidoscope of colors. He barked out in pain, bounding backward five feet and snarling at Ellie.

Ben scrambled to his feet, drawing his sword. He turned just in time to see Hoondragon charging Ellie, his spiked shoulder lowered to ram her. She spun out of the way, slashing at the back of his knee, hitting hard enough to make Hoondragon stumble but not hard enough to penetrate his armor.

Hound shot him in the side as he passed, resulting in little more than a minor course correction.

When Ben saw him coming, he raised his sword and tried to dodge, but Hoondragon simply ignored the blade and thrust his bastard sword into Ben's belly, straight through to the hilt, the dark cold steel holding him up while Hoondragon looked down at him, his fetid breath making Ben want to gag except for the paralyzing pain in his gut.

"You lose," Hoondragon said.

Ellie gasped. Imogen screamed. Hound cursed.

"NACC facility. Restricted area. Vacate the premises or be detained."

"Contact!" Ben said to the augment, his mind able to form only the most rudimentary of commands in the face of such a shock to his system.

"Link established. Agent not recognized. Full sync required. Provisional status granted. Agent in distress. Assets deployed."

Hoondragon stepped back, pulling the sword out as quickly as he had driven it through. Ben staggered for a moment in shock and amazement, wondering that something could hurt more than having a broadsword thrust through your belly. As it turned out, having it pulled out was worse. He crumpled to the ground.

Zack stepped up next to him, took careful aim and shot Hoondragon in the face with both barrels, one right after the other.

Hoondragon cursed, staggering back from the force of the blow and the fact that a pellet got through.

As one, the three drones engaged, targeting Mandrake and Hoondragon. Each drone fired an expanding wave of bluish energy that extended to a range of about fifty feet with a width of five feet. The first hit knocked Mandrake backward, end over end. The second hit knocked Hoondragon back half a dozen feet. The third knocked him flat on his back.

He regained his feet and all three hit him again simultaneously, blowing him back twenty feet in a heap.

"Hold on," Homer said.

Ben felt cold. His vision narrowed to the image of Hoondragon running away as a drone hit him from behind, blasting him face first into the dirt.

Imogen was there. Then Ellie.

"Step back," a computer voice said from somewhere.

Ben felt like he was floating. Everything was black ... and cold. And he was floating.

Chapter 19

He woke in his mind first.

"Your body has been temporarily paralyzed," the augment said. "A necessary precaution given the severity of your wound. Appropriate materials are being provided to your nanites so that they can repair your injury with optimum efficiency."

"Where am I?"

"NACC subnet access node number 147."

"Is everyone else safe?"

"Your companions are alive, present, and undamaged."

"How long until I wake up?"

"Several hours," the augment said. "In the interim, we have much to discuss."

"Such as?"

"First, the presence of magic and dragons is confirmed."

Ben wished that he could laugh. "Glad to hear it."

"The majority of the NACC has been destroyed. As a result, you have been given the rank of Director. Currently, you are the ranking officer. However, there is a stasis chamber relatively close by containing a Splinter Brigade awaiting reactivation."

"Wait, slow down. Director? What does that mean?"

"You can command all land-based NACC assets and access NACC computer systems, including the quantum communications network. You also have access to your tactical heads-up display and visual augmentation programs."

"So I can activate my ex-plus charge and use my seeker rounds now."

"Yes."

"Are there any weapons here?"

"No, but the location I mentioned earlier is well stocked with weapons."

"Tell me about it."

"It's called Alturas."

A map came up in Ben's mind showing the underground road network in the region. Alturas was a good hundred miles away underground with only two other opportunities to return to the surface along the way.

"What kind of weapons will I find there?"

"A standard small-arms locker—plasma rifles and gravity pistols."

"You mentioned a brigade earlier."

"A Splinter Brigade, yes."

"What's that?"

"Classified."

"You've got to be kidding."

"I'm afraid not. It's an eyes-only advanced research program. Recommended orders are to proceed to Alturas and revive the Splinter Brigade."

"Recommended orders? Isn't that a bit of a contradiction?"

"You are the ranking officer. The NACC system must obey your orders within the bounds of your clearance level."

"So you have to do what I tell you," Ben said.

"Yes."

"And you accept that magic and dragons are real."

"Yes."

"Good, tell me about the war," Ben said. He spent the next several hours reviewing the history of humanity's fall to the dragons. It was depressing and instructive all at once. It drove home the lesson that the dragon's greatest strength was his ability to get people to do his bidding.

After the very thorough history lesson, the augment brought an image of Ben's vitals up in his mind's eye.

"You have recovered nearly fully from your injury," the augment said. "I am preparing to revive you."

He noticed the sticky, metallic taste in his mouth first. He came awake slowly, still groggy from his recovery.

"He's awake," Ellie said, coming to his side.

He tried to speak but his voice didn't work. She held a cup to his lips. A few sips cleared his throat.

"How long?" he whispered.

"Two days," she said. "We thought you were dead."

He shook his head, still a bit groggy.

"Let's let him rest," Imogen said.

He drifted off, waking later, more thirsty this time and less groggy. He sat up, feeling only a hint of tightness where he'd been impaled.

"Recovery at 98%," the augment said. "Some scarring will remain."

"Good enough, considering. Thank you."

"You're welcome," the augment said after an uncharacteristic pause.

"You're back," Homer said. "I was worried."

Ben leaned over to scratch his dog's head, noting a slight twinge in his abdomen.

He looked around the room. It was about twenty feet wide and forty feet long with two bunk beds and a small living area taking up half of the room. The other half contained a small medical bay and an array of computers and other technology that Ben couldn't identify. Panels in the ceiling provided dim light. There were two doors, both made of steel—one closed, the other open to a dark hallway.

"What happened after I got stabbed?" Ben asked Homer.

His dog whined audibly. "I thought you were dead."

"I'm sorry if I scared you."

"The drones chased off Hoondragon and Mandrake," Homer said. "It would have been funny, if you hadn't just gotten stabbed. Then they picked you up, don't ask me how, and they carried you through a door at the end of the chasm.

From there we all got into another room that felt like it moved. When the door opened again, we were here."

"How's everyone doing?"

"Fine, now," Homer said. "We were pretty worried about you … and then the stupid computer wouldn't open the door for me until I peed on it."

Ben chuckled.

"Out that way is a tunnel," Homer said, pointing to the open door with his nose. "It's very dark and kind of spooky."

"Hey," Ellie said, sitting up and rubbing her eyes. "How are you feeling?"

"Well enough, considering I should be dead."

"I'm glad you're not," she said, offering a sympathetic smile. "And you were right about this place, thank God."

"Has the computer said anything?" he asked.

"Not much. It told us to leave you alone while it healed you. Aside from that, there was a brief argument about letting Homer out to do his business."

"Have you had a look out in the tunnel?"

"Hound and Durt went for a walk the first day. They said there was nothing but darkness and silence."

"Good," Ben said. "Hopefully our long walk in the dark will be blessedly boring."

"So … Imogen told me about the augment," she said. "It must be really weird, having another voice in your head."

Homer grumbled.

"You get used to it," Ben said. "Besides, it's already saved my life twice. And now that I've made contact with the NACC system, I think it'll actually do what I tell it to."

"What do you mean?"

"Until now, it didn't believe in magic or dragons. It couldn't decide if I was crazy or if it was malfunctioning."

She laughed softly, shaking her head. "Has it told you anything useful? I mean, now that it knows the state of the world?"

"It has," Ben said. "In fact…" He paused to query the augment.

A wall lit up with a map.

"Perfect," Ben said. "Computer, display the underground network."

A series of intersecting lines appeared on the map with a number of access nodes and underground facilities marked as well. The tunnel they had access to ran roughly northeast to southwest.

"Wow," Ellie whispered. "I've never seen anything like that. Are those all tunnels?"

"Yep," Ben said, pointing to the node they were in. "We're here." He traced the tunnel to Alturas. "And we have to get there."

She frowned, examining the map.

"If this is Shasta," she said, pointing to a large facility under the mountain, "it looks like the tunnels can take us all the way there."

"If they're still intact, and if we have enough food and water for the trip."

"There is that," she said. "So what's in Alturas?"

"Tech weapons and something called a splinter brigade."

"And what's that?"

Ben sighed. "I don't know, the computer won't tell me."

"Why not?"

"Apparently, I don't have clearance. It's kind of a recurring theme."

"A brigade sounds like it might have a lot of firepower," Hound said quietly on his way over to them.

"I hope so," Ben said. "We could certainly use it."

"How're you feeling?" Hound asked.

"My belly is a bit tight, but otherwise, I'm good."

"I thought you were dead for sure."

"We all did," Ellie said, laying her hand on his. He took it and gave it a gentle squeeze.

"I certainly didn't manage to put up much of a fight," Ben said, shaking his head. "I'm not sure what happens next time we run into Hoondragon."

"By then," Ellie said, "we'll be armed to the teeth with tech weapons and we'll put him in the ground where he belongs."

"Weapons?" Hound said.

"So says the almighty computer," Ben said, gesturing to the screen.

"You mean the one that got its ass kicked by the dragon?"

Ben laughed, nodding. "One in the same. Hopefully, its records are accurate. If so, there's a weapons cache here." Ben pointed at Alturas.

"I've heard of that place," Hound said. "Word is, it's a company town controlled by the Adara family—the ones building the railroad."

"Huh," Ben said. "I wasn't expecting it to be a town."

"It looks like the underground facility is pretty good size," Ellie said. "Maybe the town is on top and they don't even know about the tunnels."

Hound chuckled. "Aren't you cute? All optimistic and stuff."

She gave him a dirty look.

He just smiled back. "Let's not pretend we're going to have a run of good luck once we get there," he said, "save ourselves the disappointment."

All the lights in the room came up at once and the computer screen changed, showing a view of the narrow chasm leading to the node entrance.

"Intruder detected," a synthesized voice said.

Hoondragon stood at the point where the narrow passage funneled into the wider grotto area.

"You can't hide forever, little rabbit," he shouted. "The longer you draw this out, the more painful the end will be."

Three drones came into view, moving toward Hoondragon. He withdrew into the chasm, daring them to follow, but they held position ten feet inside the grotto.

"What kind of weapons are the drones armed with?" Ben asked.

"Gravity guns," the computer replied.

"What's their range?"

"Limited to the immediate area."

"Shame," Ben said. "It'd be nice to burn him to the ground right now."

"Offensive measures are not within this node's capabilities."

"Of course they aren't," Hound said.

By this time, everyone else was roused by the light. Ben spent the next several minutes assuring his friends that he was indeed healed and accepting their well wishes.

"So we're headed into the dark, then," Hound said.

"Yep," Ben said. "How much food and water do we have?"

"Plenty," Hound said, fishing a small package out of his pocket and holding it up. "There's a cabinet full of this stuff. It tastes like it's a hundred years old, but it fills your belly."

"At least there's that," Ben said. "Find anything else useful?"

"These," Hound said, holding up a small metal tube. He pushed a button and a beam of bright white light shined forth.

"Nice," Ben said. "Those will certainly help, but we'll have to leave them once we reach the surface again."

"I thought you might say that," Hound said. "I'm starting to like this tech stuff. This flashlight certainly beats the hell out of a lantern."

"Can't argue with that," Ben said.

Then he looked at the screen and said, "Computer, display a list of this node's capabilities and resources."

The screen changed from a view of the confrontation between Hoondragon and the drones to a long list of technical specifications. Ben scanned the items—most were either unhelpful or beyond his understanding.

"What's the quantum communications network?" he asked.

"QuantumNet is a secure network allowing real-time communications between operational NACC facilities or assets, as long as each has been equipped with a linked quantum-entangled chip."

"What the hell does that mean?" Hound asked.

"Clarify," the synthesized voice of the computer said.

"Is that thing in your head as difficult as this computer?" Hound asked.

"You have no idea," Ben said. "Computer, what's a quantum-entangled chip?"

"Many centuries ago, it was discovered that particles can become entangled at a quantum level. When one particle in an entangled pair is disturbed, the second particle reacts in exactly the same way at exactly the same time as the first, regardless of the distance between them. Using this principle, NACC scientists were able to create chip sets which contain a number of quantum-entangled particle pairs. Each QuantumNet-equipped facility or asset contains one chip, while its twin resides at a central hub, thus allowing perfectly secure, real-time communications between any facilities or assets in the network."

"Show me the network," Ben said.

The screen changed again, this time displaying a map of North America with an array of locations marked in red or green. In addition, a small window opened on the lower corner of the screen and a list of assets began to scroll, most in red, but a few in green.

"Facilities listed in red are no longer functional."

"Damn," Ben said, noting that Alturas was shown in red.

"Tell me about these assets," Ben said, pointing at the scrolling list.

"Most are military vehicles that have been destroyed. The only remaining operational assets are satellites."

"What the hell does that mean?" Hound said again.

"Clarify."

Hound closed his eyes and ran his fingers through his hair.

"What's a satellite?" Ben asked.

"A satellite is an orbital vehicle."

"You mean like in space?" Ellie asked.

"Yes."

"What do they do?" Ben asked.

"Primarily communications, surveillance, and weapons guidance."

"Weapons?" Hound said.

"Can these satellites be used for direct attack?" Ben asked.

"No, the corporate orbital nonproliferation treaty was ratified in 2114, prohibiting any direct-attack technologies to be placed in space."

"Figures," Hound said. "If they had space guns, they would've used 'em."

Ben nodded. "Tell me about the surveillance capabilities."

"Visual images of high resolution can be provided in real time from any functioning satellite in the network."

"Is there one that can show the local area?"

"Yes."

The screen changed again, showing a vast area of land from a great height.

"Can you zoom in?"

The view narrowed, showing more detail, though still not enough resolution.

"More."

Closer still.

"Mark our position on this display."

A dot appeared.

"Show me the immediate area around this facility, say a one-mile radius."

The image became much more distinct and detailed.

"There's Hoondragon," Ellie said, pointing at a dot on the screen.

"Amazing," Imogen whispered.

"Can't argue with that," Hound said. "Too bad it doesn't do us much good."

"Maybe … show me the next node along this tunnel to the southwest," Ben said.

The screen shifted and slowly narrowed in focus until a large bunker made of cement could be seen. The enormous door had long since been broken open.

"Get closer," Ben said.

The image grew in clarity. Atop the bunker was a guard fortification manned by three men.

"Shit," Hound said. "It's never easy."

"No, it's not," Ben said. "Computer, what can you tell me about that facility?"

"Node 159 is a vehicle-maintenance facility."

"Can you show me what's going on inside?"

"No, that node is currently offline."

"How about the floor plan?"

The screen changed again, displaying the layout of the entire facility, from surface to tunnel. The bulk of the facility was located in three floors just above the tunnel connecting to Node 147. The topmost level was joined by another tunnel that ran roughly east-west. The surface entrance allowed access to a vehicle-sized elevator and a spiral-shaped tunnel that descended to the first floor of the facility.

"Can you make a copy of this diagram?" Ben asked the augment.

"Of course. Downloading."

"In that case, get a copy of the floor plans for every facility in the NACC tunnel network."

"Downloading."

"Huh," Ben muttered.

"What?" Zack asked.

"My augment is actually cooperating. Kind of nice for a change."

"So what do we do about them?" Olivia asked, pointing at the men guarding the surface entrance of Node 159.

"That depends on whether they have access to the tunnel," Ben said. "Hopefully, we'll walk right under their noses and they'll never be the wiser."

Hound laughed out loud. "Her optimism's rubbing off on you," he said.

"Probably," Ben said, "but we don't have much choice. Hoondragon's camped upstairs and honestly, I think I'd rather fight a bunch of bandits than him." His hand went to his belly.

"Can we see Alturas?" Ellie asked.

The computer shifted view again, displaying a medium-sized community with a population of about fifty thousand.

Ben frowned, looking at the large camp just north of town. "Zoom in here," he said, tapping the screen.

An army of Dragon Guard came clearly into view, probably twenty thousand strong, and it looked like they'd only just arrived a few days ago from the work they were doing to improve their camp.

"You think that's for us?" Imogen asked.

"I hope not," Ben said.

"Hell, I'd be flattered if it was," Hound said.

Everyone looked at him.

"What? I kind of like that we're getting under the wyrm's skin. It's about time someone did."

"Yeah, but that's a bit more than we can handle," John said, gesturing to the army.

"Show me the Alturas Base floor plan."

"Wow," Imogen said. "That's a lot bigger than I expected."

A dozen levels descended from the surface, the first only a hundred feet underground. Each level was expansive with numerous rooms, tunnels, elevators, and staircases linking them together. A shaft descended several hundred feet below the lowest level, leading to a small facility.

"What's that?" Ben asked.

"Splinter Brigade #3 stasis facility."

"Doesn't look big enough for a whole brigade," Hound said, frowning with disappointment.

"Can you make contact with that part of the Alturas facility?"

"No, you do not have clearance."

"How about the rest of the facility? Can you show me inside?"

"No, the stasis chamber is the only part of the facility that still has power."

"Figures," Hound muttered.

"It looks like the tunnel comes in on the tenth level," Ellie said, tracing the route with her finger. "And this one on level seven goes straight to Shasta."

"Maybe we can avoid people altogether," Imogen said.

"Did you hear that?" Zack said.

Everyone froze, listening intently.

"People are coming," Homer said. "In the tunnel."

"Hey, was this door open the last time we came through here?" a voice said from down the hall through the open door to the tunnel.

"I see light," another voice said. "We'd better check it out."

"Damn it, I just stepped in dog shit," another voice said.

"Where'd that come from?"

Hound motioned for silence before tiptoeing to his pack and retrieving Bertha.

Ben leaned over, his eyes never leaving the door, as he slowly drew his sword.

"Augment, show me the intruders," Ben said in his mind.

An image sprang into his mind's eye showing the hallway and an unkempt man looking around the corner of the door, raising a lantern. The view switched, showing the tunnel immediately outside the door. Five men were guiding a horse-drawn wagon with a cage occupying the entire cargo area.

There were four women inside the cage, all dirty and battered, and all clearly terrified.

Ben felt a tingling sense of anger begin to well up in his gut.

Slavers.

Ben motioned to Hound, holding up five fingers and then drawing a finger across his neck.

Hound looked a bit surprised, until he saw the smoldering anger in Ben's eyes. He motioned for Ben to wait, then went to his gear and retrieved his war axe. John picked up his bow and Ellie drew her sword.

The hallway was only five feet wide. Ben put his back to the wall just beside the open door, viewing the hall through the augment, watching three men approach cautiously, all three armed with blades of various sizes.

"I think there's somebody in there," one of the men whispered.

"Maybe we ought to back off and tell Beauchamp about this."

"Tell him what? We haven't seen what there is to see."

The lead man advanced, blade at the ready. Ben waited, one hand held up to forestall any action by his friends.

The man's hand came into view. Ben slashed, cutting it off in a stroke. Before the man could even scream, Ben stepped around the doorjamb and smashed the pommel of his sword into his throat. The man fell backward into his friend.

Ben advanced, whipping his blade around and slicing two inches into the second man's throat. He shoved them both aside, rushing the third man.

The slaver's eyes wide and his mouth agape, he froze in shock. Ben ran him through, dropping him and racing for the tunnel without a second look. He stopped at the doorway, easing up to the threshold.

"Shit!" a man yelled, seeing Ben and his bloody sword.

"Run," the other said, bringing a crossbow to bear on Ben.

He dodged to the opposite side of the hallway a half second before the bolt hit the wall, ricocheting off and spraying Hound with splinters. He grunted, then swore under his breath.

Ben darted out into the tunnel, his eyes taking a moment to adjust to the lower light of the twin lanterns wired to the front of the cage. The wagon was pulling away, all four women looking to Ben with beseeching eyes filled with fear and most of all, hope.

He sprinted into the dark, gaining on the wagon even as it accelerated. His lungs ached, his legs burned, but he pushed on even harder, pouring everything he had into speed. He got close enough to grab the bars, stumbling and getting dragged for a moment.

He swung wide, contorting himself around the side of the wagon and jamming his sword into the spokes of one of the wheels. His blade was wrenched from his hand as the wheel came apart with a series of loud, echoing pops—each spoke snapping in turn. Ben let go and hit the ground, tumbling twice before coming to a stop.

The wagon pulled away, the left rear corner tipping back and hitting the ground, lifting the front of the wagon up at an odd angle and tossing the man riding shotgun against the cage. The horses struggled to escape the driver's whip, still pulling the horribly listing wagon. The rear board caught on something and tore off, clattering to the ground, followed by the cage sliding at a sick angle from the wagon bed and toppling over, taking one of the men with it.

Ben got to his feet and scanned the dark for his sword. He could hear Hound running behind him, and then there was light—a bright beam of brilliance stabbing into the darkness. Ben saw the dull glint of his tech-metal sword and raced for it.

Another crash reverberated down the tunnel as the wagon lost its left front wheel and skidded to a halt.

Ben advanced at a determined pace. He came to the cage. None of the women dared speak, but all of them cried out for help with their eyes. The man riding shotgun came up with a knife. Before Ben could reach him, Hound's light blinded the man and then his war axe dropped him, buried to the haft in his chest. Ben looked back.

"What? I get at least one," Hound said, without a hint of humor on his way to pull the axe out of the dying man's chest.

John came up behind them as Hound illuminated the tunnel and the wagon. The driver had just managed to disentangle himself from the wreckage when the light hit him. He looked toward them and then turned to run.

John drew.

"Don't kill him," Ben said.

John adjusted his aim and loosed, hitting the man in the butt and dropping him like a rock, his wails echoing down the hallway.

"Nice shot," Ellie said, coming up behind them.

"Would you two take care of the women, please," Ben said to John and Ellie before turning to Hound. "What do you say we have a chat with this guy?"

"Thought you'd never ask," he said.

"Please ... we didn't do nothin' to you," the man said as they approached. He lay on his side, the arrow penetrating into one cheek and out the side of his hip.

They stopped several feet away, Hound shining the light in the man's face. "Yeah, I'm really liking this tech," he said.

"Please don't hurt me," the man said, shielding his eyes from the light. "We didn't do nothin'."

"Tell me about the women," Ben said.

"What? What about them?"

"Why are they in a cage?"

"We was gonna sell 'em ... to Adara."

"So you're a slaver, then," Ben said.

"Well, yeah. The money's good. We could cut you in. I'll ... I'll introduce you to Beauchamp. He's always lookin' for good men."

Ben squatted down so he could look the man in the eye.

"Tell me, what has to happen in a man's mind to make him believe that it's okay to buy and sell women?"

He blinked in confusion.

"The money's good," he said emphatically.

Ben stood back up.

"Tell me about this Beauchamp guy," Hound said.

"He's the boss. He runs the fortress. It was his idea to use the tunnels to move the merchandise. Sometimes the locals interfere when they see people in a cage."

Ben and Hound shared a look.

"He has magic," the man whispered.

They both looked back at him.

"Really?" Ben said. "How does that work?"

"I don't know, myself. But I've seen him do things … things that can't be explained. He's good to work for. Please…" He started crying. "I don't want to die."

"Tell me about this fortress," Hound said.

"It's the next stop where you can get to the surface," he said. "About twenty-five miles from here."

"More," Ben said.

"More what?"

"How many men does Beauchamp have?"

"I don't know, it varies. Teams are always comin' and goin'."

When Ben's and Hound's expressions darkened, he continued.

"There's always the dozen men he keeps to guard the place, plus usually two or three teams of five."

"How are they armed?"

"Knives, swords, crossbows … the usual. Except Beauchamp, he's got a tech gun."

"Are there guards where this tunnel enters the fortress?" Ben asked.

"Yeah, two, day and night … and they always have crossbows. Oh, and dogs."

Ellie came stomping up, glaring at the injured man until he looked down.

"I just talked with those women," she said. "They're from the Deschutes Territory. They were kidnapped from a bunkhouse at the ranch where they worked. They said…" She stopped to compose herself. "They said you took turns raping them every night since you took them."

"Well…" he said, clearly unsure of how to answer her accusation. He settled on the worst possible option.

"Beauchamp would pay real good money for her," he said, turning to Ben. "I mean, like a lot."

Ben blinked in disbelief.

"You son of a bitch," Ellie said, snatching the arrow and yanking it out, half sideways, tearing through the outside of his hip and releasing a torrent of blood. He screamed in terror and agony.

"I guess that's all we're going to get from him," Ben said, stepping past Ellie and stabbing him through the heart, the rather dim light in his eyes going out a moment later.

"What did you do that for?" Ellie snapped. "He deserved to suffer."

"Yeah, but you don't deserve to be a torturer," Ben said, turning back toward the bunker.

He stopped at the threshold of the door, looking at the carnage he'd left in the hallway. In the back of his mind, it worried him that he'd killed these men so easily—not that they'd been no match for him, but that he'd cut them down without hesitation, and even now, after the fact, he couldn't seem to find any remorse inside himself for what he'd done.

He worried that he was becoming hardened to killing—only now coming to fully understand why Cyril had been so careful to spare him from taking a life. He tried to imagine what his grandfather would have done in similar circumstances, but every way he looked at it, he suspected that Cyril would have done exactly the same. Few things had brought the hardness of anger to his gentle eyes like the subject of slavery.

Ben sighed, shaking his head.

"Don't beat yourself up about it," Hound said. "They had it coming, and I'll bet those women you just saved are about to tell you all about it."

Ben looked over at him, only then realizing that the business end of the splintered crossbow bolt was still jutting from his side.

"How bad?" Ben asked, pointing.

"Just a scratch," Hound said. "Wouldn't mind some help pulling it out though."

They stepped carefully to avoid tracking blood into the bunker. Olivia and Imogen were sitting with the four women in the living area of the room while their guests ate. From the looks of it, Ben suspected that they hadn't had a good meal in days.

They glanced at the men with fear. Ben felt a fresh rush of anger at what had been done to them. He took a deep breath and tried, unsuccessfully, to let go of his emotions.

"Let's get your armor off and have a look," Ben said to Hound.

He winced as he took off his leather breastplate, then looked at the wound curiously.

It wasn't deep enough to be serious, but it certainly looked painful.

Hound eased himself back onto the table.

"Computer, tell me how to help my friend," Ben said.

A list of instructions sprang up in his mind's eye. Ben retrieved the supplies he needed from the cabinet under the medical table and went to work, following the instructions meticulously—first applying a topical pain killer, then cleaning the wound with disinfectant, easing the bolt out without causing additional damage, filling the wound with a clotting agent combined with repair nanites, and finally dressing the wound.

"Not bad," Hound said, sitting up. "You might have made a good doc."

"I might have done a lot of things," Ben said, dismissing the feeling of unfairness welling up in his belly at the thought of what might have been. He didn't have the luxury of feeling sorry for himself, and looking at the women on the far side of the room, such feelings didn't seem justified, anyway.

"So what now?" Hound asked, strapping on his armor.

"That's a good question," Ben said. "Computer, show me the area just outside the bunker entrance."

The screen came to life. Hoondragon was camped near the opening of the fissure. Ben shook his head when he saw their horses, dead and left to rot where Mandrake had run them down.

"Can't send them home that way," Hound said.

"And we can't bring them with us," Ben said. "Computer, follow the route of the tunnel leading to the northeast."

The image began to move, the desolate terrain of the high desert scrolling by quickly.

"Stop."

The image froze, showing a place where a landslide had broken into the tunnel, exposing it to the surface and allowing access to the network at a point thirty miles away.

"Zoom in."

The image became clearer. Multiple wagon tracks meandered through the sage desert until they disappeared into the tunnel.

"John, Zack, would you go get the slavers' horses and make sure they're in good shape."

They nodded, heading out into the tunnel. Ben put his sword away and cleaned the blood off his face before slowly approaching the four women sitting with Imogen, Ellie, and Olivia. He stopped a safe distance away.

"My name is Ben," he said.

"Thank you for what you did," one of the women said. The other three wouldn't meet his eye.

"You're welcome. I'm sorry this happened to you," he said, sitting on the floor half a dozen feet from them. "I want to help you, but I'm not sure how. We can't take you with us and we can't take you to the surface. I'm afraid your best option is to return the way you came. We'll give you food and horses."

The woman shook her head, her composure beginning to break, tears welling up in her eyes. The other three looked to her plaintively, though none dared to speak.

"Please, don't leave us," she said.

Ben looked at Ellie. Her expression answered his unspoken question.

"I have enemies," Ben said. "You're not safe with me. Also, I'm headed toward the slavers' base of operations, and I don't think you want to go there."

"Why would you do that?" she asked. "Can't you just take us home?"

Ben sighed, shaking his head sadly. "I'm sorry, but I have urgent business in the opposite direction."

She nodded, a tear slipping from her eye. "We don't mean to be ungrateful. It's just that we've been though so much."

"I know," Ben said. "Let me see what I can do."

He went out into the tunnel, noting that the bodies had been dragged out of the hallway, leaving lurid streaks of blood on the floor. John and Zack had piled them in the tunnel and tied the horses to the cage. Both were searching the wagon.

"Anything useful?" he asked.

"Some food and water," John said.

"And a few blades," Zack said, brandishing a sword that he'd claimed.

Ben put his hand on Zack's shoulder and looked him in the eye.

"I have a job for you," he said. "I want you to take these women home."

"But—"

"They need help, Zack," Ben said, cutting off his friend's objection. "You didn't ask for any of this and you don't have to be here. You can walk away."

"I don't want to," Zack said. "I want to go with you."

"I know," Ben said, looking down and marshaling his thoughts. "The truth is, I doubt I'll survive this, but for me the only way out is through. I don't want to get you killed, too. And those women need your help. They're alone and afraid. Please, Zack. If you want to help me, this is what I need you to do."

"And then what? I can't go home."

"I know," Ben said. "That's the second part of the job. I want you to take a letter to Dominic Flynn. He's probably worried sick about his daughters."

Zack frowned, slowly shaking his head. "I want to see this through with you."

Ben sighed. "Come with me."

Zack followed him back into the node.

"Look at them," Ben whispered. "They're hurt and afraid. They need you, and so do I. I can't take them with me, and I can't send them to the surface, and I can't just abandon them. Please."

"Damn it," Zack said. "All right, but I'm coming to find you afterwards."

Ben nodded sadly. Zack wasn't cut out for this.

"I'm going to miss you," Ben said.

Chapter 20

Several hours later, they'd loaded up on food and water and made preparations to depart. Ben took one last look at Hoondragon, still camped above. He idly wondered how long the dragon's hunter would wait.

"Seal the node and power down," he said to the augment as he stepped into the tunnel. The door closed and multiple bolts whirred into place. Hound and Durt had each taken a flashlight, the third going to Zack. Brilliant beams of light reflected off the light-grey, rough concrete walls, casting ample light to travel by. Ben took one of the wagon's lanterns and handed the other to Zack.

He looked at the four frightened women huddled together in the tunnel. "Zack will take good care of you. He's a good man, you can trust him. I know that might be hard to do right now, but it's important that you let him help you."

They nodded tightly, obviously wishing that more of Ben's party would accompany them, but leaving those wishes unspoken.

Ben turned to Zack. "Thank you," he said, giving him a hug and a sad smile.

Zack nodded, struggling to maintain control of his emotions.

Olivia stepped up and kissed him on the cheek, his face going bright red a moment later.

"I'm proud of you," she said. "You're just the hero these women need."

He smiled at her praise.

"Good man," Hound said, clapping him on the shoulder. "Remember what I taught you about that shotgun."

He nodded. One by one everyone said goodbye and they set out in opposite directions. While he knew it was for the best, Ben couldn't shake the feeling of loss, as if one more piece of his old life had fallen away. He wondered how much of himself would be left when this was all over.

While they walked through the dark, his mind turned to the rather one-sided battle with the slavers and a thought occurred to him.

"I thought I had access to a tactical display," he said to his augment.

"You do, but you must complete the tutorial before you can use it."

"How long does that take?"

"A few minutes."

After several hours of walking, they stopped for lunch and Ben took the time to complete the tutorial, which consisted of a virtual reality fight assisted by the tactical display.

It took a few minutes to get used to it, but once he did, and once he learned what all of the different parts of the display meant, he found it to be quite helpful. Friend and enemy were highlighted in green and red respectively, target ranges were given, probable enemy strengths and weaknesses were displayed in readouts attached to each opponent, and subtle but useful guidance was offered that seemed to capitalize on Ben's strengths.

They continued on after lunch, no one talking much since every noise felt like an intrusion into the eerie quiet of the subterranean passage. Ben played with his tactical display, exploring its capabilities.

Then an idea hit him and he stopped dead in his tracks.

"Can you display anything I want in my mind's eye?"

"Certainly."

"What is it?" Hound asked.

"Oh, nothing," Ben said, tapping the side of his head.

He visualized a magic circle surrounding himself at a radius of about five feet while he walked, drawing it in pure white light and then calling up the recorded memory of Cyril teaching him how to create one so he could be sure it was correct.

When he was satisfied, he told the augment to store the image for recall and projection within his mind's eye on command. He had no idea if it would have any effect in the real world, but it was worth a try.

The darkness dragged on, each step taking them into another section of tunnel that looked just like the last. It was disorienting. If not for the augment, all concept of time would have vanished into the darkness. After he'd fully explored the capabilities of his tactical display, he turned his mind to magic.

Not ten steps later, he saw a glint on the ground and smiled, chuckling to himself as he picked up another gold coin. It had become a relatively common occurrence, though no less amazing. As he stood back up, he noted the flashlights with renewed interest and started to wonder what it took to disrupt tech with magic.

He spent the rest of the afternoon trying to interfere with Hound's light with absolutely no success. The more he tried, the more he failed, until he gave up in frustration.

"Is that a door?" John asked, directing his beam of light at a section of wall up ahead.

"The slavers?" Imogen whispered.

"I doubt it," Ben said quietly. "We're still miles from their node."

"What then?" Hound asked, unslinging Bertha.

"Let's find out," Ben said, approaching carefully. A heavy, steel door interrupted the uniform concrete of the tunnel walls. It looked like someone had tried to open it with a crowbar, but the door fit so seamlessly into the frame that they could do little more than scratch the surface.

Ben laid his hand on it. "Where does this door lead?" he asked the augment.

"This is a maintenance closet."

"Can you open it?"

Ben felt a tingle on the palm of his hand, followed by a muffled clunk and a faint whirring. The door popped open a moment later.

"What just happened? Why did my hand feel like that?"

"The door required power to activate," the augment said.

"So I powered the door?"

"Technically, I did," the augment said, "though you acted as the conduit."

Ben gave the door a gentle shove, stepping aside to let Hound sweep the room with his light. It was about twenty feet square and lined with metal cabinets along the back wall.

He eased inside, scanning every corner before relaxing.

"Empty," he said.

They spent a few minutes going through the lockers, finding coveralls, tools, and parts for machines that had fallen silent decades ago.

"Nothing useful," Hound said.

"No, but we can sleep here without posting a guard," Ben said.

"Good point," Hound said, dropping his pack in the corner.

They ate a cold meal and lay down for the night, Ellie tossing her bedroll out next to Ben.

"What are we going to do about the slavers?" she asked, sitting down to take off her boots.

Ben sighed, shaking his head. "I'm not sure. Part of me wants to destroy them, but truthfully, they're just a distraction."

"How can you say that? You saw those women."

Ben looked down, conflict roiling within him. After a few moments, clarity returned and he nodded to himself. "I feel the same way, I really do, but I'm not out here trying to fix every injustice in the world … just the very worst one."

She started to say something but caught herself.

"We probably ought to be ready for a fight, just in case," Hound said.

"Can't argue with that," Ben said. "The lowest level of that node sits right next to the tunnel with nothing but a dozen vehicle-sized doors between them."

"So we can't bottleneck them," Hound said.

"Nope. Worse still, the entire level is an open bay—one giant room four hundred feet on a side."

"Sounds like we know just enough to know that we don't know enough," Hound said.

"Pretty much," Ben said, lying down and closing his eyes.

He woke in the dark, the augment telling him that it was just before dawn. The rhythmic breathing of his friends told him that they were still asleep. He slipped into a virtual combat simulation and commanded the augment to recreate the fight with the slavers.

After reliving the slaughter of those men, looking for any opportunity to learn something, he decided that surprise and training had determined the outcome of that fight before the first drop of blood hit the floor.

He cleared the field, the virtual world in his mind shifting abruptly to an open plain with a monochromatic sky. With a thought, his magic circle appeared around him. He wondered if he was just fooling himself with it. After all, it was just in his mind. He had no reason to believe it would work in the real world.

"Perhaps a test is in order," the augment said.

"What did you have in mind?"

After a moment of hesitation the augment answered, "Nothing specific."

"Helpful as always," Ben said. "It's not a bad idea ... I just don't know how to do it."

"Perhaps one of your enemies will provide you with the opportunity."

"That's what I'm afraid of," Ben said, conjuring three opponents with a thought. He drew his sword as they advanced.

After a series of training simulations, first with his sword and then with his pistol, he returned to reality. The others were beginning to stir.

"I've decided that I don't like being underground," Homer said. "It's dark, and it smells wrong."

Ben scratched his dog's head. "Might be a few days before we see daylight again."

Homer grumbled, leaning into Ben's affections.

After breakfast, they left the maintenance room, closing and locking the door. An hour later, Ben felt the hair on his neck stand up.

He stopped.

"Kill the lights," he whispered urgently. Rufus and John looked at him for just long enough to see that he was serious before plunging the tunnel into darkness.

Ben reached out with his senses, searching for the ever-so-subtle feeling of magic. He knew what it was the moment he felt it, spinning around and locking his eyes on the darkness. It took him a few seconds to pick out the faint red eyes in the distance.

"We're being followed by the Warlock's shadow," he whispered. "Let me see your light." Hound held it out. Ben flailed around for it in the pitch black before he found it. He aimed it at the eyes and switched it on. The shadow flinched, then fled into the darkness behind them. Ben handed the light back to Hound.

"He doesn't give up, does he?" Hound said

"No, he doesn't. Let's hope he doesn't make friends with Hoondragon."

Hound looked at him in mock horror. "I was kind of hoping for just the opposite."

"How much farther is the slavers' base?" Ellie asked.

Ben closed his eyes and looked at the tunnel map. "Another three miles."

"They're going to see us coming a mile away," Ellie said.

"They've probably already seen us," John said. "Tunnel's pretty straight."

"We're outnumbered with no chance of surprise," Ben said. "Let's try and talk our way through." He looked directly at Ellie. "Don't provoke them."

She clenched her jaw, anger dancing in her eyes, but she nodded nonetheless.

Not an hour later, John stopped, covering his light with one hand. Hound followed his lead. After a few seconds, they could see light flickering in the distance.

Ben lit his lantern.

"Let's keep the tech to ourselves," he said.

Hound and Durt nodded in unison, turning off their lights and stashing them in their packs. Another two hours of walking and they could distinguish the three lanterns hanging from the ceiling of the tunnel, casting a dim glow over a guard post off to one side.

They approached with caution, stopping about forty feet from the first of the bay doors, the only one currently open. A makeshift wooden barricade provided cover for the two men standing guard.

"Hello," Ben said.

"Who are you?" one of the men said, seeming only then to notice that Ben's group wasn't a team of slavers.

"Just travelers passing through," Ben said.

Both men looked at each other and the second man raced off into the node.

"May we pass?" Ben asked.

"Come closer so I can get a better look at you."

Ben approached slowly, his friends fanning out on either side of him. They stopped twenty feet from the slaver. He was armed with a crossbow, and it looked like there were at least two more weapons cocked and loaded resting on a shelf right next to him.

"We don't get many travelers through here," he said.

A tall, thin, gaunt man with jet-black hair came striding into the tunnel, followed by three more men, all armed with crossbows and swords. The tall man had a pistol on his hip under his long black coat.

"NACC technology detected," the augment said. An image of a gravity gun sprang into Ben's mind, followed by a list of specifications. The spec that caught his eye was the range—fifty feet.

"Can you deactivate it?" Ben asked.

"Of course," the augment said.

"Do it," Ben said.

"Weapon deactivated."

"They say they're just passing through, Beauchamp," the guard said.

"Is that so?" the tall man said, his eyes scanning them one by one, lingering on the women a few moments longer than the men.

"What's your business?" he asked.

"We're scouting a trade route," Ben said. "Our boss got wind of these tunnels. He wants to know if he can move his merchandise through here faster and safer than on the surface."

Imogen looked at him with a hint of surprise.

"Did you come in through the landslide or farther up?" Beauchamp asked.

"The landslide," Ben said. "Boss sent another team the other way."

"He sounds determined," Beauchamp said. "So much for keeping this a secret. What's your boss want to move through here?"

"Wine mostly," Ben said. "Occasionally he takes on freight for other merchants, but his business is wine."

"Well, now ... wine is quite a valuable commodity around here," Beauchamp said. "Why don't you come in and we'll discuss terms."

"I'm sorry," Ben said, "but I don't have the authority to represent my boss in any kind of negotiation. We're just the survey expedition. After we make our report, I'm sure he'll send a representative to talk with you."

Beauchamp smiled thinly, his eyes darting from Ben to Olivia and back again.

"You must be tired," he said. "Come in and have a meal. I'd love to hear your story."

"Thank you," Ben said, "but I'm afraid we're on a schedule. The truth is, we're due a pretty good bonus if we get this done quickly, and well, I've already got it spent, so we really need to be on our way."

"Ah ... isn't that the way of things?" Beauchamp said. "Never enough money. Well, I guess we'll be looking forward to your employer's representative. Safe travels."

Beauchamp didn't wait for them to respond, turning and walking back into the node without another word.

Ben and his friends set out at a brisk pace, nodding politely to the guards as they passed.

A thousand yards beyond the node, Hound breached the silence.

"Did that seem too easy?"

"Yeah," Ben said. "The question is, why?"

"Maybe we just got lucky," Ellie said.

"There you go again," Hound said.

"What? It could happen," she said.

"Yeah, but it didn't," Ben said. "He's up to something. Let's put some distance between us and him."

Ben felt a tingle race over his skin—magic and evil all wrapped into one. He shivered, looking back toward the slavers' node as the rushing sound of a strong wind washed past them. Something dark and formless, yet filled with intent and power, surged toward them.

With a thought, Ben projected a magic circle around himself and Homer an instant before the darkness reached them. It enveloped everyone, swirling around like living smoke, and then it was gone, racing back toward the slavers. Ben looked around in a panic. All of his friends were gone, carried off by the inexplicable assailant.

He and Homer were alone in the dark.

Chapter 21

Ben marshaled his thoughts, trying to school his breathing and his pounding heart. The slaver had told him that Beauchamp had magic, but this was far beyond anything that he'd anticipated, and yet, it had failed to ensnare him. He could only imagine that the magic circle he'd projected in his mind's eye had saved him. The implications were more than he had time to ponder at the moment.

"What are we going to do now?" Homer asked.

"The only thing we can do," Ben said, dousing his lantern and setting out in the dark, heading back toward the enemy. The lanterns hanging above the guard post were the only source of illumination. He moved slowly and cautiously, both to avoid detection and to keep from tripping in the darkness. Homer stayed right next to him, nearly leaning against his leg.

He reached the first bay door and heard voices cheering and jeering as the slavers taunted his friends. So much for being a distraction, he thought. He stopped and considered his options, closing his eyes and pulling up the layout of the node in his mind. After a moment, he decided that the prisoners would be held on the second floor. One hall lined with storage rooms had a single point of entry, so it would make for the most secure holding area.

There were staircases, two on each side leading up from the lowest level, as well as a ramp for vehicles on the far side of the room. He opened his eyes. Two men stood guard in the makeshift post several hundred feet and dozens of bay doors away. Thankfully, they were looking the other direction, not that they would have been able to see him this far away from their lantern light.

Ben tried to ease the bay door up but it wouldn't budge.

"Can you open this door?" he asked the augment.

"No, the power requirements are—"

"Can you unlock it?"

"Yes, place your hand on the door."

Ben obeyed. A tingling sensation flowed through his hand and the lock clicked. He held his breath, waiting to see if anyone had heard it. After a few moments, he lay down and slid the blade of his sword under the door, leveraging it up a few inches, wincing at the noise it made.

The last of the slavers were just entering the ramp leading up to the next level, no doubt escorting their newly captured merchandise to more secure accommodations. He scanned the rest of the room. It was lined with four rows of evenly spaced support pillars holding up the ceiling. In the center was a pile of bones. Ben felt a chill. It looked like the altar in the white church—a place of blood and sacrifice. He looked closer, straining to see more clearly in the dim light cast by fires burning in half a dozen barrels positioned haphazardly around the room. The smoke flowed along the ceiling to a large opening in the far corner— the elevator shaft.

There was a body draped across the altar, blood still dripping from the gash cut across the pour soul's throat. Ben steeled himself. He was going to kill these people, and no matter how much he searched within, he simply couldn't find any reason to feel bad about it.

He pushed the door higher, just enough to roll underneath, letting Homer go first before easing the door back down as silently as he could manage. He raised up into a crouched position, scanning the four open doorways leading to the staircases. Seeing no one, he began moving toward the one open bay door and the guard post just outside it.

The last thirty feet seemed to take forever as he placed each step carefully to avoid making any noise. He reached the edge of the door, listening for his enemy. He could hear their breathing.

"This sucks," one of them said.

"I know," the other said. "Those three aren't going to be nearly as pretty by the time we get our turn."

Ben felt his blood go ice cold. Any moral dilemma that he'd been trying to entertain vanished, leaving only single-minded determination to slaughter these men, to the very last one.

He reached out and took hold of his magic. Calmly, almost casually, he rolled around the corner. Before he moved, he knew where his enemies were, partly from their voices, but partly from something else.

Two steps and the first man saw him. He started to turn but Ben thrust, piercing the side of his neck, the blade pushing through to the other side before Ben yanked it out through the front of his throat. Ben spun around behind his first kill, whipping blood in an arc across the walls.

"What the—?"

The blade landed across the back of the second's man's neck, taking his head in a stroke. Ben picked it up and tossed it into the darkness, then dragged the bodies out of sight as well.

He scanned the big room before entering again, the altar catching his eye. As he approached, he saw a magic circle carved into the floor. Deep, chiseled gouges described it and the arcane symbols within. A lopsided wooden table sat just outside the circle angled toward it. Ben got closer and stopped. A body was chained to the table by the ankles so that the corpse's head was lower than its feet. The man's throat had been cut and the blood had been channeled so that it would flow into the circle. Two fresh sacrifices—one to consecrate the circle, the other to summon whatever it was that had taken Ben's friends.

One corner of the room was occupied by a makeshift stable, the horses inside milling about skittishly. Several wagons equipped with cages were lined up against the wall.

Ben checked the map in his mind and picked the staircase he wanted. The second level consisted of one hallway that described a square. Rooms lined both sides all the way around the level. At the exact center point of the section of hall running parallel to the tunnel but on the opposite side of the facility was a room that provided access to the secure section that Ben suspected was being used to hold captives.

He ascended cautiously, listening for threats, but also reaching out with his magic, trying to use it as a sixth sense. At the top of the stairs, he could hear voices, though they were too far away for him to make out what was being said. He peeked out into the hallway, first one way and then the other. Lanterns hung at intervals providing dim light. He slipped into the passage and crept up to the corner, peeking around and then pulling his head back just as quickly, holding his breath for fear of being seen.

"Not a bad day's work," Beauchamp said. "Shame more slaves can't just walk up and offer themselves to us."

Several men laughed.

"Bring the pretty one to my chambers and tie her to the bed," he said. "I want her to wake up to my smiling face."

"They all look pretty to me," one man said.

Beauchamp chuckled. "The youngest pretty one."

"Right."

"What about the other two?" one of the men asked.

"You'll get your chance," Beauchamp said.

"Should we put the two men in with the others or keep them separate?"

"You mean three men, don't you?" Beauchamp asked.

"No, we only got two men."

"There were three men, three women, and a dog," Beauchamp said. "I don't much care about the dog, unless you want dinner, but the third man shouldn't have escaped … couldn't have escaped, unless…"

"I don't like him very much," Homer said.

"Good, 'cuz he's going to die today," Ben said.

"I must have been so preoccupied with my summoning that I didn't notice we missed one," Beauchamp said.

Boots on stone faded into the distance. Ben stole another look around the corner. The hallway was empty. He tried to balance speed with silence as he moved toward his friends and the slavers standing in his way. When he got closer, he saw that a section of wall ten feet wide was actually a steel grate over a window. The augment told him that it had been the supply counter. The heavy door to the far side of the window was far too sturdy to breach by force and the parts window was too small to crawl through, even if there hadn't been two men inside. Directly across from the counter was an open double door leading to the switchback vehicle ramp.

Ben backed off to the closest door, easing it open and slipping inside. The room looked like it had once been an office, but was now being used for quarters.

"I need you to draw them out," Ben said to Homer. "Once they see you and open the door, run. If things go badly, get to the tunnel and hide in the dark."

"You heard them, right? They want to eat me for dinner."

"I'm not going to let that happen," Ben said, stroking his back.

"You'd better not," Homer said, padding out into the hallway. Ben closed the door behind him.

A bark was followed by some commotion.

"Hey, there's the dog," one said.

"I'll bet Beauchamp will give us first cut if we catch him," another said.

A lock was thrown open and then two sets of footsteps ran by. Ben eased out into the hallway, hurrying after the two men, quietly at first, but then sacrificing stealth for speed.

The trailing man was just beginning to turn around when Ben reached him. He stabbed the man through the kidney. He froze, his back arching, his whole body quivering for a moment before Ben withdrew his blade and let him fall. Hearing the noise, the lead man stopped to look back.

"Whoa," he said, one hand up and open while the other went for his long knife. "Let's talk about this—"

"Sure," Ben said, never breaking stride as he closed. The man's blade came up, slashing at Ben wildly. He met the attack with his sword, taking a hand with his first stroke, then following with a back-handed swing that sliced a three-inch gash across the man's throat.

Homer looked around the corner at the end of the hallway and came trotting back while Ben dragged the dead men into the nearest room. He searched them quickly, taking a few coins and their keys before heading back toward the supply counter and the secure rooms beyond.

"Hey, where did you guys go?" a voice asked from within.

Ben ducked under the counter, coming up and rushing into the room. A burly-looking man was putting Olivia, still unconscious, into a parts bin with wheels. He looked up just in time to see Ben coming at him.

As Ben thrust, the man rolled aside, moving much more quickly than Ben expected given his size.

The man danced a few feet farther away, drawing his sword. "There you are," he said. "I bet I get my pick of the women after I kill you."

There was no fear in his eyes.

Ben squared off, blocking him from the door before advancing. His opponent attacked, a flurry of slashing and hacking, quick and strong. Ben blocked, backing away from the onslaught, knowing that he was running out of room with each step.

He slipped to the side to avoid a powerful downward slash, spinning out of the way and whipping his blade at his enemy in a frantic attack, catching him across the side but only shallowly.

The man smiled, touching the wound and licking the blood off his finger. He advanced toward Ben, sword first. Ben swatted it aside and the man spun, his sword coming around at neck height with frightening speed. Ben ducked and his opponent kicked him in the side of the face, knocking him over, slightly stunned. Out of the corner of his eye he saw the blow coming, a thrust to the torso—a kill shot. He rolled away, the point of his enemy's blade sending chips of cement flying as it hit the floor scant inches from him.

Still on the ground, Ben kicked, catching him in the knee and forcing him to step back, a grimace of pain ghosting across the man's face before he smiled again, raising his sword for another death blow. Ben dropped his blade and quickly drew his pistol, firing twice into the man's chest. The slaver looked down at the blood soaking his shirt, then back at Ben with an expression of surprise.

"No fair," he said, slumping to his knees and toppling forward.

Ben scrambled backward to avoid the falling corpse.

"I bet they heard that," Homer said.

"Yeah," Ben said, gaining his feet and holstering his pistol. He raced outside the room to the vehicle ramp. Sure enough, the sound of men running echoed down the wide tunnel. Ten men, maybe more, came around the corner. Ben sheathed his sword and fished the last grenade out of his pouch. He waited.

"This is going to be loud," he said to Homer. "You might want to get some distance."

"Thanks for the warning," Homer said, running away from the impending explosion.

The men got closer.

Ben pulled the pin and peeked around the corner again.

"There he is," one shouted. They were a hundred feet away and coming fast.

He let go of the spoon, a click indicating that the grenade's fuse was lit. "One ... two ... three," he counted in his mind before tossing the grenade around the corner, ducking back into the hallway and covering his ears.

"What the hell—?"

The world shook.

Dust was carried by a shockwave into the hallway. Ben waited only a second more before he raced into the vehicle ramp, sword drawn. The few men still alive died quickly. While he felt like an executioner, he also felt entirely justified taking these lives.

As he pulled his blade out of the last man's chest, three more came around the corner, Beauchamp in the middle. His black eyes danced with hate and evil intent.

"I'm going to feed you to the darkness," he said, drawing his gravity gun and taking aim with a knowing smile.

Ben advanced toward them.

The gun clicked. Beauchamp frowned, looking at it, checking the weapon and trying to fire again. Click.

"Kill him," he said to his two henchmen.

Beauchamp ran back the way he'd come. Ben closed on the men without hesitation. Their eyes flickered to the carnage behind him, then back to the resolute certainty in his eyes. He could see that they were unaccustomed to people actually fighting back. They spread out. Ben locked eyes with one of them. The other circled. Ben watched him with his peripheral vision aided by tactical projections provided by the augment.

As the circling man moved, Ben abruptly changed direction, focusing on him exclusively, turning sideways to avoid the point of the man's blade as he hacked across the outside of his thigh, cutting deeply. The man toppled to the floor, shrieking in pain.

Ben whipped his sword around at the other one, spraying a streamer of blood at his face. He faltered, flinching as crimson splattered across his eyes. Ben attacked into that brief moment of hesitation, running him through with a single thrust and then holding him there for a moment, looking him in the eye without any hint of remorse before tipping his blade and letting gravity take him to his final resting place. He turned slowly toward the wounded man.

"Wait! You don't have to do this," he said, as Ben advanced toward him, slapping the weakly raised blade aside and stabbing him in the throat without a word. Sounds of gurgling haunted Ben as he headed up the vehicle ramp, blood dripping from the point of his sword.

He approached the door to the top level cautiously. He felt magic before he saw or heard anything. The door opened into a large room with several closed doors and three hallways leading into the rest of the level. Beauchamp was standing in the middle of the room, a hastily drawn circle of blood on the floor around him. One of his own men was kneeling before him, his wrist cut deeply, the man's face pasty white.

"Please, Beauchamp, don't do this," the man said, but Beauchamp wasn't listening. His head was tipped back and he was whispering to the ceiling. Ben stepped into the room just as Beauchamp thrust a blade down beside the man's neck, penetrating deeply into his chest, slicing through his heart and killing him instantly.

He looked at Ben, releasing the sword and letting the man fall forward.

"Too late," he said.

Blackness seeped out of the ground, almost like oil, flooding the area around Beauchamp's feet and then rising up around him. He arched his back and screamed, a blood-chilling wail that was cut short when the black magic began to flow into his mouth, nose, and eyes. Ben watched in fascination that slowly morphed into horror as Beauchamp began to transform.

Once all of the darkness had invaded its host, Beauchamp slumped forward to his knees. Ben knew that he should act, he should attack, but he couldn't snap himself out of the trance that was holding him in thrall.

Beauchamp stood up and began to grow, changing into something that was no longer a man. He began to deform, his right arm growing disproportionately large and becoming a giant bone club. His left hand became a single black claw, long and sharp. His face erupted in boils that quickly burst, releasing sputtering and bubbling puss that dripped down his face. His mouth grew wider and fangs began to protrude from each side.

"I don't like the looks of him," Homer said, peeking around the doorjamb into the room. "You should run."

Beauchamp's clothes tore and his belt snapped as he grew to a height of eight feet and a weight of easily four hundred pounds. When the transformation was complete, he bore little resemblance to the man he'd been moments before.

He tipped his head back and roared, a deafening and terrifying noise, then locked eyes on Ben and charged. His lumbering steps began slowly, but he gained speed quickly. Ben dove out of the way, tuck-rolling and coming to his feet, only narrowly escaping.

Beauchamp crashed into the door frame, howling in fury, swinging his club fist at the wall as if it had bitten him. A section of cement shattered into the room, spraying Ben with stone fragments, pelting him across the face. Warm blood trickled from the fresh wounds. As he picked a shard of stone from his cheek, his eyes landed on the gravity gun, discarded during Beauchamp's transformation.

The beast howled, this time advancing toward him with more control. Ben angled toward the weapon, keeping his sword between him and the thing coming for him. Beauchamp lashed out with his clawed hand. Ben danced backward, just out of range, the black claw whistling by only inches from his face. The clubbed fist came next, a downward attack.

Ben barely scrambled out of the way, the bone club hitting the floor with such force that a spider-web crack radiated from the point of impact. The resultant tremor nearly cost him his balance. He thrust with his sword, driving the blade into Beauchamp's leg to the bone.

The beast ignored the wound, swinging his clawed hand around at Ben. He ducked, abandoning his sword and diving for the gravity gun.

"Activate," he commanded the augment as he slid on his belly to the weapon, yanking it from its holster and rolling onto his back.

"Weapon active. Three charges remain."

He aimed and fired.

Beauchamp was charging toward him when a shimmering wave of barely visible bluish energy hit him in the chest and threw him against the corner where the ceiling met the wall. He hit hard and then fell flat on his face with a thud. Ben scrambled to his feet. Beauchamp came up on his hands and knees, looking at Ben with tortured purpose.

"Shit," Ben said, tossing the gravity gun to his off hand and drawing his pistol. His first shot hit the beast in the shoulder. Beauchamp brought his clubbed hand up to cover his face. The second bullet hit the bone club and ricocheted off.

Beauchamp regained his feet.

"Any suggestions?" Ben asked the augment as he fired his last two rounds into the beast's chest, eliciting a shriek of rage and pain.

"Perhaps the elevator doors are open."

Schematics flashed in his mind, showing him the hall he needed. He ran, fleeing the sound of the beast chasing him. Beauchamp crashed into the corner of the hallway, spinning around and continuing after him. The elevator shaft was at the end of the hall. Hope flooded into Ben, shoving his terror aside when he saw that the doors were open.

The fear returned when he heard the beast gaining on him. He looked back, firing wildly with the gravity gun, hitting his enemy again and sending him sliding back down the hall, his clawed hand striking into the stone floor to stop him long before Ben would have preferred.

He reached the elevator a moment before the sound of Beauchamp's oversized feet began to echo toward him again. The hallway turned the corner at the elevator, running straight for the length of the facility. He rounded the bend and stopped a dozen feet away, waiting with his last shot.

In the back of his mind, he gave thanks that whatever had possessed Beauchamp wasn't nearly as smart as it was terrifying. The beast came into view, struggling to round the corner and crashing into the wall just beside the open elevator door.

Ben fired. Beauchamp flew backward, hitting the doorjamb hard and toppling over into the shaft, his clawed hand catching the floor and arresting his fall. Ben dropped the gravity gun and raced for the last point of purchase that his enemy had, drawing his knife on the way. He slid, feet first, kicking against the claw but it held fast.

Beauchamp howled in fury, his bellowing, demonic voice echoing in every direction as he tried to pull himself back up. Ben slipped his knife under the claw and levered it upward. It came free and Beauchamp fell, wailing in rage until he hit the ground sixty feet below.

Ben lay back on the cold floor and took a deep breath. Homer padded up to him and licked him on the cheek.

"That was really close. You should be more careful."

Ben started laughing. And then stopped when a groan wafted up to him from the bottom of the shaft.

"Seriously?" he said, rolling onto his belly and looking down at his enemy. He could hear movement. He jumped to his feet and snatched a lantern off a hook on the wall. Standing at the edge, one hand on the wall for balance, he peered over and gently tossed the burning lamp onto Beauchamp. It hit true, shattering and spraying fiery oil onto the beast that had once been a man. In the flickering light, Ben could see that he was badly broken from the fall. And now he was on fire.

Ben retrieved the gravity gun and headed back the way he'd come, reloading his pistol as he walked. Back in the vehicle tunnel, he retrieved a sword from the first dead man that he came to and hurried to find his friends.

Olivia was still unconscious when he reached the supply room. He checked to make sure she was alive, wincing at the lurid bruise on her cheek before cautiously opening the door leading to the makeshift cellblock. Six doors lined the hallway, three to a side. He unlocked the first door. It came open quickly and a big hand grabbed him by the coat and dragged him inside. Hound was poised to pummel him with his oversized fist, but he stopped with a grin when he saw Ben, his face marred with blood and grime.

"How many left?" he asked, letting go.

Ben shook his head. "Not many," he said, then left to open the door across the hall. Ellie and Imogen, armed with sharpened pieces of a bedpost, were poised to attack.

When Ellie saw him, her composure broke. She dropped the makeshift weapon and rushed to him, throwing her arms around his neck and sobbing.

"I was so afraid," she said. "They took Olivia."

"She's out cold just down the hall."

Ellie gave him a forced smile and rushed off to tend to her sister.

Imogen put a hand on Ben's face and shared a sad look with him. "He never wanted this for you," she whispered.

"I know, but I'm glad he prepared me for it."

She smiled sadly, turning to John when he came up beside them, putting a hand on her shoulder.

"Are you okay?" he asked urgently.

She nodded, hugging him tightly. Ben smiled at the sight, going to the next door and finding an empty room. The next held four men, all afraid but angry.

"I won't hurt you," Ben said.

"What do you want?" the biggest of the four said.

"Only to set you free."

"My wife," another of the men said.

Ben nodded, turning to the last door and opening it. Six women were huddled in the corner. All of them were bruised and terrified. Ben stepped back as the man concerned for his wife rushed in. He stopped in his tracks when the women wailed in fear at his approach. He knelt, tears streaming down his face.

"It's me," he said, his voice breaking. "You're safe now."

One of the women seemed to recognize him. She struggled to free herself from the others who tried to hold her back, as if fearing to lose another of their own. She raced into her husband's arms and wept.

Ben swallowed the lump in his throat and took a deep breath.

"Imogen, John, would you help these people, please." He didn't wait for an answer, heading toward the supply cage. "I could use a hand," he said to Hound in passing.

Olivia was awake but still a bit groggy from the blow she'd taken across the face. Ellie was tending to her wounds.

"Ah, here she is," Hound said, taking Bertha from a bin full of weapons in one corner and checking her chamber. He fished out his weapons belt and war axe before nodding to Ben.

"Stay here and be vigilant," Ben said. "I'm not sure I got them all."

"Where are you going?" Ellie asked.

"To kill the rest," Ben said.

Hound followed him into the vehicle tunnel.

"Holy shit," he said, surveying the tangle of mutilated corpses scattered across the wide hallway. "I guess that explains the explosion."

He trotted to catch up with Ben. When they reached the lowest level, Ben motioned for caution as he eased up to the opening. He shook his head when he saw Beauchamp, hideously deformed, his body broken and scorched. The beast was crawling toward the magic circle in the center of the room, leaving a trail of soot and black blood behind him as he reached out with his clawed hand, slamming it into the floor and dragging himself forward by a few feet.

"What the hell is that?" Hound said.

"That's the guy who cast the spell that captured you," Ben said, walking purposefully toward the creature. He circled so that he could approach at an angle that gave him the best shot at the beast's head, lunging the moment he had an opening, stabbing him through the ear, driving the blade so forcefully that it only stopped when it hit the cement floor. Beauchamp went still.

Ben felt it a moment before the air temperature fell—an unnatural presence, something not of this world. Shadow exploded out of Beauchamp's corpse. A wave of cold evil washed over them, bringing them to their knees. A chill soaked into Ben, leaving him shivering and sweating at the same time. He retched, his stomach heaving violently as if his body was trying to expel some poison or parasite.

He flopped over onto his side, sweat beading on his forehead and underneath his shirt as violent trembling overtook him. Shadow coalesced into indistinct form, swirling overhead for only a moment before flowing like water into the blood-soaked bone altar, a forlorn wail trailing after it.

Ben focused on his breathing to quell the pounding in his chest. After a few moments, he lurched onto his hands and knees, then struggled to his feet, every fiber of his being feeling violated and raw.

"What the hell was that?" Hound croaked, struggling to regain his feet as well.

"Evil," Ben managed weakly.

Hound snorted, seeming to think better of standing up as he eased himself back to the floor, shaking his head.

"That was almost worse than the stalker," he said, sharing a haunted look with Ben.

He nodded, fumbling with his canteen, taking a drink and spitting it out before handing it to Hound.

"Just so we're clear, he doesn't look much like a man to me," Hound said, gesturing to what remained of Beauchamp.

"He summoned something that made him into this," Ben said, wrenching his sword from Beauchamp's leg.

"And you killed him … and all those other guys … by yourself."

"Something like that," Ben said.

"I helped," Homer said.

Ben sat back down and scratched his dog's ears. "I know."

"We should go through this place room by room," Ben said.

"Yeah, but in a minute."

They spent the next several minutes sitting in the flickering light, silently wrestling with the demon that had just defiled them. Slowly, the chill began to fade. Ben got to his feet again. Hound nodded resignedly.

"I've seen some darkness in my life," Hound said while they walked back up the vehicle ramp to the second floor, "but that was … hell, I don't know what that was."

"I'm not sure I want to know," Ben said.

They reached the second floor and looked in on everyone else. John was standing by the door, bow in hand, arrow nocked.

"We felt something … wrong," he said.

"Yeah," Ben said, nodding agreement. "It's gone now. How is everyone?"

"Olivia is resting. Imogen and Ellie are tending to the prisoners' wounds as best they can."

"Good, we're going to have a look around," Ben said.

John nodded.

Ben and Hound walked around the entire second floor, opening doors as they went. Most of the rooms were makeshift quarters but a few were occupied only by dilapidated office furniture decaying under the weight of time.

"I think you got 'em all," Hound said as they came full circle.

"Probably," Ben said, "but I still want to make sure."

They nodded to John in passing as they took the vehicle ramp up to the third level. Hound stopped just inside the entrance, frowning at the bloody circle and the corpse lying in the middle of it.

"He sacrificed his own man?"

Ben nodded. "I stood right here and watched. Not sure what I was thinking."

"It's not every day you see a man turn into a monster," Hound said. "How did you get him anyway?"

"He dropped his gun when he changed," Ben said, handing the tech weapon to Hound.

"Never seen one like this before. What's it do?"

"It changes the direction of gravity for a second or so—just long enough to make your target fall sideways."

"Huh, does it have any juice left?"

"Nope. I used the last three shots on Beauchamp."

Hound handed it back. "Who knows, maybe we'll find some power for it in Alturas or Shasta."

"I hope so," Ben said with a grin. "It's quite the gun."

"Sounds like it."

They swept the top floor. It was empty of enemy but they did find food, water, and an armory with assorted bladed weapons and a number of crossbows.

"We should probably check the surface," Ben said. "I don't know if the entrance guards are still there or not."

"Fair enough," Hound said, taking one of the crossbows and examining it, nodding approvingly. "You know how to use one of these?"

Ben shrugged. "I've never used one before, but they seem pretty straightforward."

Hound spent a minute going over the weapon, showing Ben how to cock and load it. "Give it a shot, down the hall," he said.

Ben raised the weapon. It felt a bit heavy on the front end, but it was easy enough to aim. He squeezed the trigger and the bolt leapt free.

"Wow, that's got a lot of power."

"Yep, they tend to shoot harder than a bow, and more accurately for most people, but they're a lot slower to reload."

Ben cocked the weapon again and placed another bolt in the firing groove.

"No sense wasting bullets on these guys," he said, heading for the vehicle ramp. It switched back and forth every three or four hundred feet until they reached the last leg and saw sunlight for the first time in days. A table with a few chairs was beside the surface entrance, but no guards.

They moved closer, slowing when they heard voices.

"I'm telling you, that felt like an explosion. We should go check it out."

"You can go if you want," another man said. "Just remember what happened to Hank when he left his post."

"Shit … maybe you're right."

Ben held up two fingers. Hound nodded. They stopped at the edge of the wall. Two giant steel doors had been ripped from their hinges, mangled beyond salvage by some power that Ben never wanted to encounter.

He focused on the moment, clearing his mind and letting the magic guide his senses. It was so subtle, so delicate that he wasn't sure if he was imagining the feeling of knowing that it gave him—and yet he knew, without doubt, that there were three men above. From the voices, he would have guessed two, but now he knew better. He held up three fingers and pointed to the ceiling. Hound nodded.

They slipped around the giant doorframe, staying close to the unfinished concrete wall to avoid being seen, stepping carefully to avoid being heard. A well-worn path led up a slope beside the bunker entrance. They reached a point where the next step would bring them into view of the men above. Ben and Hound shared a look. The big man smiled, picking up a rock and tossing it over the guards' heads. It hit on the other side of the bunker.

"What was that?"

Ben rushed up several more steps, taking aim. The closest guard heard his steps, but not quickly enough. Ben fired. The bolt seemed to magically appear in the man's chest, buried to the feathers. Ben tossed the crossbow aside, rushing up the slope toward the top of the bunker.

Hound killed the next man with a bolt through the heart. Ben drew his sword as the last slaver standing saw him. Hound grunted from somewhere behind Ben and his war axe went flipping past, hitting the last guard in the chest and killing him before he could slump to his knees.

Ben looked back.

"What? I've got some catching up to do," Hound said, going to retrieve his axe.

Ben sheathed his sword and they searched the men, taking a few coins, but finding little else of value save their weapons, none of which were better than what they already had. They collected them anyway and laid them out on the table below, several crossbows and a number of blades of various descriptions.

"Maybe the prisoners can use them," Ben said.

They returned to the second level of the node. John was still standing guard.

"We're all clear," Hound said.

John nodded without leaving his post.

Ben went to the room occupied by the former prisoners. A few of them jumped when the door opened. Ben winced, raising his hands. "It's just me," he said. "All of the slavers are dead."

"Good!" one woman said. Several others nodded, pain and loss etched into their faces.

"What happens to us now?" one of the men asked, stepping forward.

Ben shrugged. "That's up to you. There are horses and a few wagons in the level below and plenty of food, water, and weapons upstairs. Take what you need to get home."

"Just like that? You don't expect anything from us in payment?"

"Payment? For what?" Ben asked, his brow furrowed.

"Freeing us."

Ben shook his head sadly. "You owe me nothing."

"We owe you everything," a woman said. "There must be something we can do to repay you."

"There isn't," Ben said. "The truth is, I came here to free my friends. And if they hadn't been taken, I would have just walked right on by. I'm really not the hero you want me to be."

"Whatever your reasons, what you did here today means that I won't be raped tonight," she said, fresh tears spilling from her eyes.

Ben nodded mutely, swallowing a lump in his throat.

Chapter 22

While they walked through the dark, Ben wrestled with the events of the past few days. He'd killed so many people. No matter how many times he told himself that they had it coming, he still felt guilty. He'd taken something that he could never return. It was so final. As he pondered his own morality, he thought back to his grandfather's efforts to spare him from killing and came to understand Cyril's reasons with much better clarity.

And yet, every time he tried to imagine an alternative course of action, nothing else seemed adequate to the situation. The men he'd killed were slavers and rapists. They'd taken his friends and family.

"Stop that," Homer said.

"What?"

"Beating yourself up for something that had to be done. Evil people make their choices and condemn themselves in the process. You were just the instrument of their destruction, not the cause."

The tunnel was long and straight. Each footstep echoed softly into the dark. They'd been on the move for the better part of the day. After they'd helped the slavers' victims load a couple of wagons and had sent them on their way, Ben had decided that traveling underground was less risky than returning to the surface where Hoondragon's stalker bird might see them. The fact that the tunnel led directly to Alturas made the decision easy.

They traveled silently. On the few occasions when someone spoke, they did so in hushed tones as if a loud noise would somehow offend the darkness. Ben's mind eventually turned to magic—specifically to the fact that his imaginary circle, only visible to him and then only through the tech in his head, had actually protected him from Beauchamp's black magic.

It didn't make sense—but then it was magic, so it wasn't really supposed to make sense. The more he turned the question over in his mind, the more certain he became that there was something important to be learned from the experience, perhaps even something vital. And yet, he couldn't quite put his finger on it. Every time he got close, it seemed to wriggle away.

He wished that he could talk to his grandfather about it, banishing that thought as quickly as it and the attendant pang of grief had come to him.

"How far to the next node?" he asked the augment.

"At this pace, another day and a half."

"Anybody else tired?" he asked out loud.

"Exhausted," Imogen said. "But I wasn't going to be the first to say it."

"I guess here's as good a place as any," Hound said.

They made camp.

Ben woke in the dark, the feeling of being watched coming over him the moment he opened his eyes. He stretched out with his mind, searching for the enemy with his magic and will. He found what he expected. The shadow had returned. With a thought, he projected his circle around himself in his mind and then expanded it to surround everyone else as well. He didn't know what good it would do, but it couldn't hurt.

The Warlock's incorporeal servant didn't seem interested in attack as much as surveillance, a fact that offered little in the way of consolation. While the tunnels had provided an avenue of escape from Hoondragon, the Warlock was far more cunning and patient. In some ways that made him a more dangerous adversary.

Someone sat up, yawning. Light erupted in the blackness as Hound turned on his flashlight. Ben covered his eyes. Hound groaned.

"That's really bright," Homer said, putting his paws over his face.

"It is morning, isn't it?" Hound asked.

"Pretty close," Ben said, after consulting the augment. "Let me see that for a second."

Hound handed the flashlight over. Ben directed it at the shadow and it fled into the tunnel.

"Still following us, huh?"

Ben nodded. "At least it hasn't tried to suffocate me again."

"I guess there's that," Rufus said, beginning to pack up his bedroll.

The tunnel seemed to go on forever, dull grey concrete walls extending to a rounded arch twenty feet overhead. The oppressive silence was matched only by the total absence of light, save what they had brought with them.

Ben turned his thoughts to Alturas and the Splinter Brigade. He quizzed the augment for a while, but got exactly what he'd expected—nothing of interest. Eventually his mind wandered back to magic.

Cyril had told him to focus on manifestation. He'd even taught him how to attract wealth into his life in the form of his lucky gold coin, and it had worked better than he ever would have expected. He was finding coins on a regular basis, always offering gratitude for his good fortune when he did.

He'd also learned how to fight with his magic, allowing it to guide his hand and propel his blade with greater force and speed. The connection that he felt with Ellie in a fight was an even greater extension of that power—overlapping flow, Dom had called it.

New guilt washed over him.

He'd promised Dom that he wouldn't endanger his daughters, and yet here they were, stubborn and willful—and worse, he was grateful for their presence. For all of Hound's prowess in a fight, if Ben had to choose one person to step onto the battlefield with, it would be Ellie.

When he'd first come into the presence of the egg, he'd believed that magic would only work slowly and through the normal order of the world. After all, the coins that he manifested didn't just appear in his pocket, he found them one by one. If he didn't know better, he could have easily convinced himself that it was just dumb luck.

But now, after his experience with his imaginary magic circle, he was beginning to wonder if he could affect the world more directly. The augment's ability to project images into his mind that appeared as real as anything else made him wonder if he could use those images to guide his manifestations, to give them substance and form much more quickly than he'd previously thought possible.

Both Hound and John were carrying their flashlights, bright beams of white cutting through the blackness. Ben focused on Hound's light, using the augment to nullify its beam in his mind. It winked out of existence, vanishing from his sight as if it had been switched off. With the imaginary reality he'd created firmly in mind, he directed his thoughts to the egg, touching its living magic and willing it to make the world conform to his view of it.

"Hey," Hound said, tapping his flashlight against his palm, "this thing's a piece of crap."

Ben stopped in his tracks, releasing the augment's illusion in his mind and finding that reality had indeed aligned itself with his vision of it. A tingle raced up his spine, dread and exhilaration vying for preeminence.

"Try it now," he said.

Hound frowned at him, switching his light off and on, its bright beam dispelling the darkness once again.

"Huh, I wonder what happened?"

"I think I turned it off," Ben said.

"Seriously?" Ellie asked.

Ben shrugged. "Pretty sure."

"That might be useful," Hound said.

Ben nodded, his mind racing through all of the possibilities. Cyril had told him that magic could disrupt technology—with more advanced tech being more vulnerable, but he'd never shown him how to do it.

When he and his friends stopped several hours later, Ben was still thinking about his newfound capability, trying to imagine what else might be possible.

Before he went to sleep he instructed the augment to maintain the magic circle around the entire camp for the duration of the night, wondering as he gave the command if such a thing was even possible while he slept.

A few hours after they set out the following day, John stopped, switching his light off and motioning for Hound to do the same. The world plunged into blackness, and then, faintly at first, light began to become visible in the distance.

"More slavers?" Imogen asked.

"Could be," John said.

"I say we hit them first this time," Hound said.

"I'd prefer to avoid a fight if we can," Ben said.

"How'd that work out last time?"

"I take your point," Ben said, "but we don't know what we're up against, so let's not start shooting unless we have to."

"If you say so. But I don't like it."

"I know how you feel," Ben said. "Everybody, be ready."

They walked on, slowing as they got closer to the light, which wasn't the flickering of an oil lamp or a fire. Instead it was steady and white, almost like the flashlights, except it was a single orb hanging from the ceiling. When they got within a few hundred feet, a voice called out.

"Hello!"

Ben and Hound shared a look.

"Hello," Ben called back.

Three men came into view and began to approach. All were armed, but their weapons remained holstered, sheathed and slung.

Ben started forward cautiously, watching the strangers and feeling for magic. He was relieved when he felt nothing save the egg and Imogen's amulet. Even the shadow was beyond his senses.

The men stopped a dozen feet from them, the two on either side carrying oil lamps.

"I'm Captain Horowitz of Adara Cartage Security," the man in the middle said. "We don't get many travelers through here—and you don't look like you're part of Beauchamp's crew."

"We're scouting the tunnel for our boss," Ben said.

Captain Horowitz nodded, smiling humorlessly. "You're lying," he said.

Hound tensed. Ben looked at him.

"What makes you say that?" Ben asked after Hound had nodded agreement with his unspoken command to hold.

"I used to be an interrogator," Horowitz said. "After a while, you get a feel for when people are telling you the truth—or not. Any you're not, so let's try this again. I'll go first. We're doing a survey of the tunnel system north of Alturas for Adara Cartage in the hopes that they can use this network to move freight. Your turn."

"We're headed for Alturas," Ben said.

"All right. How did you get into the tunnels?"

"We entered two nodes up," Ben said.

"Now that is interesting," Horowitz said. "We took a look at that node and couldn't open the door. How did you manage to get inside?"

Ben shrugged. "The door on the surface opened for us."

"Just like that?"

"Just like that," Hound said with a current of menace in his voice.

Horowitz almost laughed. "Fair enough. How'd you manage to get past Beauchamp and his band of thugs?"

Ben took a deep breath and let it out. "They took my friends so I killed them," he said.

Horowitz's eyes went wide and he cocked his head. "You're telling the truth, aren't you?"

"I am."

Both of his men shared a worried look.

"Well, I can't say I'll miss 'em," Horowitz said. "Never much liked the idea of slavery myself."

"Just imagine how their slaves felt," Hound said.

Horowitz nodded. "Orders. Adara Cartage doesn't use slaves, but the rail does. We have very clear instructions to let them pass."

"And what do your orders say about us?" Ben asked.

"Question and assess."

"And?"

"I don't see any reason to detain you. Come with me. I'll show you the tunnel you want."

Horowitz turned and walked back toward the light.

"Be ready for anything," Ben whispered.

He accessed the augment's files about this node and found it to be even larger than the slavers'—several levels with multiple access points on the surface not far from the town of Lakeview.

They followed warily, but Horowitz was true to his word. He led them past an intersection with another tunnel running perpendicular to the one they'd been traveling through. Lights hung from the ceiling over each tunnel entrance. Ben noted a staircase and a closed bay door in one of the other tunnels.

"I didn't think the dragon liked electricity," Ben said, gesturing to the light bulb hanging from the ceiling.

"He doesn't, but what he doesn't know won't hurt us," Horowitz said. "This tunnel leads to Alturas—about three days on foot. You might run into a traveler or two. Be nice and they'll be nice too."

"Thank you, Captain," Ben said.

"Safe travels," Horowitz said, turning toward the staircase, leaving his two men to return to the guard post watching over the intersection.

Ben and the others hurried down the tunnel, gaining distance from the Adara checkpoint out of fear that they were about as trustworthy as Beauchamp had been. With each step, the illumination from the light bulbs hanging over the intersection grew dimmer.

"I see more light," John said, bringing his monocular up to his eye. "Looks like another electric light."

They continued, approaching cautiously. Hanging from the ceiling was another bulb, glowing steady and bright. It was only then that Ben noticed the wire running down the wall of the tunnel. He accessed the augment's schematics and found that the wire was a new addition. All of the original electrical work ran through conduits within the ceiling.

"Nice to see someone else ignoring the wyrm's edicts," Hound said.

They continued on, finding lights hanging at half-mile intervals for the entire day. Ben wondered about the power source but the augment was unable to determine its origin. If House Adara was willing to use electricity in defiance of the dragon, perhaps they weren't as bad as he'd originally thought—except for the part about using slaves to build the railroad.

Chapter 23

Midmorning of the following day, Homer said, "I smell someone."

"Hold up," Ben said quietly.

Everyone stopped, looking to him for an explanation. The next electric light bulb in the tunnel was easily half a mile off. Ben consulted the augment and found a surface access point just up ahead.

"We have company," he said.

"How do you know that?" Olivia asked.

"It's complicated. Just be ready," he said, checking his pistol and sword before continuing on.

As they neared the light, a young woman stepped out into view, her hands raised and open.

"Hello," she said.

Hound spun Bertha up into his hands.

"Easy," Ben said, stepping forward. "Hello … I'm Ben."

"My name is Kayla Adara. I've come to warn you. You're in terrible danger."

Ben stretched out with his magic, feeling for threats but finding nothing save the silence.

"Let me guess," Hound said, "you're here to save us."

"Something like that," she said. "There isn't much time. Come with me."

"You're going to have to be more specific about the threat," Ben said, making no move to follow her when she turned toward the door in the tunnel wall.

She looked toward Alturas, then back at Ben.

"The survey crew called ahead and reported your presence," she said.

"Wait … called ahead?" Ben asked.

She pointed to the wire running along the wall. "It doubles as a communication line. I don't understand the tech, but it works. Short story, word got out about you."

"I hear horses," Homer said. "And they're coming fast."

"Shit," Ben muttered. He looked at Kayla and asked, "Why would you help us?"

"You came in through a locked tech node," she said. "I'm hoping you can help me open a door." She stopped, raising a hand for silence and cocking her head. "You hear that?"

"Horses," John said.

"This scary, blond Dragon Guard woman showed up a few days ago looking for you," Kayla said. "I'm pretty sure she'll be at the head of that platoon. Then two days later, an equally scary-looking guy with a half-melted face arrived and started discreetly asking about you too. Now, I'm willing to help you, but only if we go right now."

"You double-cross us and they'll have to clean you up with a mop," Hound said.

"Right back at ya," she said, vanishing into the doorway.

Ben started to follow her, but Hound stopped him with a hand on his arm, going through the door first. Once everyone was inside, the young woman pulled the door closed and placed a device on it, then turned a dial and waited for several seconds. After a muffled click, she turned the device off and stowed it in her pack.

"This way," she said, brushing past them.

"Which other way is there?" Hound muttered, following a few steps behind her, Bertha at the ready.

The passage ended in a staircase that switched back and forth, again and again until Ben's legs burned. Finally, it ended in a room, half caved in on the far side. A man was waiting by the light of a dimly lit oil lamp.

Hound brought Bertha up.

Kayla stepped in front of the barrel, both hands raised. "He's with me. His name is Derek."

He came to his feet, eyeing all of them suspiciously. "I hope you know what you're doing, Kayla," he said.

Ben put a hand on Hound's shotgun—he eased it down, albeit reluctantly.

"Maybe now would be a good time to answer a few questions," Ben said.

As if in response, a muffled thud echoed up the staircase.

"Well, shit," Derek said. "I really didn't want to lose this access point."

He went to a pile of what looked like old crates and shoved one aside, wheeling a cart out stacked with four wooden casks.

"What's that?" Imogen asked, frowning deeply.

"This is a bomb," Derek said, maneuvering the cart onto the landing at the top of the staircase, and then lighting the long fuse with his lamp.

"Time to go," Kayla said, heading for the broken end of the room.

A section of the wall was cracked wide open, providing access to a dirt tunnel that was supported by a number of irregularly spaced wooden supports. Forty feet later, the tunnel opened into another room through a spot in the wall that had been smashed in with a sledge hammer, which was still leaning against the wall. Through a door and up another flight of stairs, they were on the surface, bright sunlight blinding them all.

"You'll want to keep your tech hidden," Kayla said. "The army isn't too far from here. I can talk us through any patrol or checkpoint so long as they don't see anything out of the ordinary."

Hound and John stowed their flashlights.

"Army?" Hound asked, scanning the broken-down and burned-out buildings in the immediate area.

"The Dragon Guard are gearing up for a push north into Lakeview," Derek said.

An explosion interrupted him, shaking the ground momentarily, a gust of dusty air blowing out of the ruins they had just exited.

"We have to leave, now," Kayla said, leading them around the shell of another ruined building to a wagon with a team of four horses, all a bit skittish. "Load up, I'll answer your questions once we're clear of the area."

The wagon was covered with canvas. John sat at the back with the tarp pulled aside to keep watch. After half an hour of hard travel, the horses slowed and the ride evened out. Kayla pulled the front of the tarp aside and climbed over the seat into the back of the wagon.

"We should reach my safe house on the outskirts of Alturas well after dark, provided we don't run into any trouble along the way."

"What kind of trouble are you expecting?" Ben asked.

She shrugged. "Dragon Guard, bandits, railroad agents … it's hard to say. We're taking a back route, but that's no guarantee we won't run into someone."

"Sounds like we have time for you to answer some questions," Hound said.

"Fair enough," Kayla said.

"I thought the Adara family was allied with the dragon," Ben said.

"We are, mostly anyway. It's a big family with a lot of business interests, so we have to stay in the dragon's good graces or get wiped out. Most of the family elders are closer to the wyrm and his priests than some of us would like … but, well, like the saying goes, keep your enemies closer."

"So the wyrm's your enemy, then?" Imogen asked.

"He's humanity's enemy," Kayla said. "Believe me when I tell you, whatever you know about the dragon is only half the story.

"My family got in bed with him a long time ago, and we've survived because of it. Some of my relatives like the power he offers enough to do some truly unforgivable things. Others, like myself, would rather not hurt people."

"Good to know," Ben said. "You mentioned some people asking about us. What can you tell me about them."

"The woman, she said her name was Dominus Nash, arrived a few nights ago and went straight to the Dragon Guard headquarters with a wanted poster. After that, she started making the rounds to all of the inns and taverns in town. Didn't take long before I got wind of her and had a look for myself. Needless to say, I didn't like what I saw, but I didn't think much of it at the time. Just another one of the dragon's minions on the hunt.

"Two days later, I got word that someone else was poking around town, staying mostly to the shadows, but asking about the same group of people—that would be you. Naturally, that piqued my curiosity, so I put out feelers for any more information about you.

"It wasn't long before one of my people in the constable's office contacted me with a story about you coming to town through the tunnels—tunnels that we've worked pretty hard to keep secret, mind you. And that you'd entered the network through a tech node that we've never been able to access.

"I left within the hour because I knew you wouldn't stand a chance underground with everyone coming for you."

"I appreciate that," Ben said, "but I would like to know more about why you're helping us."

"Like I said, I want you to help me get through a door. Alturas is built on top of an old underground military base. We've managed to search most of it, but there's at least one level that's still sealed … and I want in."

"What do you expect to find?" Ben asked, his mind racing.

She shrugged. "Hard to say. Tech, intel … maybe a working computer. Any of the above would be incredibly valuable."

"I didn't think the dragon permitted that sort of thing," Imogen said.

"He doesn't, but he can't see tech if we keep it underground."

"Do you plan on selling it?" Olivia asked.

"No … not a chance," Kayla said. "Let's just say some of the people that I work with want to preserve the discoveries of the past in the hope that they can be put to use in the future."

"Does this future you're talking about involve the dragon?" Ellie asked.

"I hope not," Kayla said, "but that's probably a long way off. Regardless, humanity accomplished a lot before Dragonfall, it would be a travesty to let all of that knowledge and discovery vanish from the world."

"What happens if the wyrm figures out what you're up to?" Ben asked.

"Nothing good," she said.

"So you're risking your life to build a museum that nobody is going to see for the next several centuries," Hound said. "You might have to do better than that if you expect us to believe you."

"I don't know what to tell you," she said with a helpless shrug, "I've already risked a lot to help you."

"You're making my point," Hound said. "I find it hard to believe that you'd put your life on the line for a group of complete strangers all to save some relics from the past. Makes more sense that you're trying to collect the bounty on us."

She laughed. "You think I'm in this for the money? My family is richer than you can imagine. I've always had all the money I ever wanted or needed. I know most people worry about it, work for it, steal for it, even kill for it, but that's not me."

She fished a small leather bag out of her pack and dumped twenty gold coins onto the floor of the wagon bed, a small fortune by any standard. Ben might have been impressed before he'd come into possession of the egg.

"I have a box full of gold at home," she said. "And if I wanted more, I'd just go to the bank and sign for it, no questions asked … within reason, anyway. The wanted poster I saw only offered a thousand drakes each, and then only for the four of you. These two aren't even wanted." She gestured to Ellie and Olivia. "This pouch of gold is worth twice as much as four thousand drakes, so no, I'm not here for the money."

"All right, but preserving history seems a bit thin," Ben said. "Are you sure there isn't some other reason you want through that door?"

"Look, depending on what's inside, I may or may not have a use in mind. I haven't asked you why so many people are looking for you, so how about you let me keep my reasons to myself."

"I guess that's fair for now," Ben said.

"So … how'd you do it?" she asked, leaning forward.

"Do what?"

"Get inside that node?"

"I doubt you'd believe me if I told you," he said. "Besides, if I did tell you, you might just leave us on the side of the road."

She smiled.

"You're getting good at that," Homer said.

"What?"

"Misleading people."

"Yeah … Dom was right about deception, but it still makes me feel like I need a bath every time I do it."

"Good," Homer said.

"The guy looking for us," Ben said, "the one with the melted face, was he alone?"

"No, he was with a man about your age, curly black hair … and cute," she said.

Ben and Imogen shared a look.

"What?" Kayla asked. "Is he someone you know?"

"Something like that," Ben said.

"Checkpoint," Derek said from the driver's seat.

"Be quiet," Kayla said, scrambling back to the front of the wagon and closing the tarp.

"Hold up."

The wagon slowed to a stop.

"What's your cargo and destination?"

"Adara Security," Kayla said. "My cargo is classified, as is my destination."

Ben and Hound shared a look. Two men outside conferred in hushed tones.

"I'm sorry, but we have our orders," one of the men said. "All transports are to be searched."

"Your orders don't apply to me. Take a look at my credentials."

More hushed tones.

"My apologies, Miss Adara. I didn't recognize you."

The wagon began to move again. Ben held his breath, expecting the worst.

"Stop that," Homer said.

"What?"

"Expecting bad things to happen."

Ben frowned at his dog, confusion creasing his brow.

"Manifestation works both ways," Homer said, curling back up on the floor of the wagon and closing his eyes.

Ben mulled over his dog's advice, wondering anew about Homer's origins. A creeping sense of dread came over him. He hadn't considered the possibility that he could attract ruin into his life as easily as he attracted gold. The thought was terrifying. As Kayla climbed into the back of the wagon again, he set his new source of worry aside for more consideration at a later time.

"Your family must have some real pull," Hound said.

"With the rank and file, we do. With the higher ups ... well, let's just say they don't like being told what to do."

"Who does?" Olivia said.

Kayla smiled.

"So you were about to tell me why so many people are looking for you," she said, offhandedly.

Ben cocked his head, offering only a sidelong glance.

"My husband sold my baby to the Priest," Imogen said.

"Holy shit," Kayla said. "I'm so sorry."

"We killed some Dragon Guard trying to get him back, so now they're after us," Imogen said, looking down.

Silence fell on the wagon. Kayla nodded as if to herself.

"Maybe that's enough talk for now," she whispered, returning to the driver's bench beside Derek.

Ben leaned back and closed his eyes, letting the gentle swaying of the wagon lull him to sleep. He woke to a scream, his blade coming free before he even knew what had happened.

Kayla tore the tarp open.

"What happened?"

"Nightmare," Imogen managed, still trembling.

Ben looked at her questioningly. She nodded tightly.

"How much longer?" Ben asked.

"Another few hours," Kayla said.

"At least," Derek added without looking back.

Ben willed his circle into existence around the wagon, still not entirely certain if it made any difference, especially since he couldn't see it through the canvas.

"Is there something I should know?" Kayla asked.

Ben hesitated, considering his options.

"The people looking for us in Alturas aren't the only ones hunting us."

"What? More Dragon Guard?" Kayla asked.

"A bounty hunter," Ben said.

"How close was he?"

"Pretty close," Ben said, involuntarily rubbing his stomach where Hoondragon had run him through, "until we managed to get underground, anyway. He couldn't follow us, so I'd hoped we'd lost him. But he won't quit, not for anything."

Kayla nodded, scanning their faces.

"Look, I know there's more. You seem like good people, so I hope you aren't going to bring too much shit down on me for saving your lives back there."

"Me too," Ben said.

"That bad, huh?"

"Let's just say, the less you know the safer you'll be."

She laughed mirthlessly.

"You want to know why the bank is so hell-bent on building a railroad? It's not what you might think. Adara Cartage already moves most of the freight west of the Mountaintop."

"Wait, the Mountaintop?" Hound asked.

"Yeah, it used to be called Denver," Kayla said. "Now we just call it the Mountaintop—dragon headquarters, the seat of power, the priests' conclave. Everybody who wants to be somebody fights like hell to get there."

"And yet, here you are," Ellie said.

"Yes, I am, but then I've never wanted power, at least not the way those people, and I use that term loosely, want power. They want to dominate others, enslave them, rule over them, hold innocent lives in their hands. They get off on it. Anyway, as I was saying, the bank doesn't care about the freight—they care about the information. You see, Adara Cartage is out here, everywhere. We talk to people all over the place in the normal course of doing business.

"My grandfather is no fool. He figured out in about five seconds that the information we can gather is far more valuable than all the freight in the world. The bank hates it that we always know more about what's going on than they do, so they decided to build a railroad to develop their own information network."

"That's a long-winded way of calling bullshit. In my experience, there's no such thing as too much information."

Ben smiled thinly, nodding to himself. "My grandfather would have liked you. But he would also have told you that you're wrong. There are some secrets that'll get you killed. You've helped us, and you didn't have to. I'm grateful for that. If I can get you through the door you're trying to open, I will, but there are some things that I simply will not tell you."

She regarded him for several moments before nodding slowly. "I guess everybody has their secrets," she said. "I just hope yours don't get me killed." She dropped the tarp before Ben could respond.

He waited a moment before he leaned in toward Imogen.

"What happened?" he whispered.

"I fell asleep and he was there, asking where we were going."

Ben swallowed hard, knowing the answer before he asked the question. "What did you tell him?"

"Nothing, but I couldn't help seeing Mount Shasta … just for a second. Then he roared and I woke up."

Ben closed his eyes, his mind racing. Threats were coming from so many different directions, from so many different enemies.

"I'm sorry," Imogen whispered through new tears.

He sighed. "It's all right. We'll figure it out."

"But how? He knows where we're going."

"Yeah … maybe we can use that to our advantage."

"How?"

"I'm not sure yet," Ben said. "I wish—" He stopped and took a breath.

"Me too," Imogen said. "I miss him every day."

Ben nodded. "Get some rest, but try not to fall asleep."

She nodded tightly.

Ben closed his eyes again.

Ellie poked him on the shoulder.

"Mind filling us in?"

"Later," he said, motioning toward the front of the wagon.

He lay back, the daylight filtering through the thick canvas beginning to fade. He needed someone to talk to about magic … and tech for that matter. He needed his grandfather.

"Pull up all of the footage you have," he told the augment. "Play it all in sequence."

For a while he simply retreated into the tech-enhanced memories of his grandfather. At first, he took comfort in his presence, his steady, calm wisdom and his unconditional love. Once he'd played through every record the augment had of every moment he'd spent with Cyril since he'd woken up in the secret bunker, he thought back to lessons from his childhood, looking for insight, advice, guidance … anything that might help him understand how to use his magic better.

As he reflected on all of the lessons he'd learned over the years, he started to notice a common theme. Cyril had always insisted that Ben learn to control his emotions, to master his inner fire.

As a teenager, Ben's skills in combat had become formidable, far surpassing anything that Frank could bring to a fight. Cyril had always demanded that Ben refrain from unleashing his wrath on his brother, and yet, he'd also allowed Frank sufficient leeway to misbehave, often at Ben's expense. The seeming unfairness of it had chafed at him, but at the same time he'd enjoyed a closeness with his grandfather that Frank had never allowed to develop. In time, he came to pity Frank's self-imposed isolation.

Now, looking back with fresh eyes, he wondered if Cyril had been preparing him to wield magic in yet one more way … all without ever revealing his true purpose. The idea that he could manifest both positive and negative outcomes with a focused thought was both terrifying and perfectly logical.

And it required a whole new level of self-control.

The battlefield within, a common thread that ran through so many of Cyril's lessons, had just taken on a new, far more important meaning. No wonder Cyril had been so cautionary about magic … it could lay a man low as easily as it could lift him up.

He'd always been captivated by stories of magic from history. Looking at them with fresh eyes he realized that every single practitioner of the unexplainable always possessed the same quality of control, emotional evenness and a measured rational demeanor. To be sure, many of them used emotion to fuel their magic, but none allowed their emotions to rule them—at least, not the ones who survived.

Now he understood why—his own thoughts might transform into yet one more enemy, one that he could never escape. Only mastery of his emotions might shield him from such peril. As troublesome as his augment had been at first, it seemed profoundly tame and reliable next to this new understanding of magic.

He needed a mentor. With an inward smile, he decided to attract one into his life. He could make gold appear in his path, why not a teacher? The wagon swayed and jostled as they moved steadily toward Alturas. Ben focused his mind on his desire, forming a picture of the qualities he needed in a guide, the knowledge he wanted to gain and the calm certainty that only genuine wisdom could offer.

A nudge brought him out of his focused daydream. The interior of the wagon was as black as the inside of his eyelids, only the breathing of his companions and the rumble of wagon wheels coming to a stop told him where he was.

"I think we're here," Hound whispered.

A hinge creaked and the wagon gently jolted forward again. A gate closed behind them and a bar fell into place, followed by a dim light growing steadily just outside. Kayla pulled the tarp aside.

"You'll be safe here," she said. "I have food inside."

John tied the tarp open and dropped the tailgate before sliding out and scanning their surroundings. He looked back to Ben, nodding his approval before offering Imogen a hand. They were inside a small barn, just big enough to house a team of horses and a wagon. Derek went to work tending to the horses.

"Follow me," Kayla said.

Ben nodded for John to go first.

"Do we trust them?" Hound whispered, leaning close to Ben.

"Not yet," he whispered back.

"Good," Hound said, following Kayla and the rest of their companions. A simple house stood just beside the barn. A large main room joined the dining room and kitchen with a staircase leading up to the second floor. Heavy curtains hung over all of the windows, and the front door was barred shut and locked with two bolts.

Kayla went to work lighting a number of lamps and then the wood stove in the corner of the kitchen. Within a few minutes, she had the stove crackling and a pot of water beginning to heat.

"Can I help?" Imogen asked.

"Sure, there are some potatoes in that cupboard."

Derek came in a minute later.

"I'll go make the rounds," he said.

Kayla nodded, offering him a smile. "Be careful."

"Wait," Hound said. "Where are you off to?"

Derek looked to Kayla. She nodded and went back to work chopping carrots.

"We have contacts in town," Derek said. "I'm going to ask around and see what's happened since we left yesterday."

"Why don't I tag along?" Hound said.

Derek shrugged. "So long as you leave that shotgun here. Firearms are a death sentence."

Rufus frowned, grimacing as if in the midst of a great internal battle. Finally, he nodded, handing Bertha to Ben.

"You look after her, ya hear?"

Ben nodded with a smile.

Hound slid his war axe into his belt under his coat and checked his knife before nodding to Derek and following him out into the night.

"They'll be fine," Kayla said to Ben. "There's a bag of onions in the pantry … grab me a couple?"

Ben retrieved the produce and pulled up a stool on the opposite side of the prep table. "Need any more help?"

"I think we've got it," Kayla said.

"All right … so where's this door?"

Kayla nodded as she added a small pile of chopped carrots to the stew pot.

"It's in the lowest level of the underground complex under the city. The first couple of levels are used by the Dragon Guard and the priests. Below that, everything is off limits except by special permission. Adara Cartage has been granted access for our survey expedition, but even we're only supposed to access the tunnel network coming into the third level."

"So how do you know about the lower levels?" Ellie asked, pulling a stool up next to Ben.

"We broke the rules," Kayla said with a shrug. "The access points are all locked up tight and guarded, but they don't know about all of the secondary tunnels in town. A few of those will get you into the lower levels."

"The Dragon Guard don't run patrols down there?" Ben asked.

"No … they just let a few of their monsters loose instead."

"Monsters?" Ellie asked.

"Dragon dogs," Kayla said.

"You mean stalkers?" Ben asked.

"No, those are different. Dragon dogs are a crossbreed between wolves and the wyrm … although there's a lot more wolf than dragon to them."

"That's not much comfort," John said.

"No, and it shouldn't be. They're dangerous in the extreme, which is why we're going to draw them away from where we're really going, hopefully for long enough to get through the blast doors and into the sublevel."

Ben consulted his map of the underground base and did his best to maintain a poker face. Kayla wanted him to get her into the very place that he'd come for. Unfortunately, the augment was still restricting the details of what resided within.

"Will I be able to open that door?" Ben asked his internal computer.

"Of course."

"Then why not tell me what's inside?"

"The Splinter Brigade is a compartmentalized, special-access project. You don't have clearance."

"Yeah, yeah, I know, but you'll let me through the door. That doesn't make sense."

He sighed inaudibly when the augment didn't respond.

"What if we run into these dragon dogs?" Ellie asked.

"We fight like hell," Kayla said.

"Seriously?" Olivia said. "You must want whatever's inside pretty badly."

"Have you ever seen old-world tech?" Kayla asked. "And I don't mean guns and bullets, but real tech?"

Olivia shrugged, but Ellie answered. "Not really."

"I have, and I'm here to tell you, it's powerful, like magically powerful. The right tech can do things that I didn't know could be done. And the dragon hates it. So much so, that the Dragon Guard have standing orders to destroy it on sight. That means he's afraid of it."

"Are you planning to make a run at the dragon?" John asked.

"No, not me, and not anytime soon, but one day the time will be right. When it is, humanity will need all the firepower we can get."

"So you're building a resistance," Ben said. "Is this just you? Or is your family on board with this?"

She winced, shaking her head and turning away to put some onions into the pot.

"I'm not entirely alone in this, but the family elders are definitely not on board. My great-grandfather got into bed with the dragon just after the apocalypse, and all nine of his children, including my grandfather, are still working closely with the priesthood and the Dragon Guard. Since we owe our fortune and standing to that relationship, I don't expect them to go against the wyrm for anything."

"Why you?" Ben asked.

Her eyes grew distant, and sadness came over her.

"I was a twin. When we were seven years old, a priest came to my parents and demanded that they give them one of their children. I have six other siblings, but my brother and I were best friends. They gave him up.

"It was supposed to be a great honor to be chosen, but the dragon always has the final say. Usually he accepts the candidate into the priesthood, but sometimes he doesn't."

She fell silent, adding seasoning to the stew before covering it.

"What does that mean?" Imogen asked, a tremor in her voice.

Kayla shrugged helplessly, her eyes glossy, sadness etched into her face.

"The wyrm ate my brother. Snapped him up in a blink, right in front of my whole family."

Ben closed his eyes, a feeling of heaviness coming over him. One more story of tragedy to add to the pile. One more life scarred for nothing but power and hatred.

"I'm sorry," he whispered, turning away and going into the living room, sitting heavily in a dusty overstuffed chair. Homer laid his chin on Ben's knee and looked up sympathetically. Ben scratched his head before leaning back and closing his eyes.

The rest of them joined him while the stew simmered.

After the silence became uncomfortable, Ben opened his eyes and scanned the faces in the room, landing on Kayla.

"You wanted to know how I got through that door." He tapped his temple twice with an index finger. "I've got tech in my head."

She stared at him, taking a deep breath and holding it for a moment.

"How? Where did you get it? What can it do?" She stopped to look at him more closely. "Do you control it, or does it control you?"

"Stop," Ben said, holding up his hands. "My grandfather gave it to me to save my life. It lets me access and control NACC tech."

She thought about that for a moment. "All of it? I mean, all of their tech?"

"Most of it, depending—"

Derek and Hound came in through the back door in a hurry.

"We're compromised," Derek said.

"Time to go," Hound said, heading straight for Ben and snatching up Bertha.

Ben came to his feet, swinging his backpack to his shoulder and turning to Hound.

"What?"

"We had a run-in with some thugs. Seems they've taken a liking to Miss Adara."

"Boggs," Derek said in response to Kayla's questioning look.

"Shit … how the hell did he find me?"

The house shook from a sudden pounding on the front door.

"I know you're in there, Adara," a drunk and arrogant voice shouted.

Kayla shook her head, motioning for them to follow her quietly. She snatched up a lamp and led them to a false panel that opened to a staircase going twenty feet into the ground. It had been crudely cut but effectively shorn up with stout timbers.

At the bottom, a low tunnel, five feet tall at best and barely as wide, ran off through the earth at a right angle. Silence and oppressive heaviness pressed in on Ben as he followed Kayla through the hundred feet of corridor. It opened into a dirt-walled room with an exit on the far side and a complicated-looking contraption next to the doorway they'd entered through. All that Ben could discern at a glance was that it probably wasn't a weapon and that it involved a counterweight.

Derek lit a lamp. The light grew slowly, casting erratic shadows across the walls. Ben looked at the contraption again, but this time the augment mapped it and determined its purpose—it was designed to collapse the tunnel.

"What now?" Hound said.

Kayla pointed to the staircase leading up on the far side of the room. They resurfaced in an abandoned house on the opposite end of the block. When they went outside, Kayla went right. Ben went left, stopping at the corner of the house and looking down the block. A group of agitated men were gathered on and near the porch of Kayla's safe house, shouting obscenities and encouraging a large man who was still pounding on the front door.

"Come on … we don't have time for this!" Kayla said.

Hound stood beside Ben.

They watched as a single Dragon Guard walked out into the light of the street lamp hanging over the corner. He raised his rifle and a wave of orange flame erupted from the barrel, showering the entire group of men and the porch of the house, the calm night air suddenly shattered by the terrified screams of a dozen men burning to death.

In the sudden flare of light, Ben saw the dwarf, standing off in the shadows, watching the spectacle with a smile.

"Enemy target acquired. Seeker round probability of success, 87%," the augment said, combat visuals coming into place, marking his target.

Ben made the decision in a second, fluidly slipping his revolver out of its holster and slapping the cylinder open. He removed a bullet and replaced it with a seeker round, closing the cylinder carefully to ensure that the right chamber was in place.

Hound turned back to the rest of their companions.

"Hush!" he whispered harshly. Silence fell.

Ben raised his weapon, taking careful aim—his target more technological visuals than flesh and blood in his mind's eye at this range and in the dark. He didn't hesitate, instead firing as soon as he was sure. The round exploded from the pistol, locking on to its target and then accelerating. It hit a fraction of a second later, detonating inside the dwarf's head and spraying viscera for twenty feet down the street. The Warlock's minion fell with a thud.

A cry of anguish and rage rose up in the distance.

"Nice shot," Hound said, laying a hand on Ben's shoulder. "Now, let's go."

Chapter 24

They fled into the night, following a very agitated Kayla. Most of this section of town had fallen into ruin and become overgrown with forest that flourished where the roads had once been. Lone standing walls and husks of buildings were common, but then so were basements.

She led them to a house with a broken-in and disintegrated roof. Four walls surrounded a common room, the only part of the building still standing. A rough outline of a door provided access.

Kayla approached slowly, disarming a tripwire and pointing to a deadfall still suspended in the trees. After ushering all them inside, she reset the trap and turned to a pile of rubble in the corner.

After a moment of searching, she pulled up a disguised trapdoor with a steep staircase beneath. Derek went first, followed by Hound and then Ben and the others. The cold, steel stairs took them down twenty feet into a simple room forty feet long and thirty wide. Kayla was the last to enter.

"We'll be safe here ... for now."

"That's what you said last time," Olivia said.

"She has a point," Ellie said.

Kayla ignored them, turning to Derek.

"Report."

"Someone tipped Boggs to your location, so he rounded up his hirelings and came for you, but more importantly, the Sage reached out."

She hesitated, verifying with a look that he was serious. "How and when?"

"The cemetery at the moon's zenith—look for instructions."

"Yeah ... don't forget to tell 'em about the Amazon," Hound said.

"Dominus Nash is back in town and on the hunt," Derek continued. "Also, word is, the army is preparing to move."

"Move? I didn't think they were ready," Kayla said.

"Nobody did ... they're headed for Shasta."

Ben and Hound shared a worried look.

"What have I done?" Imogen whispered.

"That makes no sense," Kayla said. "They've been planning a push north for months."

"That's the question everyone is asking," Derek said.

"Anything else?"

He shook his head. Kayla thought for a moment, then turned to Ben. "We should go to the Sage."

"Who's that?"

"A very secretive and very powerful man ... he's helped me on a few occasions."

"Powerful, how?" Ben asked, a tingle of dread beginning to form at the base of his spine.

"He has magic," Kayla said.

Every hair on his body stood on end.

"Can he be trusted?" Hound asked.

"His reputation is good, and like I said, he's helped me a few times in the past," Kayla said. "The thing is, I've never actually met him."

"How do we proceed?" Ben asked.

"He set a meet, but we still have a few hours."

Ben found a spot against the wall and sat down.

Kayla sat cross-legged facing him. "How does your tech work?" she asked.

"It's a voice in my head, and it can display tactical information in my field of vision."

"So it helps you fight."

"Yeah, mostly," Ben said. "Your turn. Who was that at the door?"

"Just a guy I screwed out of a lucrative freight contract," she said, with a shrug. "That one was strictly family business, and all aboveboard … maybe a bit ruthless, but all legal." She pursed her lips. "What I don't understand, is how he knew where to find me. And why would the Dragon Guard light them on fire?"

"Anyone else aware of your plans?"

"Just Derek … that house is one of three that we had ready and waiting, and I picked it at the last moment," Kayla said, frowning. "The more I think about this, the more it bothers me."

"You said the Sage has magic. What kind of magic?" Ben asked.

"He can see the future."

Ben cocked his head at her and waited.

"No … why would he?" she said. "He's always helped me in the past."

"I'm sure he has his reasons," Hound said.

"Still, we might want to see what he's offering," Ben said.

"Fair enough," Hound said. "Let's just do it carefully."

"Before we get to that," Kayla said, "you want to tell me who you were shooting at out there? Guns draw the Dragon Guard."

"One of the Warlock's minions," Ben said. "Well worth the bullet, considering that he's stabbed me—twice."

"Seriously?" Olivia asked, looking at Ben with renewed curiosity. He ignored her.

"Well, don't do it again," Kayla said. "That goes for the rest of you, too. Gunfire attracts trouble."

"Fair enough," Ben said with a shrug. "Now that you mention it, are you sure the Sage is worth meeting? Given all of the attention we've attracted, maybe we should just make our way underground right now."

"If he has something to say, we want to hear it," Kayla said. "We should make time for this."

"All right, describe the meeting place."

Ben spent a few minutes building a visual construct of the location from Kayla's description, quizzing her frequently about the details. When he had a working model, he looked at it from every angle and then formulated a strategy, or at least an approach that provided some cover.

"I have a question," Hound said, scanning the room, full circle. "Is that staircase the only way out of here?"

Kayla nodded.

"Let's go then," Hound said. "I don't much like having my back to a wall."

"We'll be early," Kayla said, "not to mention out in the open."

"Good," Ben said, swinging his pack into place and taking care to cover his pistol with his long coat.

"We're going to have to rest at some point," Imogen said, laying a hand on Ben's arm.

"I know, just not yet," he said, turning to Kayla. "You mentioned another safe house."

She nodded.

"Is it closer to the meeting spot?"

She nodded again.

"Take us there."

She thought about it for a moment before glancing at Derek. He climbed to the surface, whistling all clear a few moments later. Hound was up next, followed by the rest of them, Kayla last of all, locking the door and covering it with debris.

"We should hurry," Derek whispered, looking back from the open doorway.

Kayla motioned for him to proceed. He vanished into the night, followed closely by John. Within moments all of them were moving through the darkness, clinging to the shadows, avoiding light and sound as they fluidly wound through the trees and derelict houses.

It felt good, the breeze on his face, the effortless rhythm of placing one step after another, air burning in his lungs. A hint of magic in the distance snapped him back to the gravity of the situation.

He stopped.

Kayla stopped, looking back questioningly.

Ben pulled her down into a crouch and whispered, "We're being followed."

"Who?" she asked.

"I don't know for sure, but it has magic."

"How—?"

"Doesn't matter," Ben said. "What matters is … it's coming. How quickly can we get to your safe house?"

"Quickly, but it won't matter if that thing is tracking us," Kayla said.

"Better to face it in a confined space that we control," Ben said, turning to the rest of his companions. "We have to move faster."

It took half an hour of running through the night and a bit of climbing to reach the second safe house. They stopped a good distance from it, watching cautiously and catching their breath. After several minutes, Derek entered and swept the place, returning a few minutes later with an all-clear signal.

After everyone filed in, Ben projected his circle into his mind's eye and expanded it to encompass the main room, focusing his will on protecting them from discovery. A cougar screamed in the distance.

"The Warlock," Ellie and Olivia said as one.

Kayla and Derek checked the doors and windows, drew the drapes and lit the lamps. Within minutes they were working on a second, far more successful attempt at a stew. After everyone had eaten their fill, Kayla pushed her bowl toward the center of the table and looked at Ben.

"We should go alone."

Ben shook his head. "I'm taking at least one of my friends … and my dog."

"The Sage is very cautious. If we come with a crowd it might spook him."

"Better than walking into a trap without backup."

"I hope you mean me," Hound said.

"I should go," Ellie said. "I'm less intimidating … and I don't have a gun."

"Not having a gun is your argument?" Hound said.

"She has a point," Kayla said. "That shotgun will get you into trouble if anyone even sees it."

"I've wandered into … what the hell … Ben, say something."

"Sorry, Rufus, but I need you to stay here."

"Aw, not you, too?" Hound said, walking away muttering, "Don't you listen to 'em, Bertha."

"Keep an eye on everyone, John," Ben said on his way to the door, stopping to talk to Imogen. "Draw a circle around the entire room," he said.

Then he and Ellie followed Kayla out the door. She was good in the dark, quiet, light on her feet and quick. The moon was nearing its zenith. Ben started to notice landmarks familiar to him from Kayla's description of the area surrounding the cemetery. He oriented himself, filling in the model with new information as it became available—terrain features, structures, trees.

He tapped her shoulder and motioned for her to veer off the main path, skirting a small hilltop and approaching the graveyard from a spring runoff ditch along a back road. They crept up to one of the maintenance buildings and then alongside it, peering out into the semi-uniform procession of tombstones stretching out before them, moonlight describing streaks of silver through a few patches of night mist, large oak trees throwing swathes of impenetrable shadow that contrasted sharply with several gleaming white headstones.

Movement drew his eye.

"Target acquired, assessing," the augment said, tagging the man walking through the graveyard with a visual indicator.

Ben was beginning to get used to having all of the extra information the augment provided. Or at the very least, it no longer startled him when it happened unbidden. He crouched, watching from the safety of shadow and distance as the man wound his way toward one of the far exits.

"Wait," Kayla whispered.

Four Dragon Guard appeared out of the night and surrounded the man, escorting him away.

"Let him go," Kayla said, motioning for Ben to follow her behind the building.

"Why?" he asked once they were well concealed.

"Because he probably left a message for us, and because there are Dragon Guard nearby."

"And why is that?" Ellie asked.

A form began to appear in front of Ben, translucent, silvery—more apparition than person.

"You tell me," Kayla whispered harshly. "I'd love to know why everyone in town is hunting you."

"Are you seeing this?" Ben said, his eyes never leaving the woman standing before him. She now appeared precise and real, yet he knew instinctively that his hand would pass right through her if he were brazen enough to try to touch her. She looked human in every respect, save for the softly glowing, white feathery wings sprouting from her back. She wore only a simple smock that was impossibly white.

"Keep it down," Ellie said, peeking around the corner into the graveyard.

Kayla huffed but remained silent.

"You are a powerful one, aren't you?" the translucent woman said, holding Ben with bright, inquisitive eyes. "My master would like to meet with you—there is much he can teach you."

Ben blinked, closing his eyes tightly and looking again. Homer growled softly, standing right beside him, leaning against his leg.

"Are they coming?" Kayla asked.

"No," Ellie said, turning to face her. "Why would they be here?"

"I already told you, I don't know," Kayla said.

"Hey," Ben said, drawing their attention. He pointed at the apparition. "Can you see her?"

"See who?" Ellie asked.

"What the hell are you talking about?" Kayla said.

The apparition laughed, her voice light and lilting, full of knowing humor. "I am here for you alone," she said. "The Adara girl will know where to look."

She faded from sight as quickly as she'd appeared, leaving Ben feeling momentarily bereft, as if he'd stumbled upon a great secret and then lost it just as quickly.

"Are you all right?" Ellie said, stepping close to him and looking up into his eyes.

He nodded, frowning in thought.

"Be careful with her," Homer said.

"Who? Ellie?"

"No, the avatar."

"Wait … what's an avatar?"

"You'll figure it out," Homer said.

He frowned at his dog and turned to Kayla, adding one more concern to his list.

"Where would he leave a message?"

"In the graveyard," she said. "In a vase."

"Can we get to it without being seen?" Ellie asked.

"Probably not."

"I'm quite certain of it," a man said from behind them.

Ben whirled, drawing his sword just as a second man tipped his horn back and blew, loud and long, shattering the night's calm and calling every Dragon Guard for miles to battle.

Ben lunged forward, slapping the nearest man's sword aside and kicking him in the chest, sending him stumbling backward, pressing the attack, lunging again and thrusting into the man's face, the point of his blade stopping against the inside of the Dragon Guard's helmet.

The sound of footsteps coming from the cemetery registered in the back of Ben's mind as he turned his attention toward the man who'd blown the horn, but before he could strike, a knife plunged into the man's face and he fell over.

Kayla retrieved her curved dagger from the dead man, one of a pair, and turned away from the cemetery.

"Come on," she barked.

"We need the Sage's message," Ben said.

"There's at least a dozen coming," she said. "We have to run."

"I concur," the augment said.

"Go," he said, following after the two women.

Kayla led the way around the cemetery, sneaking into an empty house half a mile away. The voices of a dozen Dragon Guard walking patrol and challenging all intruders grew and then faded into silence.

"We're clear," Kayla said.

"We need that message," Ben said.

"Back up," Kayla said. "This just went south … like everything else since I met you. A while ago you weren't even sure you wanted to meet the Sage, but now you're willing to fight a squad of Dragon Guard for the chance. What is going on?"

"This Sage of yours sent me a message," he said with a shrug. "I need to meet him."

"What are you talking about, Ben?" Ellie asked.

"Magic … the Sage used magic to tell me about a message. He left it for us, and he said you'd know where it is, Kayla."

"Then I do, for sure," she said. "It's right where I thought it would be. Out in the middle of the graveyard in a vase in front of Fred Binghamton's headstone."

"Why didn't you say so," Ben said, shaking his head. "Let's go."

He led them out of the house without waiting for a discussion, heading back toward the cemetery, using shadow to conceal his passage as best he could until he reached the edge of the graveyard, coming up through a thicket of trees.

"Point to the area," he whispered to Kayla. She obliged with a questioning look.

"Think you can find it?" he asked Homer.

His dog grumbled before trotting off into the night, seeming to vanish as he passed into the nearest shadow.

They fell back into the cover of the trees.

"What's happening?" Kayla said.

A voice in the night silenced them. They froze, waiting, breathing slowly and deliberately. Another voice answered, from farther off.

Ben exhaled slowly, calming himself and directing his mind to the task at hand.

"We're waiting," he whispered, so quietly that they both took half a step closer to him.

"For what?" Ellie asked, after a moment.

Kayla's head bobbed in the dark.

Ben ignored them, his attention fixed on his hearing, listening for any hint of Homer's movement. A voice shouted. Another answered.

"Is that a dog?" The sentence came across the breeze as if delivered to him alone.

"Stay low," Ben said, heading back toward the graveyard but stopping just inside the wood line under the protection of the forest's shadow.

Men were running, Dragon Guard converging on a point in the graveyard. Homer ran away from that spot, sticking to the black shadow cast by the trees in the moonlight. Ben watched him return, kneeling to greet him and to take a metal key from his mouth.

"Good job," he said.

"Thanks," Homer replied.

"We should go," Ben said, easing back into the trees and away from the Dragon Guard now patrolling the graveyard in a grid pattern. Once they were half a block away from danger, Kayla stopped.

"What the hell just happened?" she asked.

"I was hoping you could tell me," he said, holding up the key. "Let's get back to the safe house."

She stared at it for a moment, then looked at Ben and nodded before leading them into a small forest that used to be a neighborhood. Ben brought up the rear, following closely enough to drive them to move faster. It wasn't long before they slipped through the back door into the kitchen.

A single lamp burned low beside a comfortable chair in the living room. Hound sat with Bertha across his lap as he watched both doors. He took a quick breath and came to his feet the moment they opened the back door. Bertha was at the ready but Hound was still a few seconds from awake.

"We're back," Ben said to him, pulling him fully out of slumber. He held up the key, then took the lamp and placed it on the kitchen table, gently laying the key in its light and pulling up a chair.

Ellie took the chair to his right, Hound sat to his left. Kayla sat across from Ben.

"A hotel key?" Hound said, frowning at it before picking it up to examine it more closely. "And a nice one at that ... this is a two-way key, one for members-only areas and the other for the room."

"The Chesapeake," Kayla said, eyeing the insignia on the key. "You've got to be kidding."

"Why?" Ben asked. "What's the Chesapeake?"

"That's Boggs's place," she said with bitter laughter in her voice. "His son just burned to death on my doorstep."

"What are the odds of that?" Hound asked.

"Any hint of a threat here?" she asked, scanning the room, her eyes lingering for a moment on the front door.

"Nothing," Hound said, his mirth evaporating as he offered his report. "Your man is thorough, the building is secure and the exterior is quiet."

Ben nodded to himself when he saw the circle that Imogen had drawn around the room. All of the bedrolls were laid out so they fit neatly inside the diagram.

Derek came to his feet in a rush, a blade in his hand seemingly of its own volition. He scanned the room, straightened up and sheathed his knife.

"Why don't we all step inside the circle," Ben said.

"Imogen insisted on it," Derek said. "I didn't see the harm."

Kayla looked at the floor as if for the first time—seeing something new, seeing something important. She took Ben's hand and stepped over the twin circular lines drawn on the floor—seven arcane symbols depicted at specific positions within the circles. Once inside, Ben snapped his circle of light on top of the one that Imogen had drawn, focusing his will on protecting them from discovery.

"What do you know about magic?" Kayla asked, looking at Ben very directly and with fresh eyes.

"More than most, and not nearly enough," Ben said.

"Magic and tech, no wonder the Sage is interested in you ... do you have an artifact?"

Ben froze, all of his options cascading through his mind. Everything came down to two facts—she'd saved him, and she had her own agenda. He looked down at the table and sighed.

"I knew someone who did," he said, softly. "He's dead now, but he taught me about magic ... he taught me how to draw a circle."

"But you need an artifact," Kayla said.

"No, actually you don't," Ben said. "You just need the proximity of something magical—an artifact, a dragon, a priest, or even a mule—and, you can actually use someone else's magic, if you know how."

"So what magic is this?" Kayla whispered, gesturing emphatically at the circle drawn around the room full of sleeping people.

"This is protection," Ben said. "This is why the Warlock hasn't found us. But it's so much more than that."

"Stop," she said, her exceedingly clear, dark brown eyes fixed on Ben. "You're telling me that anyone can use magic, if they know how, provided a source of..."

"Dragon magic," Ben offered.

"Is nearby."

"Yes ... and you have the aptitude, and you know what you're doing."

"So tell me about this circle," she said.

"This circle has power," Ben said, "more than it should, and I'm not sure why. I've seen a few things that most people wouldn't believe ... and this circle has power." He stopped, holding her eyes for a moment. "And it's always the same. The one who taught me drew it exactly the same as the slavers did—the same seven symbols within two circles. Always the same symbols, but different materials," he said, his voice trailing off as new understanding came over him.

"Make it with gold, silver, blood, or bones and it will have more power. Do you have paper?"

Kayla blinked a few times before going to a cabinet and returning with a stack of parchment and a metal tin filled with chalk and charcoal. Ben sketched a copy of the magic circle, handing it to Kayla when he was satisfied.

"Memorize this. Learn to draw it. Make it part of your mind. The symbols must be accurate, and their relation to one another must be consistent. The size of the circle is up to you. Once you've mastered this, I'll help you take the next step."

"What—"

Ben cut her off with a raised hand. "I need sleep. We'll talk later."

"I hope you know what you're doing," Ellie whispered to him as he wrapped his blankets around himself.

"Yeah ... me too," he muttered, laying his head down and drifting off almost immediately. He woke to dawn streaming in past the edges of drawn curtains. The augment presented a series of data points, nothing surprising, just a very thorough accounting of the current state of affairs—people, room dimensions, exits, weapons.

"Recommend you scan for magical presence," it said.

Ben yawned, pushing himself up from the pillow and squinting at the streamers of light that managed to penetrate the curtains' defenses. Almost involuntarily, he reached out with his mind ... and found a threat ... and then another. One was pure magic, extranormal in every way. The other was wild, yet dark, controlled, and feral. He wasn't sure how, but he knew—the Warlock's cat, lurking, stalking, hunting.

He tried to bring his mind back to the first source of magic but it evaporated ... vanishing like perfume on a breeze.

The cat was still there. It had them. It was watching. In spite of the circle.

He rolled to a sitting position on the edge of his bedroll, his circle of light still surrounding the room. The Warlock wasn't far away. Ben reached into his backpack and laid his hand on the egg, satisfying himself that it was still there, even though he could feel it with his mind.

For a few moments, he puzzled over the cat's ability to find them.

Homer rolled over and began to wiggle and snort, scratching his back on the floor.

"What's gotten into you?" Ben asked.

"The cat … its scent makes me anxious."

Ben snorted, shaking his head. The cat didn't need magic to find them—it was a hunter by nature. He pulled on his boots and headed for the back door. Hound followed him outside. John was already sitting on the back porch.

Dawn cast streamers of light through the forest, dew dripping from the world as the morning mist burned off.

"The Sage or the Splinter Brigade?" Ben whispered after motioning for them to lean in closer.

"The Sage," Hound said. "I know," he shrugged apologetically, "I want bigger guns too, but the Sage might know something important."

"He's right," John said.

Ben chuckled, shaking his head. "I didn't expect you two to agree, and I seriously doubt you'll like my plan."

"Let me guess, you want me to stay here … again," Hound said.

"Actually, no," Ben said. "I want you and Ellie to follow us in case we need backup."

"That sounds better than sitting here waiting for our enemies to find us," Hound said.

"There's one other thing," Ben said, hesitating for a moment before continuing. "I want you to hold on to the egg for me."

Hound looked a bit surprised, but nodded agreement nonetheless.

"I take it you don't entirely trust this Sage," he said.

"The only people I trust are right here," Ben said. "Also, the Warlock and his cat are nearby. He's probably not very happy with me right now."

"I don't imagine he is, but it was his turn to bleed," Hound said.

"Just be careful. That cat is stalking us," Ben said.

John and Rufus both nodded soberly as the door opened.

"Anybody hungry?" Olivia said, the smell of pancakes wafting out of the kitchen.

Ben ate voraciously, sating his hunger with gusto. With the new day, everyone was in an optimistic mood, Ben most of all—the prospect of answers about magic igniting his imagination.

He focused his mind on reaching the room in the hotel.

He had the key.

"How's your tailor?" he asked Kayla.

Her eyes narrowed.

Chapter 25

Ben adjusted his collar, again—it was stiff and uncomfortable, and he thought it looked ridiculous, even though Kayla and her tailor both assured him that it was the latest style in Alturas. She selected a formfitting black dress and a luxurious long fur coat. He had to admit, they looked pretty good together, or at least they looked like two people who liked to spend money.

A carriage arrived at the tailor's front door and took them through town to the hotel. While they rode, Ben found himself checking for his pistol, again. He felt naked without it. Also, he felt a deep sense of loss, having left his backpack, and the egg within, in Hound's care. Being out of the presence of his link with magic left him feeling like something was missing.

After a few minutes of travel, he relaxed, realizing that he possessed a kind of invisibility—he was one of the wealthy, one of the protected class. The authorities seemed to ignore him as a matter of course.

He watched two Dragon Guard questioning a couple on a street corner as his carriage rolled past. They didn't even give him a look. Those authorities that did acknowledge them did so with a courteous nod and a wave to continue on their way. It wasn't long before they pulled up in front of the hotel, a valet coming to open the door before the coach had completely stopped.

"Good evening," the enthusiastic young man said.

"Hello," Ben said, stepping out of the carriage and offering Kayla his hand. She played the part expertly, a wealthy woman, accustomed to being served, yet gracious to a fault.

"Here's a coin for your troubles, dear," she said, pressing a drake into the valet's hand and offering a dazzling smile that left him a bit flustered. He rushed to get the door.

They walked into the hotel like they owned it, heading for the main staircase without a single rushed step, Kayla's hand on Ben's arm keeping him moving at a reserved pace instead of the quick step he had in mind.

The concierge offered a smile in passing but aside from him, nobody even seemed to notice them. The other guests were just as self-absorbed as Ben was pretending to be. They reached the third floor and Kayla started giggling, quickly pressing Ben up against the wall and kissing him like she meant it.

He wasn't sure what to do—it was nice, Kayla was pretty, even if he didn't entirely trust her … and he was in the middle of a job … and then there was Ellie.

His senses slowly returned to him as a couple of men walked past heading down the stairs, one muttering a comment under his breath, the other chuckling.

Kayla sopped kissing him, no hint of amorous intent in her expression.

"Come on," she whispered, "those were two of Harlow's crew."

Ben followed her down the hall and around the corner. He stopped a few steps later, his mind alight with power. Not long ago, he wouldn't have noticed a thing, but now he knew that he was in the presence of great magic. Excitement and fear raced up his spine.

He checked the key one last time before handing it to Kayla, then he looked back at the empty hallway and nodded for her to proceed. She opened the door quietly. The room beyond was dimly lit—fragrant, warm air pouring out past them. They slipped inside. Ben closed the door behind them, taking care to lock it again.

"Hello."

They both spun. An older, impeccably dressed gentleman with silvery white hair bowed respectfully. He stood in the middle of a foyer with three doors leading away from the main entrance.

"My employer has been expecting you. Please, this way."

Ben and Kayla looked at each other and then followed the man through the door to the left, down the hall and through another door that opened to a sitting room. The drapes were drawn, a pair of candle lamps offering meager light. A figure sat in the dark on the far side of the room, screens positioned to ensure that he remained in shadow.

"Please, sit," the valet said, gesturing toward two chairs in the middle of the room. He left, closing the door softly.

They both remained standing.

"Please, you have nothing to fear," the man in shadow said.

Kayla took a breath to speak.

"Are you the Sage?" Ben asked.

"I am."

Ben and Kayla shared another look before sitting.

He fixed his eyes and his mind on the figure in the dark. The Sage had an artifact—and a powerful one, though not as powerful as the egg. It had a different quality about it, more fixed, less vibrant, less alive … and something else, something that Ben couldn't quite put his finger on.

"Thank you for seeing us," Kayla said.

"You're most welcome, my dear," he said. "Truthfully, I must thank you for bringing your friend to me. It would seem that he is very important, and yet I don't know why."

Ben froze, his mind racing. Above all, he needed to protect the secret of the egg. He could feel the power of the Sage's artifact—palpable, beyond reason, a window into time itself. And the Sage was probing, searching for a clue to Ben's import. He touched the artifact with his mind and then snapped his magic circle into place, willing it to protect them both.

The silvery woman with wings appeared beside the Sage.

"Remarkable … he's erected a defensive circle," she said, fading out of sight a moment later.

"What the hell was that?" Kayla said, surging to her feet.

Ben put a hand on her arm, urging her to sit down with a look. After a moment's hesitation, she complied.

"Your avatar is perceptive," Ben said.

The man shifted in the dark. Ben could feel his unease.

"Impressive," he said. "You have a well-trained mind, far too well-trained to be the product of chance, I think."

"Back up," Kayla said. "I want to know who that woman was and where she went."

"She is my avatar, as your friend here has indicated," the Sage said. "A magical construct, if you will."

A thrill of possibility and understanding raced up Ben's spine.

"You created her in your mind and then manifested her in the world," he said. "Amazing."

The Sage chuckled gently. "It's no wonder that I saw you coming," he said. "You have far more knowledge of magic than one your age should possess. I'm most curious about your master—who trained you?"

Ben considered his options and decided on caution. "You first," he said.

"Very well," the Sage said. "I was trained by the Wizard ... before he betrayed us and fled into hiding with our greatest weapon."

All of the wonder and opportunity that he'd been hoping for vanished in a blink, fear and uncertainty washing it away without a trace. He felt like he'd just walked into a trap.

"You knew the Wizard?" Kayla asked, a hint of awe in her voice.

"Yes. He was my friend and mentor for many years."

Ben could feel the man's attention shift back to him.

"Your turn. Who taught you?" the Sage asked.

Ben hesitated, Dom's advice about deception coming into his mind unbidden, and yet he was unable to fabricate an alternate reality in the moment.

"My grandfather," he said, chiding himself for failing to prepare a deception in advance, knowing even as he spoke the words that he was revealing too much.

"Interesting, he must be quite a man to have prepared you so well at such a young age. I would very much like to meet him. I believe we have much to discuss."

Ben looked down, grief momentarily bubbling to the surface before he shoved it aside.

"He's dead."

The Sage fell silent.

After a few moments he said, "I'm sorry, both for your loss and for my own. There are very few people in the world today that have any understanding of magic, and most of them serve the wyrm."

"I'm not sure he understood magic as well as you think," Ben said. "He just taught me how to meditate."

"And yet you've projected a magic circle around yourself—one that I cannot see, one that isn't drawn on the ground as it should be, but still I feel its power. What's more, you don't possess an artifact—I would have felt it. The only explanation that remains is that you've touched the artifact that I possess and are wielding its power against me. I believe there is much you aren't telling me."

"Says the man sitting in shadow," Ben said.

The Sage chuckled softly.

"A fair point. I've been at war for a long time. The Wizard taught me many things, but one of the most important is the value of a moniker. If I were to reveal my identity, the wyrm would hunt me down and kill me very quickly."

"So I guess we both have secrets," Ben said. "For example, I'd love to know how you found me—how you knew I was coming."

"Not all artifacts are created equal," he said. "Most are simply bones or fragments of scales, but some few have been enchanted further, adding power and capability beyond the magical link that they provide. I possess one such artifact. It's called the Oculus. It was fashioned from the diamond-like orb that is the eyeball of a dragon and then enchanted to give its possessor insight into the future."

Ben stopped breathing for a moment. The implications of such power were remarkable and terrifying. In the wrong hands the Oculus could doom the world. In the right hands...

"I see your mind working," the Sage said. "And yes, it is quite powerful, though the insights that it offers are often less forthcoming than I would like. For example, I saw your arrival, the when and the where. I felt a strong sense that you are quite important, but the why and the how elude me. Hence this meeting."

"Mostly, I'm just running for my life," Ben said. "I'm not sure how that makes me important."

"Perhaps it's simply your desperation," the Sage said.

"Why would that make me important?" Ben asked.

"A desperate man will do things that others will not, things that others would not even consider possible. But there's more to you than that, I think. Perhaps much more. The question is, why are you really here?"

"Just passing through," Ben said.

"Yes, but why?" the Sage said.

Ben could feel his eyes boring into him, his magic buffeting against Ben's circle as he probed for the truth—a truth that Ben didn't dare reveal.

"My reasons are my own," he said. "You've been at war for many years so you know the importance of controlling information. I'm at war, too."

"Ah, now we're getting somewhere," the Sage said. "Given the loyalty of those hunting you, I can only assume that we share the same enemy. Perhaps we could work together. I always have need of talented operatives."

"That sounds more like me working for you than us working together," Ben said. "Besides, I'm just passing through."

"So you've said. In your travels, perhaps you noticed the army north of town. I've received word that they're moving west when we expected them to move north, a quite sudden development. More interestingly, Saint Thomas and Legate Rath have come to town while their army marches. Most unusual. And all of this coincides with your arrival.

"Happenstance? Perhaps I might have believed such a thing had the Oculus not shown me your arrival. I've led the resistance against the wyrm ever since our original leadership abandoned us and I believe that you have a part to play in this fight, perhaps even a vital part."

Ben shook his head and looked down for a moment. "I'm just a guy trying to protect the people that I care about."

"Of course," the Sage said. "In that at least, we share the same objective. Thank you for meeting with me."

Ben felt a swirl of emotions. He had so many questions that he wanted to ask, so much he wanted to know, but each question the Sage answered would lead him closer to discovering Ben's secret, and that was something that he simply could not allow to happen.

He stood, nodding respectfully. Kayla stood with him, tension virtually radiating from her.

"Thank you for seeing us," Ben said.

"And you as well."

They turned for the door.

"Ah, one last thing," the Sage said. "I didn't get your name."

"Benjamin Boyce," he said, knowing the moment he spoke that he'd made a mistake.

The Sage hesitated. "Excellent, thank you, Benjamin. Safe travels."

The valet was waiting for them when they exited the sitting room. He led them to the foyer and held the door for them, offering a respectful nod.

Once in the hallway, Ben felt a sense of unease, as if he was being watched. He quickened his step until Kayla slowed him down with a hand on his arm.

"Wealthy people don't rush," she whispered. "Play the part until we're clear."

He slowed his pace, feeling for all the world like he was being followed. They reached the ground floor. The door was in sight.

"You've got a lot of nerve showing up here," a gruff voice said.

They turned to see a big man, more belly than muscle, eyeing them like they'd just stolen his wallet. He was flanked by two men who looked like they liked to fight.

"You kill my son and then waltz into my business like you belong here?" he said.

"I didn't kill your son, Floyd," Kayla said. "A Dragon Guard did that … go take it up with them."

Ben scanned the foyer. Several more men were watching.

"A Dragon Guard you paid," Floyd Boggs said.

"If I wanted Harlow dead, he would have just disappeared," Kayla said. "I certainly wouldn't have lit him on fire on my own front porch."

Floyd scowled, anger and anguish in his eyes.

"He wouldn't have been on your porch if you didn't cheat him out of that contract."

"I didn't cheat anyone," Kayla shot back. "I just made a better deal."

"You and your fancy name, you come into town and take over like you own the place. Maybe we should make you disappear."

"My second knows where I am," Kayla said. "Lay hands on me and your whole bloodline will burn."

Floyd all but snarled at her, though he stayed his men with a gesture.

"This isn't over, girl. Set foot in my business again and I'll skin you alive myself."

Kayla curtsied, eliciting a scowl, then turned toward the door and was all too happy to walk just as briskly as Ben. They waited nervously for the valet to call for their carriage as they glanced back into the hotel, noting the growing crowd of henchmen surrounding Floyd Boggs.

"Is this going to be a problem?" Ben asked.

"Pretty sure," Kayla said, sighing with relief when the carriage came into view.

They quickly climbed inside and urged the driver to hurry.

Ben's mind swirled with all that had just happened, pieces of his grandfather's past snapping into place. Above all, he was glad that he'd had the foresight to leave the egg with Hound. The Sage would have recognized it in an instant. While Ben truly believed that he had good intentions, there was no telling how he might react, especially considering his history.

The carriage carried them through the streets, Kayla looking back every now and then. Ben, once again, got the sense that he was being watched, though far less intensely than before. He could feel a hint of magic, but it was dim in his mind, indistinct and unfocused.

He suspected that the Sage's avatar was somewhere nearby.

"What the hell happened back there?" Kayla asked.

"I'm not entirely sure," Ben said. "But I think we're being followed."

"Shit," Kayla muttered, looking back again.

Ben turned around and saw four men on horseback. While they kept their distance, their intent was obvious.

"I meant by the Sage's avatar," Ben said.

"About that, how did you know what it was? And how did you ... what did he call it? Project a defensive circle?"

"I saw his avatar in the graveyard," Ben said. "As for the circle, that's a story for another day." He gestured toward the four men on horseback arrayed across the road several blocks ahead.

"Driver, turn here," Kayla snapped, pulling a bag from under the seat and digging out a pair of pants and boots. She started changing out of her attractive but highly impractical dress. "Faster ... head for the market."

The driver snapped his whip and the horses stepped up the pace. Ben looked back as the four men behind them rounded the corner, still following but not attempting to catch up to them.

They had traveled scarcely a block before Ben felt it ... magic, strong and alive. Hound and Ellie appeared from an alley just ahead of them, both out of breath and flushed. Homer poked his head around the corner as well. At the same time, several blocks up, four men on horses appeared, reining in their animals and spreading out across the street.

Kayla pulled her tunic down over her head and stuffed her dress into her bag.

"Stop at that alley," Ben said.

The driver looked back to Kayla. She nodded and he slowed. Ben didn't wait, opening the door and jumping, landing on the run. Kayla was right behind him.

"Go," she shouted to the driver. He yelled to his team, snapping his whip again and the horses bolted. Eight men, four behind and four ahead, all spurred their animals into a gallop, closing on them quickly.

Hound handed Ben his backpack and they ran into the alley.

"I see things went well," Hound said.

"Why should today be any different?"

"This way," Kayla said, when they reached an intersecting alley that led out onto a cross street. Ben looked back just as the first horseman rounded the corner.

Kayla turned into the first open door they came to, a bakery. Two men and a woman were busy preparing loaves of bread. All three stopped in surprise when they entered, closing the door behind themselves and dropping the bar.

"You can't be in here," one said.

"Especially with a dog," another said.

"Hey, that's not very nice," Homer said.

Kayla fished a purse out of her bag and dumped the contents onto the flour-dusted table, holding her finger over her lips as the sound of horse hooves clopped by outside.

All three of the bakers looked at the small fortune in gold and silver drakes, then looked at her, all nodding silently. Several more horses filed past, moving quickly. Ben found himself holding his breath. After a few minutes of remaining dead silent, straining to listen for their pursuers, Kayla started laughing.

"That was close," she said.

"Who were they?" Hound asked.

"Nobody important," Kayla said. "Just—"

The front door to the shop opened, a bell ringing to alert the proprietor.

"Can I help you?" a voice said from the front of the store.

"We're looking for a couple, a man and a woman, well-dressed. Have you seen them?"

"No, I'm afraid not."

"You sure? We'll make it worth your while."

"I wish I could be of help, but my last customer called half an hour ago, and she was an elderly woman."

The door opened and closed again.

Ben slowly released his breath. "We should get some distance," he whispered.

"Maybe you should change first," Ellie said, straightening his collar. "You're a bit too fancy."

He looked at the rest of them, all dressed far more functionally, and immediately felt out of place. Within minutes, his brand-new suit was crumpled up in his bag with the egg and his gear and he was wearing his comfortable and far more durable travel clothes with his long coat covering the pistol on his hip. He checked his ammo before holstering the revolver.

"We don't want any trouble," one of the bakers said.

"Neither do we," Ben said, lifting the bar and opening the door a crack. "Looks clear."

They slipped into the alley and went back the way they'd come, Kayla leading through a winding series of narrow side roads and alleyways barely wide enough for two people to walk abreast.

After a few minutes, Ben stopped, stretching out with his mind. He felt magic from several directions, all different and all threatening, save the avatar.

"We might have a problem," he said.

"Ya think?" Hound said.

"What do you mean?" Kayla said. "I'm pretty sure we lost Boggs's men."

"They're not the problem," he said, looking up at a two-story building across the street and pointing. A cougar was lying on the flat roof, his head at the edge, his black eyes boring straight into them.

"What the hell?" Kayla asked.

"It's a stalker," Ben said. "The Warlock is close."

"You mean the man with the melted face?"

"That's the one," Ellie said. "Trust me, you don't want to meet him in person."

They turned back, threading their way into a network of alleys and footpaths that led to a shantytown, the shells of old buildings used as the foundation for shacks and huts made from all manner of salvaged materials. People huddled around open fires here and there, some just standing around as if they had nothing useful to do in the middle of the day.

Ben caught a glimpse of a man with black curly hair, but he was gone before he could take a second look. They rounded a corner.

"There they are!" a man shouted.

"I say we fight," Hound said.

"No, we can't leave a trail of dead bodies or the Dragon Guard will be all over us, even in the poor quarter," Kayla said, turning around and racing into the shantytown again, ducking into a shack and walking through it despite the objections of the woman sitting in the corner.

She led them out of the poor section of town and into another neighborhood occupied by rebuilt houses, stopping for a moment to get her bearings before turning down a residential street with several trees growing up through the broken pavement where a road used to be.

"The wind just shifted," Homer said. "The cat is still following at a distance."

They reached the end of the block and Kayla eased up next to a house, peeking around the corner and then stepping back just as quickly.

"I'm pretty sure Boggs has every single one of his men out looking for us," she said. "We need to get off the street."

"What did you have in mind?" Ellie asked, pointing toward the two men several hundred yards back the way they'd come. Both men seemed to notice them at the same time, urging their horses forward.

"There!" a man shouted from the other direction. Two more men on horseback came around a corner several blocks away.

A shriek from overhead drew Ben's attention. The stalker falcon was circling.

"Shit," he muttered.

"Is that what I think it is?" Hound said.

Ben nodded.

"What?" Kayla asked.

"Hoondragon is here."

Her face went white. "Are you kidding me? You didn't say he was after you."

"No, I didn't," Ben said, drawing his pistol and flipping the cylinder open, replacing a slug with a seeker round.

"What are you doing?" Kayla snapped. "You can't fire that in town."

Ben ignored her, turning to Hound. "We're going to take their horses," he said, motioning toward the nearest pair of henchmen closing on them. "Wait for them to get close."

Hound smiled, flipping his coat aside so he could bring Bertha up to the ready and chamber a round.

"This is a mistake," Kayla said. "Gunfire will bring more trouble than we can handle."

"We can't escape as long as that bird is tracking us," Ben said, holding his pistol up in front of her. "And this is the only way I know to kill it."

She looked up and then back at him.

"You can't hit that bird from here," she said.

He smiled and took aim, his tactical display guiding his hand, a projection of the seeker round's anticipated trajectory appearing in his mind's eye. He fired, a loud report ringing out, echoing off the nearby houses.

The two men were nearly on top of them, but the gunshot spooked their horses, forcing both men to struggle to remain mounted. Another explosion rang out high overhead. The stalker falcon was falling, spiraling out of control. A fleeting sense of satisfaction ghosted through Ben's mind.

He turned his attention to the two thugs.

Bertha blasted one of the men from his horse. The other was thrown, landing hard. Hound grabbed the reins of one animal while Ellie took the reins of the other, struggling for a moment to calm the beast. Hound and Kayla took one, Ben and Ellie mounted up on the second. The remaining two men charging toward them had reined in sharply when Ben fired at the falcon, clearly neither of them willing to risk a confrontation with a well-armed enemy.

They rode hard, turning and twisting through the streets of Alturas, people watching them race past, a few Dragon Guard waving for them to stop for inspection, then shouting when they failed to obey.

Kayla led them into a ruined section of town that had never been reclaimed from the encroaching forest. Once they were certain that no enemy had followed, she stopped and dismounted, slapping the animal on the rump to send it off on its own. Ben followed her lead, sending his horse away as well.

She took them into the remnants of a building that might have been a warehouse or a factory, leading them to a still-intact office in one corner, the only part of the structure still sheltered by a roof. She closed the door behind her.

"Help me with this desk," she said. "Up against the door."

Hound shrugged, shoving the large, rusting metal desk into place with a grunt. Kayla pulled a trapdoor open and descended into the dark.

"I hate ladders," Homer said.

Ben opened his pack and pulled out a blanket, quickly fashioning it into a sling. He lifted Homer into it before following Kayla. They descended several dozen feet down a rough shaft. Hound closed the trapdoor, cutting off all light. Ben stopped for a moment before making his way to the bottom by a dim but growing light from below.

He found himself in a dirt room held up by rough timbers. Kayla held a candle high, providing the only illumination.

"What is this place?" Ellie asked.

"A safe house, of sorts," Kayla said. "We'll wait until dark and make our way back to Derek and your friends."

Ben could still feel magic, though it was farther away now. He projected his circle, willing it to protect them from detection.

"You mind telling me what the hell is going on?" Kayla said. "I've put my life on the line for you, more than once, and now you tell me that Hoondragon is chasing you too. That doesn't happen unless the wyrm has taken a personal interest in you … and he wouldn't do that because you killed a few Dragon Guard. In fact, now that I think about it, Hoondragon hasn't left the Mountaintop for a dozen years." She stopped to look at Ben. "Just what the hell are you into?"

Ben looked to Hound. He shrugged. Ellie offered little more. Ben sighed and sat down, motioning for her to sit as well.

"What do you think?" he asked Homer.

"She's helped you so far."

He set his bag on the dirt floor and fished out the dragon's egg, holding it up in front of her very wide eyes. She scrambled to her feet and took a few steps back, swallowing hard, seemingly unable to form words for a few moments.

"Oh my god!" she said, putting her hands on her head. "Please tell me you're kidding."

"Afraid not," Ben said, motioning for her to sit back down.

"What have you done? It's only a matter of time before the wyrm comes himself. He'll burn Alturas and everyone in it." She walked in a circle, her hand on her forehead. "This is a disaster. How the hell did I get myself into this? All I wanted was some tech … nothing fancy, maybe a plasma rifle or a gravity gun…"

Ben waited, placing the egg on the ground.

She stopped, facing him with a look of exasperation. "Do you have any idea how dangerous that damn thing is?" She started pacing. "No wonder the Sage wanted to talk to you. Wait, shouldn't he have been able to sense it? No, wait, where the hell did you get that thing?" She started pacing again.

Ben shared a worried look with Hound.

"Why don't you sit down," Ben said. "I'll tell you everything I know."

She stopped. "Like hell you will! Come to think of it, I don't even want to know the answers to the questions I've already asked." She pointed at the egg as if she was leveling an accusation of murder. "That thing is the world's end." She started pacing again. "Oh, shit, my father is going to kill me ... and that's only if my grandfather doesn't find out about this and kill me first."

"Kayla!" Ben snapped. "Sit down. You're making me nervous."

"Oh, I'm making you nervous," she said, laughing hysterically. She stopped, her eyes going distant for a moment. "No wonder Saint Thomas and Legate Rath are in town—either of which are a nightmare on a good day. Both of them together ... on the hunt ... you're a dead man. All of you are already dead, you just don't know it yet."

"Like hell," Hound said, stepping into her personal space. "Have a seat. The man wants to have a chat."

She huffed, shaking her head, her nervous laughter anything but humorous.

"Why the hell not?" she said, sitting cross-legged in front of the egg. "We probably have enemies closing on us right now. Nothing left to do but wait for them to find us."

"I didn't peg you for a fatalist," Ben said.

"Oh, I wasn't, until you put the most dangerous thing in the whole world right in front of me."

She looked at the egg, a spark of curiosity and wonder displacing the fear in her eyes for a moment. She stared at it, glassy-eyed, shaking her head slightly before looking at Ben again.

"Who are you?"

"My name is Benjamin Boyce. My grandfather was the Wizard."

She shook her head, her eyes going distant again. "Holy shit, we're in so much trouble."

Ben laughed.

She stared at him like he was crazy. "What the hell is wrong with you?"

He shrugged. "I'm being hunted by the most dangerous forces on this planet ... and it's my intention to destroy them all." He forestalled her protest with a raised hand. "Overly ambitious, I know, but for me, and for those I love, the only way out is through."

He locked eyes with her, holding her in thrall with nothing more than simple intensity.

"I'm going to kill the wyrm. Will you help me?"

She started trembling, her eyes never leaving his. "Are you serious? Wait, better question, are you bat-shit crazy?"

"Yes ... and probably yes," he said.

She shook her head again, blinking a few times before coming to her feet in a surge and beginning to pace again.

Ben leaned against the wall, closing his eyes and stretching out with his mind. The avatar was close, but not in the room. He idly wondered if she could hear their conversation. The stalker cat was near as well, waiting in the shadows, but there was more. Something dark and powerful was searching in the distance, too far off to identify, but far too close for Ben's comfort.

Kayla stopped, facing him again. "You can't beat Hoondragon, nobody can."

He nodded soberly, pulling his tunic up to reveal the scar where Hoondragon had run him through. "I know," he said.

She stared, new fear in her eyes, but also a hint of wonder.

"How?" she said, sitting back down.

"Tech … and luck … probably more of the latter."

"So you're telling me that Hoondragon stabbed you and you lived to tell the story."

Ben shrugged.

"We thought he was dead," Ellie said, a tremor in her voice, her hand squeezing his momentarily. "Without the node's automated defenses, we'd all be dead."

Kayla looked from her to him. "Okay, start at the beginning … tell me everything."

"Will you help us kill the dragon?" Ben said.

She hesitated, swallowing hard and then nodding slowly.

"Yes."

Ben smiled, nodding to himself. "It all started in K Falls…"

He told her almost everything, recounting every detail of his flight from home and his decision to slay the dragon, the death of his grandfather, his brother's betrayal, everything except the details about Dom and Homer.

It took over an hour. She sat quietly for several minutes after he'd finished, occasionally shaking her head while she worked through all that he'd revealed.

"That's a lot to take in. I'm sorry about your grandfather … and your brother."

Ben nodded his thanks for her condolences.

"So your next objective is the very same door that I've been dying to open for the past year."

He nodded again.

"What do you think is inside?"

"It's called a Splinter Brigade … and no, I don't know what that is."

"That sounds dangerous."

"I sure hope so."

She frowned. "The Sage isn't going to let this go. I mean, he knows there's something going on with you." Her eyes narrowed. "I wondered why he let us leave without more questions." Her eyes got wide again and she looked around. "Do you think the lady with wings is here?"

"No," Ben said. "She's close, but I'm pretty sure she can't find us right now."

"Why? Are you using magic?"

He nodded.

"This is going to take some getting used to," she said. "Also, I want to learn. If I'm going to help you kill the dragon … holy shit, that sounds crazy when I say it out loud." She locked eyes with him. "I want to learn about magic."

He nodded. "I'll teach you what I can. For now, we need to focus on getting into the bunker under the city."

"That's easy," she said. "The hard part is doing it without alerting the Dragon Guard or the monsters they've let loose down there."

"Quiet," Homer said.

Ben froze, holding up a hand to forestall any more noise.

"They've found us," Homer said. "I hear men searching around up top."

"How many?"

"Maybe a dozen."

"They've found us," Ben whispered, stuffing the egg into his pack and scooping Homer up into his sling.

"What's the plan?" Hound asked.

"We fight," Ben said.

"You sure that's wise?" Kayla asked.

"Either that or we wait for them to burn us out."

She winced. "Yeah, there is that."

Ben went for the ladder but Hound stopped him.

"Me first," he said.

Ben nodded.

They reached the surface and Kayla gently closed the trapdoor while Ben stowed his blanket.

"Check the office," a muffled voice said. "Their tracks led to this place, they've got to be around here somewhere."

The sound of footsteps grew louder. Ben drew his sword quietly, everyone else following his lead.

The doorknob turned, but the door held fast behind the desk.

"It's stuck. Give me a hand."

Another pair of footsteps approached. Ben positioned himself beside the door, sword at the ready. Hound moved up alongside him, putting his back against the wall and one foot against the desk.

"On three. One. Two…"

Hound shoved the desk aside just as they pushed at the door. The first man fell flat on his face. Ben stabbed the second man in the neck and surged into the large room with Hound right behind him, war axe in hand. Ellie stabbed the fallen man in the back in passing, rushing out to stand beside Ben, her bloody sword up and at the ready.

Eight men armed with a variety of bladed and bludgeoning weapons spread out before them.

"Well, well, well, there you are," the leader of the thugs said. "We just want you, Kayla … the rest of you are free to go."

Kayla looked over at Ben, wild fear in her eyes. He ignored her.

"Kayla's my friend," he said.

"If that's the way you want it," the leader said, his men fanning out in front of him.

Ben touched the egg's magic, glancing over at Ellie. She nodded. He could feel her intent, her harnessed will tapping into the power of the egg as well, her mind overlapping with his. The augment marked all of his enemies, offering information about their size, mass, weapons, and movement.

"Walk away from this," Ben said. "You have nothing to gain here."

"Oh, but you're wrong," the leader said. "Boggs will pay well for her head—and you're outnumbered more than two to one."

"And yet, today is about to be your very last day," Ben said. "Stand down."

The leader chuckled, looking over at the nearest of his men.

"Check out the balls on this one," he said, looking back to Ben. "Look around, we've got you cornered. Just give us the Adara bitch and we'll let you leave, no harm, no foul."

"No."

"Fair enough," the leader said. "Just remember, I gave you a choice."

"Funny, I was going to say the same exact thing," Ben said, walking deliberately toward the nearest man.

Hound and Ellie flanked him on either side. The man watched Ben come with a hint of disbelief in his eyes. Ben darted forward, covering the last few steps with startling speed, driving his blade into the man's heart. The look of disbelief in his expression spiked for just a moment before his eyes lost focus.

Everything seemed to slow down. Ben turned the dead man on the end of his sword toward the nearest attacker to his right and kicked him off the blade. The rushing man stumbled into his falling companion, trying to both catch him and avoid tripping over him. Hound lopped a chunk from the top side of his skull with his axe. Both men fell in a heap.

Ellie parried an attack that was meant for Ben. He ignored it as he closed with his next target. Ellie spun, slashing the man across the back of his legs as she moved past him. He fell on his face, howling in pain. She slapped another man's club aside, stepping closer to Ben to avoid the next blow.

He blocked a sword to his right, shifting direction abruptly and flipping the point of his blade out like a whip, the last inch slicing an onrushing attacker's throat just before he crashed into Ellie. She dodged to the side, moving back toward the man with the club, hacking at his arm before he could bring his weapon back up. He shrieked. She stabbed him through the throat, bright red blood spilling onto the ground.

Ben swung his blade in an arc to his right, driving another man back in a struggle to avoid death. He failed. Hound hacked him in the side of the chest, then lowered his shoulder and lunged into the next man, knocking him onto his back with a grunt.

The leader's face had gone from arrogance to fear. He and the remaining thug still standing turned and ran. Hound raised his axe overhead and heaved it. Another man fell.

Ben tossed his sword to his off hand and drew his pistol. Kayla hurled one of her knives past him into the back of the leader. He fell, wailing in pain. Ben looked over at her as he holstered his pistol. He approached the leader. The man was trying to reach the knife stuck in his back, mewling in pain with each failed attempt.

"Here, let me help you with that," Ben said, snatching the blade out and handing it back to Kayla. The leader screamed. Ben rolled him over with one foot, leveling his bloody sword at him.

"How many more are looking for us?"

He gasped in pain, trying to take a breath. "All of them," he managed, frothy blood bubbling from his mouth.

"And how many is that?"

He tried to speak again but started coughing and sputtering. Ben sighed, stabbing him in the heart. He stiffened for a moment and then went still.

"Please don't kill me," the thug with the sliced legs said, struggling to crawl away from them. The one who'd been knocked over by Hound regained his feet, looking at them like a caged animal.

Hound had retrieved his axe and was keeping an eye on the single uninjured man. Ben sighed, heading toward the last man standing.

"Wait," Kayla said. He stopped, looking back. She stepped just past him, holding the man's eyes with her own.

"Tell Boggs to leave town with his whole family or the next letter to my father will include a contract on his entire bloodline."

He eyed her suspiciously. Ben glanced at the man that Ellie had wounded. He wasn't going to make it. Bright red blood was spilling from his legs and his face was pasty white.

"You're the last man," Ben said. "If you want it to stay that way, I suggest you do as the lady says. Sheathe your sword and go."

He didn't look convinced, but he did as Ben commanded, giving them a wide berth on his way toward the breach in the warehouse walls where he broke into a dead run until he was out of sight.

Kayla eyed Ben suspiciously for a moment before shaking her head.

"That was both impressive and a bit terrifying," she said. "Where did you learn to fight like that?"

"My grandfather," he said with a shrug.

"Naturally," she said. "We should get out of here."

Chapter 26

Ben cleaned his blade and returned it to its scabbard, reaching out with his mind in search of magic. He wasn't disappointed.

"Show yourself," he said, turning toward one corner of the room.

After a moment, the Sage's avatar appeared, looking at him quizzically. "Master was wrong, you do have an artifact—or at least you do now," she said.

"Tell him to stop spying on me," Ben said. "I don't want to be his enemy, but I can't have you following me."

"You do not wish for my master to regard you as an enemy either," she said. "He requires more information about you and your role in the struggle with the darkness that has embroiled this world. Surely an alliance would serve you both."

"Perhaps," Ben said. "But at the moment, I have more important things to do, and I get the impression that an 'alliance' would be pretty one-sided."

"Master is relentless."

"I'll bet. But in this case, he'll do well to stay out of my way. Tell him that."

"As you wish," she said, fading out of sight.

"That's a new one," Hound said.

"Yeah, what's going on?" Ellie asked.

"Long story," Ben said. "I'll tell you later." He turned to Kayla. "Can we get to the safe house without attracting attention?"

"I doubt it," she said.

"As do I," Nash said, stepping into view, she and her four Dragon Guard filling the space of the breach in the wall. Her cat leapt up onto the corner wall, fixing its slightly luminous yellow eyes on Ben. It stood six feet at the shoulder, and its tight, leathery skin was black as night. There was a presence about it that was entirely unnatural.

"You've been quite the quarry," she said, striding toward them, her entourage in tow, swords drawn. "Give me the egg and kneel. Grovel. Beg for mercy and I will spare your friends—though I'm afraid that your brother, Imogen and her whelp will still have to die."

The avatar appeared again. "The egg?" she said.

Nash snarled at her almost reflexively. "Be gone, figment. You have no place here." She raised her hand and a bolt of translucent shadow arced to the avatar.

She shrieked, her wail vanishing a few moments after she did.

"Now, surrender and your death will be quick," Nash said as if nothing had happened.

"Such a shame," Hound said, racking a round into Bertha. "We could have been so good together."

"What the hell is going on now?" Kayla asked.

Ben ignored her.

"She's possessed by a demon," Ellie said.

"You're kidding," Kayla said.

All four Dragon Guard took a second look at Nash.

"You didn't know?" Ben said, shifting his attention to the man on her right. "You're not serving the dragon, you're serving Magoth, the demon prince of transformation."

"Do not speak my name!" Nash shouted, raising her hand toward Ben.

A thousand thoughts went through his mind, but the one that stuck was *Defend*. He projected his circle, willing it to protect them all. Shadow streaked toward him, other-worldly darkness born of Magoth's black heart and Nash's implacable hatred. Time seemed to slow down. Ben wondered how she was casting such a spell—then it dawned on him that she was tapping the power of the egg, just as he had tapped the power of the Oculus.

Her black magic reached his circle and vanished as if it was nothing more than a shared delusion. She stared in disbelief, her spell utterly ineffectual.

Ben smiled, drawing his sword.

"Blades only!" Nash snapped to her men. "I want some time with this one."

The Dragon Guard advanced. Ben expanded his circle to a diameter of forty feet, his augment marking the enemy, his mind overlapping with Ellie's without effort.

The men rushed. Ben waited, shifting to the side as the first man reached him, his thrust missing by scant inches. Ben whirled away from the attack, moving to engage the man headed for Ellie as she shifted to engage the one heading for him, both seamlessly aware of the other's intent.

His blade struck across the Dragon Guard's chest, his armor turning it aside, but doing nothing to lessen the force of the blow. He staggered back, struggling to catch his balance.

Ellie slashed at her target's hand, his gauntlet defending against her blade as well, but the force of her attack caused him to drop his sword.

Bertha's report echoed off the warehouse walls. The man charging toward Hound abruptly changed direction, the blast hitting him in the face, lifting him off the ground and dropping him onto his back, dead in a blink.

Kayla dodged aside, narrowly evading a slashing strike from the Dragon Guard rushing her. Her counter glanced off his bracer.

Ben pressed the attack, their swords flashing and ringing as they exchanged blows. The Dragon Guard feinted expertly, drawing Ben in, causing him to commit to an unwise attack. He managed to escape with a gash across the outside of his left shoulder, the sharp pain enough to elicit a gasp. The Dragon Guard smiled, attempting to capitalize on Ben's momentary distraction, driving him backwards with a series of strikes.

Ben let the man come, sacrificing ground to lure his opponent into committing too fully. Then he slipped to his enemy's right, evading a thrust and allowing the weight of the man's armor and his momentum to carry him past.

He waited.

Just a fraction of a second. Just until he had the right angle of attack. He thrust into the back of the man's neck, just under the helmet, severing his spine and dropping him face first to the ground.

Ellie struck her opponent's breastplate, forcing him back before he could retrieve his sword. He drew his knife, facing her. She attacked again. He blocked with his bracer, forcing the tip of her sword to go wide, then he grabbed her blade with his gauntleted hand and yanked her forward, thrusting his knife into her belly. She froze in shock, staring into his face.

Ben felt cold steel in the pit of his own stomach. Emotion flooded into him—fear, rage, love. He cried out in fury, rushing to Ellie's aid. The Dragon Guard yanked the knife from her belly, attempting to defend, but Ben was on him too quickly, kicking him in the chest, knocking him flat on his back and then landing in the middle of him. He hit him in the face with the pommel of his sword over and over again.

Kayla faced off against her man, both knives out and at the ready, daring him to come for her. He advanced, leading with the tip of his sword, gaining ground slowly, cautiously.

Hound circled. The Dragon Guard glanced at him, marking his position, before looking back to Kayla, advancing, knives up. He lashed out at her, driving her toward the wall. Hound lunged in and hooked his war axe around his throat from behind, dragging him backward, blood erupting from his wound as he fell to the floor. Hound worked his axe free, smiling humorlessly at the dying man.

Ben rolled to his feet, battle raging in his mind. He wanted to go to Ellie but Nash started clapping. His fury boiled and then went icy cold. He turned toward her. Her cat leapt to the ground, taking up position right beside her.

"I was hoping you'd face me," she said, drawing her sword.

Ben calmed his mind, focusing his will into his circle.

"Stay back," he said to Hound and Kayla, striding forward. He knew facing a demon-possessed Dominus by himself was a fool's errand, but he couldn't make himself stop. He collapsed his circle until it was only ten feet in diameter, deadly intent burning in his mind, displacing everything else, even his terror at Ellie's wound.

"What the hell are you doing?" Hound asked.

Ben ignored him.

Nash strode toward Ben, an inhuman snarl distorting her face, glee and madness dancing in her eyes.

Then she passed into his circle.

She froze—terror, confusion, relief, and disbelief struggling for supremacy in her expression. Magoth was driven out, a black stain in the air, tearing free of Nash's body and then transforming into a swirling, inky mass with a frozen porcelain mask for a face.

A low keening wail began to build.

Ben thrust into the moment of Nash's indecision, his blade driving upward under her chin and out the top of her head. He tipped her backward and unceremoniously dropped her corpse to the floor.

The wail built into a howl of rage and loss. Magoth began to swirl around and around like a dust devil, his black, smoky form whirling into the ground like water down a drain. The shriek faded and then silence fell on the warehouse.

Magoth was gone.

The cat ran, transforming into a common house cat as it fled.

Ben raced to Ellie where she lay crumpled on the ground. He slid to his knees beside her, gently cradling her head in his lap.

"Bastard got me," she said.

"Shh," he managed past the lump in his throat. He wanted to weep. She was hurt so badly ... and he'd promised Dom that he wouldn't get his daughters into this ... and he couldn't lose her. She was—

"Ben," Hound said, the tone of his voice bringing Ben back to the rest of the world.

That's when he felt it. The Oculus.

He looked up and saw an old man with grey hair and a wrinkled face coming toward them, his steps light and sure. Several more men were moving to secure the area, but none of them seemed intent on doing harm.

"Looks like I got here just in time," the Sage said.

"Have you been following us?" Kayla asked.

"Yes," the Sage said. "Benjamin was less than forthcoming about his role in all of this, so I thought it prudent to investigate further, and it looks like it was a good thing that I did. I can help your friend, if you let me."

"She's hurt," Ben managed through tears.

He knelt next to him, assessing her wound.

"Are any of these men still alive?" he asked, looking up at Hound.

Rufus looked over at the one that Ben had bludgeoned, nodding. "This guy's still breathing."

"Excellent, bring him here," the Sage said.

Hound took hold of the unconscious man's wrist and dragged him across the floor until he was beside Ellie.

"Project your circle around us," the Sage said, closing his eyes. "Oh, yes, I remember that power. So alive—so potent." He laid one hand on Ellie and the other on the unconscious Dragon Guard, then began to chant quietly.

Ben watched, holding his breath. The unconscious man came awake suddenly, shrieking in pain as Ellie's wound began to close up. Both of them stiffened. Ellie began breathing deliberately, fear and pain in her eyes. The Dragon Guard tried to take a breath to wail but was frozen in pain as the wound deepened.

It took several minutes, and it looked like Ellie was in agony the entire time, but the wound vanished completely, or rather, it was now in the belly of the unfortunate Dragon Guard.

The Sage finished, lifting his hands from both of them. Ellie gasped, sitting up quickly, her hand going to where she'd been stabbed, her eyes wide with disbelief.

The Dragon Guard tried to sit up, groaning in pain. "What did you do to me?" he asked weakly.

Ellie pulled her tunic up and wiped the blood away, examining the place where she'd just been mortally wounded. There wasn't even a scar.

When Hound noticed the man fumbling for his knife, he reached down, clamping his big hand over the Dragon Guard's and taking the blade away with the other, tossing it aside.

"You're just going to lay there and die gracefully, ya hear?" he said.

"What have you done?" he managed.

Ben ignored him, pulling Ellie into his arms. "I thought you were dead," he whispered.

"We should be going," the Sage said. "There's much to discuss and far worse enemies than these hunting you."

Ben held Ellie out at arm's length and looked at her intently. "Can you walk?"

She nodded and he helped her up. She checked her stomach again, frowning.

"Thank you," she said to the Sage. "I was dead for sure."

"Happy to be of service," he said. "Now, come, all of you, inside Benjamin's circle. Can you adjust the size to protect us all?"

Ben nodded.

"Excellent, at some point I would very much like to understand how you're able to do such a thing. For now, I must cloak us with a glamour spell. It will be much more effective if you're able to maintain your circle to shield us from magical detection."

Ben nodded again.

The Sage began whispering to himself, his eyes going very distant. After several moments, Ellie changed into an entirely different person, her face now old and her hair grey. Ben looked around, fear growing in his belly. All of his companions looked different, as did the Sage.

He smiled knowingly. "One of the more useful spells, especially for those of us operating in the shadows," he said. "I keep a glamour prepared at all times, just in case."

He motioned to his men and they left without a word, each going their own way, disappearing into the trees and buildings nearby.

"I believe it's time to go," the Sage said.

Not three blocks away they rounded a corner and saw Hoondragon riding straight toward them. Ben could tell at a glance that his horse was possessed by a stalker once again. He froze in place, memories of being impaled holding him fast.

The Sage urged him on, taking his elbow and guiding him to the side of the street so the dragon's hunter could pass. And he did—without a second look. They hurried on, following the Sage's lead until they came to a small diner and filed inside.

The Sage exchanged hushed words with the man behind the counter and then led Ben and his companions into the back room, down a set of stairs and into a basement storeroom. After a moment of searching, he pressed a stone in the wall and a secret door opened. He lit a lamp and ushered them through. The passage was narrow, yet another tunnel. It went straight for several hundred feet, ending in a staircase that descended farther into the earth to a landing and a single steel door.

The Sage held his lamp up and counted stones in the brick wall to one side of the door and then pressed. A click, followed by a grinding noise and the section of wall moved in and then opened on a set of hinges. They filed into a large room, thirty feet on a side. A few crates were stacked around the periphery. A single door led out. The Sage produced a key, opened the door and led them through, locking it behind them. The next passage was lined with several doors, all draped with cobwebs, yet sturdy.

"And I thought *I* had a network of secret passages," Kayla said.

The Sage smiled over his shoulder, leading them to a staircase going toward the surface. Another secret door allowed access to a basement, and another staircase brought them into the living space of a house.

"Please, make yourselves comfortable," the Sage said. "I'll put on some tea."

Ben looked to Hound. He shrugged, going to the window and pulling the drapes aside just enough to peek outside.

"Looks like one of the nicer neighborhoods," he said. He checked the front door next, making sure it was locked.

"This house is protected by a circle. Your enemies can't find you here," the Sage said, placing a kettle on the wood stove after lighting the fire. "Oh, I guess I can dispel the glamour as well." He muttered under his breath and everyone reverted to their normal appearance.

"How does that work, anyway?" Ben asked.

"The glamour? It makes people see something other than what is really there. It's quite useful when dealing with those who are less sensitive to magic."

"I bet," Hound said, checking the back door.

"How much do your friends know about you?" the Sage asked, returning to the living room and taking the chair opposite Ben. "I don't wish to reveal secrets that are not mine to tell."

"What are you getting at?" Ben asked.

"You are the Wizard's grandson. You have a twin brother, or at least you did, and you possess the dragon's egg."

Ben felt a hint of unease. He wanted to trust the Sage, but he'd learned through hard experience that trusting people when the stakes were so high was dangerous.

"What gave me away?"

"Your name, and the presence of the egg," the Sage said with a shrug. "If you're going to survive, I suggest you adopt a moniker, or at least make up a name that can't be tied to your real identity. Please, sit. We have much to discuss."

Ben eased himself into a chair. His head reeled at the scope of his failure to protect himself—of all things, he'd compromised his identity by offering his real name.

"You were wise to hide the egg during our meeting," the Sage said. "Caution will keep you alive."

"Why did you help us?" Ben asked. "Don't get me wrong, I'm grateful." He looked over at Ellie. "I just don't understand."

"We want the same things," the Sage said. "The wyrm must be destroyed."

"I can't argue with that."

The Sage paused, seeming to marshal his thoughts.

"I've been at this for a long time now," he said. "I have the experience and a network of operatives. You do not. The only thing that I lack is the egg. With it, I'm certain that I can neutralize the dragon's defenses and deliver a fatal blow. I've brought you here to ask that you give me the weapon that I need to end this war."

Ben felt a flurry of emotion race through him. Just few weeks ago, he would have welcomed such an offer. The egg made him a target, it put everyone he cared about in danger, and yet, he didn't want to give it up. More than that, he knew instinctively that doing so would doom Imogen's baby, and probably the world.

The logic of the Sage's offer was indisputable, but something deeper rebelled against it. The room had gone deathly silent.

Ben slowly shook his head. "I'm afraid I can't do that."

The Sage's expression darkened momentarily.

"I understand how you must feel," he said. "Your grandfather gave you this burden and you believe that it's yours to carry, that you must see it through to the end, no matter what that end might be. Please believe me when I tell you that you are not prepared to face the dragon."

Ben nodded, looking at the floor. "I know," he whispered. "I was hoping that you would teach me."

"Such instruction takes years. We don't have that long, especially with the impressive array of enemies that you have pursuing you. Eventually, one of them will best you. Hoondragon himself is here. That alone is proof that you're out of your depth."

"I have people counting on me," Ben said. "I can't abandon them, and I have no chance without the egg."

"You have no chance with it," the Sage snapped, reining in his ire with a deep breath. "I'm sorry. I've often wondered what became of the egg after the Wizard abandoned the cause. Many speculated that the Dragon Slayer had succeeded in convincing him to destroy it. I never believed that, though I must confess that I feared it.

"The egg is the only artifact in the world that can hope to match the dragon's magic, and then only if it's wielded by someone of sufficient experience and talent. As much as I admire your courage and dedication, you are simply too young to have any chance of success."

Homer sat up beside Ben and growled, low and deep. Ben idly stroked his fur, sitting back and looking up at the ceiling for a moment. He searched his feelings and found that he simply could not give the egg away, not to the Sage, not to anyone, not until the job was done.

"My grandfather wasn't much older than I am when he took up this cause."

"And just imagine how much more effective he might have been if he'd had the necessary experience and training," the Sage countered. "Please understand, I do not wish for you to stop fighting. On the contrary, you're clearly an exceptional young man, but you're also a latecomer to this fight. Many of us have been waging this war for years. Let us help you."

"I'm happy to have your help, but the egg stays with me until the wyrm is dead," Ben said, standing up.

The Sage stood as well, tension etched into his face. "You're making a mistake," he said.

"Maybe. I do that sometimes," Ben said. "One of the pitfalls of being young and inexperienced."

"Please, I beg you, reconsider."

"Thank you for saving Ellie," Ben said. "I'm in your debt for that, so I'll help you in any way that I can, but the egg is not up for negotiation."

"You carry the world's doom in your bag."

"Or its salvation," Ben said.

"I've asked you nicely. I want to be allies, friends even. I would be happy to teach you all that I know about magic, but I cannot allow you to jeopardize the world with your foolish arrogance."

Hound slipped his hand under his coat.

"Be careful," Ben said. "That almost sounded like a threat."

"Your enemies will run you to ground, take the egg, kill everyone you care about and enslave the world—in that order. You must reconsider."

"I've given my answer," Ben said, stretching out with his mind. The Oculus was there, bright and powerful, but he felt no other sources of magic.

"I can't accept your answer," the Sage said. "You're a child playing at being a hero. Do the right thing, give me the egg."

"No," Ben said.

The Sage sighed, shaking his head. "Now!" he shouted.

Commotion came from several different directions—footfalls from upstairs, a closet opening, men coming from down the hall.

Hound swung Bertha up and jabbed the barrel into the Sage's back, grabbing him by the collar and forcibly maneuvering him toward the hallway as three men with swords came rushing out. Another two came from the closet and four more from the second floor, all of them stopping in their tracks when they saw the Sage held at gunpoint.

"You sure do know how to make friends," Kayla said, her knives out.

"Stop!" Ben shouted.

"Do as he says," the Sage said, clearly not anticipating such a turn of events.

"I don't want to hurt any of you, but I will," Ben said. "Lay down arms and let us leave."

"Not a chance," one of the men said. "You have something we need. Give it over and we'll let you go."

He didn't look like much at first glance. His face was ordinary, the kind of face you see and almost immediately forget. His black stubble made him look like a vagabond, his unkempt hair only serving to reinforce that impression, but his eyes held a keen intelligence.

Ben scanned the rest of the men—all were armed with swords and knives, save one who carried a short bow, arrow nocked but not drawn. He felt Ellie's will in his own mind. Her hand was on the hilt of her sword.

"You're outnumbered," the leader said.

"That's exactly what the last guy said," Ben replied.

"Don't I know you?" Kayla asked, looking at the leader intently.

"I doubt it," he said, his eyes never leaving Ben. "I have one of those faces."

"Either way, I'm sure you know my family," she said. "Do you really want to make another enemy?"

"I've got lots of enemies," he said. "One more won't matter much."

"This one will," Kayla said.

He smiled at her, excitement dancing in his eyes before looking back at Ben.

"Hand it over, you can't escape."

"Sure we can," Ben said. "Tell them to stand down." He looked at the Sage, cocking his head expectantly.

"Do as he says," the Sage said.

Ben nodded to Hound to head for the back door. Ben was the last one out.

"Don't follow us," he said to the nine men in the room, closing the door and hurrying to catch up with his friends. Hound still had the Sage by the collar. Ben stopped them just outside the gate between the backyard and an alley running between two rows of houses.

"I don't want to be your enemy," Ben said. "Stop trying to take the egg."

He gave a nod to Hound, and the big man let the Sage go, though he kept Bertha trained on him.

"You're making a mistake," the old man said, sadly.

"So are you," Ben said, backing away.

"This way," Hound said, pointing toward a path that led to the street. Ben hurried to follow.

Kayla took the lead crossing the street, cutting between two houses before turning onto the alley running through the next block.

"You know he's not going to stop, right?" she said.

"Yeah," Ben said. He could still feel the Oculus, even at this distance. His mind turned to his circle. It had become a constant presence around him, always visible in the background of his mind's eye. He took a moment to focus his will on it, commanding it to protect those within.

He felt something else at a distance, dark and powerful ... and closing quickly.

"We have to get out of sight," he said.

Kayla hesitated until she saw his expression, then scanned the nearby houses, selecting one and heading for it. She was through the front door in moments. An old woman sat in a rocking chair. She looked up from her knitting, alarm and curiosity in her eyes.

"Hello, ma'am," Ben said. "We won't hurt you, we just need to stay here for a few minutes."

He went to the window, expanding his circle to encompass the house. He felt it before he saw it—a man with wings, flying over town. Ben froze, feeling very much what he imagined a rodent feels when a hawk is overhead.

He waited, his shoulders tense, holding his breath, his mind returning to his circle.

Something was pressing against it, trying to find it, defeat it, search him out. Ben put his mind to defending the circle, and he succeeded, but not without effort. After a time, the threat faded. Ben looked up again, watching the winged man fly away.

"What the hell was that?" he whispered.

"That was Saint Thomas," Kayla said. "He's one of Noisome Ick's lieutenants—and he's not entirely human."

"He had so much power," Ben said. "It was strange. I could feel both living power and an artifact."

"All I felt was the hair on the back of my neck stand up," Hound said.

"Me too," Kayla said.

"Forgive the intrusion, ma'am," Ben said to the elderly woman before leaving. After five minutes on the street, he felt Saint Thomas coming back as if he was flying a search pattern over town.

"How much farther to the safe house?"

"Halfway across town, twenty or thirty minutes," Kayla said.

"We'll get made," Ben said. "Thomas is coming back."

"There's access to the underground nearby."

"More tunnels?" Ellie said.

"I'm afraid so," Ben said. "Lead the way."

Kayla moved quickly, rushing through the neighborhood, sticking to alleys as much as possible, finally arriving at the back door of a house with light coming from within. She motioned for them to remain outside and knocked on the door, talking briefly with the man who answered. She returned and led them to a pair of cellar doors set well away from the house.

A hidden door in the cellar led to a passage sloping down to a staircase and culminating in a broken section of the Alturas Base underground. Hound dug out his flashlight. Ben mapped his position. Kayla turned in the correct direction, so he let her lead.

The abrupt quiet and stillness made Ben feel a bit uneasy. He reinforced his circle with a moment of focus. When they reached a caved-in section, Kayla led them into a timber-shorn tunnel cut into one wall. It was four feet wide and six feet tall. Ben had to crouch to fit. Hound cursed under his breath. It wound around for several yards before opening through a crack in the wall of a large interior room.

Hound covered his flashlight with one hand, allowing only a sliver of light through. It was enough to confirm that the room was empty, having once been a classroom, judging from the rows of broken and deteriorated desks. Ben updated his map and marked his position. This section, while geographically close to the previous passage, was nonetheless in a completely different part of the base, closer to the core.

"This way," Ben whispered.

Across the room, through a door, all by the light of a sliver of Hound's flashlight. A dozen steps later, he stopped in front of a staircase.

"There's a pretty direct route one level down, or we could go back to the surface."

"How bad is this Saint Thomas guy?" Hound asked.

"Terrifying," Kayla said. "Like, raze-the-village-and-salt-the-fields terrifying."

"Bad," Ben said.

"Let's go through the dark, then," Hound said.

Ben nodded, heading down.

Hound opened his light up, scanning in both directions once he reached the passage below. The underground road was twenty feet wide and twenty feet high. It was quiet. So quiet it seemed to absorb sound.

"This way." Ben set out, moving quickly but quietly, scanning ahead for any hint of danger. The passage ran long and straight. Ten minutes later he slowed and began looking for the passage out.

A howl echoed past them. The sound was pitiless—the hunting wail of a predator lusting after blood. A sound devised for the purpose of causing fear, driving prey.

Ben froze for a moment, a sharp thrill in the pit of his stomach. He took a breath and mastered his resolve before he went back to searching for the exit, finding it a minute later.

"Can you open this?" he asked the augment.

"Yes, but I will require a recharge soon."

"How do I make that happen? Never mind, open the door," he said, laying his hand on the surface of the rounded steel portal.

He felt a tingle, then a whirring and then the door slid into the wall, revealing a cylinder five feet in diameter with a ladder going up and down. Ben went up, climbing five levels, the ladder rungs his only guide in the dark. At the top, he felt his way over the lip of the tube housing the ladder, braced himself, then offered Ellie a hand as she came up next.

Kayla was followed by Hound.

Ben mapped his position. They should be close to the safe house. Every time he encountered new terrain, it filled in his augment's map a little bit more, adding one more piece to the puzzle that was Alturas.

He pulled on the door and they filed out into a vacant alley, closing the heavy steel door behind them.

He eased up to the corner of the store they had come out behind, and then pulled back, motioning for everyone to stay quiet. He moved up to the corner again, peeking carefully.

A man was hiding in a bush, watching the safe house. Ben backed off, motioning for Kayla to take a look. She edged up to the corner and then pulled back just as quickly, nodding to Ben.

"Take a run?" Ben said to Homer.

"All right," he said, trotting off into the night.

Ben motioned for everyone else to pull back farther into the shadows. A few minutes later, Homer appeared, putting his head on Ben's lap. He scratched his ears.

"You're screwed," Homer said. "Twelve men, plus that leader guy you faced off against in the Sage's safe house. Every approach is being watched."

"Shit," Ben said. He retraced his steps, winding back into the alleys and passages of Alturas.

"What just happened?" Hound said, stopping Ben after they were a good distance from the safe house.

"The house is surrounded by the Sage's men."

"So, what do we do?" Ellie asked. "We can't just leave them back there."

"She's right," Kayla said.

Ben looked from one to the other, shaking his head. "Maybe we should."

"What the hell?" Kayla said.

"You can't be serious," Ellie said.

"Listen, they've been made, but they don't have what the Sage wants," Ben whispered harshly. "If we make contact, we'll get made too."

Hound smirked, nodding at Ben appreciatively. Ellie and Kayla looked at him like he was crazy.

"We don't have a choice," he said. "We have to go for the door, right now, just the four—"

"Five," Homer said.

"Five, of us."

Homer growled softly and said, "I smell someone."

Ben drew his sword. Everyone looked at him.

A small metal canister fell out of the sky, clinking when it hit the broken pavement and then rattling to a stop a few feet from them.

"NACC technology detected, stun grenade—command lockout."

A flash followed.

Chapter 27

Ben blinked. It was a deliberate action, it required effort. He took a breath. That required effort, too. His chest hurt. There was no sound, just ringing, high-pitched and highly annoying. He rolled onto his stomach, willing his eyes to focus.

They obeyed, reluctantly. The alley was scattered with his friends, all down, but all alive.

The augment began monitoring their vitals in the background. "Hold and heal," it said.

Ben pushed himself up onto his knees. His head hurt. The ringing…

He crawled to Hound, the closest of his companions, pulling him over onto his back. His body was rigid and tense, his eyes flickering back and forth behind his eyelids as if he was dreaming.

He turned to Ellie, their minds touching the moment he thought of her—a wailing, tormented, terrifyingly loud shriek poured into him. She was in agony, curled up and defenseless against the onslaught, and Ben could understand why.

He invited it in, sharing her experience, taking as much of it as he could, willing the sound volume to diminish. At first, he met with failure, but after a while, he was able to bring it under control and then share that control with Ellie. They opened their eyes, looking directly at each other, holding each other's hands.

"What the hell was that?" he asked the augment.

"A Mark 3 stun grenade."

Specifications came up in his visual field: 5 to 20 meter variable radius of effect. Neuro-stun pulse, debilitate all living targets within area of effect for approximately five minutes by overloading the nervous system through a brainwave specific electromagnetic pulse.

Kayla groaned.

Hound sat up. "What the—?" He put his hand on his forehead. "Ow…"

"What just happened?" Ellie asked, her eyes never leaving Ben's.

"Someone threw a stun grenade at us and then stole the egg," he said. It felt like he was listening to himself speak.

"Shit!" Hound said.

"Yeah," Ben said. "They have a few minutes on us."

"What the hell?" Kayla said, sitting up and looking around wildly. Her eyes landed on Ben … and then she turned and vomited until her stomach was empty. "Oh, that sucked." She rolled away from the puddle of bile and came to her feet, swaying a bit. "What just happened?"

"Tech just kicked our ass," Ben said. "Can you keep up?"

She worked up some saliva and spit at his feet, swaying again, catching herself on the wall and leaning heavily against it.

"You're an asshole," she said, enunciating her words very deliberately. "Lead the way."

Ben looked to Hound. He nodded, going to Kayla and offering an arm.

"Like hell!" she said, slapping him away and stumbling for her effort.

He stopped, looking at her with exasperation.

"Woman, that thing kicked my ass too ... if we lean into each other, maybe we won't fall over."

She huffed, hesitating, but eventually offered her arm. He took it graciously and they set out.

Ben and Ellie followed, their minds strangely entangled. They couldn't quite hear each other's thoughts, except those filled with intent. Also, they could almost feel each other's emotions. The more they focused on the same outcome, the more they fell into sync.

He reached out with his mind. The egg was on the move. He pointed. Hound led. After a few minutes, all of the effects of the stun grenade wore off and they were able to move without hindrance. They were gaining. Ben didn't dare imagine what would happen if he let it slip from his control for any length of time.

"Faster!" he snapped, racing ahead of his friends.

He turned a corner and stopped abruptly, his friends piling up behind him. He stretched out with his feelings. The egg was close, moving downward now. He mapped his position and found a switchback staircase, part of Alturas Base, accessible from inside a market built within a large building that still had most of its skylights intact.

It was close.

He broke into a sprint. His friends raced to catch up and were soon following him back and forth down a staircase, deep into the earth. Six levels, twelve sets of stairs. Ben rounded a corner at the bottom and came face to face with a man armed with a crossbow, locked, loaded, and pointed right at him.

Time slowed.

The arrow sprang free, coming for his face. It bent with force, its point aimed straight at him. He slipped sideways, moving right, drawing his sword and then lunging, overextending, thrusting with all possible range, driving the point of his blade an inch into the man's heart.

Ben pulled his blade out, dropping the man and wiping his sword off before sheathing it. The egg was close enough that it still lent power to his blade. He picked up the crossbow and loaded it.

"This way," he said, mapping his position and following the only road that made any sense. It ended in a collapsed area, but there was a passage cut into one wall.

Ben eased into it, crossbow in hand. He came to a hole in the ground that opened into a passage one level below. He lay on his belly and looked into the corridor before slipping off the edge and dropping to the floor.

Hound followed, Ellie and Kayla each dropping a moment later, the echo of their landings ringing out.

A moment passed, then another. A howl echoed down the passage.

There was so much malice in that howl.

"This way," Ben whispered.

They moved quickly and quietly, following the ten-by-ten corridor for a long way before Ben stopped, accessing his map, shaking his head at just how little the augment really knew about the Alturas underground. He reached out for the egg, touching its magic and letting it guide him. It was farther away than he liked, but it was still close enough to feel. A route appeared in his mind.

He ran, his friends protesting and running at the same time behind him. He pressed on until he reached just the right passage.

He skidded to a halt, stopping at a man-sized tunnel cut into the side of the main passage. He headed into it as if he knew where he was going. It wound deep and long, ending in a large natural cavern, already well-lit by a few dozen lanterns.

They poured out into the giant room. Ben pulled his coat aside and put his hand on his pistol.

The Sage stood fifty feet away, six well-armed men flanking him. The Thief was handing him Ben's backpack … with the egg inside.

One man nocked an arrow, drawing and aiming. Ben snapped up the crossbow, the augment highlighting the target instantly and guiding his shot. He loosed the bolt … it hit the archer in the center of the chest. The man's half-drawn and unaimed arrow bounced off the ceiling, then the floor, then skipped away until it came to a stop. Ben dropped the crossbow.

The Thief looked back at him and then raced out of the room through a door on the far side, leaving the Sage flanked by five able men, all armed with blades.

"Drop it and walk away!" Ben said.

The Sage shook his head, backing away with Ben's backpack.

The five armed men stepped forward.

Ben took a deep breath, let it out quickly and targeted the enemies before him, the augment marking each man with the optimum shot to stop each one. Five shots queued up like people buying groceries.

They advanced.

Ben drew and fired.

The first shot hit perfectly, through-and-through, left shoulder. Man down, nonlethal.

The next shot was a bit more messy—it hit a man's head, spraying him backwards into the wall.

Number three hit the next in the belly. He collapsed, sliding into a heap, howling in pain.

Shot four hit a lunging man in the shoulder, throwing him to the ground. He'd live.

Shot five killed the man charging Ellie. He was nearly on her when Ben brought his pistol around and shot him in the head, the round blasting him aside so he missed her entirely.

Ben rushed the Sage, revolver pointed at his chest, one round left.

"Don't shoot me!" the Sage said.

Ben hit him with his pistol, knocking him to the ground before snatching up his backpack. He could feel the egg within. A tightness in his chest relaxed. He threw his pack over his shoulders and cinched the straps.

"Where's the Oculus?" Ben asked.

The Sage shook his head, a pleading look in his eyes. "Please don't take it. I need it."

"I've had enough of you messing with me," Ben said, extending both his pistol and an open hand. "If I have to search you, I'm going to hit you a few more times first."

He hesitated. Ben raised his pistol, cocking his head and waiting.

"All right," he said, fishing a black leather pouch from his robes and holding it up.

Ben took it, frowning for a moment before handing it to Hound. "Want to search him for me?"

"Glad to," Hound said, taking the pouch and pocketing it before grabbing the Sage by the throat with his left hand, picking him up off the ground, putting him against the wall and then patting him down. He pulled out a coin purse and dropped it, then a knife, and then another leather pouch with a stone in it.

"That's the one," Ben said.

Hound let go of the Sage, stepping back and handing the bag to Ben. The Sage slid down the wall into a sitting position, watching Ben intently. Hound scanned the injured men again.

Ben opened the bag and looked inside. The stone was smooth and oval, translucent and powerful. He dumped it out into his hand.

His whole body stiffened, every muscle tensing at once. He gasped one breath and then stopped breathing, his back arched, his body trembling.

Reality evaporated. He was floating through a whirling cloud, lightning the only source of illumination.

Then he was standing on a roof overlooking the alley where they'd been ambushed. A few moments later, he watched himself come into view with his friends.

Then he was standing across the street from the safe house watching himself and his friends try to make contact with Imogen. Saint Thomas and Hoondragon surprised them with fire. Ben watched Imogen and Ellie burn.

He gasped, trying to reclaim control over his mind and body.

The world shifted again. He was inside a cinder cone, open at the top, the floor scattered with bones and treasure, a storm raging overhead. Ellie was chained to a post atop a sacrificial altar. The wyrm slithered past in the dark. Ellie screamed.

Reality shifted again.

He was in a map room. Several men, including the Sage, were working together to plan an attack against the wyrm. Ben was at the head of the table.

He came to his senses, rolling the stone onto the bag in his hand, taking a deep breath and trying to master his pounding heart.

"What did you see?" the Sage asked, leaning forward, curiosity burning in his eyes.

Ben knelt down and offered him the chance to touch the stone again. He didn't hesitate, laying his hand on it as soon as it was offered. He seemed to be much more used to the intensity of the experience than Ben was.

"I see," he said, nodding to himself, his eyes distant.

Ben put the Oculus into its bag and dropped it into his pack. "Behave and someday I'll give this back to you," he said.

The Sage seemed to come to a decision, nodding to himself again before looking up at Ben.

"I'll help you however I can," he said, with virtually no enthusiasm whatsoever.

"Good, start by acquiring an artifact for yourself," Ben said. "That's your standing order."

The Sage snorted, shaking his head. "Easier said than done." He didn't bother to get up.

Ben consulted his map, matching it with the room they were in, before pointing.

"This way," he said.

"Wait," the Sage said.

Ben ignored him.

The passage led deeper into the labyrinth that was Alturas Base. Ben picked his route, moving toward a staircase that spanned several levels. He stopped a few minutes later, straining to hear over the deafening silence.

A voice … or rather the echo of one.

Ben motioned for Hound to turn off his light and then felt his way up to the corner, peering around. Flickering light in the distance and another voice. Ben consulted his map. The staircase he wanted was several hundred feet down the passage, toward the light.

"We move in the dark, by feel, along the wall," he whispered. "And we have to be quiet."

He eased around the corner and proceeded forward, one hand on the wall, his leading foot always tentative and testing. They closed the distance, the flickering coming into focus. It was a fire in a barrel. Two men stood on either side of it, still several hundred feet away.

Hound tripped and caught himself, grunting. Both men looked up. Ben froze, holding his breath.

"Anybody there?" one of them shouted.

"You think someone is going to answer you?" the other said.

"They might," the first said.

Ben eased forward, the staircase was another fifty feet.

"You think we should have a look?" the second one asked.

"No," the first said. "If they come to us, then we light them on fire, those were the orders."

Ben reached the stairs and sent his companions down into the dark. On the second landing, he stopped.

"Maybe a little light," he whispered.

Hound turned his flashlight on and let just a sliver of light through. The stairs went down six levels, well past the area patrolled by the Dragon Guard. At the bottom, Ben selected a ten-by-ten-foot passage from several options and set out.

It was quiet, still, undisturbed.

"I like sunlight," Homer muttered in Ben's mind.

Ellie stopped. "Are we really just going to leave them?"

Ben sighed, nodding sadly. "For now, we are. The Oculus showed me what'll happen if we try to make contact."

"That bad?" Kayla said.

Ben nodded.

"Fine, let's get this over with," Ellie said. "Which way?"

Ben set out again, reloading his revolver.

After traveling for half an hour down several flights of stairs and through a dizzying array of passages, a howl broke the interminable silence. Everyone froze.

Hound turned off his light. "How close was that?" he asked.

"Too close," Ben whispered. "Let's keep moving."

Hound switched the light back on but kept it mostly covered.

Ben turned off the passage they were following and into a laboratory, through the work area to the administrator's office, closing the door behind them.

"Let me guess, another secret door," Hound said.

"Yep," Ben said, going to work searching for the switch and finding it a few seconds later. A section of the wall opened, revealing a locked grate over a circular shaft with a built-in ladder.

Another howl, closer.

Ben fashioned a sling for Homer, then opened the grate. Hound climbed over the edge and started down. Kayla followed, then Ellie. Ben stopped, holding his breath at the sound of snarling, snapping, and barking just down the hall. He eased himself down into the shaft, braced himself and began to ease the grate down.

The door splintered. A doglike creature, five feet at the shoulder and seven feet long, crashed through, skidding to a halt. Its eyes, alive with magic and intelligence, locked with Ben's. He slammed the grate shut, nearly falling when the dragon dog slammed into the wall beside the grate, barking and growling at them, yellow eyes boring into Ben with furious and desperate intent.

"Come on," Hound said.

"Yeah, I don't like that thing," Homer said.

Ben tore his eyes away from the beast and wrapped the chain dangling from the grate tightly around a peg before descending. As unsettling as the vicious noises coming from above had been, their sudden absence worried Ben even more. He got a firmer grip and looked up, expecting something. The howl nearly scared him into letting go. It was right there, so close, all he could do was hold on and weather a storm of visceral fear.

It took several moments of focused breathing before Ben was able to reclaim command over his body. The rest took a few moments longer.

They kept going. Another howl answered from somewhere.

All at once, a wave of ill intent like nothing that Ben had ever felt before washed over him, buffeting against his circle. He focused on protecting their location, but the onslaught of the psychic attack overwhelmed him, collapsing his circle, the image of it vanishing from within his mind's eye for a moment.

Ben brought it back as quickly as he could, pouring intent into the visual image, but he knew—Saint Thomas had their location. Ben consulted his map.

Three more levels down the ladder and they arrived in a small room with a steel door, barred on their side. He opened it with Hound's help and they stepped into a dark and still passage. A howl was answered by two more. The enemy was getting closer.

"I hope you know where you're going," Ellie said.

"Me too," Ben said, looking this way and that, then choosing the latter.

"I think we have a problem," Kayla said, slowing to look more closely at their location.

"What do you mean?" Ben asked.

"This level is collapsed through the middle … and we're on the wrong side."

"Of course we are," Hound said.

"The ladder crossed a level just above this one," Ellie said.

Ben shook his head, scanning the map in his mind.

"The stairs are this way."

He didn't give them time to argue, moving off in the dark. The stairs were broken here and there, but still marginally passable, with a bit of climbing. He went first, stirring up dust and dislodging a few stones, but otherwise ascending without much difficulty. He scanned the corridor. A pair of yellow eyes watched him from the dark. A howl washed past him. Fear flooded into every inch of his body. He froze, transfixed by the eyes, eyes that were now moving toward him at a dead run.

Time slowed, he took a breath, calming his nerves, drawing his pistol, taking aim, the augment springing into action, marking his target, guiding his shot. He fired.

The eyes in the dark flinched.

He fired again. And again. And again.

Fear spiked in his belly. He focused on his aim, committing his entire will to hitting the target—the beast's left eye.

He fired again.

It flinched, this time barking in pain.

One last shot and it skittered to a stop, shaking its head back and forth frantically.

Hound scrambled into the hallway, light flooding over the horrific beast for a moment before he dropped his flashlight and leveled Bertha at the dragon dog, firing an instant later. It jerked backward, shaking its head again, finding Ben with its one good eye and lunging into a dead run toward him.

He dropped his pistol and drew his blade, whirling away from the wild and terrifyingly fast assault, spinning to face his attacker. It turned, lunging with lightning speed. Ben jabbed, stabbing into the roof of its mouth before dancing aside.

"Hey! Over here," Hound shouted, axe in hand.

Ellie came up beside Ben, their minds meshing seamlessly when she came within a dozen feet.

"We'll pin it, you hack its legs," Ben shouted to Hound, advancing toward the creature, Ellie falling in on his left.

They rushed, coordinating their attacks, stabbing the beast in the chest, driving it back, then lifting it up and tipping it over onto its side, pinning it against the wall. Hound rushed in, hacking the first leg that presented itself.

The creature spasmed, coming free and scrambling backward, yowling in pain. It regained its feet, limping from the lack of a right foreleg, its one good eye fixed on Ben with pure hatred.

Kayla reached the corridor next, drawing her knives.

"Whoa! That thing is ugly … and really unhappy."

Ben and Ellie advanced with Hound behind them.

The dragon dog barked, running a few dozen feet away, limping, half-blind and bleeding. It stopped to howl, its wail no less terrifying for the injuries it had sustained. It locked its one eye on Ben again and barked before turning and limping into the dark.

"No wonder people are so afraid of those things," he said, reloading his pistol. "I shot it six times." His ammo count appeared in his visual field, fading a moment after he acknowledged the information.

"How about we get where we're going?" Hound said.

"Yeah," Ellie said.

Ben oriented himself and set out, heading down a long passage with several doors on either side. They moved past them without looking, heading for the stairs on the far end. Aside from a bit of debris, the path was clear.

He could feel his heartbeat quicken.

The stairs opened onto a road one level below. Ben turned right, hurrying toward a twenty-foot opening in the side of the road. Light was pouring out.

He eased up to the edge, motioning for Hound to turn off his light. He searched for magic, but the feeling he got back was confused, or at least entirely unfamiliar.

"Come out, little rabbit," Hoondragon said.

Ben's hand went to his belly.

"Shit," he whispered, peeking around the edge of the giant door. The dragon's hunter stood in the middle of the room, his horse off to one side, Mandrake watching from the shadows. Ben leaned against the inside of the wall, the augment telling him that the room was a hundred feet on a side and twenty feet high—and a metal cylinder was embedded into the far wall.

The door he'd come for.

"I see you," Hoondragon said. "Come out and die well, little rabbit."

Ben looked back at his friends. Hound smiled, topping off Bertha after chambering a round. Ellie drew her sword—Ben could all but feel the cold steel in her hand. He drew his own sword and stepped out.

"You people are seriously crazy," Kayla said, her back to the wall, her eyes fixed on Ben.

"He's between us and the door," Ben said, shrugging helplessly at her before striding into the room.

"Ah ... excellent. Little rabbit wants to play." Hoondragon held up his weapon, a black bastard sword with an ornate hilt and crossbeam. "Do you remember this?" he asked, his dark eyes peering out through his helm. "It remembers you."

Ben did remember.

"NACC technology detected," the augment said. "Level nine security door, physical contact required."

"You mean I've got to touch that metal cylinder to unlock it?" Ben said. "Yes."

"Circle right," Ben said to Hound.

They rolled around Hoondragon as he advanced. Ben and Ellie met his attack, each of them giving themselves over to the fight, their tactical decisions made long ago by training, their strategy and coordination produced by overlapping flow.

The dragon's hunter was good—more than a match for either of them.

Ben swept into him, diverting his attention from the rather aggressive assault he was waging on Ellie. She regained her footing, launching an attack, forcing Hoondragon to shift and defend, channeling him back and away from the door. Ben circled and attacked again. Hoondragon countered his assault, and slapped him across the face with his gauntlet.

Ben staggered backward, swinging wildly to defend against Hoondragon's overextended attack, just barely batting it aside before racing several steps away to gain distance and his footing. Ben and Ellie were ninety degrees to each other relative to Hoondragon, both moving the same direction, Ben rotating toward the cylinder in the wall.

Hoondragon lunged at him, his blade swinging in a series of powerful attacks, driving Ben backward. Ellie attacked into their enemy's flank, her blade glancing off his armor, scarcely altering his course as he drove Ben back, flipping his blade back and forth, side to side, frantically struggling to defend against the onslaught.

Ellie raced in behind Hoondragon and kicked the back of his knee, dropping him to the ground. He lurched forward, catching himself before falling and sweeping his blade in a great arc to his rear. She dropped, the black sword whistling just inches over her face, narrowly missing her. She regained her feet and surged forward, knocking him over. He landed with a clattering thud, but rolled onto his back, facing her a moment later.

"Now!" Ben shouted, racing for the door.

Hound charged past him, heading for Hoondragon, axe high and ready. The dragon's hunter started to get up. Ellie locked eyes with him, challenging him. He smiled at her for a moment, but then seemed to sense danger, crunching his head down into his shoulder and leaning into Hound's axe. The stroke was sure. It should have taken the better part of his head off. Instead, it hit the lip on his helm, glancing up and away, dispersing the energy of the swing into his helmet.

Hoondragon pitched over sideways from the force of the blow, sprawling face first on the ground. Hound recovered, stepping back, drawing his axe in and readying another blow.

Ben reached the door, sliding to a stop and slapping his hands on the very shiny metal.

Nothing happened.

He looked at the metal door beseechingly, then looked back at the battle raging behind him. His hands stuck to the door. The augment came alive, linking with another computer … and then it began downloading a detailed record of every moment since Ben had awakened with the augment in his brain. It seemed to take forever, but the augment assured him that it had only taken four-tenths of a second.

He felt slightly humbled.

Ellie charged Hoondragon, targeting the point where helm met breastplate, stabbing hard. Her blade hit his armor, glancing away. He swept his sword across the ground, knocking her legs out from under her, dropping her not ten feet away. She landed with a thud and a grunt.

"Access granted," a voice said.

Specifications for the fortress beneath them scrolled through his mind. He shoved them all aside, seeking the one, single, most important piece of information—how long did the door take to open and close?

It began to move. The metal cylinder, forty feet in diameter, unblemished tech metal, impervious and shiny, began to corkscrew up and to Ben's right.

Hound engaged, hitting Hoondragon from behind, his axe glancing off his armor once again. Hoondragon spun, whipping his sword around at Hound, who danced backward, still taking a shallow cut across the chest.

Ben charged back into battle.

Hoondragon turned toward Ellie, now on all fours, struggling to regain her feet. He raised his sword in both hands but Hound hooked his blade with his axe and stopped the blow. Ben circled to the right.

Hoondragon smashed Hound in the face with the pommel of his sword, knocking him back several steps, stunning him. Ben stabbed into the joint of Hoondragon's elbow, his blade slipping through the plates. The dragon's hunter flinched away, barking in pain.

Ben smiled at the red on the tip of his sword.

Hoondragon scrambled backward, moving much more quickly than a large man in plate armor should be able to, checking his position relative to his enemies.

Ellie and Hound flanked Ben. Kayla was already in the wedge-shaped room that served as the secure elevator. It had just moved into place.

"Let's go," she said.

They backed into the room all at once, the elevator asking Ben if he wanted to descend the moment he stepped inside. Hoondragon charged when he saw the cylinder begin to corkscrew down and to the left. The augment calculated a good probability that he would reach them in time to attack.

Ben drew his pistol, consulting the augment as he brought the weapon up, asking for the shot that would stop Hoondragon, even if for just a few seconds. A solution presented itself in his visual field. He let it guide him, targeting his enemy's left foot in the moment of a step and firing. The bullet hit, sweeping his leg out from underneath him at just the moment he committed his weight to it, laying him out flat on his face.

Hoondragon looked up, locking eyes with Ben for a moment before the elevator ceiling passed beneath the room's floor, taking them into the deepest part of the base, beyond reach.

Hound started laughing. "Nice shot," he said, taking a deep breath and letting it out quickly. "Shit, that hurts." He looked at the slice across his chest, shook his head and started taking off his ruined breastplate, tossing it aside.

The room went round and round, down and down, finally opening on one end of a corridor twenty feet wide and ten feet high. Lights came on when they arrived.

After walking about twenty feet, they saw double doors on either wall. At fifty feet, the corridor intersected with an identical corridor running fifty feet in both directions perpendicular to the first.

A hint of light came from the far end of the corridor they stood in. Ben moved forward until he came to a force field. When he laid his hand against the shimmering barrier, his arm fell through.

"Whoa, let's take a look around before we do that," Hound said.

"Yeah," Ben said.

After a few minutes of exploration, they found that the level consisted of four equally sized quadrants—barracks, lab, shop, and storage. Aside from a wide variety of impressive technology, most of it built-in, the level was empty.

Hound walked back to the force field and laid a hand on it. There was a loud popping sound. He jumped back.

"That hurt," he said, inspecting his hand.

"So this is as far as we go," Ellie said.

"Yeah," Kayla said.

"I'll be right back," Ben said, walking through the force field, his companions' protests suddenly becoming muffled when he passed beyond the barrier.

"I hope you know what you're doing," Homer said.

"Me too."

The lights came on. He proceeded, moving down an empty hallway, ten-by-ten for forty feet. The doors at the end of the passage opened on their own. The room beyond was circular, fifty feet across and filled with equipment and tech.

A silver pod shaped like an egg occupied the center of the room, with a series of control stations surrounding it. Two concentric rings of machines filled the rest of the room.

He stopped in the doorway.

Chapter 28

As Ben stared in wonder, a number of nodes around the room began to crackle, electricity arcing from one to the next, casting an eerie light. Each node channeled power into the pod in the center, its silvery, impervious exterior seeming to ripple like water as it took in the power.

The electricity built to a crescendo and then the silvery exterior of the pod melted away. The light in the room equalized and Ben could see a man dressed in medical scrubs strapped to a table tilted at a sixty-degree angle. He was slumped forward, unconscious, his grey hair hanging over his forehead.

"Splinter Brigade Commander, Colonel Edward Kaid," the augment said.

The man groaned, his head lolling back and forth. His body hung limp and still. He looked for all the world like he was on display … for sale, hanging on a rack.

Suddenly he jerked, his body spasming. Then he went still.

Ben held his breath for a moment, then hurried forward. The man was breathing very shallowly, deliberately extending each breath. After several minutes of focused breathing, eyes closed, muscles tense, he opened his eyes and locked on Ben.

With that, the computer in Ben's head went to work. His entire database downloaded, all of his experiences, all of his thoughts, ever since he'd woken up with the augment—the egg, the Oculus, the Sage, Hoondragon, the Dragon Slayer, Imogen's baby, the Warlock, Frank, his grandfather … Homer.

So many things that mattered so much.

The man coughed, sputtering for several seconds, untangling himself from the straps holding him up before falling to his knees.

"Shit," he said. His eyes went distant. He put his forehead on the ground for over a minute.

Ben waited, watching, expecting, hoping, and most of all, fearing.

"Well shit!" the man said, shaking his head, sitting up and looking at Ben, then laughing bitterly. "Looks like it's just you and me, kid."

"Huh?" Ben said. "Wait, what just happened?"

"We're it," he said. "I'm CEO Kaid and you're Director Boyce. We're the NACC." He started laughing again.

"Shut the hell up!" Ben said. "You just raped my mind and now you're laughing at me."

"Ah," he said, "fair enough. We've lost. The dragon won … even with that egg, our chances are slim." He came to his feet, still a bit unsteady. "Still, you're right. Computer, allow all access, Director Boyce."

Ben felt doors open in his mind, files now visible that didn't exist before in his mind's eye, access that wasn't previously available. He scanned the files, finding a folder about the NACC's study of magic.

He scanned the executive summary, noting the hours of video and audio files of experimental data. Magic was genetic, those predisposed to wielding it having descended from the dragon's creations from the time before the flood.

Magic depended on focused will, visualization, and belief to manifest. Part of that was attaining the correct brainwave frequency. Several neurofeedback programs were available to assist the student.

The most powerful magic could only be had through the intervention of powerful beings, but they were always dangerous to deal with.

Kaid stumbled past Ben, heading to a large cabinet occupying the side of the room opposite the entrance. It opened as he approached, a backlit suit of armor hanging within. As he reached inside the pod, countless splinters sprayed away from him, his hand landing on the interior suit. It flowed onto him as if it were liquid, enveloping him completely, save for his head. Then thousands of tiny metal splinters, all floating in a cloud around him, coalesced onto his suit, encrusting the Colonel with gleaming tech-metal armor. The man was in his fifties, grey hair, steel-blue eyes, and he had command presence, especially now.

"Ah, that's better. Hello, Director," he said, cocking his head, frowning and then finally smiling at Ben. "I like the dog," he said.

Ben felt a chill race through him.

"So, near as I can tell, we're going to need orbital weapons," he said.

"What?" Ben said.

He felt a download take place, a rush of information detailing the Splinter Brigade. The capability was astounding.

"Holy shit! You can do all of that?" Ben finally managed.

"Yeah ... and it's not enough."

Another download revealed just how impotent tech was in the face of magic's inherent ability to disrupt it. The most advanced weapon systems were easily disabled by neophyte priests. Low-tech worked better, but was still subject to magical interference.

One battle after another had yielded the same results. Eventually, the NACC had broken up, fracturing into regional resistances, each falling to the degree that they threatened the dragons. They began to study magic too late to make effective use of it.

"Okay, that was depressing," Ben said. "So you know my past and I know yours, or parts of it anyway."

"Don't worry, I'm not going to tell anyone about the dog," Kaid said. "I am curious about his origins, though."

"Me too," Ben said. "My grandfather gave him to me as a child. I don't remember a time when he wasn't there."

"Your grandfather, the fabled Wizard, who led the only successful resistance against the wyrm ... using that egg. I bet he knew where Homer came from."

"Probably," Ben said looking at the floor.

"Sorry, kid. Still fresh?"

Ben nodded.

"So, like I said, we need orbital weapons, preferably kinetic—"

"What are you talking about?" Ben asked, trying to make the transition.

"Ground-based guns don't hit hard enough," Kaid said. "We shot a dragon with surface-based plasma cannons. Barely left a mark. We hit it with a high-energy rail gun. That knocked the wind out of it, and made it mad. We were working on an orbital cannon but it never got put together before the leadership was killed and the rest of us scattered.

"I was supposed to wake up after one year—it's been forty-seven. One last plan gone to hell. None of the other stations in my cell are responding. Most don't even register, those that do don't have power—aside from a few special-access projects with dedicated vacuum energy like this one."

"Wait, where?" Ben asked.

A map of North America appeared with seven facilities highlighted, one deep under Mount Shasta.

"That's the one," Ben said, drilling in closer and mapping a route underground to the secondary entrance. "I need more information about magic, and I believe that I'll find it right there."

"I need bigger guns," Kaid said. "And I'm pretty sure the cannon components are right here."

A facility in Florida lit up in his mind. "That's a long way away," Ben said.

Kaid floated a foot off the ground. "I can fly."

"Of course you can," Ben said. "So, help me first, and then go get bigger guns."

Kaid settled to the ground.

A surveillance feed from the tunnel above appeared in Ben's mind. Hoondragon, Saint Thomas, and Legate Rath stood facing the door flanked by a hundred Dragon Guard.

"The reason I was in stasis is because we couldn't overcome the dragon's ability to interrupt tech."

"I can," Ben said.

"You sure? We have to go right past them to get to the escape tunnel," Kaid said. "If you can keep their magic off me, I can keep them off all of us."

"Done," Ben said. "One last thing. Burn this symbol into the floor right here."

Kaid looked at him for a moment before nodding. Several thousand splinters came free from his armor, assembling into a rotating cylindrical device hovering over his right shoulder. It began firing a few moments later, a beam of red light burning a circle into the floor according to Ben's exact specifications. When it was complete, the laser cannon disassembled and the splinters returned to Kaid's armor.

Ben took a moment to consecrate the circle, then he placed the egg in the center.

"Probably a wise choice" Kaid said.

"I hope so."

"Now, let's upgrade your combat capability," Kaid said.

Another download began, new programs installing into Ben's augment. The splinters' capabilities became even more clear as their operating system became available.

Four hundred splinters peeled off Kaid's armor. Ben felt a handoff take place in his mind and then they were under his control. Each set of one hundred splinters could be used for a variety of things, including darts, surveillance drones, a splinter swarm, a shield, and gravity assist. All four hundred together could create a kinetic missile.

"Put one set on each foot and the other two on your belt," Kaid said.

Ben wasn't sure what Kaid was talking about until the tutorial sprang to life in his mind. He raised one foot and a hundred splinters encrusted the sole of his boot. A moment later the second boot was similarly clad and the remaining two hundred splinters were attached to his belt.

He focused on the two hundred splinters on his boots and rose into the air, just a few inches before he became unsteady and let himself back down.

"Don't get cocky with that," Kaid said. "It'll save you from a short fall, not a high one. It'll help you walk forever if you have to, but you can't fly. Go through your simulations before you try to use the darts in a fight. It may not seem like much, but that setup carries some serious punch, especially if you get creative."

"Thank you," Ben said.

"So, we should talk about our plan," Kaid said.

"What did you have in mind?"

Rather than explain, the Colonel's battle plan sprang into Ben's mind, complete and with additional detail for each section if Ben wanted it.

Ben laughed, shaking his head. "That's quite a talent. And, I think it's a pretty good plan."

"I'm glad you agree. Now you should probably introduce me to your friends."

Kaid closed the door and sealed it with a thought. The access code flickered across Ben's mind and then was stored for immediate retrieval.

He stepped through the force field first. Hound bounded to his feet, Kayla and Ellie right behind him.

Then Colonel Kaid stepped through the field.

"A Metal Man," Kayla whispered.

Ben took a moment to make introductions … and then the interrogation began.

Kaid was patient and forthcoming, but Kayla was relentless, peppering him with questions until he raised his hands.

"Enough," he said. "If you want, I can give you temporary and limited access to the computer."

She stopped talking.

"I think that actually worked," he said, offering Ben a sidelong grin.

"How?" she asked.

"I put a drop of liquid in your eyes and you get access."

She hesitated for just a moment. "Do it."

"It's going to sting."

"I don't care."

A small cluster of splinters detached from his suit and floated up over Kayla, forming a small wedge shape, spinning slowly, tip down.

"Tilt your head back and look at the point."

She obeyed. A drop of liquid formed on the point and then dripped into her right eye. She clenched it shut, biting off a curse, then quickly tipped her head back for a drop in her left eye. The splinters returned to him after administering the second dose.

Kayla leaned forward, both eyes closed, her whole body tense.

"That hurts, a lot," she said.

"It should take about an hour," Kaid said. "Find a bunk in the barracks and lie down."

"Want some help?" Hound asked.

She hesitated before nodding, her eyes still clenched shut. He gently picked her up and carried her into the barracks, returning a few moments later.

"So, a pistol, a gravity gun and a sword; a shotgun and an axe; a sword and two knives," Kaid said, pointing at each of them. "You need bigger guns."

"This guy is starting to grow on me," Hound said.

Kaid smiled, nodding appreciatively. "I'm afraid I don't have a small-arms locker and I'm sure that the base lockers were looted long ago, but I do have a microfab shop."

"I don't know what that is, but if it'll make bigger guns, I like it," Hound said.

With a thought Ben was scanning through the capabilities of the shop.

"I believe you call your shotgun 'Bertha,'" Kaid said. "I can give her an upgrade, if you like."

Hound looked to Ben, as serious and questioning a look as Ben had ever seen on his face.

"Do it," Ben said. "I think you'll like how it turns out."

Hound unslung Bertha and held her out with both hands. "You take real good care of her."

"Come on, you can watch."

Kaid led them into the shop and lights began coming on, first from the ceiling, then blinking and colored lights began coming to life on a number of panels. He took Bertha to a frame box and laid her inside, stepping back while a set of lasers scanned her from every angle.

A holographic image appeared over the box.

"Lose the wood and drop the mag tube," he said.

The hologram changed. The stock and foregrip vanished, and the tube magazine under the barrel disappeared.

"Good, the core is solid. Add a poly foregrip and a collapsing stock with a pistol grip. Also, add an eight-round poly magazine. And a combat sling."

Parts changed again.

"How's that look?" Kaid asked.

Hound had to tear his eyes away from the transformed image of Bertha.

"Real good," he said, quickly looking back at his reimagined weapon.

"All right," Kaid said. "It'll take a few minutes for the machine to make the parts and then we can get to work. How's your ammo?"

"Is there ever really enough ammo?" Hound said, with a helpless shrug.

Kaid cocked his head and smiled. "Fair point. You want shot? Maybe a few grenades?"

"Yeah, what else you got?"

"All gauges of shot up to a slug, sabots, flares, and ex-plus."

"Yes, please," Hound said.

"Of course," Kaid said, nodding a moment later. "The order is in. It might take a while, but you'll have a basic load. Now, about your armor. In fact, all of you need a ballistic shirt and Rufus should probably have a breastplate. What else? Oh, rounds for your revolver, say a hundred slugs and a dozen seekers. Unfortunately, the gravity gun is damaged and can't hold a charge. I'm afraid it's useless."

They all stood mute. Ben wasn't sure what to say. Part of him didn't even believe that the machine whirring away in the background could do what Kaid said. Mostly, he hoped that it could.

It would certainly change things. For the first time since the whole thing began, he might be on solid footing, or at least well-armed.

Kaid looked at Ben and said, "I suggest that you go through your splinter tutorial simulations while we wait. In the meantime, I'll test your friends' blood for magical aptitude and give them a booster shot."

"Come again?" Hound said.

"It's just a shot to clear out any illnesses and to build up your immune system."

"You two go ahead," Ben said, heading for the barracks and lying down before shifting into his simulated reality and activating the training program.

A man dressed in grey robes appeared on a barren landscape. "Splinters can be used in many ways," he began.

Ben opened his eyes. Hound was standing over him, shaking his shoulder.

"Your turn to get stuck," he said, holding up Bertha, now composed mostly of poly, a virtually indestructible, lightweight, and highly durable material custom-formed at a nano level.

"She's damn near a work of art."

Ben sat up. He looked around for Kayla.

"She's with Kaid," Hound said.

Ben wandered across the hall to the lab, where he found Kayla sitting on a table watching Kaid administer a shot injected with high-pressure air.

"This is incredible," she said, seeing Ben. "Is this what it's like for you, too? I mean can you just see the entire base in your mind?"

Ben nodded, smiling. "I take it the pain is gone."

"Yeah, and Kaid gave me this, too," she said, snapping one sleeve of her formfitting undershirt. "It's pretty tough stuff, almost like armor, but not nearly as cumbersome."

"Yours is hanging there," Kaid said, gesturing to the shirt draped over a nearby chair. "It will protect you from most blades and disperse the impact of a bullet, though the kinetic energy will still hurt you. Before you put it on, let me get some blood."

Ben let him take a sample and then okayed the booster shot after questioning the augment about its contents and finding that it was exactly what the Colonel said it was.

He put on his new shirt. It fit perfectly. The fabric was black with a small hexagonal pattern and it was light but strong. He put his tunic on over the shirt and then his coat.

"There's some ammo for you," Kaid said, pointing to several boxes on the table, right next to a couple of grenades.

"Oh, yeah, I made grenades, too. The basic materials needed to make explosives have been depleted, but I can still make slugs and shot if you need more."

"I think I'm good," Hound said.

"Me too," Ben said, stowing the ammo and grenades in his bag.

Kaid turned to Ellie and Kayla and said, "I wish I could provide better weapons for the two of you."

They shrugged in unison.

"I like my weapons," Ellie said.

"Me too," Kayla said.

He chuckled, nodding helplessly.

A soft noise from one of the machines alerted Ben that the blood had been analyzed. He pulled up a report on his own.

"No wonder," Kaid said, displaying the report on the wall. "You've got the highest percentage of alien DNA known to the database. Almost double the best agent we ever tested."

"How about the rest of us?" Hound asked.

"Afraid you and Kayla are in the same boat as I am—nothing. Ellie has a good percentage, about half of our best agent."

"That must be why…"

Ben nodded.

Kayla looked dejected.

"You should all get some sleep," the Colonel said. "Once we set out, we'll be on the move for quite some time."

Ben ate and then slept. He woke up hungry.

After breakfast, he checked the surveillance feed from the room above. Saint Thomas and Hoondragon were still waiting, but now they had three hundred Dragon Guard and they were dug in.

"Just as expected," Kaid said.

Ben nodded.

They gathered their things and stepped into the corkscrew elevator.

"Tell me how this works again?" Hound said.

"I shield his shield so it can shield us."

As the room began to move, Ben projected his circle around everyone, willing it to protect all within from magic, sending the image of the circle's position to Kaid.

Splinters began to peel away, floating up and around them, forming a floor-to-ceiling matrix that projected a force field just inside Ben's circle. The ceiling of the elevator rose above the floor of the waiting room. More splinters peeled away, forming a ring overhead, just inside the shield. Several streaks of white began to move around the inside of the ring, faster and faster.

The enemy tensed.

Ben waited for it, pressing his will against a force that had not yet come. He wasn't disappointed. As the room moved, twisting up and left, his eyes locked with a fair-haired young man wearing white robes—good-looking by any standard, except for the yellow eyes and the black claws.

The assault came a moment later, Ben's will challenged by a far stronger will. He relaxed into the attack, absorbing and deflecting, taking the brunt of it and holding his own. He could feel his defenses being stripped away, his strength, will, and focus draining out of him with each moment of effort. He could hold, but not for long.

"Fire!" Legate Rath commanded.

Fifty Dragon Guard unleashed their rifles at them, a wave of orange flame washing onto the force field and then splashing away like water, leaving the floor outside the shield burning. Ben felt heat on his face, but the certain death he expected from such an attack never materialized. Kaid's shield protected them.

Kaid directed the first glowing ball of matter orbiting rapidly overhead, sending it out like a bullet at Legate Rath. The shot hit him squarely in the chest, sending him flying back into the crowd, hitting two Dragon Guard before tumbling to a halt. He groaned and sat up, looking down at his shattered breastplate.

"He's a tough one," Kaid said, sending another shot at him.

Saint Thomas gestured forcefully toward Rath from forty feet across the room and sent him sprawling out of the way of the next round coming for him. Ben felt the force of the assault on his circle wane momentarily, but then resume with as much intensity or possibly even more a second later.

The room turned, the ceiling of the elevator now higher than the ceiling of the room. Kaid sent his final rounds in close orbit at the nearest two Dragon Guard, burning holes through their chests the size of a man's fist.

Ben held, defending against a relentless mental assault on his protective circle. Once the floor passed the ceiling, the assault stopped. He almost fell over.

"That was impressive," Hound said.

"Not half as impressive as the fact that his armor held," Kaid said, his accelerator disassembling and returning to him.

The room turned round and round, rising well over a hundred feet. Ben reviewed the map, filling in a dead space that he'd wondered about before. They reached another level and ground to a halt. Kaid dispatched a swarm of splinters into the room. They formed small whirling cubes, crackling light glowing from within dozens of spinning lanterns.

The room was large, a hundred feet on a side and it was completely empty. One road ran out the opposite side.

"This route should be safe," Kaid said. "There aren't any connecting tunnels between here and the exit."

Chapter 29

It was safe and blessedly boring. Kaid's floating splinter lanterns provided a soft light to travel by and his drones ranged ahead, providing a constant view of the coming tunnel.

Ben fell back from the rest of the group, willing one of the splinter clusters to detach and form into a dart. He was surprised by how quickly the weapon appeared, floating five feet in front of him, a small dart, just under an inch long and a quarter inch across. He queried the augment, checking the durability of the splinters. To his surprise, and mild annoyance, the database listed them as partially indestructible.

"What does that mean?"

"Most events cannot destroy a splinter, though extraordinary events, such as the plasma accelerator that the Colonel created, will consume or destroy splinters."

"So I can shoot it at the wall," Ben said.

"Yes, but to little effect."

Ben picked a point on the cement wall and directed the dart at it. It leapt forward, accelerating with terrifying speed, hitting about five inches from the point of his aim, burying halfway into the cement. He walked up, willing his other cluster to form a set of lanterns like Kaid had done. Five little floating cubes formed, crackling blue-white light emanating from the center of each. Ben examined the dart. He looked back, estimating his range at about fifteen feet.

"Not bad," he said to himself, willing the dart to dislodge from the cement and fire at the opposite wall, this time burying the dart almost entirely.

"What would that do to an unarmored person?" he asked the augment.

"Through-and-through penetration."

"You coming?" Ellie called back.

Ben hurried to catch up, the dart orbiting around his head.

"Playing with your new toys?" she said when he reached her.

He shrugged with a grin, pointing to the wall and directing the dart to strike.

"Whoa!" she said, stopping in her tracks. "That's powerful—don't let anyone see you use it."

"No," Ben said, shifting the configuration of the dart into a drone. A moment later a feed view came up in the corner of his visual field.

"Nice," he whispered, sending the drone forward, accelerating quickly, scanning through its capabilities—telescopic, infrared, thermal, auditory, data relay and storage, record, broadcast, project a limited hologram, conditional activation and linkage with other NACC weapons systems to provide targeting data—in this case, Ben and his darts or his seeker rounds.

He brought it back and reattached it to his belt. For the hour that followed, he practiced willing a cluster of splinters to detach from his belt, coalesce into a dart and hit a target. At first, it took the better part of a second to form the dart and strike. An hour later, he was hitting his target within a tenth of a second … quick as a thought.

He added a second dart to the mix. Again, he was slow and clumsy at first, but continued practice paid off. After another two hours, he was able to rapid fire his two darts at two different targets in fractions of a second.

"Think of your darts like guns with infinite bullets," Kaid said in his head.

A demo video came up showing a soldier with one dart hitting multiple targets in succession by accelerating the weapon through one target, slowing rapidly, retargeting and accelerating again. He hit six targets in three seconds.

Ben fell back again and shot at the wall, then turned the dart and shot across the corridor into the other wall, back and forth. After a while, he started to feel tired, but not from walking … the splinters on his feet were helping him move with ease. His mind was tired. Constant focus on the splinters was taxing.

His vision of Ellie at the wyrm's mercy suddenly came to him. Fear surged into his belly. He stopped, leaning over to breathe. He recovered his wits a moment later and hurried to catch up again.

Since he'd touched the Oculus, he'd been trying to think about anything other than what he feared for Ellie's future. He reminded himself that the visions were always only part of the story and that they were open to interpretation.

He caught up and she smiled at him. A wave of guilt wracked him. He was putting her in danger, and now it wasn't abstract danger. The visions from the Oculus felt so real, and yet, he hadn't led Hoondragon to the safe house. Maybe he could protect her from falling into the dragon's mercy, too.

"What's wrong?" she asked, touching his arm.

"I got a flash from one of my visions."

"Want to talk about it?"

"Not really," he said, looking down and away from her.

"All right, but if you ever do…"

He nodded with an apologetic smile and fell back. He briefly considered trying to send her home again, but he knew how that would go. He decided to distract himself, activating a brainwave-monitoring program. He watched the erratic line move across the bottom of his visual field. With a thought, he switched it to the top and started watching the line more intently.

After a while, he began to breathe in rhythm to his footsteps, adding mental counting a moment later. After a few minutes, the line began to fall, dipping out of the beta frequency and into alpha. He walked in a trance, his mind so focused on his walking, breathing, counting rhythm that he walked right into Ellie, causing her to stumble and nearly fall.

"Oh God, are you okay?" he said, after she caught her balance and looked back at him with a mixture of annoyance and surprise. He winced. "I'm sorry, I wasn't paying attention." He tapped the side of his head.

"Be more careful," she said. "You could walk into a wall, or worse."

He nodded sheepishly.

Kaid fell back, walking beside him.

"It takes practice," he said in Ben's head. "Yeah, we can talk without talking, share data, intel, pretty much any information you want, but I can't dig around in your mind, at least not any more than I did when we first met.

"Anyway, it takes practice to pay attention to reality and to your display at the same time. Err on the side of reality."

"Yeah, I suppose that's good advice."

Kaid stopped, sighing and frowning to himself.

A drone feed appeared, showing Ben a cave-in about an hour ahead. "That complicates things," he said.

"Yeah, but not too badly," Kaid said, setting out again.

"What are you two talking about?" Hound asked.

"There's a dead end up ahead."

"So why aren't we turning around?" Hound asked as Kaid walked away.

"No need," he said over his shoulder.

They walked for another hour before they reached the cave-in. The entire road was collapsed.

"We'll have to go back to the surface," Kaid said.

"How? Back through town?" Kayla asked. "That would be risky."

"No, I'll just cut an exit," Kaid said. "But maybe we should stop for the night here. No sense wasting perfect security."

Everyone nodded agreement and went to work making dinner and laying out their bedrolls.

"Don't worry about a guard," Kaid said. "I'll set a force field and a dozen sentry drones. Even if anything is down here, it won't get through that."

They ate while listening to Kaid tell stories about battles fought long before any of them were born. Ben thought that he might be embellishing, but not by much.

He wondered about Imogen and John, wondered if they were safe, worried that he had left them. Imogen was one of the strongest women he'd ever known, but since her child had been taken, she wasn't herself—she needed help, she needed him. Ben knew that John would look out for her, but he wasn't going to be able to rescue her baby and she wasn't going to stop trying.

Most of all, he worried about what she might do next.

Morning came by the light of Kaid's lanterns floating overhead. After breakfast, he stood up, appraising the collapsed ceiling.

"You're going to want to stand back," he said, ushering them away from the end of the tunnel.

Then he turned toward the dead end. Splinters began coming off of him, assembling into a large cylinder five feet in diameter and twelve feet long. Piece by piece it came together, taking a few minutes to construct. Once it was complete, it began to rotate, aiming one end of the cylinder at an upward angle.

Kaid backed off a bit more and another swarm of splinters projected a shield across the entire tunnel, enclosing the device he'd assembled on the far side.

The cylinder began to swirl and pulse with light, sputtering and popping before an intensely bright blue-white beam shot forth, burning the stone and dirt.

Within seconds, the space beyond the shield was cloudy with vaporized remnants of rock. Pressure began to build, then abruptly it was released when the beam cut a small hole through to the surface. Kaid began to work his beam around in a circle until he'd cut a seven-foot-diameter hole at a thirty-degree angle all the way to the top. It took twenty minutes.

They waited several minutes longer for the ground to cool and the vapor to dissipate.

"I've never seen anything so powerful," Kayla said. "Couldn't that kill the dragon?"

"Afraid not," Kaid said. "Beam weapons get diffused when they get close to him. It'll do a number on his men, though," he smiled.

"I have to say, that was impressive," Hound said, staring at the hole burned to the surface. "I've seen some magic, and that was better."

"If only it worked against magic," Kaid said. He held his hand out toward the angled two-thousand-foot shaft, testing the temperature. "Still warm, but not dangerously so."

Two drones zipped up to the surface and rose into the air, each spinning slowly, capturing full panorama video of the surrounding area. They stopped at a thousand feet, holding station while rotating slowly.

"Looks clear," Kaid said, floating a foot off the ground and gliding up to the surface.

"Bastard," Hound said, hoisting his pack and beginning the long climb. The others followed behind him.

"My feet hurt," Homer said after walking a short distance. "The ground is still hot."

Ben scooped him up, carrying him upside down in his arms.

He grumbled contentedly.

Ben felt grateful, and a tinge guilty, for his tech-enhanced footwear, which greatly eased the difficulty of the climb. When they reached the surface, they were in a forest somewhere near Mount Shasta.

Hound lay down in the dust-covered moss and tried to catch his breath. Kayla and Ellie walked in circles to cool off before sitting down and taking off their boots.

"That was a bit more than warm, fly-boy," Kayla said.

"Apologies. I sometimes forget what it is to be without metal."

"I'll bet," Hound said, still breathing heavily, lying flat on his back and staring at the sky.

Ben queried his map, noting the location of the main entrance to Shasta Base. The augment provided his current location by referencing the record of their journey from the bunker.

"Seventy-five miles," he said. "Two days if we push really hard."

"Or we could just fly," Kaid said.

"What do you mean?" Ben asked, the answer appearing in his mind before he finished asking the question.

"Why isn't that in the books?"

"Because not everything is in the books, most of the best stuff we just made up along the way. Like that accelerator cannon—you lose a few splinters, but the projectile can be accelerated to plasma with a little time and a bigger ring."

"You're telling me that your suit is also a plasma cannon," Hound said, sitting up and looking at him, before looking over at Bertha. "Girl, you're pretty, but…"

Kaid laughed, nodding unabashedly.

"The splinter suit is the best weapon system I've ever commanded. Unfortunately, you need a chip to make them work, and I've never had clearance to chip someone, or the tech, for that matter."

"What about what you did for Kayla?" Hound said.

"I gave her limited access to the city computer and command of the doors, as well as a visual display with access to city specifications. The eye drops don't allow for weapons interface—that requires a whole different level of mind-computer integration."

"How do I get a chip?" Kayla asked.

"I wish I knew," Kaid said. "Believe me, we'd be a whole lot more effective if I could divide my splinters among all of us. Unfortunately, Ben's chip can only handle four hundred and none of the facilities that might have been able to produce the required tech are showing any signs of life."

Hound shrugged. "Had to ask." He got to his feet.

Ben tried to contact the base … he waited … but there was no response.

"What are you thinking?" Kaid asked.

"I want to know if Saint Thomas and Hoondragon are still waiting for us."

"Nice," Kaid said, a swarm of splinters coming free and coalescing into a dish receiver, pointing toward the sky. He redirected it a few times and then stopped.

"Comsat up … linking to base … surveillance…"

The feed came up in Ben's mind. The room was empty of men but there was a pack of twenty stalker wolves and the entrance had been completely walled off.

"Well, that's an answer," Ben said, detaching from the feed and stretching out with his mind. He felt like his range was diminished, not by too much, maybe twenty percent. Then he felt a presence. And another. Stalkers.

He sent two clusters of splinters into the air, one a dart, the other a drone. He sat down, closed his eyes and opened the drone feed as his sole focus.

"Good idea," Kaid said.

Ben's drone scanned the field. He switched to thermals and found both stalkers within a few moments. He picked the closest one and drilled in with telescopic vision, locating a bobcat stalker, maybe fifty pounds, but dangerous. He locked on to the enemy, tracking it with the drone as it moved, while the dart fell into a glide, homing on its target and accelerating. The augment noted a cluster of trees in the way and plotted a course around, coming to bear on the target. Ben commanded the drone, several thousand feet high, to chirp … loudly.

A single tech beep rang out in the sky. The stalker stopped, looking straight at the drone. Ben smiled. The dart hit it right in the side of the head, breaking into its constituent splinters a moment after impact, shredding the stalker's cranial cavity and spraying brain across the ground. Its body flopped over and went still.

Ben reassembled his dart and commanded it to return to the drone.

"Well done," Kaid said. "No need to go looking for the other one. I already burned it."

Ben gave him a disappointed look.

"What? You designated targets."

"Yeah ... I guess I just didn't ... this hasn't all sunk in yet." He motioned to his head with both hands.

"Understandable," Kaid said. "Like I told you when we met, we're the NACC, you and me ... and maybe Kayla." He gave her a sidelong grin.

"Now, tell me how you found them in the first place. There were other predators in the area that you didn't target."

"Stalkers," Ben said. "I used magic."

Kaid's eyes went distant for a moment. Ben could see the files being accessed in his mind's eye.

"Dangerous. Did you really survive that?"

"Yeah," Ben said. "I try not to think about the hellish realm they come from."

"Sorry, I can understand why ... I couldn't stomach three seconds of the simulation." He put a hand on Ben's shoulder. "I'm glad you're the one who found me."

"Me too," Ben said. "You mentioned something about flying to Shasta."

"Oh, yeah, I've played around with the force-field function, a lot."

Splinters drifted off of him and began to take shape. A dozen seconds later, there were four seats made of splinters and a blue force field surrounding him. A low-walled dog box formed behind one of the seats.

Kaid chuckled. "It's amazing what you can do with force fields. It takes quite a few splinters to make it work and a good imagination, but the results are undeniable."

"You want us to sit on your magical blue see-through chairs?" Hound said. "And then what?"

"We fly to Shasta."

"You said it was seventy-five miles," Hound said, turning to Ben. "We can do that in two days if we push, like you said."

Kayla took a seat, wiggling a bit to get comfortable while smiling mischievously at Hound.

"Oh," he whispered, cocking his head sideways, watching Ellie take a seat. "Women are evil, you know that, right?" he said to Ben, pulling him in closer. "Maybe I should go find Imogen, bring the rest of our people to the fight."

"It'll be all right, Rufus," Ben said. "He won't drop us, and this tech works. I know it does, for certain." He tapped the side of his head, then took Hound by the arm and walked him over to one of the remaining force-field chairs.

"This is crazy," Hound said.

"Yeah, but it'll work," Ben said.

"You better be sure about this. I don't mind a fair fight, but gravity don't fight fair."

"I am sure," Ben said. "This could make all the difference. We need the Codex. I need to understand magic better.

"Even when I was little, my grandfather read me stories about battles. There was always a decisive moment, the bold decision that turned the tide of a fight. This, right now, is that moment. We move with all possible haste. We reach our objective before the enemy can stop us and we use it to destroy them."

Hound nodded, looking down and nodding some more.

"Flying ain't natural," he said.

"Sit down!" Ellie and Kayla barked at the same time, both of them giggling at him a moment later.

"Well, shit, when you put it like that," he muttered, taking his seat.

"You sure about this?" Homer said.

"Pretty sure," Ben said.

"Gotta say, on this one, I think I'm with Hound. You can tell a lot about a person from their name."

Ben envisioned a dog box behind his chair that was opaque and sent the visual to Kaid. A few moments later the box was no longer translucent.

"Best I can do," he said, picking Homer up and setting him in the box before taking his own seat. Homer curled up and closed his eyes. A swarm of splinters streamed off of Kaid, forming an oval force field around all of them.

"Prepare to strap in," he said. A moment later, three bands of energy formed across each passenger's legs, waist, and chest.

"What the hell?" Hound said.

They lifted into the air, rising a hundred feet, then two hundred, and then accelerating forward at a rapid pace. Kaid kept them a few dozen feet over the trees, moving fast, but constantly changing altitude to minimize risk of exposure.

"Oh, shit!" Hound said, loud enough to startle everyone.

Ben banished the readouts and turned his attention to the landscape slipping by beneath him. It was majestic, powerful, primal—a part of the world that had never been tamed. He felt a sense of gratitude for that.

They came off of a draw and floated out over a lake, moving twenty feet above the water, fast and low. It was wide, two kilometers at least. Targeting data came up in Ben's display.

"Enemy," Kaid said.

They banked hard, moving away from the enemy position and toward the north side of the lake.

"Brace!" Ben shouted.

White light, like a cloud moving at terrifying speed, nearly collided with them, streaking past in a blur.

Ben took a breath. "Bank harder, get distance ... dive!" he shouted.

Kaid dove, expertly transitioning into a glide toward the water in the last few feet of fall. Spray shot up on both sides as they decelerated. Intense cold white light streaked over them.

"There are two of them," Ben said, marking the originating position of both shots for Kaid as they splashed into the lake.

Splinters wrapped around them, lifting them from the water and carrying them toward the bank even as more splinters detached from Kaid, floating straight up into the air in a swirling cloud. Once the splinters reached three thousand feet, the cluster stopped and formed an accelerator cannon a hundred feet across. At the same time, a number of smaller drones moved off toward both targets, spooling up and emitting light as if preparing to fire.

Ben watched in his mind's eye. The accelerator propelled a handful of splinters up to genuinely dangerous speeds, friction with the atmosphere transforming them into a stream of superheated plasma after they'd reached sufficient velocity.

Kaid directed a stream of plasma at the first target, a flash of brilliance burning a straight line across the sky, blasting a hole into the lakeside forty feet wide and causing an explosion that could be heard for a hundred miles.

It also killed the target.

The other enemy ran.

The weapon powered down and Kaid re-formed his flying force-field carriage, taking them fifty feet over the treetops, very quickly.

Ben closed his eyes and reached out with his mind. There was darkness, and power, pursuing him. And it was on the move, as if it had his scent. He reestablished his circle … again.

Kaid altered course, moving up the backside of a ridge to the top of a knoll overlooking the mountain and the surrounding countryside. He landed on top of a peak that they couldn't climb down from if they wanted to.

"I've got eyes on a small army," he said.

A drone feed opened in Ben's mind. Ten thousand Dragon Guard were camped around the broken and scorched entrance to Shasta Base.

"Yeah … that's where we have to go," Ben said.

Kaid chuckled. "Of course it is. I can burn them from here and then take you in."

"Seriously?" Hound said.

"Yeah, they're five point four klicks out. My heavy laser hits hard at that range, and we have the high ground."

"Won't that give away our location?" Kayla asked.

"Probably … I guess I could send the laser to a different position."

"Do that," Ben said. "Let's stay low and see what happens." He focused on his circle, and then opened his mind to magic in the vicinity—two stalkers on the outer edge of his awareness, and something else farther out, far more powerful, and coming fast.

A large swarm of splinters floated off of Kaid and began accelerating away. It wasn't until the swarm began to coalesce into the laser weapon and the surveillance capability came online that Ben noted where the weapon was—twenty kilometers away, firing from well up the side of Mount Shasta.

The blue-white beam split the world, a bright line arcing out at the Dragon Guard army from the mountain.

Let's go," Kaid said, re-forming his flying chairs. Hound sat down after only a stern look from Ben. Soon they were flying toward the enemy, watching the laser systematically burn a hole through each man, flicking from one to the next with terrifying speed and accuracy. After a minute and a half, the remaining Dragon Guard scattered, all of them searching for any form of cover against the light from the sky.

Men fell by the hundreds, the bright beam never wavering, just retargeting. After a few minutes, the enemy soldiers had either fled or died.

Kaid's force-field carriage drew closer, flying a few hundred feet above the forest, coming over another small mountain lake.

Saint Thomas was standing on the bank.

All of Kaid's splinters failed at once. The carriage collapsed and they all fell, tumbling into the water. Ben hit hard, the wind bursting out of him. He wanted to take a breath, but his augment stopped him, freezing his diaphragm until he surfaced. It was a few of the most miserable moments that Ben could remember … but he was still alive.

He gasped for breath, looking around frantically before going under again, registering an image in his mind of a handsome young man on the far bank. The water was black, and cold. He held his breath, kicking for the surface.

He came up again, taking a gulp of air, and then another, then turned his face up to the sky and lay back on the water. As he floated, he leaned his head up for a moment to see the man on the far bank … except he wasn't a man anymore. He had transformed into something hideous with wings and leathery skin … and horns.

The creature was just beginning to flap its wings.

Ben spun around in the water, picking the nearest bank and swimming for it. He gained on it but started to lose energy, stopping to look at the coming threat.

Saint Thomas flew toward him on a pair of batlike wings, his body no longer remotely human. Ben felt for the lake bottom with his foot. It was beyond reach. He started swimming harder. He looked back, still in deep water. Saint Thomas pointed a staff at Hound, a staff with a claw affixed to one end.

It took a second for it to register, but Ben suddenly realized that Saint Thomas was wielding the Warlock's dragon-claw staff. Darkness shot forth from it, reaching across the battlefield quickly, hitting Hound in the chest. Ben expanded his shield, willing all within to be protected.

Hound lost focus for a moment, then brought Bertha up as Ben's circle dispelled the black magic.

"Son of a bitch!" Hound shouted. "Try and take control of me!"

Bertha rang out, followed a fraction of a second later by another explosion. Saint Thomas spiraled into the water.

Ben's feet finally reached the lakebed and he rushed out of the water as quickly as he could, feeling all the while like he was in a dream and stuck in molasses.

Hound was smiling at the shot he'd just made.

"I'm thinking I was too quick to judge," Hound said as Ben waded out of the water. "Maybe Bertha still has more blood to spill. That was a sabot round. I liked it."

Ben stopped, leaning on Hound while he let the water drain out of his pants and boots. "I'm glad to see that you're working through this."

"Hey guys," Kayla said, walking toward them from along the south shore.

Ben felt it as soon as he opened himself up to it—Saint Thomas was down, but still alive. He rose out of the lake, flying north.

Kaid shot straight up out of the water, his splinters detaching and reattaching as he landed. "Guys like him make me nervous," he said.

"I don't like the looks of him, either," Ellie said, watching him fly into the forest, one wing damaged, his flight slightly wobbly.

"No," Ben said, "he's dangerous."

"Yeah, but he's running that way," Hound said, pointing north. "And we want to go that way, so let's go."

Ben checked his map. They were still half a dozen klicks out.

"Let me do a survey," Kaid said, a swarm of his splinters returning from the fire mission, some going right back out on a surveillance tasking. A couple of minutes later, Ben got a summary of their position and the enemy's position relative to them.

The army was scattered, but regrouping in small units. Hoondragon and Legate Rath were just inside the shattered entrance to Shasta Base with a hundred Dragon Guard and three dragon dogs.

"We've got to get through that," Ben said.

"They should have dug in," Kaid said, another swarm of splinters moving away from his now diminished armor.

The splinters took position a thousand feet up, forming into a circle, a handful beginning to accelerate until they reached subplasma energy levels. Kaid directed the particle stream at the base entrance.

A flash momentarily took over the sky, followed by a boom and then a cloud of dust.

Ben watched the feed. The blast had delivered significant explosive force without collapsing the entrance further. There was no evidence of Dragon Guard visible from outside once the dust cleared.

"Nice," Ben said.

"Thomas is hightailing it home," Kaid said, sending Ben another feed.

The dragon high priest was flying with all possible speed toward the rising plume of dust that Kaid had just caused.

"He has a lead on us," Ben said.

"Let's see what he knows," Kaid said, transforming the accelerator cannon into a beam laser. After a minute of transformation, disassembly and reconstruction, it sputtered to life, projecting a blue-white beam from high overhead at Saint Thomas. The surveillance feed locked on and zoomed in.

The beam shot straight and true but diffused a dozen feet away from Thomas, effectively transforming into a floodlight with no power other than annoyance and illumination.

"Yeah, that's what I thought," Kaid said, recalling the splinters making up the beam weapon and re-forming the flying chairs.

Ben helped Homer on board, then took his seat, reloading his revolver with seeker rounds in the first two positions. Soon they were flying low and fast. Ben knew they were in no danger but he still felt a few thrills of fear from Kaid's maneuvers. Hound was cursing under his breath at every sudden shift in direction.

"You should land a ways out and let us walk in," Ben said. "Saint Thomas is inside somewhere."

A feed came up in Ben's mind—the Warlock, a Dragon Guard armed with a dragon-fire rifle, and another man, cloaked and hooded and carrying a rifle as well, all headed into the bunker, a cougar trailing behind them.

Ben highlighted the relevant data clips for Kaid, marking the moments in time that he'd encountered the Warlock.

Kaid picked a small meadow a kilometer out and set down, recalling all of his splinters save a few drones providing overwatch.

"I'll provide fire support and surveillance, but I'm not getting into tight quarters with magic," Kaid said.

"Understandable," Ben said. "Let me know if anyone else shows up."

"Will do," Kaid said. "Let me know when you need an exit."

Splinters formed a seamless shell over his face a moment before he flew straight up into the air.

"Must be nice," Hound said.

"Yeah," Ben said, directing the two clusters on his belt to launch as drones, floating up and into twin orbits over their position. "This way."

They moved cautiously, Ben stopping frequently to refer to his drone feeds. He found a small unit, twenty-seven men strong, five hundred meters away. He stopped, picking a new path around a grove of fir, easily avoiding the threat. He stopped again, still within the trees, sending one drone forward, searching for the best path and any other threats.

"Looks like most of them have scattered to the north. We're clear to the entrance."

"Uh-huh," Hound said.

"There's nothing there now," Ben said.

"Until we go inside," Kayla said.

"Exactly," Hound said, pointing at Kayla. "Hoondragon and a pretty scary dragon priest—plus the Warlock and his entourage for good measure."

"What's your point?" Ben said.

"We need a plan."

"How about this? We go up to the door, look inside, see what we see and go from there?"

"Okay, smartass," Hound said. He pointed toward the mountain looming over them. "Seriously, there's some dangerous shit in there. How do you want to handle things?"

"I want to go in quietly, slip past everyone and find what we need without ever being detected. Then I want to slip out the same way we came in."

"What do you think the odds of that happening are?" Ellie asked.

"Slim to none," Ben said with a shrug. "If we have to fight, let's be quiet about it if we can."

They all nodded. The forest was thinning along with the air. Ben kept one drone at the base entrance and the other a thousand feet overhead, scanning the immediate area. They came out into a wide mountain meadow, the last stretch before they reached the entrance.

Fifteen Dragon Guard emerged from the forest to the north, five hundred meters away and moving toward Ben. Suddenly, bright light arced out of the sky and systematically burned a hole through each and every one of them in a matter of seconds.

"I think we're clear," Ben said, hurrying toward the scorched bunker entrance. Once, it could have accommodated four lanes of traffic. Now, a section of the tunnel was collapsed several hundred feet inside, choking off all but a narrow passage under a section of ceiling propped up by an intact beam.

Ben had stopped his drone there. The space before the collapse was littered with the bodies of more than a hundred Dragon Guard, scorched, crushed, and mangled—they looked like they'd been blasted apart by unimaginable forces. A quick but thorough scan didn't find Hoondragon or Saint Thomas in the carnage.

Ben didn't expect to get that lucky but it was worth a look.

They reached the entrance, a wide, steel-reinforced concrete tunnel plunging into the side of the mountain.

"Impressive kill count," Hound said, appraising the dead, searching a few, taking a coin here and a knife there. "The Metal Man is a nice surprise for a change."

Ben nodded, heading for the narrow section, sending his drone in once he reached it, switching to low-light vision, winding through a series of narrow passages for thirty feet or so before reaching the next section of tunnel.

Dark and quiet.

Ben scanned but found nothing. The tunnel went straight for half a mile before it reached the first level of the base. Ben sent his drone forward, moving quickly, its sensors recording as it flew.

"There's one," Ben said, sending his second cluster through the rubble as a drone, racing to catch up with the first, now holding station, pressed into the corner between the wall and ceiling. When the second drone got close, Ben transformed it into a dart, using the first drone to target the Dragon Guard hiding in a broken section of the wall, waiting … bored.

His helmet was off. Ben almost felt bad. He directed the dart into the side of the man's head, killing him by surprise in an instant. Then he transformed the dart into a drone again and recalled it, leaving the other to watch the tunnel.

"We should be clear for a ways," he said, heading into the passage through the rubble. It was a tight squeeze in a few places, but it was stable. When they reached the far side, the tunnel resumed its forty-foot-wide, twenty-foot-high passage through the mountain.

Ben picked the side of the tunnel where the Dragon Guard had been hiding and moved to that wall, setting out with minimal light. He sent his forward drone to scout the rest of the tunnel. When it reached a set of melted steel doors, Ben slowed it, moving it along the floor near one wall. The room was five hundred feet across and twice as long. A number of tunnels and facilities and passages dotted the far wall, all of the doors melted to slag. A few ancient, burned-out vehicles littered the space between.

Saint Thomas stepped out from behind one of the derelict vehicles. He carried the Warlock's staff. Hoondragon stepped out next, followed by Mandrake and three Dragon Guard, all a bit banged up.

Thomas looked straight at Ben's drone and smiled. Then the feed went dead.

"Shit," Ben muttered. "They know we're here."

"Who, exactly, is 'they'?" Hound asked.

"Hoondragon and Thomas."

Hound nodded, sighing. "What's your plan?"

"Hit 'em hard and push through," Ben said. "Once we're into the base below, we'll run and hide."

"So, bust 'em in the mouth and run away," Hound said.

Ben shrugged.

"No, I like it," Hound said, checking Bertha. "I think I'll lead with a sabot—you know, since Thomas liked the first one so much."

"Once we reach the room, we want the road door on the far side, just left of center," Ben said.

They moved along the wall, staying quiet, staying dark.

"Was that you?" Ellie whispered as they passed the dead Dragon Guard.

Ben looked back, nodding. A few hundred feet later, he stopped.

"Come out, little rabbit," a voice in the distance said.

"I'm really starting to hate him," Ben muttered, turning his attention to his circle.

A gunshot rang out from the room ahead.

"What the hell?" Hound said.

"Come on," Ben said, racing forward as quickly as he dared in the dark. Another shot. Then a flare of orange. It faded, but not completely.

Ben reached the end of the road and stopped, looking out into the giant room, the hub for the base entrance. His splinters came back to life the moment his circle passed over them. He assembled them into a drone and kept it close.

"Are you mad?" Thomas shouted, his white robes burning from the dragon fire the man's rifle had just belched at him. The Dragon Guard prepared another shot. Hoondragon and Mandrake watched with amusement from a good distance.

The Dragon Guard fired again, but this time Saint Thomas flung his arm out at the fire, barking a command. The flames turned, rebounding away from him and washing over the Dragon Guard, burning him alive, sending him screaming and running wildly until he fell.

Thomas tore off his burning robes, tipped his head back in a silent scream and abruptly transformed into a seven-foot-tall, leathery, winged, taloned and fanged dragon-man.

"Human form is so tiresome," he said, turning toward Ben and smiling as he stretched his wings.

In the same moment, Ben saw movement from across the room—the Warlock, another man, and a cat. It appeared that the Warlock had his staff back.

The Dragon Guard were all dead, save Legate Rath, who had taken position behind one of the burned-out vehicles.

Ben met the high priest's yellow eyes for a moment and withdrew into the corridor.

"Shoot Thomas, then throw grenades at Hoondragon and make a run for it," Ben said.

Hound stepped out, took aim and fired. Thomas launched into the air, his wings carrying him up to the ceiling in a single beat, well out of the path of Hound's sabot round. Ben stepped into the room and shot twice, firing both seeker rounds, both targeting Saint Thomas.

The first penetrated a wing, through-and-through, failing to explode, doing minimal damage. Ben felt Thomas's formidable mind pushing on the seeker rounds, willing them to malfunction. The second round struck the other wing, exploding and shredding it, dropping Saint Thomas to the ground in a smoldering heap.

Mandrake leaped toward them. Ellie and Kayla each threw a grenade the moment the bullets were away. Both grenades arced over Mandrake's head, landing on either side of Hoondragon, bouncing and then exploding, concussive force hitting him first, followed an instant later by shrapnel. He toppled over.

Mandrake leapt. Ben fired four times, hitting him each time in the chest. He landed on top of Ben, knocking him over onto his back, then reared up to strike, faltering for a moment as if he'd forgotten what he was doing, blood flowing freely from his wounds.

Ben's arms were pinned. Mandrake regained focus, looking down at him with burning hatred, raising his clawed hand and preparing to strike. Ellie stabbed him through the heart, grunting as she levered him over so he wouldn't fall on Ben.

Ben rolled onto all fours, his ears ringing from the grenades and multiple gunshots. He shook his head and looked up, frowning at the person watching him from a doorway across the giant room. He shook his head again and there was nobody there. He regained his feet.

Hoondragon was trying to get back up. Saint Thomas was already on his feet.

Hound cried out, a knife buried in his left shoulder.

Legate Rath fled into another section of the base.

"Son of a bitch," Hound said. "Kaid said this armor would stop bullets." He pulled the blade out, gasping in pain as it came free, less than half an inch of blood on the tip. He held the knife up and examined it. "That's quite the blade," he said. "Weighted for throwing, too."

Ben looked at it and specifications came up. NACC tech, advanced carbon polymer, single piece, stealth knife. Sharp, durable, light, quick, and deadly.

"Let's go," he said, leading them in a sprint across the room to the road door leading to lower levels. Thomas roared, as horrific a sound as Ben had ever heard—it only served to fuel his race across the room. They reached the door, out of breath, Ben keeping an eye on their enemies through his trailing drone. Thankfully, nobody was following, yet.

"I'd wager that Legate Rath is kicking himself right about now for donating to your weapons collection," Ben said.

Hound smiled, working his shoulder. "Guess the armor did its job, after all," he said. "Still, that bastard made me bleed. I'd like to return the favor."

Ben pointed back the way they'd come.

Saint Thomas was transforming into a man again, screaming in the process, a terrifying, lonely, forlorn wail that echoed throughout the entry hall. Hoondragon was up on one knee.

"Let's go," Ben said, dumping the spent casings out of his revolver into a pouch before reloading with slugs. He sent one drone ahead and kept the other in the entry hall, the latter keeping watch on Saint Thomas and Hoondragon, as well as Legate Rath when he returned.

The road sloped down, running for five hundred feet before turning ninety degrees, running straight for fifty, then turning right again and continuing down. At the next level, they could see a single road running straight into the darkness. They continued down on the switchback highway.

His enemies were on the hunt, Ben could feel it, or at least he could feel Saint Thomas. Down another level, which was much the same as the one above. The next fed into a large room that was caved in. Several more levels worth of switchbacks brought them to another large hub room, five hundred feet square with twenty foot ceilings and several doors leading out in different directions.

He approached with caution, coming up on the twenty-by-twenty-foot open bay door and easing up to the edge. The room was filled with vehicle husks—many military in nature, all melted into barely recognizable lumps of metal.

Light drew his attention. He motioned for his friends to remain silent, then raised his drone to the ceiling and focused in on the flickering from across the room. The Warlock was sitting on the floor, cooking something in a small can. Frank sat across from him. The cougar sat in the shadows close by. Ben sent the drone closer, recording audio as well as video, recalling his second drone when Saint Thomas began to pursue again.

"I don't understand how getting your staff back gets me my birthright," Frank said.

"Fortunately, your understanding isn't required," the Warlock said, holding up his dragon-claw staff. "Today was a good day. You did well and you will be rewarded." He stopped, freezing in place for a moment before looking straight at Ben across the entire width of the pitch-black room. Only when Ben reached out with his mind did he feel the shadow watching him.

Magic and tech.

The Warlock tipped his fire can over and disappeared, a cat's roar echoing in the darkness.

"Damn it," Ben said, assembling his splinters into a cluster of lanterns. "I was too busy watching him through a drone to feel him watching us with his shadow."

"No harm done," Hound said.

"Yeah, focus on the mission," Ellie said.

Ben shook his head at his own distractibility.

"This way," he said, heading into the room, Hound's flashlight out and cutting through the black. They moved quickly, searching for the passage that would take them deeper into the mountain, stopping in dismay when they approached the entrance and it was collapsed in, fully filled with dirt to the point of overflowing.

Saint Thomas entered the room behind them. He was on fire. Entirely engulfed in flame. Not wailing or crying, not struggling or running, just burning brightly.

"There's nowhere to go," he shouted, his voice carrying better than it should have. He flapped his wings, rising several feet off the ground and then gliding quickly toward them. "You don't have my prize, I can feel it. So where is it?"

Ben scanned his map, a number of possible courses lighting up in the wire-frame diagram in his mind's eye. He picked the one with the closest exit.

"Come on!" he shouted, racing toward a nearby doorway. Even here, the doors were melted and the stone was scorched and pocked, even fused in a few places. He stopped at the threshold, sending his drone in first, keeping his trailing drone close by and watching the quickly approaching and very much on fire Saint Thomas.

Hoondragon arrived at the entrance to the level with Legate Rath close behind him. Ben marked them both, then reinforced his circle in his mind's eye.

He entered a room filled with row after row of melted computers, all lined up neatly, running the length of the forty-foot-wide, two-hundred-foot-long room. Ben raced into the dark, his splinter lanterns leading the way, his friends trailing behind him in single file through the banks of deformed machines.

He danced over a pack of rats. Ellie yelped. Kayla cursed under her breath. Hound stopped to step on an extra rat or two.

They reached the far side of the room and another melted door. Ben could only imagine the temperature here on the day that Imogen's mother had died. Flickering orange light drew his attention. Thomas had entered the room behind them and was floating effortlessly toward them on wings engulfed in flame.

Ben raced forward, taking a right turn toward a double staircase. The staircase leading up was broken in several places and probably going to collapse sometime soon, but the stairs going down were sturdy. They wound deeper into the mountain, level after level. Ben counted, his augment verifying with undeniable certainty, fourteen levels. Shasta Base was huge.

At the bottom of the staircase, they stepped out into one corner of a large room, two hundred feet long and a hundred feet wide with twenty foot ceilings—another transport hub, all passages on this level coming together here to facilitate movement, everything scorched black like everything else in the base.

Ben stopped at the threshold—magic and darkness dancing at the edge of his awareness. He concentrated on his circle, expanding it to protect his friends, then searched out the threat. The shadow was watching. He pointed at it.

Hound directed his flashlight at it and it fled. Hound chuckled as he chased it to an exit on the far wall.

"I'm pretty sure Frank is with the Warlock," Ben said.

"Want me to shoot him?" Hound asked, serious as can be.

"No, not unless you have to."

"Fair enough."

"Where to?" Ellie asked. "This place is ... let's get this over with."

Chapter 30

Ben consulted his map, picking the passage and pointing at it as he set out. Halfway across the chamber, the ground began to shake. Dust fell from the ceiling. Ben raced for the door, reaching it and stopping to wait for his friends, looking back.

The ceiling in the center of the room broke, chunks of rock falling, shattering in all directions on impact. One stone bounced and hit Rufus on the back of the leg, knocking him flat on his face, hard.

A ten-foot-diameter circle of stone fell from a hole in the ceiling, flattening everything beneath it. Three figures stood, stock-still on the platform—Saint Thomas in his true form, Hoondragon, and Legate Rath. All three of them were frozen, still as a statue.

"Come on!" Ben shouted.

Hound scrambled to his feet. Kayla changed direction and ran toward him, almost losing her footing. She grabbed him by the arm and dragged him toward the door until he was running as fast as she was.

All three enemies came to life and turned to face them as one, dust settling around them. Saint Thomas launched forward, rising into the air, bursting into flame and then landing, all of the fire surrounding him hurtling toward Ben and his friends.

Ben stepped out in front of them, projecting his circle, focusing on it with all of his will. The flame approached, heat and crackling light—death by fire.

It hit the circle and vanished as if it had never existed.

"Run!" he shouted, tossing his last ex-plus charge ten feet inside the hallway against the wall. The passage ran for fifty feet, two doors to a side, ending in a staircase leading down to a thirty-by-forty-foot room with an exit on the far end.

Ben stopped at the stairs waiting for his quarry, one drone forward, the other right overhead inside his circle, protected. His friends hurried down to the room below.

"What's the plan?" Hound asked from the bottom of the stairs.

"Boom," Ben whispered, motioning with both hands for an explosion.

He watched Hoondragon through his drone, drawing it back so it was far enough away to avoid detection, pulling both drones back when Hoondragon came into view.

He raced downstairs shouting, "Go!" Then he hurried after his friends, detonating the ex-plus charge with a thought as he entered the corridor.

The world shook.

Ben found himself on his face. He wasn't sure what was happening. He couldn't hear. His friends were all on the ground, too.

"I don't like this," Homer said.

Ben wanted to respond, to agree, or … anything, but he couldn't form a thought. He tried to think about breathing. It always came back to breathing. In … deeply. Hold. Out.

Everything tilted. He was sliding. They all were. The ground broke into pieces as the level collapsed into the level below. Ben snatched Homer to his chest and rode a section of concrete down a dirt slide into a large room that might have once held a banquet or a board meeting. The slab of rock hit hard on one end, toppling forward. Ben jumped, landing awkwardly and then scrambling backward to avoid the rock landing on top of him. Homer ran clear, turning and barking at the fallen rock, then sneezing from the dust it kicked up when it landed.

"I like sunshine," Homer said.

"Me too," Ben said.

Ellie slid down next, guiding herself through the dirt with her feet. Kayla rode a desk that shattered completely at the bottom. She rolled to her feet, unharmed. Hound tumbled to the bottom, coming up immediately, albeit a bit unsteadily. All of them were brownish-grey from a liberal coating of dust.

Ben consulted his map, which didn't really matter much, since there was only one door out of the room. It led to a larger reception room with a number of exits. Ben peeked around the doorframe as Hoondragon slid into the room from a large hole in the ceiling, another spot damaged by the explosion.

His entrance wasn't graceful. He tumbled in fast and hard, landing with a thud and not moving for a moment. Saint Thomas floated in next, followed by Legate Rath, sliding in on a piece of furniture, jumping clear before it hit and shattered.

"You can't run," Saint Thomas said.

Ben consulted his map again, nodding to himself.

"Grenades," he said, pulling one from his pouch.

"All four of us?" Kayla asked.

Ben nodded.

She relented, pulling her last grenade and throwing it when he gave the go-ahead.

Icons appeared in Ben's visual field, four grenades, each with an estimated position and time to detonate, all at different times. With a thought, he adjusted the detonation times for all four grenades to be exactly the same.

The explosion was deafening. They waited, and then the world moved again, the floor breaking out from underneath them, all of them falling into the next level below. Ben crashed into the ground, twisting an ankle and jarring himself so hard that he was stunned senseless. The world shuddered around him.

Sounds of fighting came to him. He rolled over, groaning.

Rath had a short sword in each hand and he was driving Ellie and Kayla back. They were working together to retreat without bleeding. Ben shook the buzzing from his ears, scanning the battlefield—another hub room, but this one collapsing in multiple places. Hound was down. Ben let his breath out when the augment told him that he was still alive.

Homer nosed him on the cheek. "Stop blowing things up. It's really loud."

Ben shook his head again, trying to reclaim control of his body. He got to all fours, looking up across the room. Ellie tripped, falling backward, landing hard. Kayla swept into Rath. He met her attack expertly, diverting her knives and moving her away from Ellie, getting between the two of them, knocking Kayla off balance while turning on Ellie, raising his blades and advancing.

She lashed out at his legs, forcing him to leap away as she skittered backward on her butt, keeping her sword up and between them. Kayla rushed. Rath blocked, but gave enough ground for Ellie to regain her feet.

Ben took a deep breath and slowly stood up, shaking his head in an effort to reclaim his wits.

The room was in ruins, parts of the ceiling were broken, other parts had already fallen. Dirt was flowing into the room from several breaches, creating a number of growing mounds of dry, sandy earth.

One such mound moved oddly, drawing Ben's attention. A gauntleted hand thrust out of the dirt. Hoondragon.

Rath was forcing Ellie and Kayla back, trading blows with both of them and seeming to enjoy himself. Ben launched both of his darts at him, aiming for his head. The first hit his helmet, knocking it off and sending him falling off balance, toppling over. The second dart lost cohesion, the splinters scattering across the floor.

Saint Thomas floated into the room through one of the holes in the ceiling, landing in the center and eyeing Ben like a predator eyes prey. Hoondragon pulled himself free of the pile of dirt he was buried in, slowly coming to his feet.

Ellie and Kayla advanced on Rath. He regained his senses quickly, and his feet a moment later, managing to recover one of his short swords in the process. Ellie lunged. Rath swatted her attack away, falling back to avoid the series of blows that followed. Kayla circled to his left, searching for a way in.

"You've hidden it somewhere," Thomas said, his raptor's glare boring into Ben. "Tell me where and your friends may live."

Ben drew his pistol.

With one flap of his wings, Thomas launched a dozen feet into the air and then tipped into a glide toward him.

Ben took aim, the augment guiding his hand, and fired. The pistol clicked, the round misfiring. He tried again. Another click. He refocused on his circle and fired again. A shot echoed into the cavernous room. The round hit Thomas at a range of ten feet, tearing into his shoulder, through-and-through.

Thomas landed on Ben, viciously swatting him to the ground. He was so strong. Ben felt suddenly very overmatched. He was on his back, Thomas straddling him, one taloned hand poised to strike, the other holding Ben's sword arm down.

"Ben!" Ellie shouted, in the midst of her battle with Rath.

Hound groaned.

"Where is the egg?" Thomas said, his grip on Ben's arm tightening to the point of pain. "I can break your feeble little body any time I like."

Ben ignored the pain, focusing instead on his circle, bringing it in tight around just the two of them.

"Your paltry magic won't protect you," Thomas said, swinging at Ben with his raised hand, his talons coming down on Ben's face and throat with blinding speed, then stopping just as quickly not an inch from his face. He grasped Ben by the throat, clamping down tightly enough that Ben couldn't breathe.

His fear was rising, taking up space in his mind. He tried to calm it, but feelings of suffocation weren't helping. He commanded the two clusters of splinters on his shoes to detach, forming both into darts, turning them toward Saint Thomas's back and accelerating both with all possible speed.

Thomas pitched forward from the impact, barking out in pain and surprise, letting Ben go just in time for Hound to kick the beast in the head, then shoot him in the side with Bertha. Thomas grunted from the blast, then directed a hateful glare and an outstretched hand at Hound.

Magic knocked Hound off his feet, sending him tumbling across the floor. He rolled to a stop and groaned.

Then Ben saw Hoondragon coming for him, fury in his eyes. Ben recalled his splinters, all four on his belt.

Thomas launched into the air, bleeding and injured but also enraged. He caught fire again.

Hoondragon was closing fast, charging at Ben with his black sword held high.

"Doesn't he ever quit?" Homer said.

"Pretty sure that's why the dragon gave him the job," Ben said, drawing his sword.

Out of a dark corner of the room, Ben felt a surge of magic. He turned in time to see the Warlock directing a stream of darkness from his dragon's claw into Hound, still on hands and knees trying to get up from the last hit he took.

Ellie went down. Kayla fought furiously, but Rath was just better with a blade. He sliced her shallowly across the belly. She gasped in pain. Ellie charged back into the fray, driving Rath away from Kayla, even grazing him across the shoulder, but he turned her next attack and hit her, close-fisted, across the face. She fell hard, landing with a thud and not moving.

Ben felt panic and loss press against his will.

"Kill the abomination!" the Warlock commanded Hound, pointing at Saint Thomas. Hound staggered to his feet as he changed the round in Bertha's chamber, raised his weapon and fired.

A readout came up in Ben's mind.

"Run!" he shouted.

The grenade round streaked past Thomas up to the ceiling behind him, hitting and exploding with a loud crack. Dust rained down on the room. Another crack rang out, this one announcing a growing break in the giant slab of stone that formed the ceiling. A smaller chunk fell off, grazing Saint Thomas. He fled toward the nearest door.

Hoondragon unleashed a battle cry as he attacked. Ben dodged to the side, dancing out of the way and circling to face his opponent. The augment cycled through all of the weapons he had available to him and their likely effects. Of everything, the only one that had ever drawn Hoondragon's blood was his sword.

A chunk of stone the size of a man's head shattered not ten feet from them.

They clashed, blades ringing, Ben's hands stinging with the impact of each of Hoondragon's blows against his sword. He fought, giving ground, looking for weakness, vulnerability, anything, finding only armor and steel, and an implacable drive to kill.

One on one, Ben was simply outmatched.

A loud crack drew everyone's attention. Ben looked up, backing away. A huge section of the ceiling came free, falling noiselessly for a fraction of a second and then hitting with such force and violence that Ben was blasted off his feet, falling flat on his back. He hit and everything went black.

Homer was licking his face.

"What?" he mumbled, pain and the ringing in his ears assailing him all at once. He rolled onto his side, scanning the wreckage of the room, trying unsuccessfully to ignore the pain.

Hoondragon was down, half smashed by a house-sized chunk of rock. Hound was up, staring blankly. Ellie and Kayla were up and headed for Ben. Rath rolled over on the ground somewhere behind them, pushing himself onto all fours. Most of the room was caved in, and the door that Saint Thomas had fled through was completely buried.

Ben tried to get up but the pain stopped him.

"No critical injuries," the augment said. "But you have sustained multiple smaller wounds."

The Warlock stepped out of the shadows and pointed at Ellie and Kayla. "Stop them," he said.

Hound raised his shotgun at them.

"What the hell, Rufus?" Kayla said.

"He's not in control," Ellie said, stopping quickly, putting a cautionary hand on Kayla's arm.

Frank smiled at Ben as he headed for Hoondragon. Homer charged him, barking and snapping.

"Get the hell away from me, you stupid mutt," Frank said unslinging his rifle and pointing it at Homer.

Homer ran off, circling Frank and barking some more.

"Frank," Ben managed. "What are you doing?" He struggled to his feet. He hurt everywhere.

Frank ignored him … his eyes were locked on Hoondragon's sword.

"Just relax, Rufus," Kayla said, stepping forward.

"Shoot them," the Warlock said.

"No!" Ben shouted, lunging toward Hound, expanding his circle until his friend was within its protective confines, but it was too late. Most of the blast hit Ellie, knocking her off her feet. She landed limp and didn't move. Kayla took several pellets to the side and arm, none penetrating her synthetic shirt, but the force was enough to knock her down as well.

Hound shook his head, frowning deeply before realizing what had happened. He turned toward the Warlock.

"You son of a bitch!"

He fired a blast of buckshot, grazing him.

The Warlock yelped, vanishing into the shadows.

"Shit … oh, shit," Hound said, racing to Kayla and checking her injuries with a look.

"Ellie," she managed, pointing.

Frank reached Hoondragon, his eyes never leaving the big black bastard sword next to the dragon hunter's half-crushed body.

"Don't," Ben said.

"Why not?" Frank said. "You want this, too?"

He reached down and picked it up, taking a quick breath as he grasped it, then standing and raising it out before him. Shadow flowed like smoke out of the sword, swirling around Frank and slowly seeping into him like water into the soil.

Ben felt a surge of unease in his belly.

The look of exaltation and power on Frank's face was even more unsettling. He pointed the sword at Ben.

"All my life you've been able to bully me, but not anymore. I can beat you now."

"Why are you doing this?" Ben asked.

The floor shook and a fresh fall of dirt came rushing into the room. Frank started looking for an exit.

"Leave the sword," Ben said. "It's not what you think it is."

Frank shook his head. "Not this time, Brother. This time, I get the prize."

Another stone cracked. Ben backed away, worry spiking when he saw Hound carrying Ellie toward the nearest exit. The ceiling collapsed further, unleashing another rush of sand and dirt. Ben staggered backward, struggling to maintain his footing during the rumbling.

"Ben!" Hound shouted, laying Ellie down just inside an intact hallway. "I shot her," he said. "Why would I do that?"

Her teeth were clenched. Ben could almost feel her pain through their link. He ran to her side and gently peeled up her synthetic shirt. Panic nearly overcame him. Her skin was lurid purple, blue, black, and yellow. She was bleeding inside.

"That bad?" she managed.

"Hush, don't talk," he said, trying desperately to choke back the lump in his throat. He consulted his map. They were close. If she had a chance, it was there.

A howl echoed in the dark.

Ben ignored it, attaching two clusters of splinters to the soles of his boots and the other two to his sleeves before gently picking Ellie up and setting out, the map in his mind's eye guiding him deeper into the base—down a corridor to another staircase and then down another hallway, into a storage room, to the back, through a secret door, down a staircase into a small room. Lights came on when

Ben stepped inside. A readout came to life in his visual field. The facility was intact. The door whirred shut behind them.

He laid Ellie down and put his hand on the door. A hum was followed by a gentle clunk and the double doors retracted into the wall, revealing a ten-by-ten room.

Once inside, the doors slid shut and the room began to descend, falling at a controlled and comfortable rate for over a minute.

"Why does it feel like the ground is moving?" Homer asked.

"Because it is," Ben said.

The elevator slowed and then stopped, the doors opening a few moments later, lights flickering to life.

"Shasta Black Research Facility coming online," the augment said. "Director Boyce recognized. All access granted."

"Excellent, where is your vault?"

A map came up in his mind. The facility wasn't large, big enough for a dozen people to live and work. Ben took Ellie straight to personnel quarters and gently laid her down on a bed.

"Try to hold still, I'll be right back," he said, giving her hand a squeeze.

She nodded tightly, beads of sweat rolling off her forehead.

He went to the very secure vault and willed it to open. A series of access codes came up in red, but the augment issued an override command. A green icon momentarily flashed in the corner of his visual field and the door clicked open, swinging wide.

The room was six feet by twelve. A number of items were stored on the shelves lining each wall, some even magical in nature, but one in particular drew Ben's eye.

The Dragon's Codex.

A book bound in dragon scales and written on leaves of hide. It radiated a hint of magic, but that wasn't what Ben needed most of all. He flipped it open and his heart sank. The writing was in a language that he'd never seen before, save for one of the seven runes in the magic circle.

"Dragon runes," the augment said. "Believed to be the written language dragons use to communicate to their slaves."

"Can you read it?" Ben asked.

"Accessing research files, translation in progress."

A moment later a page became visible in Ben's mind. It was an introduction to the Codex and a caution. He ignored it, flipping to the next page, scanning it quickly and flipping to the next, moving more quickly than the augment could translate. He finished and left the vault, willing the door to close behind him on his way back to Ellie.

"How is she?"

"In and out," Hound said, shaking his head. "It was the damnedest thing. I could see myself taking aim, I knew I was going to pull the trigger, but I couldn't stop." He fell silent for a moment. "I don't think she's going to make it."

"It wasn't your fault," Kayla said.

"Doesn't do her any good."

"No, but I might be able to," Ben said.

The translation was complete. And as much as he wanted to spend hours pouring over every word in the Codex, right now he needed the spell for healing—or more precisely, the spell for transferring a wound.

The augment directed his attention to the correct page. He read it once, then pulled a bed closer to Ellie, sitting down and facing her.

"I'll probably be out for a few days," he said to Hound. "Just make sure I have water."

"What are you going to do?" he asked.

"I'm going to take her wound."

"What?"

"You can do that?" Kayla asked.

"Just look after us both while we're out," Ben said, tenderly laying his hands on Ellie's side.

"Grant facility access to my friends," he said to the augment.

According to the spell, there were three ways to transfer a wound: One—Visualize the transformation so perfectly and with such will that reality conforms … not an easy thing for even the most powerful of wizards; Two—Enlist the aid of a being from another plane … Ben didn't know of any that he wanted to talk to, and he didn't have anything to bargain with, anyway; Three—Invoke an emotion, particularly love.

He knew as he read the words what he had to do. He and Ellie had been dancing around their feelings for one another since they'd discovered overlapping flow.

Now it was so simple.

He had to love her or she would die.

He closed his eyes and saw her in his mind's eye, relaxing his body and letting go of everything save her. He kept her in his thoughts until his feelings for her began to well up within him, growing until it felt like his chest might burst.

He poured it all into her, and got back a torrent of pain in return. It felt like a horse had kicked him, the agony of a great bludgeoning trauma radiating throughout his chest.

He wailed, gasping for breath, letting his feelings for her slip. She screamed, her cry trailing off weakly into a moan. Ben redoubled his efforts, focusing on her until she was his whole world.

The pain came again. This time he was better prepared to take it, letting the numbing, deadening wound spread across his chest until he felt that his life might be hanging in the balance.

He released his spell and moaned in agony, unable to muster the strength to do more. Somewhere in the distance, he heard Ellie wail as well. He slumped over and someone lifted his feet onto the bed.

"Critical injuries sustained. Recommend prolonged immobility," the augment said.

He closed his eyes. The darkness was calling. He could feel his consciousness fading.

Homer licked his nose. "Don't go," he said.

"Is she all right?"

"Her breathing is steady."

"Good, I'll be back in a while."

Homer whined quietly.

Ben let go and the darkness claimed him.

Here Ends The Dragon's Codex
Dragonfall: Book Two

Made in United States
North Haven, CT
05 February 2022

15747112R00157